A
SCHOOL
FOR
UNUSUAL
GIRLS

A
SCHOOL
FOR
UNUSUAL
GIRLS

A Stranje House Novel

KATHLEEN BALDWIN

**TOR®
TEEN**

A TOM DOHERTY ASSOCIATES BOOK

New York

A SCHOOL FOR UNUSUAL GIRLS

Copyright © 2015 by Kathleen Baldwin

Exile for Dreamers excerpt copyright © 2015 by Kathleen Baldwin

Reading and Activity Guide copyright © 2015 by Tor Books

A Tor Teen Book
Published by Tom Doherty Associates, LLC
175 Fifth Avenue
New York, NY 10010

www.tor-forge.com

Tor® is a registered trademark of Tom Doherty Associates, LLC.

The Library of Congress Cataloging-in-Publication Data is available upon request.

ISBN 978-0-7653-7600-8 (hardcover)
ISBN 978-1-4668-4927-3 (e-book)

Tor Teen books may be purchased for educational, business, or promotional use. For information on bulk purchases, please contact the Macmillan Corporate and Premium Sales Department at 1-800-221-7945, extension 5442, or write to specialmarkets@macmillan.com.

First Edition: May 2015

Printed in the United States of America

0 9 8 7 6 5 4 3 2 1

To Brett, my real-life hero.

Words make such weak meals, but let me try . . .
You live the truth of love. Day in. Day out.
And through the long night.
You believed in me when I did not.
Even after all these years, when I see you
I still want to run and fling myself into your arms.

Contents

CONTENTS

A
SCHOOL
FOR
UNUSUAL
GIRLS

One

BANISHED

- London, April 17, 1814~

What if Sir Isaac Newton's parents had packed him off to a school to reform his manners?" I smoothed my traveling skirts and risked a glance at my parents. They sat across from me, stone-faced and icy as the millpond in winter. Father did not so much as blink in my direction. But then, he seldom does. I tried again. "And if the rumors are true, not just any school—a prison."

"Do be quiet, Georgiana." With fingers gloved in mourning black, my mother massaged her forehead.

Our coach slowed and rolled to a complete standstill, waylaid by crowds spilling into Bishopsgate Street. All of London celebrated Napoleon's abdication of the French throne and his imprisonment on the isle of Elba. Rich and poor danced in the streets, raising tankards of ale, belting out military songs, roasting bread and cheese over makeshift fires. Each loud toast, every bellowed stanza, even the smell of feasting sickened me and reopened wounds of grief for the brother I'd lost two years ago in this wretched war. Their jubilation made my journey into exile all the more dismal.

Father cursed our snail-like progress through town and drummed impatient fingers against his thigh. We'd been traveling from our estate in Middlesex, north of London, since early morning. Mother closed her eyes as if in slumber, a ploy to evade my petitions. She couldn't possibly be sleeping, not while holding her spine in such an erect fashion. She refused herself the luxury of leaning back against the seat for fear of crumpling the feathers on her bonnet.

Somehow, some way, I had to convince them to turn back. "You do realize this journey is a needless expense. I have no more use for a schoolroom. I'm sixteen, and since I have already been out in society—"

Mother snapped to attention. "Oh, yes, Georgiana, I'm well aware of the fact that you have already been out in society. Indeed, I shall never forget Lady Frampton's card party."

I sighed, knowing exactly what she would say next.

"You cheated."

"I didn't. It was a simple matter of mathematics," I explained for the fortieth time. "I merely kept track of the number of cards played in each suit. How else did you expect me to win?"

"I did not *expect* you to win," she said in clipped tones. The feathers on her bonnet quivered as she clenched her jaw before continuing. "I expected you to behave like a proper young lady, not a seasoned gambler."

"Counting cards isn't considered cheating," I said quietly.

"It is when you win at every hand." She glared at me and even in the dim light of the carriage I noted a rise in her color. "And now, given your latest debacle—" She stopped. Her gaze flicked sideways to my father, gauging his expression. I would've thought it impossible for him to turn any stonier, but he did. Her voice knotted so tight she practically hissed, "I doubt I shall *ever* be allowed to show my face in Lady Frampton's company again, or for that matter in polite society *anywhere*."

Trumped. She'd slapped down the Queen of Ruination card, *Georgiana Fitzwilliam, the destroyer*. I drew back the curtain and stared out the window. A man with a drunken grin tipped his hat and waved a gin bottle, as if inviting us to join the celebration. He tugged a charwoman into a riotous jig and twirled away.

Lucky fellow.

"Bothersome peasants." My mother huffed and adjusted the cuff of her traveling coat. *Peasant* was her favorite condemnation. She followed it with a haughty sniff, as if breathing *peasant* air made her nose itch. A roar of laughter rocked the crowd outside entertained by a man on stilts dressed as General Wellington kicking a straw dummy of Napoleon.

"Confound it." Father grumbled and consulted his pocket watch. "At this pace we won't get there 'til dark. All this ruckus over that pompous little Corsican. *Fools*. Anyone with any sense knows Bonaparte was done for a month ago."

Without weighing the consequences, I spoke my fears aloud. "One can never be certain with Napoleon, can they? He may have abdicated the throne, but he kept his title."

"*Emperor*. Bah! Devil take him. Emperor of what? The sticks and stones on Elba." Father bristled and puffed up as if he might explode. "General Wellington should've shot the blighter when he had the chance. Bonaparte is too arrogant by half. The man doesn't know when to give up. Let that be a lesson to you, Georgie." He shook a finger at me as if I were in league with the infamous emperor. "Know when to give up, young lady. If you did, we wouldn't be stuck here in the middle of all this rabble waiting to get across London Bridge."

Never mind that during the last ten years Napoleon Bonaparte had embroiled all of Europe in a terrible war—today I was the villain.

But I forgave my father's burst of temper and heartily wished I'd kept my mouth shut. His anger was understandable. My brother Robert died in a skirmish with Napoleon's troops shortly before the Battle of Salamanca. Reminders of the war surrounded us. Perhaps if we had been the ones burning Napoleon in effigy it would have been liberating. Although it had been more than two years, each redcoat soldier who sauntered past, each raucous guffaw jarred our coach as if we'd been blasted by the same cannonball that killed Robbie.

My father would never admit to a weakness such as grief. I didn't have that luxury. Gravity could not explain the weight that crushed my chest whenever I thought of Robbie's death. He had been the best and kindest of my brothers. We were closest in age. I hardly knew my two oldest brothers; they'd been away at Cambridge and had no interest in making my acquaintance. Robbie, alone, had genuinely liked me. He never looked at me as if I was an ugly mouse that had crawled out from under the rug. I missed how he would scruff my unruly red hair and challenge me to a chess game, or tell me about books he'd read, or places he'd visited.

Napoleon stole him from us.

If we'd been home, Father would've stomped out of the house and gone hunting with his beloved hounds. Some hapless hare would've paid the price of his wrath. Instead, this laborious journey to haul me off to Stranje House kept him pinned up with painful reminders. Unfortunately, Napoleon wasn't present to shoulder his share of the blame. Father furrowed his great hairy eyebrows at me, the troublesome runt in his litter.

If only I'd had the good grace to be born a boy. *What use is a daughter?* How many times had I heard him ask this? And answer. *Useless baggage.* Three sons had been sufficient. Even after Robbie's death, Father still had his heir and a spare. I was simply a nuisance, a miscalculation.

The leather seats creaked as I shifted under his condemning frown. He'd never bestowed upon me more than a passing interest. Until now. Now I'd finally done something to merit his attention. Not as I'd hoped, not as I'd wished, but I had finally won his notice. He squinted at me as if I was the cause of all this uproar.

I swallowed hard. "We could turn back and make the journey another day."

My father growled in response and thumped the ceiling with his walking stick alerting our coachman. "Blast it all, man! Get this rig rolling."

"Make way," the coachman shouted at the throng and cracked his whip. Our coach lumbered slowly forward. With each turn of the wheel, my hope of a reprieve sank lower and lower. Before we crossed the bridge, I took one last look at the crowds milling on boardwalks and cobblestones, reveling and jostling one another. One last glimpse of freedom as I sat confined in gloomy silence on my way to be imprisoned at Stranje House and beaten into submission.

With a weary huff my mother exhaled. "For heaven's sake, Georgiana, stop gawking at the rabble and sit up like a proper young lady."

I straightened, prepared to sit this way forever if she would reconsider. She sniffed and pretended to sleep again.

We passed the outskirts of London with the sun high above us, a dull brass coin unable to burn through the thick haze of coal soot and smoke that hung over the city. We traveled south for hours, stopping only once at a posting inn in Tunbridge Wells to change the horses and eat. As evening approached, the sky turned a mournful gray and the faded pink horizon reminded me of dead roses. Except for Father's occasional snoring, we traveled in stiff, suffocating silence. Two hours past nightfall, we turned off the main road onto a bumpy gravel drive and stopped.

Sliding down the window glass, I leaned out to have a closer look and inhaled the sharp salty tang of sea air. The coachman clambered down and opened a creaking iron gate. A rusty placard proclaimed the old manor as STRANJE HOUSE, but I knew better. This wasn't a house. Or a school.

This was to be my cage.

"It must be well after eight. Surely, it's too late to impose upon them tonight. We could stop at an inn and come back tomorrow."

Father hoisted his jaw to an implacable angle. "No. Best to get it over and done with tonight."

"The headmistress is expecting us." Mother straightened her bonnet and sat with even greater dignity.

Our coachman coaxed the team through the entrance and clanged the gate shut behind us. The horses shied at the sound of barking in the distance, not normal barking—howls and yips. Seconds later, dogs raced from the shadows. It might have been two, two dozen, or two hundred. Impossible to tell. They seemed to be everywhere at once, silent except for their ferocious breathing. One of them pounced at the coachman's boot as he scrambled to his perch.

I jerked back from my window as one of the creatures leaped

up against the coach door. Black as night, except for yellow eyes and moon-white teeth, the monstrous animal peered in at me as if curious. I couldn't breathe, couldn't move, could do naught but stare back. Our coachman swore, cracked his whip, and the horses sprang forward. The beast's massive paws slipped from my window. With a sharp yip, he fell away from the coach. These were no ordinary dogs.

"Wolves." I slammed the window glass up and secured the latch.

"Nonsense," my mother said, but scooted farther from the door. "Everyone knows there are no more wolves in England. They were all killed off during King Henry's reign."

"Might've missed one or two," my father muttered, peering out his window at our shadowy entourage.

Whatever they were, these black demons would devour us the minute we stepped out of the coach. "Turn back. Please. I don't need this school." I hated the fear creeping into my voice.

Mother laced her fingers primly in her lap and glanced away. I cast my pride to the wind and bleated like a lamb before slaughter. "I'll do exactly as you ask. I promise. Best manners. Everything. I'll even intentionally lose at cards. I give you my word."

They paid me no heed.

Stranje House loomed larger by the second. Our coach bumped along faster than it had all day, the coachman ran the team full out in an effort to outpace the wolves. My heart galloped along with the horses. Faster and faster we rumbled up the drive, until the speed of it made me sick to my stomach.

The sprawling Elizabethan manor crouched on scraggly unkempt grounds. Dead trees stood among the living, stripped of bark by the salt air they stretched white skeletal hands toward the dark sky. The roof formed a black silhouette against the waning moonlight. Sharp peaks jutted up like jagged scales on a dragon's back. Fog and mist blew up from the sea and swirled around the boney beast.

Gripping the seat, I turned to my parents. "You can't mean to leave me in this decrepit old mausoleum? You can't." They refused to meet my frantic gaze. "Father?"

"Hound's tooth, Georgie! Leave off."

My heart banged against my ribs like a trapped bat. No reprieve. No pardon. No mercy.

Where could I turn for help? If Robbie were alive, he wouldn't let them do this. My stuffy older brothers would applaud locking me away. Geoffrey, the oldest, had written to say, "She's an embarrassment to the family. About time she was taught some manners." I doubt Edward remembers I even exist. Thus, I would be banished to this bleak heap of stones, this monstrous cage surrounded by hellhounds.

All too soon, the coach rolled to a stop in front of the dragon's dark gaping mouth. I couldn't breathe. I wanted to scream, to shriek like a cat being thrown into a river to drown.

Only I didn't. I sank back against the seat and gasped for air.

From my window, I watched as an elderly butler with all the warmth of a grave digger emerged from the house and issued a sharp staccato whistle. The wolves immediately took off and ran to the trees at the edge of the old house. But I saw them pacing, watching us hungrily from the shadows.

To my dismay, our coach door opened and a footman lowered the steps. I hung back as long as possible. My parents were almost to the house when, on wobbly legs, I climbed out and followed them inside, past the grizzled butler, and up a wooden staircase. Every step carried me farther from my home, farther from freedom. Each riser seemed taller than the last, harder to climb, and my feet heavier, until at last, the silent butler ushered us into the headmistress's cramped dimly lit study.

We sat before her enormous desk on small uncomfortable chairs, my parents in the forefront, me in the back. Towering bookshelves lined the walls. More books sat in haphazard piles on the floor, stacked like druid burial stones.

Concentrating on anything, except my fate, I focused on the titles of books piled nearest my chair. A translation of *Beowulf* lay atop a collection of John Donne's sermons, a human anatomy book, and Lord Byron's scandalous vampire tale, *The Giaour*. A most unsettling assortment. I stopped reading and could scarcely keep from biting my lip to the point of drawing blood.

The headmistress, Miss Emma Stranje, sat behind her desk, mute, assessing me with unsettling hawk eyes. In the flickering light of the oil lamp, I couldn't tell her age. She looked youthful one minute, and ancient the next. She might've been pretty once, if it weren't for her shrewd measuring expression. She'd pulled her wavy brown hair back into a severe chignon knot, but stray wisps escaped their moorings giving her a feral catlike appearance.

I tried not to cower under her predatory gaze. If this woman intended to be my jailer, I needed to stand my ground now or I would never fight my way out from under her thumb.

My mother cleared her throat and started in, "You know why we are here. As we explained in our letters—"

"It was an accident!" I blurted, and immediately regretted it. The words sounded defensive, not strong and reasoned as I had intended.

Mother pinched her lips and sat perfectly straight, primly picking lint off her gloves as if my outburst caused the bothersome flecks to appear. She sighed. I could almost hear her oft repeated complaint, *"Why is Georgiana not the meek biddable daughter I deserve?"*

Miss Stranje arched one imperious eyebrow, silently demanding the rest of the explanation, waiting, unnerving me with every tick of the clock. My mind turned to mush. How much explanation should I give? If I told her the plain truth she'd know too much about my unacceptable pursuits. If I said too little I'd sound like an arsonist. In the ensuing silence, she tapped one slender finger against the dark walnut of her desk. The sound echoed through the room—a magistrate's gavel, consigning me to life in her prison. "You *accidentally* set fire to your father's stables?"

My father growled low in his throat and shifted angrily on the delicate Hepplewhite chair.

"Yes," I mumbled, knowing the fire wasn't the whole reason I was here, merely the final straw, a razor-sharp spearlike straw. Unfortunately, there were several dozen pointy spears in my parents' quiver of *what's-wrong-with-Georgiana.*

If only they understood. If only the world cared about something beyond my ability to pour tea and walk with a mincing step. I decided to tell Miss Stranje at least part of the truth. "It was a scientific experiment gone awry. Had I been successful—"

"Successful?" roared my father. He twisted on the flimsy chair, putting considerable stress on the rear legs as he leaned in my direction, numbering my sins on his fingers. "You nearly roasted my prize hunters alive! Every last horse—scared senseless. Burned the bleedin' stables to the ground. *To the ground!* Nothing left but a heap of blackened stone. Our house and fields would've gone up next if the tenants and neighbors hadn't come running to help. That ruddy blaze would've taken their homes and crops, too. *Successful?* You almost reduced half of High Cross Greene to ash."

Every word a lashing, I nodded and kept my face to the floor, knowing he wasn't done.

"As it was, you scorched more than half of Squire Thurgood's apple orchard. I'll be paying dearly for those lost apples over the next three years, I can tell you that. And what about my hounds!" He paused for breath and clamped his teeth together so tight that veins bulged at his temples and his whole head trembled with repressed rage.

In that short fitful silence, I could not help but remember the sound of those dogs baying and whimpering, and the faces of our servants and neighbors smeared with ash as we all struggled to contain the fire, their expressions—grim, angry, wishing me to perdition.

"My kennels are ruined. Blacker and smokier than Satan's chimney . . ." He lowered his voice, no longer clarifying for Miss Stranje's sake, and spit one final damning indictment into my face. "You almost killed my hounds!" He dismissed me with an angry wave of his hand. "Successful. Bah!"

My stomach churned and twisted with regret. *Accident.* It *was* an accident. I wished he had slapped me. It would've stung less than his disgust.

I wanted to point out the merits of inventing a new kind of undetectable invisible ink. If such an ink had been available, my brother might still be alive. As it was, the French intercepted a British courier and Robert's company found themselves caught in an ambush. It wouldn't help to say it. I tried the day after the fire and Father only got angrier. He'd shouted obscenities, called me a foolish girl. "It's done. Over. He's gone."

Nor would it help to remind him that I'd nearly died leading the horses out of the mews. His mind was made up. Unlike my father's precious livestock, my goose was well and truly cooked.

He intended to banish me, imprison me here at Stranje House just as Napoleon was banished to Elba.

Miss Stranje glanced down at my mother's letter. "It says here, that on another occasion Georgiana jumped out of an attic window?"

"I didn't jump. Not exactly."

"She did." Father crossed his arms.

It had happened two and a half years ago. One would've thought they'd have forgotten it by now. "Another experiment," I admitted. "I'd read a treatise about Da Vinci and his—"

"*Wings.*" My mother cut me off and rolled her eyes upward to contemplate the ceiling. She employed the same mocking tone she always used when referring to that particular incident.

"Not wings," I defended, my voice a bit too high-pitched. "A glider. A kite."

Mother ignored me and stated her case to Miss Stranje without any inflection whatsoever. "She's a menace. Dangerous to herself and others."

"I took precautions." I forced my voice into a calmer, less ear-bruising range, and tried to explain. "I had the stable lads position a wagon of hay beneath the window."

"Yes!" Father clapped his hands together as if he'd caught a fly in them. "But you missed the infernal wagon, didn't you?"

"Because the experiment worked."

"Hardly." With a scornful grunt he explained to Miss Stranje, "Crashed into a sycamore tree. Wore her arm in a sling for months."

"Yes, but if I'd made the kite wider and taken off from the roof—"

"This is all your doing." My father shot a familiar barb at my mother. "You never should've allowed her to read all that scientific nonsense."

"I had nothing to do with it," she bristled. "That bluestocking governess is to blame."

Miss Grissmore. An excellent tutor. A woman of outstanding patience, the only governess in ten years able to endure my incessant questions, sent packing because of my foolhardy leap. I glared at my mother's back remembering how I'd begged and explained over and over that Miss Grissmore had nothing to do with it.

"I let the woman go as soon as I realized what she was." Mother ignored Father's grumbled commentary on bluestockings and demanded of Miss Stranje, "Well? Can you reform Georgiana or not?"

There are whispers among my mother's friends that, for a large enough sum, the mysterious Miss Stranje is able to take difficult young women and mold them into marriageable misses. Her methods, however, are highly questionable. According to the gossip, Miss Stranje relies upon harsh beatings and cruel punishments to accomplish her task. Even so, ambitious parents desperate to reform their daughters turn a blind eye and even pay handsomely for her grim services. It's rumored that she even resorts to torture to transform her troublesome students into unexceptional young ladies.

Unexceptional.

Among the beau monde, being declared *un*exceptional by the patronesses of society is the ultimate praise. It is almost a prerequisite for marriage. Husbands do not want odd ducks like me. Being exceptional is a curse. A curse I bear.

I care less than a fig for society's good opinion. Furthermore, I haven't the slightest desire to attend their boring balls, nor do I want to stand around at a rout, or squeeze into an overcrowded sweltering soiree. More to the point, I have no intention of marrying anyone.

Ever.

My mother, on the other hand, languishes over the fact that, despite being a wealthy wool merchant's daughter with a large dowry, and having been educated in the finer arts of polite conversations, playing the pianoforte, and painting landscapes in pale watercolors, she had failed to bag herself a title. She'd married my father because he stood second in line to the Earl of Pynderham. Unfortunately, his older brother married shortly thereafter and produced several sturdy sons, thus dashing forever my mother's hopes of becoming a countess. As a result, her desire to elevate her standing in society now depends on puffing me off in marriage to an earl, or perhaps a viscount, thereby transforming her into the exalted role of mother to a countess.

A thoroughly ridiculous notion.

Has she not looked at me? My figure is flat and straight. I doubt I shall ever acquire much of a bosom. I have stubborn freckles that will not bleach out no matter how many milk baths or cucumber plasters Mother applies. She detests my ginger hair. Red is definitely not *en vogue*.

Not long after the glider incident, she tried to disguise my embarrassing red curls by rinsing them with walnut stain. It would infuriate her if she knew that her efforts to change my hair color increased my obsession with dyes and inks. Her oily walnut stain failed miserably. The hideous results had to be cut off—my hair shorn like a sheep. It has only now grown out to an acceptable length.

And now this. Exile to Stranje House.

I clinched the fabric of my traveling dress and wished for the millionth time that I'd been more careful while adding saltpeter to the boiling ink emulsion. If only it hadn't sparked that abominable fire.

Miss Stranje allowed an inordinate amount of time to pass before pronouncing judgment upon me.

"I knew it." Mother collapsed against the back of her chair in defeat and threw up her hands. "It's hopeless. Nothing can be done with her."

Miss Stranje rose. The black bombazine of her skirts rustled like funeral crepe. "On the contrary, Mrs. Fitzwilliam. I believe we may be able to salvage your daughter."

Salvage? They spoke of me as if I were a tattered curtain they intended to rework into a potato sack.

"You do?" My mother blinked at this astonishing news.

"Yes. However"—Miss Stranje grasped the edge of her desk as if it were a pulpit and she about to preach a sermon condemning us all to perdition—"you may have heard my teaching methods are rather unconventional. Severe. Harsh." She paused and fixed each of us with a shockingly hard glare. "I assure you, the gossip is all true."

For the first time that day, my mother relaxed.

I, on the other hand, could not swallow the dry lump of dread rising in my throat. Miss Stranje's sharp-eyed gaze seemed to reach into my soul and wring it out.

She bore down on my father. "Mr. Fitzwilliam, you may leave your daughter with me under one condition. You must grant me authority in all matters pertaining to her welfare, financially and otherwise. Should I decide to lock her in a closet with only bread and water for sustenance, I will not tolerate any complaints or—"

"Heavens, no. You can't do that." Mother swished her hand through the air as if swatting away the idea. "It won't work. Don't you think we would've tried something so simple? It's no use. You can't leave her in solitude to think. She'll simply concoct more mischief while she's locked up. You'll have to come up with something more inventive than that."

Lips pressed thin, Miss Stranje sniffed. I wasn't sure whether she was annoyed about Mother interrupting or about being saddled with such an intractable student. "Furthermore," she said with a steady calm, "if I deem it necessary to take her to London to practice her social skills, you will not only permit such an excursion, you will finance the endeavor."

"More coin?" My father ran a finger around the top of his starched collar. "Already costing me a king's ransom."

"The choice is yours." She plopped a sheaf of papers on the corner of the desk nearest him. "You must sign this agreement or I will not accept your daughter into the school."

He glanced at me and his angry scowl returned. His nostrils flared. I groaned, knowing the smell of ash and burnt hay still lingered in his nose. He would sign.

"Won't sign unless I have some assurances you can do the job." He sat back, arms crossed. "We stated quite clearly in our letters, we expect some kind of guarantee. I'm no stranger to the rod. Went to Eton. Got beat regular. All part of the training."

The lump in my stomach turned into a cannonball, and my backside began to hurt in anticipation.

"Women are too weak for this sort of thing." He glared sideways at my mother. "How do I know a female like yourself can administer proper punishment, when punishment is due?"

Miss Stranje got all prickly and tall. She didn't look weak to me. Not by half.

"I assure you, sir, although I always abide by the law and never use a rod that is thicker than my thumb—"

"Proof, Miss Stranje." Father leaned forward and tapped the stack of papers. "I want proof that you can make something of her. Then I'll sign your blasted papers."

Miss Stranje tilted her head and studied him, the way a wild turkey does before it tries to peck your eyes out. In the end, the headmistress stepped back and lifted the oil lamp. "As you wish. I believe a visit to my discipline chamber is in order." She ushered us to the door. "You, too, Georgiana, come along."

She led us down long twisting stairs, deep into the bowels of Stranje House. Damp limestone walls, gray with age and mold, closed around us, swallowing us in chilly darkness. Deeper and deeper we went. It was the hellish kind of cold, a moist heavy chill, as if the underbelly of the house had been cold for so long it had seeped into the stones permanently. It sucked the warmth straight out of my bones. We emerged in a dank hallway and shuffled through the musty passageway until the headmistress finally stopped in front of a heavy wooden door. The hinges creaked as she opened it, and we were met with the sound of human whimpering.

Miss Stranje swept her hand forward, welcoming my parents into her dungeon just as if it were a prettily decorated parlor.

Mother marched straight in, glanced about the room and shook her head. "I'm afraid there's not much here we haven't seen before." She pointed to a pale white-haired girl who was strapped waist, shoulders, and head to a thick oak slat. "See here, Henry, this is a common backboard. Very good for the posture. They had one at my finishing school. I daresay every lady in the ton has spent time in a similar device."

The girl's blue eyes opened wide and flittered fearfully as we drew close. Her forehead had been buckled so tightly to the backboard that red marks welted on each side of the leather strap. She stood perfectly still as Miss Stranje addressed her. "Mr. and Mrs. Fitzwilliam, may I present Miss Seraphina Wyndham."

Seraphina did not speak, nor did she greet us with a genial smile. She simply mewed like a strangled kitten.

Next to Seraphina stood a large steel mummy case. I'd read about Egyptian artifacts but had never seen one. Except I quickly realized the coffin was not from ancient Egypt, not with that type of a clasp. I leaned closer, thinking I heard something inside.

Breathing.

I jumped back. "Something's in there."

"Someone," Miss Stranje corrected. Holding her lamp aloft, she peered into one of the eyeholes. The metal coffin reverberated like a dull bell when she rapped on the front. "Lady Jane? Are you—"

A sharp yowl echoed inside the metal sarcophagus.

"No need to move about. Those tines are extremely sharp. I only meant to inquire after your health. I couldn't help but notice a small quantity of blood seeping out of the bottom of the case. Are you well?"

Of course, she wasn't well. Blood trickled out of the metal seams onto the floor. "This is barbaric!" I backed away from the horrid mummy case and the even more horrid Miss Stranje.

"Well enough." Lady Jane's surly response reverberated eerily from the casket.

"Well enough, *thank you*," Miss Stranje corrected. "One must be courteous regardless of the situation."

There was no answer.

"This is cruel." I glared at the headmistress. "You can't do this to a member of the nobility."

"Can't I?" She cocked her head at me, quizzically, like a raven right before snapping up a beetle.

A small Oriental woman padded silently out of the shadows and whacked the mummy case several times with a bamboo stick, setting off a sickening chime. I flinched as Lady Jane shrieked in pain and then obediently responded, "Well enough, *thank you*."

My mother's only comment was, "Well now, that *is* something I haven't seen before."

Miss Stranje inclined her head to the Chinese woman and turned to my parents. "Mr. Fitzwilliam, Mrs. Fitzwilliam, allow me to present Madame Cho. She assists me here in the discipline room and also instructs the girls in Asian history."

Small and old, Madame Cho looked crafty as a black cat. She bowed slowly and stiffly as if the effort cost her ancient bones much pain.

My parents walked on without acknowledging her, following Miss Stranje to examine a rack of various sized training rods and lashes.

Swift as a thief, Madam Cho straightened. *So much for her old bones.* Her obsidian eyes reminded me of a lizard's as she examined me with ruthless assessment. I edged away and joined my father who stood toying with the end of a whip that hung on the wall. He fingered the knots tied in the leather thongs at the beating end of the whip. Glancing sideways at me, I wondered if he might be troubled by the idea of my back, lashed and bleeding.

"*Father?*" I whispered, praying for a reprieve.

Then I remembered how, after the fire, he'd chased me with his riding crop. His face hardened into the same angry mask he'd worn that day.

He let go of the whip and rubbed his palms against the side of his coat. "I've been too soft on you," he said under his breath, and turned his back on me.

Mother stood in front of a small medieval stretching rack. The relic must've dated clear back to the Inquisition. She seemed alarmed to find such an evil contraption housed in a girls' school. But as she rubbed her fingertips together I realized she wasn't alarmed, merely perturbed that dust had smudged the tips of her glove.

I wanted to scream. *No, no, no!* People do not do this any-more. Not to their daughters. Not to anyone. And yet here we were, standing before implements of reform that even the despi-cable Miss Stranje had not invented; whips, paddles, various length training rods, and other devices, like the backboard, that were in use all over England.

I swallowed the pincushion of fear stuck in my throat and, marshaled every ounce of courage I had left, to ask, "You don't actually use this rack, do you?"

Miss Stranje turned to me, hideously pleasant, as if merely commenting on the weather. "I find it remarkably effective."

Father headed for the door. "I've seen enough. I'm ready to sign those damnable papers of yours. I want to be rid of this place."

Rid of me.

Mother and Miss Stranje hurried after him. I stared at the shackles on the rack, stunned that my parents would leave me at the mercy of this awful school. I'm not given to outbursts of weakness, but I began to tremble stupidly and my feet seemed frozen to the cold stone floor.

Hope does not shatter all at once. The mind plays tricks.

For several moments I felt certain Stranje House was no more than a ghoulish nightmare. Any moment, I assured my-self, my maid Agnes would throw back the curtains and I would awaken in my own bedroom. The world would turn right again. Sanity would return. The sun would glint through my windows. The mantel clock would tick steadily and reliably, not like the panicky thumping of my heart.

But I did not wake up. Not until Madame Cho swatted the back of my legs with her stick and pointed to the door. "You go." Then she turned and beat on the mummy case. My stinging calves roused me out of disbelief.

I ran.

My slippers skidded against the stone floor as I dashed out of that ghastly room. Faint candlelight trickled from the discipline chamber, but not nearly enough to penetrate the thick darkness in the hallway. Still I ran. Straining to see my way through the inky blackness. A junction in the corridor confused me. Which way were the stairs? Behind me, Madame Cho's banging mingled with yelps of pain. I shook my head. This wasn't a girls' school. It was a madhouse.

I had no idea what Napoleon intended to do about his imprisonment on Elba, but as for me, I planned to escape.

Two

SECRETS

I rushed down the corridor until I found an opening in the stone wall. Candles in the discipline chamber did not reach this far down the hallway. The only light came from wisps of moonlight filtering through a small mullioned window high on the wall. A narrow staircase curled up into thick impenetrable darkness. This had to be the right way, so I stepped up into utter blackness.

Moisture from damp moldy stones seeped onto my fingers as I trailed them along the wall, guiding myself as I climbed. I waved my other hand in front of my face brushing away cobwebs and spiders that dangled from the low ceiling. I had to catch up to my parents, but every step increased my uneasiness. Realizing that this couldn't be the right stairwell, I slowed my frantic steps and considered turning back. Except that would do no good. Only the discipline chamber lay behind me.

A faint glimmer caught my attention. Straining to see, I groped the wall and came upon what appeared to be a small door with a weak golden light wavering around the edges. Hopeful it might lead back to the normal part of the house, I pushed. With a loud scraping noise, the door cracked open. I shoved harder. Small pebbles and stones grumbled beneath the wooden panel and pattered on my head. Finally, it opened wide enough that I could squeeze through.

A flurry of high-pitched squeaks startled me—the unmistakable sound of bats. I covered my face and shuddered. They flapped crazily, fanning my nerves to the edge of panic, before they fluttered away. Once they quieted, I peeked out and found myself hunkered on a small ledge high on the wall of a rough-hewn chalkstone cave.

I inched to the lip of the alcove and accidently knocked stones loose with the toe of my shoe. Two seconds later a splash echoed. Far below, a hissing oil lamp hung on a docking post. It sent orange light and shadows sneaking across the walls of the cave. Seawater sloshed in through a narrow opening and splashed against the cavern walls, knocking against a dinghy tied to the post.

I'd read about smuggler's caves in North Devon and Cornwall, and everyone knew they existed along the southern coast near Penzance and St. Ives, but I hadn't expected one here. Yet, surely, this must be a smuggler's cave, and as evidenced by the boat and lantern, in recent use.

Spiders of apprehension skittered up my spine. What sort of girl's school was this? I had to find my parents before it was too late. Surely, knowledge of a smuggler's cave would dissuade them from leaving me here.

I wriggled back through the makeshift door and dashed up the passageway. A few moments later, I heard something. *Voices.* Indistinct at first, but as I darted up the steps, they grew louder. A man's voice, an irritated man, and that could only be one person. With a flood of relief, I shouted, "Father! I'm coming. Wait for me. Please!" The walls muffled my cries, sucking the sound into all the musty crooks and crevices. I called again, and raced through the dark to catch them.

I would do anything to stop my father from signing those papers. I would throw myself at his feet and beg him to forgive me. I'd vow to never *ever* conduct an experiment in the stables again. I'd even swear not to dabble with explosive components again. At least, not in such imprudent quantities. If only he would let me come back home.

A thin beam of gray light penetrated the thick darkness ahead. I ran faster and, in my rush, tripped on a crumbling step and fell to my knees. A mouse pipped in alarm and scurried past my shoulder. The floors were wood here. I leaped up, and brushed the grit and splinters from my palms. At last, I'd found a doorway out of this interminable pit. I scrambled up the remaining steps, but stopped short on a narrow wedge-shaped landing.

This was not a door.

And the voice did not belong to my father.

I teetered on the edge of a precipice overlooking a room. I stood in a small alcove facing the backside of a tapestry, one that must hang very high on the wall. Thin gauze-like peepholes in the tapestry's weave allowed me to survey the chamber below with a fair amount of clarity.

The voices belonged to two gentlemen, one young and one middle-aged. But this sparsely furnished room wasn't intended for guests. The only chairs were four uncomfortable looking straight-backed chairs from the Tudor period. There was no welcoming fire and a table stood off to the side, strewn with maps, letters, and books. It did not bode well. What were these men doing in a girls' school late at night? Equally baffling was the question of why a spy hole existed in a dark passage of that same school. It must be a forgotten hiding place from the house's Tudor days, when, according to my history books, royal families were obsessed with spying on one another.

The younger of the two men paced, while the elder stood completely still. Both tall in stature, they were opposites in every other way, angel and devil, light and shadow. The older man stood at ease. Tranquil. His golden hair thinning and his skin roughened from years in the sun. The younger man looked only a handful of years older than me and had midnight black hair and hard angular planes in his face. His eyes flashed with impatience and a sword swung at his hip as he paced.

"We're wasting time, Captain," he grumbled. "If we leave now we can make the crossing before morning. We must strike while his men still think he's dead." I detected a slight French accent in his speech.

The captain shook his head. "They already know."

"How?" The younger man stopped pacing and pressed a fist atop the hilt of his sword. "His own family has been kept in the dark."

"Face facts, Sebastian, he has eluded us for weeks. Always a step ahead. Someone is helping him. *Someone* knows he's alive."

Sebastian spun around and raked a hand through his dark curls. "Who? Thistlewood and his Jacobean cronies?"

"No. Too well-organized for that lot." He rested a hand on Sebastian's shoulder. "I think the Order of the Iron Crown is back at work. It's the only thing that makes sense. Half of France wants Napoleon restored to the throne. There must be more collaborators on this side of the pond than we suspected."

Order of the Iron Crown?

What sort of girls' school welcomed conspirators into their

private rooms? I clutched the wall to balance myself. Bits of old mortar crumbled in my palm.

Sebastian circuited the worn Turkish carpet, grumbling so low I could hardly hear. ". . . If anyone knows, mark my words, it's her."

Who? I wondered.

He circled back to my side of the room and declared, "We'll make her tell us—force her if necessary." I leaned as close as possible, straining to hear the other man's response to Sebastian's dire threat.

"Be reasonable. She's a peer. What would you do? Put her on Emma's rack?"

I covered the gasp that nearly escaped my mouth.

Sebastian shrugged and rubbed the back of his neck. "Wouldn't help. She'd only lie." He stopped in front of the Elizabethan chest directly beneath me, and smacked his fist against his palm. "We have no choice. We must cross and run him aground now."

"There is always a choice. You're allowing emotion to rule your head." The older man tucked his hands behind his back and waited until he had Sebastian's full attention before continuing. "If Emma's new student has developed a reliable invisible ink, one that can't be detected by simply running a candle under the letter, think how that will aid us. Our time is better spent here, rather than chasing the Ghost across the channel and risk using the old codes."

Codes. Ink. I couldn't believe my ears. Surely, they weren't talking about my ink formula. It had to be a coincidence. I clutched the edge of the niche and leaned closer, intent on hearing every word. They couldn't possibly know about my experiments with ink. No one knew about my research, no one except my father, and . . .

Mother. She must have mentioned it in those wretched letters she sent Miss Stranje.

Sebastian exhaled loudly and glanced about the room before blurting, "We can't be certain this girl has anything viable. We're going on too little. The strength of a few letters and one governess enamored of her student."

He couldn't mean my Miss Grissmore? Surely not. What could she possibly have to do with all of this?

The captain's stance stiffened, no longer tranquil, and if I were a sailor on his ship, I would be backing away. "I assure you, Emma has researched the matter thoroughly." His tone was terse, full of command. "She's been investigating the young lady for some time now. That is good enough for me."

Open-mouthed, I sucked in air. Had someone been watching me? Investigating? No, surely not. They couldn't be talking about me.

"Even so, she's a mere girl. New to the school." Sebastian crossed his arms. "What can she possibly know of chemistry and ink formulas? Chemistry requires an understanding of mathematics. In my experience, girls' heads are full of fripperies and trinkets. Their weightiest calculations are deciding how many ruffles they want on their next ball gown."

Fripperies? Ruffles? I curled my fingers around a decaying timber. What an arrogant jackanapes. I'd like to hit him over the head with a calculation or two.

With a shake of his head, the captain relaxed and said, "Careful, my boy. Never underestimate women. They're dangerous. Apart from that, you know how selective Emma is about her young ladies. She only takes in the ones who . . ." He stopped and rubbed at the stubble on his cheek as if contemplating his next words.

Drat! What about the girls in this school? I balanced on the edge of the landing, barely able to keep from shouting at him, *Yes, yes, go on. The ones who . . . ?*

I did shout. My foot slipped off the ledge. I screamed and scratched wildly at the tapestry, trying to grab hold of some nubbin or knot in the weave, fighting to keep my balance, but it swung open. Scrabbling in vain, midair, I dropped like a stone. Except time slowed to a torturous crawl.

My future rushed toward me in predictable angles, calculable forces, inescapable Newtonian physics.

I would be dashed to bits on the monstrous Elizabethan chest below. My lungs would be punctured on the steepled gothic finials. Other parts of me would be bruised and pierced on the metal studs hammered along the edge. In short, I would die.

I closed my eyes.

Instead of breaking my ribs against the sharp-edged chest and plummeting to the floor, I felt myself whisked sideways, swooped away from the furniture. An angel must have saved me. Or perhaps I had died and flown directly into heaven?

Unlikely, on several counts.

I opened my eyes and found myself cradled in the devil's arms. Stunned beyond words or good sense, I blinked, noting that Sebastian's eyes were a startling blue.

I ran through several explanations I might give for my sudden appearance, but decided against speaking. Instead, I concentrated on recovering my breath. I felt a distinct sense of satisfaction to see that Sebastian's impatience had completely disappeared. The young man seemed quite as astonished as I.

Introductions were in order.

So, I began. "For your information, I have *never* given a single thought to the number of ruffles on my ball gown. *Ever.*" There. That told him.

One of his eyebrows shot up to meet a shock of dark hair

that had fallen across his brow. My moment of triumph might've lasted longer if his surprise hadn't melted into a lazy sardonic smile. *Smug scoundrel.*

The captain rushed to us. "Is she all right?"

Sebastian's gaze wandered casually down my neck and kept going, brazenly surveying areas of my person that he ought not to look upon so directly. "Yes, I believe so." Finally, his wicked eyes returned to my face where they belonged. However, from the way he studied my nose and mouth I wondered if the brigand was counting my freckles. He cleared his throat, and with a sly half smile, said, "Although she must have bumped her head. She keeps going on about ruffles."

"I do not. And for your information, a ball gown doesn't have ruffles, it has flounces."

"See what I mean?" Sebastian shook his head mournfully. "Poor thing is delirious."

I buckled my lips together and then promptly unbuckled them. I meant to put a hasty end to his mockery. "Why were you discussing my ink?" I demanded.

At that precise moment, the door opened and Miss Stranje glided into the room. She took one look at me draped across Sebastian's arms, glanced up at the tapestry dangling open in front of the spy hole, and hesitated only a moment before calmly addressing us as if nothing was amiss. "Ah, I see you've met my newest student." Her gaze narrowed at me. "Miss Fitzwilliam, how clever you are to have already discovered one of our secret passages. Incidentally, your parents asked me to bid you *adieu.*"

Adieu? She was making that up; my parents didn't use French phrases. "They're gone? Without saying farewell?"

Miss Stranje inclined her head. "Your father thought it would be better this way."

Better for whom? Not me. It wasn't better. Not better, at all.

They'd abandoned me. How could they leave me in this awful place? I felt disoriented, dizzy, like I might be falling again. My stomach lurched. I bit my lip to keep from crumpling, and turned my face into Sebastian's chest, away from the wobbling light of the oil lamps.

I didn't intend to sink deeper into his arms. Sadness rendered me momentarily weak. Cradled in his arms I felt warm and comforted, yet uneasy at the same time. I'd never been held by a man before, except, perhaps, by my father, but that was so long ago I had no memory of it. *Father*—who had just discarded me, left me in this place like unwanted baggage. I suppressed the instinct to curl up, to double over against the gnawing ache in my middle. I fought it. Trembling with the effort.

Sebastian's arms tightened around me.

I mustered my pride, fought to regain my senses and take charge of the situation. To do that, I needed to get on my feet. I certainly didn't belong in this man's arms. Apparently, I didn't belong anywhere.

A surge of something, maybe it was anger at the injustice of it, or maybe it was knowing I had no one to depend upon but myself, whatever the source, I found the strength to push against his chest. "Put me down, sir."

"Lord Wyatt is a viscount, Georgiana. One must address him as *my lord*, rather than *sir*." Miss Stranje instructed me as if I were a complete simpleton. "Thus, you would say, 'Kindly put me down, my lord.'"

I didn't care whether he was a viscount or a fishmonger. I needed to get out of his arms and onto solid ground.

Sebastian studied my face. "You're still pale. After that fall, are you quite certain you're steady enough to stand?" A wash of pity colored his features. I wanted none of it.

"Quite. Now, if you would be so gracious, *my lord*, as to *kindly* set me on the floor." I emphasized his title with more sarcasm than I ought, and nearly spat the word *kindly* at Miss Stranje. My mother would've whipped me soundly for such rudeness. In my defense, I was still startled by the fall and my parents' hasty departure.

Sebastian lowered my feet to the ground. "You're welcome," he said coldly, reminding me I hadn't thanked him for saving my life. He straightened his rumpled sleeves and brushed away a cobweb I must have carried down with me on my skirts.

I couldn't risk gratitude. Not just yet. My composure hung by a thread more fragile than the cobweb he brushed off his coat. I set my jaw and turned to Miss Stranje. "Did my father mention at which inn he would be staying?"

Her bird-of-prey features softened. "No. I offered him rooms here, but he insisted on a hasty departure. To avoid a fuss, as he put it."

"I would not have made a fuss." *A lie.* I would've clung to his boots and begged like a street urchin, like one of the peasants my mother detested. The untruth made me flush with heat. Unable to look at them, I studied the intricate pattern in the Turkish carpet.

"Of course not." Miss Stranje stepped aside and gestured to the doorway. "You may be excused for the evening, Miss Fitzwilliam. Your trunks have been carried to the girls' dormitorium. You'll find it easy enough. It's up one flight, turn left into the east wing, the second room on the right."

I was not a child that she should dismiss me out of hand. I faced her squarely, just as if my knees weren't quaking. "These men were discussing my invisible ink."

Miss Stranje didn't flinch. That sharp hawk-like expression of hers returned, unreadable and shrewd. "Were they?" she said, without a modicum of surprise.

That proved it. They had, indeed, been talking about my ink. *But why?* The experiment had failed miserably, burst into flames, and Miss Stranje knew it.

"I demand to know why." I couldn't keep my wretched tongue from betraying my curiosity. I jutted my chin, defying her. I wanted answers. How had she found out about my research into invisible ink? Had she investigated me? Why? "And what does Miss Grissmore have to do with this?"

A flash of surprise lit her eyes but instantly vanished, followed by a frighteningly cold steel shuttering of her features. I stepped back involuntarily. Miss Stranje's face became an unyielding mask of civility. She gestured to the hall again. "It is late, Miss Fitzwilliam. Bid Captain Grey and Lord Wyatt good night. You really must run along and attend to your luggage."

"And your ruffles," Sebastian said under his breath, sweeping into an overly flamboyant bow, but not before I glimpsed his insufferable smirk.

I frowned at him so hard the impertinent rogue ought to have shriveled to dust. He remained annoyingly intact. Rather than give them a quick curtsey, I wanted to slam the door on them and run headlong into the night after my parents' coach. Except, that would be utter foolishness, and while I admit to many defects of character, foolishness is not numbered among them.

Three

LUNATICS AND THIEVES

C harming girl," Sebastian intoned to my retreating backside.

I didn't give him the satisfaction of turning around. What's
more I had no desire to see the cocky smirk on his face. For that
matter, I never wanted to see him or his shockingly blue eyes
again. *Ever.* I rubbed my upper arm where, for some strange
reason, I could still feel him holding me. There was no rational
explanation for this phenomenon, except Sebastian was a devil
and his fingers left scorch marks.

How dare he think I had nothing but fripperies occupying
my thoughts. It wasn't his formula under discussion, was it? No.
If I had only ribbons and lace rolling around in my brain, how
did he suppose I'd made a recipe for undetectable invisible ink?
Never mind that I'd nearly roasted myself alive while mixing
it. I had something Lord Evil-Eyes coveted. *Why* he wanted it
prickled and niggled at my brain like an unreachable itch.
I vowed to find the answer.

I stiffened my spine enough to satisfy even my mother, tramped up a flight of stairs, made a left turn, and marched down the hall. The second door on the right stood ajar. I peeked into the dormitorium. Hardly a dormitorium. The dim light made it difficult to see, but it appeared to be simply an overly long bedroom with a fireplace at the far end, a few dressing screens, and two large beds arranged along one wall, divided by armoires and side tables. Across from them stood another bed, a writing desk, and a deep window seat.

I took a deep breath and headed in, but came to a sudden halt. My mouth fell open. "What are you doing?" I balled up my fists and stomped toward the three girls leaning over my portmanteau. "Get away from *my* trunks."

The tallest of them spun around and I found myself staring at the sharp tip of a dagger. Candlelight glinted against the merciless steel. This was a fighting knife. Judging by my attacker's fierce glare, rumors about the girls in this school didn't do them justice. I realized that they might well be murderers or dangerous thieves. Or even madwomen. My bravado sank to the floor leaving me naked with terror, even my thin cloak of anger fell away in tatters. I had nothing left to keep me from shivering. Not even pride.

Her blade did not quiver. That was only me. She held it steady, the point less than an inch from my face. I dared not breathe.

The girl beside her laid a hand on my assailant's arm, gently lowering the knife. "Put it away, Tess. There's no need for that."

"She's trouble." Tess frowned at me. "I can tell."

"Obviously, or she wouldn't be here."

Tess grumbled low in her throat, but she flipped the blade, pulled up her skirt, and slid the dagger into a sheath strapped on her calf.

I crossed my arms protectively and struggled to regain an ounce or two of my dignity. "And you?" I asked the girl who appeared to have more control over her emotions. "What are you? Murderers? Or just thieves?"

It was Tess who answered. With a defiant tilt of her chin she reached back, snatched my riding boots from the trunk, and chucked them into an armoire that stood open. "Neither. We were merely helping you unpack."

I knew better. The armoire was empty except for the boots. "I see, and you're a liar, as well." I glanced pointedly at the bandage on her arm. "Now I understand why Miss Stranje locked you in the mummy case. How fortunate for you. I'm surprised she didn't give you a turn on the rack. In London they hang thieves."

"Fortunate?" she practically spit the word at me. "You don't know anything about me. I wasn't in the case." She tossed back her long dark hair and tilted her head sideways, indicating the girl who had rescued me. "That would've been Jane."

Of course, Lady Jane.

She didn't seem the sort of girl who deserved to be shut inside a spiked coffin. She seemed exactly the type of young lady my mother wanted for a daughter. Her alabaster skin and pert smile would've charmed all the women at Lady Frampton's card parties. But I didn't trust her any more than I did Tess. Nothing was as it seemed in this house.

They stood side by side, intentionally blocking my way. I peeked over their shoulders and saw Seraphina, the pale flaxen-haired girl who'd been strapped to the posture board, intently perusing the contents of my trunk, and she had my protractor in her hand.

I shoved past Tess and Jane and snatched it away from her. "You say you're not thieves, and yet here you are pawing through my things like common criminals. Obviously this sort of thing is why you're all locked away in this horrid school. And to think I felt sorry for you."

Tess glared down her patrician nose at me as if I was a bug that needed squashing. "Don't play all high and mighty with us. You've done something wrong or you wouldn't be here." She poked my shoulder. "Your turn in the dungeon will come soon enough."

Seraphina's forehead was still red, and I noticed a fading bruise on Jane's chin. Obviously something other than the sharp tines of the sarcophagus had cut Tess's arm. I backed away, swallowed hard, and fidgeted with the corner of my trunk lid. "I didn't mean—"

"Yes, you did, *Miss Holier-Than-Thou*. That's precisely what you meant. You said we deserved a go on the rack. You even mentioned the gallows, as if touching your precious things was a hanging offense."

"We only went through your things to figure out why you're here," Jane said with a huff. "We had to know, our lives depend upon it. You can't blame us for that."

I didn't see how their lives depended upon it, unless they thought I was some sort of violent criminal. Regardless of their reasons . . . "You supposed my clothing would give you the answer?"

"Don't be absurd." Jane looked askance at me, as if I was the irrational one. "We thought Sera would see something and tell us what you are."

"*What* I am?" I frowned. "You mean *who* I am." I fell back on my hypothesis that the occupants of Stranje House were all mad as hatters.

"No. Sera has a gift. She can—"

Tess flicked Jane's arm, silencing her. Jane buttoned her lip tighter than an accountant's purse.

My patience wore thin. "She can what?"

No one answered. Glancing this way and that, they retreated into a mutual pact of silence.

"Look, you lot. It shouldn't matter to you who I am, or even *what* I am. I have no intention of staying in this asylum. I'm going to escape as soon as I figure out where . . ." I hesitated. *Where would I go?* I couldn't run home.

"Escape? You?" Tess scoffed and shook her head. "You wouldn't last five minutes out there."

I didn't know if she meant the wolf dogs would tear me apart, or that I wouldn't survive in the world on my own. Before I could argue she turned to Sera and demanded, "What did you see?"

Sera tilted her head sideways and calmer than a Sunday afternoon answered, "Miss Fitzwilliam lives in a household dominated by men. She does not care much for her appearance, and is far more interested in mathematics and science." At this juncture she exchanged a knowing look with Jane.

"*Science.*" Jane nodded as if mulling over the word. "What else?"

"She has recently been involved in a fire—"

"You're guessing!" I barked. "Or worse, you've been listening to idle gossip."

"Sera doesn't need to guess," Tess snapped.

"Very well, then what is she? A soothsayer? More likely a charlatan." I whirled on the culprit. "How did you find out?"

"It wasn't difficult." Seraphina ducked her head sheepishly. But then she recovered her composure and employed the same long-suffering tone I'd used so often on my mother. "First, your dresses were thrown haphazardly into the trunk whereas your books were wrapped and stowed with great care. The scent of ash and smoke permeated this one." She picked up my most prized possession, an extremely valuable English translation of twelfth-century alchemy experiments in Persia and Arabia. It contained Al-Jildaki's notes on alloys and chemical extraction, but more important, several ancient Egyptian formulas for invisible ink.

"Be careful with that." I reached, but dared not grab it away from her. The crumbling leather binding was too fragile. "There are only five copies in existence." I'd sent dozens of letters all across Europe, hounding rare-book collectors until I finally obtained this copy.

She held it out to me with both hands. "Its importance to you is evidenced by the way your name is written so carefully on the leather cover."

I took it, exhaled with relief, and tenderly rewrapped the crumbling book in a silk scarf. I tucked it back under the clothing where it had been hidden. My parents would've been furious if they'd known I'd smuggled these books into my luggage, but I couldn't leave them behind. I lifted my lace box lid to make certain my hand-scribed compilation of Da Vinci's experiments was still safely hidden.

Tess planted her fists on her hips. "So that's why you're here? Because of a fire?"

"It was an accident," I mumbled, heartily tired of explaining. They all circled around me, waiting for more. I shrugged. "If you must know, one of my science experiments got out of hand."

To my surprise that seemed to satisfy them. Tess turned to Sera. "Anything else?" Sera studied me openly and without shame or any pretense of manners. They all did.

After what seemed like an interminable appraisal, Sera shook her head and spoke about me as if I wasn't present. "Not much, only odds and ends. Her mother or guardian does not bear her same color hair. Otherwise, she never would've selected such unfortunate colors for her clothing. She injured her left arm at some point; see how it won't hang straight or extend fully. And she's been in one of our seldom used passages." She waved her hand at the brownish green tinge of mold staining my hem. "I suspect she took a rather bad fall." She directed their attention to a rip in the seam of my sleeve. "Or two." She pointed at the stains where my knees had landed against the passageway.

"I'm sorry. Nothing conclusive." Sera cast her gaze to the floor. Her silky white hair fell across her face like a curtain. Tilting her head, she peeked out at me and added softly, "Obviously she's intelligent."

"Obviously." Tess's face twisted in exasperation. "I doubt a stupid girl would be hauling around books on ancient chemistry."

"I hope she is also generous." A voice came from the shadows. "Because I would like to borrow this excellent book on plants."

Another of my books stolen? I turned, searching for the fourth girl. As if emerging from the woodwork, the most exotic creature I'd ever seen stepped forward. I was astonished. She'd been here the whole time. How had she blended into the shadows so perfectly and moved with such quiet stealth? A delicate girl, with dark shining eyes, smooth whiskey-colored skin, she was draped in a swath of cinnamon brown fabric trimmed in filigreed saffron.

"You're from India," I blurted, and instantly felt clumsy.

"Brilliant," Tess mumbled, and cast me a look of derision.

The newcomer dipped into an elegant foreign-looking curtsey. "Maya Barrington."

Hearing her name, I became confused. "You're English?"

"Half-caste." She said it quietly, but with so much defiance and pain, that I blushed with shame for my thoughtlessness.

I didn't know what to say. "I didn't mean . . . that is to say, I was surprised. I apologize—"

"No need." Her voice flowed smooth and cooling over my awkwardness. "But you are correct. I am part English. My father met and married my mother while he was an officer in the East India Company." Clearly she'd delivered this explanation dozens of times.

I found myself responding with a silent curtsey.

She inclined her head. "You must forgive us for looking through your things. We meant no harm. One never knows who to trust." Her words washed over me like a calming mist. She held out my botanical guide as if the faded book was a peace offering.

I still felt awkward and boorish. I didn't know whether to take back my book or tell her to keep it.

"It is a most useful book. Perhaps you will let me look at it again someday?"

Her soothing tone made my tense shoulders relax and I took it from her. "Yes," I muttered, not wanting to say there would be no someday, because I was leaving.

"See. We're not all thieves and charlatans," Jane said, as if sharing a private joke with the others. "Maya is our diplomat."

Tess still brooded. She entreated Sera once more, "Are you quite certain? You didn't see anything else about her?" She said *see* as if it meant much more than observing my height or noting my abundance of freckles.

Sera tilted her head, her silken hair shimmered in the candlelight as she answered no. "Perhaps, you—"

Tess cut her off with a quick shake of her head.

"Well, that's that, then." Jane brushed out her skirts. "*C'est la vie.*"

Tess uncrossed her arms and stared at me with obvious disappointment. She turned to Jane. "I was sure it would be her."

Jane answered mournfully. "Time will tell."

Tess pressed her eyes closed for a minute as if blocking out something painful. "That's just it. There's no time left."

I didn't understand what they meant, nor did it matter. I had no intention of staying in this awful place. I grabbed my boots out of the armoire, stuffed them back in my portmanteau, and tried to ignore the disappointment of the girls surrounding me. With an exasperated sigh, I gave in and extended a small olive branch. "If there's something you would like to know about me, you could simply ask. I don't have any secrets."

"Now *that* is a lie." Tess backed away as if I'd burned her. "Everyone has secrets."

Jane merely shrugged and turned away. "Thank you, but we'd rather have heard it from Sera."

The girls of Stranje House were a peculiar lot. Apparently, they all tilted a little too far off the starboard beam. But then again, Sebastian probably thought the same about me. Was I as out of plumb as these girls? Or was I worse? I sighed heavily and closed my trunk. I couldn't ignore the fact that my parents had left me here in this madhouse for some reason.

The girls drifted apart, leaving me alone. It didn't matter. I was used to solitude. I had always played alone, eaten alone, and been sad alone. Why should tonight be any different? I sat on the nearest bed and picked at a nubbin of wool on my stocking. I needed to face facts. *I am a trifle odd.* But was I so abnormal that my own parents would dispose of me just as they would a three-legged pup?

Madame Cho barged in and struck the floor with her bamboo walking sick. "Bedclothes. Now." She thumped it again. The other girls had already scattered like quail into the shadowy corners of the room. I didn't move.

The old dragon drew up in front of me and threw open my trunk. She yanked out a night rail and flung it at me. Her dark eyes flashed like steel against flint. I swallowed any hope of defiance. She leaned close, so close I grimaced at the smell of rice and fish and leeks. "You sleep now. Unpack tomorrow."

I had no intention of doing either. I would not sleep. Nor would I unpack. And yet, I couldn't find the strength to make even a pretense of obedience. I was trapped, a rabbit paralyzed beneath Madame Cho's snake eyes. My limbs felt heavy and useless, my spirit drained of strength. I hated her, I hated this place, hated this night. So, despite her fierce glare and fishy breath, I just sat there.

Not until she pinched my leg, did I move. Her bamboo cane slapped the hardwood floor, a warning of what would come next if I didn't comply. "Bedclothes!"

I stood then, and mechanically untied the tapes of my traveling gown. It slipped off and I tossed it across the chest. What did I care if it wrinkled? My petticoats pooled around my feet and I stepped out of them. The old dragon moved away, nodding, pleased to have proven her authority over me.

The evening chill prickled my flesh. I shivered, more determined than ever to escape. All I needed was a proper plan. I may be odd and peculiar, I may be freckled and unlovable, but there's one thing I know for certain about myself: I am good at making plans. Even if some of those plans do, occasionally, burst into flames.

Four

NIGHT CREEPERS

I lay in bed, next to a stranger who may or may not be deranged, and stared into the darkness. Alone. Cast out. Discarded by my parents like so much rubbish. How could they do this? My head throbbed. How long, I wondered, how long would they leave me here?

I posed the question to my bedmate, Sera. "How long have you been at Stranje House?"

"Two years." She sighed mournfully. "And then some."

Two years. She may as well have punched me in the stomach. I turned away and curled on my side. Two years was an eternity. My parents wouldn't leave me here that long. *Surely not.* This was merely a punishment. As soon as I demonstrated proper behavior, they would let me return home. *Surely.*

The more I dwelled on it, the more I conjectured that perhaps they'd sent me to Stranje House out of love. After all, Squire Thurgood had been furious about his burnt orchard. The night of the fire there had been talk of calling in the magistrate, and loud discussions about the proper punishment for young ladies who set fire to their fathers' stables.

I squeezed the pillow around my head in an attempt to blot out those recollections, because I could not help but recall my father ranting as loud as the Squire. He certainly hadn't defended me, except to the extent that he refused to allow a magistrate to interfere. He swore he'd handle it himself, not wanting his good name tarnished by the reckless acts of his addlepated daughter.

Oh, yes, I might well be banished to Stranje House for two years.

Or longer.

It all came back to escape. I set to counting the names of people I might impose upon to house me after I escaped. The list was short. To be perfectly frank, the list was blank. My uncle, Lord Brucklesby, would promptly return me to my father. My maternal grandfather would do the same after delivering a hearty lecture and liberally applying a switch to my legs.

Then there was the problem of getting past the dogs, or wolves. Whatever they were, they posed an obstacle. I groaned and sank deeper into the pillow, wishing it would swallow me up and spit me out at home in my own bed.

I would never get to sleep. It didn't help that one of the girls prowled through the dark like a sneaky fox. For all I knew, one of my fellow students might have a penchant for strangling people in their sleep. That might account for why there were so few girls in this *supposed* school.

Tess scampered across the room, keeping to the shadows along wall. Like a ballerina doing an arabesque, she bent on one leg and peered under the thin gap beneath our closed door. She darted back and whispered, "She's gone."

Sera rolled toward my side of the bed and spoke softly next

to my ear, "Madame Cho stands guard every night until we are asleep."

Madame Cho had failed in her task.

She flung back the covers and swung her feet over the side of the bed. "Come."

Come where? I didn't move. Whatever they were up to, they could do it without me. I had plans to formulate.

Jane popped out of the darkness and thrust her face next to mine. "Did you think to pack candles in that enormous trunk of yours?"

Startled by her sudden appearance, I only shook my head. No. I hadn't thought to smuggle a firearm into my luggage either, but it might've proved handy in dealing with this lot.

"I thought you were supposed to be the smart one." She grasped my hand and tugged me out of bed. "Come on then. We'll have to make do without."

Normally, I would have demanded to know exactly what was going on and why, but given the odd inhabitants of this school and my precarious position among them, I decided it would be prudent to remain silent and cooperate. Tonight, I would emulate Captain Cook on his voyages to the aboriginal people of the South Pacific. For the sake of science, I would observe and analyze the natives in their natural habitat. Truth be told, I *was* curious.

Jane tugged me along as we crept to the far side of the room. The others huddled near an ornate oak paneled wall. Tess pressed the top corner and a latch clicked. The panel scraped against the floor as she pulled it open. We tensed. Jane and Maya spun around and stared at the bedroom door, wary as deer fleeing a hunter.

Maya exhaled and whispered, "She did not hear."

Tess disappeared through the opening and Sera followed.

I balked, having seen quite enough of secret passages for one day. I didn't relish the dust and mildew on my bare feet, or the spiders, or mice, or—

"Come." Maya took my hand and ended my standoff. "You will want to see this."

I don't know why I let Maya persuade me. *Baffling.* Perhaps it was the musical quality of her voice, or her gentle nature. I only know I felt compelled to follow her. I ducked under the oak frame, into the wall, and a blanket of dense blackness engulfed us.

Jane pushed me from behind. "Hurry."

I followed the others up the narrow stairway. Jane pulled the panel shut, and stale, musty, cupboard air closed around us. The tight quarters inside the wall magnified every sound; five of us breathing, ten feet padding on the crumbling stone stairs, and the whiskery *tick-tick* of mice chasing up the steps beside us.

"Mice!" I warned the others.

"Hush." Jane patted my back. "Keep moving. Tess will deal with the rats."

"*Rats?*"

Jane silenced me with a thump between my shoulder blades. I shivered, but not from the cold. I imagined dozens of gray, greedy-eyed vermin swarming around us, their hairless tails whipping from side to side, and their sharp teeth snapping at my heels. I tiptoed cautiously up the cold steps, hoping each splinter of rotting wood, every nubbin of broken plaster underfoot was not an angry rat's tail.

We climbed higher and higher, until at last, the air tasted less stagnant, and gray light filtered down from somewhere above us. "Ack!" I hopped aside as one of the rats, a fat dark fellow, scurried past me, racing up the stairs toward the opening.

Jane shushed me again. So I kept mum and followed Maya out of the passage into a low-ceilinged attic.

Large undraped dormer windows cut into both sides of the long garret, and moonlight bathed the room in wisps of silvery blue. Discarded paintings leaned against a monolithic old wardrobe. Crates and trunks, stacked in tall misshapen pillars, formed caverns and created weird shadows. In the center of this labyrinth, near one of the windows, sat several mismatched dilapidated chairs arranged in a semicircle. Jane lit a small tin oil lamp and placed it on the floor, but it barely illuminated the chairs.

Sera hurried to the window seat and busied herself with a sailor's spyglass. Unlatching the window, she focused it toward the east. I peered out, trying to determine our height and the distance to the edge of the property, wondering if Da Vinci's kite might serve as a method of escape. But I couldn't see a road in that direction. I wended through boxes and broken furniture to the window on the far side of the room, only to find it looked out over the sea crashing against the cliffs. No hope in that direction, not without a flying boat.

A broken mirror leaned against the wall near my feet. I might not be able to build a flying boat, but I could do something about the gloom in the attic. Selecting two large pieces, I returned to the circle and used a vase and a small wooden stool to prop the mirrors at angles around the lamp. I adjusted them so that they amplified the feeble lamplight. Jane watched my efforts with interest, but any response she might have made was eclipsed by Sera's exclamation.

"I see him!" she cried softly. "He's in the library."

"Let me." Tess rushed to the window and took the telescope.

"Who? What library?" I asked, forgetting my resolve to observe silently.

Jane pointed. "Look past our grounds, beyond that stand of trees. There. Do you see the neighboring manor?"

Our window jutted out from the peak of the house affording us an unimpeded view of the property to the north and east. The moon peeked through the mist and I saw where Stranje House's tangled woods ended and opened out onto a smooth manicured park. Farther east stood the profile of a large manor. A window on the second story glowed with orange firelight.

I nodded.

"It belongs to Lord Ravencross," she said, as if his name held some special significance. Then she whispered, "Very mysterious fellow. He returned from the war and reduced his staff to only two servants for that entire manor house."

Jane squinted at the neighbor's mansion as if she was counting the number of rooms. "He must keep most of it closed up and in covers." She shook her head. "He refuses all visitors, never pays calls to anyone in the neighborhood. Rarely does anyone go in or out." With a wry smirk she added, "We play guessing games about him. What do you say, Georgiana? Is he so horribly disfigured he cannot abide company?"

"You are the only one who plays those guessing games, Jane." Sera tugged the spyglass away from Tess. "And I do wish you would stop. The poor man is in mourning. His only brother is dead. He deserves our sympathy, not your mockery."

Maya stood beside Sera straining to see across the park. "You must think we are dreadful busybodies." She turned to me with a probing gaze and awaited my answer.

I hedged. "I suppose it's only natural all of you would be curious about a neighbor."

Sera shook her head. "No. It is much more than mere curiosity. He needs us."

I didn't see how that could be true, but I held my tongue.

"You're skeptical, but I assure you it's true." Sera sighed deeply and dove into an inscrutable explanation. "Tess had one of her dreams, a nightmare really, about a young man being brutally injured in a horrifying fight. She woke up screaming. We were all quite alarmed because she isn't like me. I only see what is. Tess has dreams and she sees—"

Tess pinched her.

"Ow!" Sera rubbed her arm and glared at Tess. "The upshot of it is, three weeks later we witnessed Lord Ravencross returning from the war, and he was limping."

Jane shook her head. "Sera fancies he is a wounded hero. She, of course, is the heroine who must heal him from his tragic past."

In lilting accents Maya explained, "Seraphina has a poet's heart."

Jane gave Sera's shoulder a teasing shove. "Because she reads too many novels."

"Either way, it's all rubbish." Tess stretched like a cat and leaned out of the window, letting the cool breeze ruffle her hair. "He's healed from his injuries well enough. I saw him this morning, riding his horse at a bruising pace."

Sera's elfin-like features widened with surprise. "You kept this news to yourself?" Moonlight illuminated her pale blue eyes and made her hair glimmer like spun silver. She pulled Tess back inside the window.

"I'm telling you now."

"How near to him did you get? How does he look?"

We scarcely breathed waiting for Tess to tell us about the man in the golden window. She slumped against the window frame and fidgeted with the fabric of her nightdress. Clearly, she did not wish to tell about the encounter. Finally, she answered, "What do you wish to know? He looks very like his older brother did, except his hair is long and wild." She shrugged. "One can assume his sole purpose for riding was to exercise the horse, because he wore neither coat nor hat. His shirt was damp with sweat, and he had worked his poor stallion into a lather. There, I have told you all about the infamous Lord Ravencross."

"Were his features twisted in pain?" Sera asked.

Tess glanced toward Lord Ravencross's manor. "Not with pain."

She peered sideways at Tess. "Is he badly scarred?"

"Not as much as we'd expected." Tess shook her head. "There's a jagged mark across one cheek."

Jane lost all patience. "What aren't you telling us?"

Tess stiffened. "I meant to spare you. You won't like it. But if you must insist on knowing . . ." The edge on her voice softened. "Sera, you ought not waste your pity on him. He's nothing like the hero you imagine him to be. Lord Ravencross is an angry heartless scoundrel."

Sera drew back. "Don't say such things."

"What's more, he's rude." Tess slid out of the windowsill and paced. Her straight brown hair fell across her cheek as she counted out more of his sins. "He's callous and unfeeling." She stopped and looked into each of our amazed faces. "It's the truth." Chin in the air she pushed past us and flopped into one of the chairs.

"Unfeeling? Why would you say such things? After everything he's been through?" Sera tilted her head and squinted at Tess. "Something happened between you, didn't it?"

Maya sat beside Tess. "Whatever occurred, it seems to be troubling you. You must tell us."

Tess crossed her arms and sank deeper into the chair. "He nearly trampled me to death, that's what happened."

"You were running in the fields again, weren't you?" Jane chided.

"Don't fuss at me. You know perfectly well, I *have* to run," Tess snapped. "As long as I go early in the morning and no one sees me there's no harm in it. There's never anyone out at dawn."

"Apparently, there is," Jane scoffed.

"I always have that hour to myself. How could I have known we'd cross his paths and I'd startle his horse."

"Of course not," Maya soothed.

"What about the wolves?" I asked. "How did you keep from being attacked?"

"Wolves!" Tess tilted her head quizzically. "Do you mean the dogs?"

"They don't look like dogs," I said, remembering their yellow eyes.

She shrugged. "I suppose they might be wolves, but—"

"It doesn't matter. Either way, they would never hurt Tess. No animal would." Jane returned to the matter at hand. "What happened when you startled his horse?"

"It reared, and I stumbled backward into the mud." Tess smacked the torn armchair. Wadding and dust puffed out. "It was so stupid. I *never* fall. And I wouldn't have today if he'd controlled his mount."

Having fallen once or twice that very evening, I pointed out, "All of us *fall* from time to time."

"I don't." Tess pressed her lips tight and stared intently into the dark side of the room. "He swore at me." When she turned back to us, her cat-shaped eyes had hardened against the sympathy we offered. "His horse reared again. They always do, don't they, when someone shouts."

"Especially where you're involved," Jane said softly.

I didn't comprehend her meaning, but the others seemed to.

They gathered closer to Tess, except for Sera, who hung back staring out the window as if she longed to hear Lord Ravencross's version of the events.

"He called me a bothersome little demon." Tess sank deeper into the chair. "Or something equally hateful. Exactly as my uncle would've done."

"It was said in the heat of the moment. He could not have meant it," Maya said in a low, calming voice.

"What happened next?" Jane demanded, like a governess expecting a child to spill all the facts of the matter onto the table.

Tess's jaw tensed. "He pointed his crop at me and told me to stay clear of his property or he would bloody well take a horsewhip to my backside. Then he galloped off and left me flat on my bottom in the mud."

"Oh, dear." Maya shook her head mournfully. "That was badly done."

"Appalling." Jane rendered her verdict. "You're right. He's rude. That explains why he carries on like a hermit."

"It certainly wasn't gentlemanly behavior," I said.

"He must be terribly sad." Sera peered through the spyglass again. "Look there. See how he limps as he paces in front of the fire. He wouldn't have treated you so poorly if he were not wracked with pain."

"Pain does not excuse him from common decency." I might've said more, if I hadn't noticed something stirring in the shadows near Tess's feet. "Don't move," I warned. Two tiny rubies glowed in the darkness. I knew immediately what creature lurked beneath her chair. "Rat!"

I did not shriek. At least, I prefer to *think* I didn't shriek. I snatched an old shoe out of a nearby box, lunged, and slapped wildly at the fiend. One knock on the head with the chunky Georgian heel and that horrid rat would cease to exist.

"Stop." Tess grabbed my arm and snatched the shoe out of my hand. "They're only hungry."

"Yes, for your toes."

Jane laughed.

Then, I registered the plural pronoun in Tess's plea. "They?"

To my horror, she pulled two scraps of bread from her pocket, stooped near the bottom of her chair, making ridiculous kissing noises, just as one might use to call a kitten. A pair of rats skulked out, scowling in my direction.

Tess held out the bread to them. "Don't be afraid. It's all right. The big, bad, new girl didn't know you're our friends."

Jane said, "Don't lump me into that category. They're your friends, not mine." She tossed a cynical smirk in my direction. "Miss Fitzwilliam, allow me to do the honors." She waved me closer. "May I present Messieurs Punch and Judy."

I cringed. Two plump rats, one dark gray and the other a white albino, greedily tore into the morsels of bread Tess doled out.

Jane shook her head at my distress. "Poor Georgiana, sent away to a school inhabited by thieves, liars, and rats."

The gray rat gobbled his crust down and then tried to snatch his cohort's bread. Tess tapped him lightly on the back and scolded, "Don't be so greedy." But she indulged him with another crust.

Jane leaned close to my ear as if confiding a secret. "The gray one ought to have been named Jack rather than Judy. Tess says they're both males. I suggested we keep the name, but think of it as a nickname for Judas. As you can see, he's a rather disloyal thief."

Sera nodded sympathetically at me. "You'll get used to them. But guard your ribbons well. They're his favorite."

Her olive branch of kindness intensified my curiosity. Why

was Sera here? Why had any of them been sent to this awful school? I couldn't figure it out. Unlike me, all of these girls were beautiful. Which meant they were marriageable. There was always a gentleman willing to marry a pretty girl, as long as she was moderately well behaved and had an enticing dowry. I doubted they would be here if their families didn't have money.

My question was impertinent, but I couldn't help myself. I had to know. I turned to Jane and asked, "Why are you here?" When she didn't answer immediately I tried to clarify. "What I mean to say is, why are you at Stranje House? You don't seem in need of . . . er . . . reforming." I couldn't think of a way to ask that wouldn't insult her.

An emotion splashed across Jane's face, but vanished so swiftly I couldn't identify it. Was it anger? Sadness perhaps? Or pain? She withdrew and turned stiff and formal. "Are you asking why I'm here, instead of in London lined up against the wall at Almack's, hunting a husband along with all the other sheep-faced little debutantes?"

She said it with such ferocity that I could only nod.

"It's simple really. I made too much money."

Even more confused, I shook my head. "You must've misunderstood my question—"

"No, you're the one who doesn't understand." She spoke loud enough to draw the other girls' attention. "I'm here for the same reason all of us are here. The same reason that brought you here."

"I doubt you burned down your father's stables," I blurted, and immediately wished I could retract the words.

"Burned it down?" Jane drew back and exchanged glances with Tess. "Well, I admit, that is a trifle unique." The corner of her mouth quirked up. I expected her to laugh at me, or mock me. She didn't. Instead, her wry smirk developed an edge of respect. For the first time Jane seemed genuinely interested in me. Her eyebrow hooked up sharply. "Surely, you realize that the fire isn't the *only* reason your parents sent you away."

Her question wormed into my mind, burrowing into dark corners I wanted left untouched. It was better not to question my parents' motives. Better not to dwell on their lack of affection for me. Better to *never* think about such things.

Ever.

But Jane waited for an answer, and the longer I hesitated the more knowing her expression became. Cruel of her to guess at their intentions. Anyway, she was wrong. I swallowed down the bile rising from my stomach. She didn't know them. She couldn't possibly know how invisible I usually was to them. No, the facts of the matter were simple. I'd caused a problem for my parents, that was all. I'd been a nuisance. Stranje House was simply their reaction to the fire. I refused to put any other construction on it.

I backed away and shook my head. "No. It's simple. Cause and effect. I started a fire and now I'm being punished."

"What were you doing when it started?" Tess asked.

"Mixing chemicals." I answered too quickly, and awakened the worm again. It started gnawing away at my raw places. *No, no, no.* I pushed it away, and threw a question back at Jane, where it belonged. "Why would anyone send you away simply because you made too much money?"

They all stared at me. The fire forgotten. Rats forgotten. Lord Rotten Ravencross forgotten.

Jane rubbed the bruise on her jaw. "You might just as easily ask why Sera is here for drawing a picture."

Tess glanced up from the rat she cradled. "To be fair, it was an extremely accurate sketch of her grandfather. Which would not have caused such a stir except he had died when Sera was only two."

"Hardly a reason to lock her in a closet with nothing but bread and water for a month," Jane protested. "Or you, Tess, exiled because your uncle's stallion kicked him."

Tess shifted uncomfortably and mumbled, "A bit more to it than that."

Jane paid her no heed. "And what about Maya, who never did anything to anyone except be born too beautiful and with a voice—"

Maya inhaled sharply. "No more, Jane. *Please.*"

But Jane ignored her, and with a sweeping gesture asked, "Can anyone here guess how the patronesses of Almack's would react upon meeting a young lady who mixes chemicals in her father's barn?" I couldn't tell if she intended to laugh or if she was choking on the words. "Never mind that it caught fire. You're not exactly the *beau monde*'s image of an ideal young lady, are you? You know how they abhor bluestockings."

Jane frowned at me, hands on hips. "You can't truly believe you were sent away solely because of a fire, Georgiana? What did you think? You would serve out a sentence for your crime and then go home, welcomed back into your family's arms? There's no going home again for us. Not really." Her eyes flashed, as if she wanted to slap sense into me. "Starting a fire is awful, yes, but you're here for the same reason we are. Because you don't fit in."

It was a cold hard slap. I edged away. I didn't want to hear anymore.

"You're here because you're odd. *Exceptional.*" Unrelenting, Jane followed me to the edge of the circle. "You're unusual, Georgiana. And *that* is far more dangerous than any fire."

My stomach lurched. For a moment it felt as if the floor might fall out from under me. I could only shake my head.

"You know it's true." Jane clucked her tongue and wagged a

finger at me. "If only you'd sat in the corner like a good little girl, doing needlepoint and reading poetry. Maybe then they wouldn't have booted you out. *Maybe*. But even that trick didn't work for Maya."

"No. You don't understand." I backed away from her. "It isn't that at all. They—"

"Oh, I understand well enough. You didn't sit in the corner, did you, Georgie?" Jane kept coming. "No. You were out doing things. Alarming people. Upsetting the proverbial apple cart." She jabbed my shoulder. "And, tell me, Miss Fitzwilliam, what did the people who are supposed to love you do about that? Did they whip you like Tess's uncle did? Or did they lock you in the attic like they did Sera? Or did they simply do what my brothers—"

"Jane! Stop." Sera's normally gentle voice echoed through the room like an iron bell. "You're hurting her."

Jane clamped her lips together for a moment, composing herself. "She needs to know."

"She's not ready." The brass telescope rested in Sera's lap. Moonlight spun a halo about her silvery hair.

With a resigned sigh, Jane dropped into the nearest chair. "You know perfectly well she's bound to figure it out."

"Not yet. Not tonight." Moonlight cast a haze over Sera. She looked like a ghostly princess holding a golden scepter and her word appeared to be as absolute as any monarch's. "You mustn't rush her."

Too late. Jane's words had already dug talons into my brain.

"You m-m-must excuse me," I stuttered. I never stutter. My mouth felt as dry as burnt toast. I backed toward the passage, bumped into a tower of crates, and glanced behind, toward the dark opening. "I've had a long journey today."

Jane waved her hand dismissively at me. "Bound to get even longer, isn't it, if you keep running away?"

I plunged into the black gloom behind the wall and ran headlong down the crumbling stairs. Fragments of jagged stone bit into the soles of my feet. I didn't care. I'd a hundred times rather face rats and spiders in the darkness than the monstrous truths Jane had unleashed.

Five

ESCAPE

I darted downstairs. Not caring if I tripped. Not caring that the passageway quickly became a pitch-dark pit. I couldn't run fast enough to escape Jane's words hammering in my head. I stopped and covered my ears with my hands, willing myself to blot out the noise.

"It isn't true," I said aloud. "Lies." My parents loved me. Underneath their anger about the fire, my experiments, the card party, and everything else, surely they loved me. They had to. They must.

And yet they'd left me in this vile place.

Was I too peculiar? Did I frighten them, as Jane suggested? I leaned my forehead against the moldy wall, mourning the fact that the lies weren't Jane's. They were mine.

Our families should've seen our worth. Instead, they'd sent us away. I felt sick. My hands dropped to my sides, useless. My life was over. I would be whipped into shape or tortured to death. One way or the other my parents would be rid of me. At least, they would be rid of the *real me*—weird, peculiar, frightening me.

I didn't cry. Oh, I may have choked on a few salty streaks of weakness that slid onto my lips. But I didn't cry. Blubbering was pointless. I wanted to kick something, not cry. I swiped the offending moisture from my cheeks, brushed the grime from my brow, and trudged blindly down the steps. Down, down into hell and forever, around another corner, up another flight, and that's when I realized I was lost.

Again.

Furious, I slammed my hand against the wall. My reward was a palm full of moldy plaster and splinters. Clenching my teeth, I knocked off the debris and plucked at the slivers. Neither anger nor despair would do me any good. This situation required a logical, analytical approach.

Fact: the panel to the dormitorium lay somewhere in this passage.

Fact two: at the very least, I should be able to find another exit into the house.

Fact three: unlike my other problems, this one was solvable.

Even in thick darkness, deep in a tangled maze, there are telltale indications of the terrain. If one stands very still, faint drafts of air tease the senses and briefly relieve the stuffiness, and there are minute sounds. I stilled my thundering heart, calmed my ragged breathing, and listened.

Blocking out the patter of mice, ignoring the surges of wind buffeting the outer wall, I heard the low whistle of air through an opening.

A panel. I hurried to check. But my toe stubbed against a block of wood. The wood flipped sideways as if on a hinge. The floor beneath my foot sagged.

My next step fell on nothingness.

No wood.

No stone.

Nothing.

My elbow smacked against the mouth of the trapdoor. I dropped into blackness. A rush of cold air swallowed my shriek. Wind billowed out my nightdress as I spiraled down a chute, falling, sliding, bumping, scraping against the rough sides. Rocks and debris peppered my shoulders and face. I flung my arms up to shield myself as I plummeted down the black pit.

It seemed to drop forever. Yet, it must've been only seconds before the shaft opened to a broad expanse of air.

No more walls.

A dim light.

Swoosh. I plunged into icy water. Suspended in murky green darkness. Salt and foam flooded into my mouth and nose. I sank amid a torrent of bubbles.

Shock held me captive. Disoriented. Lost. Sinking.

I came to my senses, owing to a desperate need to breathe. Clawing frantically at the water, I followed the rising bubbles toward the surface, paddling like a dog. A drowning dog. At last, I broke through the waves, gagging and sputtering, half blind with confusion.

It took me a moment to realize where I was. Waves sloshed against the sides of a cave. I recognized the flickering oil lamp as it hissed from where it hung on a rough-hewn docking post. I, gulping and grappling, half swimming, half drowning, bobbed my way to the rowboat. No sooner had I grabbed hold of the prow when I spotted something unthinkable sitting against the far wall. My heart nearly spewed out of my throat along with the seawater I'd swallowed.

A skeleton. Bones wearing a tattered pink gown. A noose hung around its neck and a faded placard warned: BEWARE THE HANGMAN'S WALTZ!

I screamed, lost my grip on the rowboat and sank once again beneath the dark waves.

When I burst back up through the surface my nightdress ballooned under my arms. I angrily flung away a strand of seaweed, spit out fishy seawater, and shook off my fear. Bones could not hurt me. But the monsters who'd left that girl here to rot certainly could. I swam for the boat with grim determination. Fate had offered me a chance to escape Stranje House and I intended to take it.

Except when I tried to pull myself into the rowboat the ruddy thing tipped, almost to the point of flipping over. So, I swam, or rather thrashed, toward the dock and heaved myself onto the stone ledge like a great flopping fish. I lay there shivering, a wet muddy mess. As soon as I caught my breath, I took one last look at the skeleton with her ghastly warning, and climbed aboard the rowboat.

The skiff was surprisingly well equipped. In the stern, atop a box of supplies, lay a woolen blanket, which I immediately wrapped around me. Inside the box I found a bottle of brandy and a neatly wrapped parcel containing bread and cheese. Having had very little to eat that day I ripped off a hunk of bread and took a quick bite. That would have to do for now. I needed to get under way before Captain Grey and Sebastian returned for their boat.

It had to be theirs. Most likely the two of them were smugglers. Or pirates. *Lord Wyatt*, indeed! That couldn't possibly be his real name. Sebastian was no gentleman. And even if he was, it didn't matter. Their rowboat was mine now. I set the two oars into place and tugged the rope loose from the docking post.

Rowing proved trickier than I'd expected. The boat banged against the cave walls a number of times. The oars knocked one side or the other so often, it was a small wonder the entire household did not come running. I battled the current and managed to maneuver the craft toward the small mouth of the cave. Luck was with me. I caught an outgoing wave, ducking as the dinghy thumped and bumped its way through the low arch to freedom.

Stars blinked in and out as clouds raced across the inky sky. I'd done it. I had escaped.

Surf roared in my ears and the rowboat lifted high atop a wave. I set to the oars, suddenly aware that the cave had provided shelter from the wind and this violent tide. It took every ounce of my strength to keep the skiff from crashing against the rocky shore. I rowed like mad, but the sea lifted up the boat and tossed it down as if it was a child's toy.

I'd escaped, but to what end. *Death?*

The thought of drowning in that dark sea, of sinking unnoticed and unremembered into a vast unmarked grave, of being eaten by indifferent fish and scavenging snails made a shudder run through me. Fear gave way to a warming anger. I would not surrender to death. Not without giving it a good fight.

I rowed harder, leaning into every stroke. My life depended on it. Waves pelted me. Salt bit against my cheeks. Wind whipped the blanket from my shoulders, but I dared not stop to adjust it. I put my back into the task of rowing, lifting off the seat to push harder. Even with my newfound strength the oars grew heavier and more awkward with every stroke.

Waves splashed over the sides, turning my woolen blanket into a sodden mess, filling the hull with frigid water, sloshing against my calves. I pulled in the oars, grabbed the bucket from the corner in order to bail, but the boat started to spin and tilt to one side. I rushed to put out the paddles again. The left oar slipped from the blocks. I lunged for it, but my fingers only grazed the handle before it sank in the swells.

The next wave slapped me soundly for my stupid mistake.

No time for regrets—not if I wanted to live. I struggled with the lone oar, trying to distance myself from the deadly rocky shore. It seemed like I rowed forever and yet the outline of the cliffs still loomed perilously close. My arms ached and I couldn't stop shivering. The contents of my stomach had long since left me. Over and over, the boat rose heavenward six or seven feet and then dropped like a stone into a trough. Miraculously it didn't capsize.

Exhausted from being tossed about like an unwanted doll, I yearned for solid land. The rowboat rode up the back of a gigantic swell. This time, instead of plunging off into a valley of water and being thrashed by the falling wave, we stayed atop the curl. I have never moved so fast in all my life.

Moonlight exposed the beach. All rocks. As the sea flung me toward the cliffs I realized the little boat would be smashed to pieces. I wrapped the soggy blanket around me, crouched low, and braced myself against the crosspiece.

I remember a splintering crunch, and the marvelous sensation of flying through the air. After that, I only recall my head thudding against stone.

Hot white fireworks.

And the sudden inability to draw breath.

It's quite possible I may have died. I'm not certain. It's all rather hazy. I do remember feeling terribly cold. Then sinking into a peaceful warmth.

Oblivion.

I didn't regain my senses until morning when the sun stabbed through my stupor. Light made the throbbing worse—pain at the back of my skull so intense it felt as though someone was beating me rhythmically with a big stick. I kept my eyelids closed tight until something scratchy and moist slid across my cheek. I squinted and peeked out of one eye.

Two yellow eyes stared back.

Dark fur. Teeth.

Wolf.

I gasped for air. But my lungs froze.

I meant to scream. Tried to scream. Nothing came out. Oh, God, let me drown and be eaten by fishes, *please*. Not torn apart by wolves. I closed my eyes tight, wishing to return to that comfortable oblivion that had consumed me during the night.

The wolf yipped softly and nudged my chest with its nose.

I shook. No, I trembled. Every part of me quaked, even my innermost parts—heart, stomach, *everything*. I shook with such taut rapid vibrations that nothing outwardly moved.

Something warm shifted against my back, snuffled, and pressed a wet nose into my neck. There were two of them. Two gigantic wolves very, *very* close. So close, I could smell their meaty breath and the musky scent of grass and dead leaves rising from their fur. So close, drool dripped onto my cheek as the one standing sniffed me. The wolf lying behind me licked my shoulder.

Hot pain pulsed at the back of my skull. Yet the rest of me felt intensely cold. I began to shiver more violently. The wolf standing over me stopped sniffing. With a low growl, he laid down and curved his enormous body into mine, pressing up against my belly. The other beast responded with a short low yip.

Were they warming up breakfast? Or preserving my soggy carcass for dinner? Their behavior made no sense and yet their heat had a calming effect on my quavering insides. Moments later the wolf in front of me lifted his head, his ears peaked. He startled me with a sharp bark and jumped to his feet. His mate did the same.

Their ruckus nearly deafened me. Finally they stopped. But my head pounded louder than ever. Despite the throbbing I heard boots running on the beach. "What is it, Phobos?" A man greeted my wolf. "Down, boy! Down." The animal behind me growled. "Easy there, Tromos. What have you found?"

I groaned. *It would be him.*

"Good Lord!" Sebastian knelt beside me. "Back, Tromos, stand back. There's a good girl."

I kept my eyes closed as he pressed two fingers against the artery in my neck.

"Miss Fitzwilliam?" He gently shook my shoulder. "Miss Fitzwilliam, can you hear me?"

I made no sound.

Lord Wyatt whipped off his coat and laid it over me. "Captain!" he shouted, making my head hammer ferociously. "Captain! Over here. Forget the boat. It's the girl. She's hurt."

Captain Grey ran up breathing hard. "Is she . . . ?"

"Alive. But, judging by the blood, she's injured her head." He gently lifted my shoulder. "See? Do you think it's safe to move her?"

"We've no choice. In this cold, it's a wonder she survived the night."

Sebastian scooped me up. "I expect Phobos and Tromos had something to do with it."

So, these wolves had names, Greek for fear and trembling. It suited them.

Captain Grey shed his coat, too, wrapping it about my legs. "There now. Steady on, Miss Fitzwilliam. We'll get you back to the house. " He tucked the coats around me, speaking as one does to an injured animal, soothing it, but not expecting an answer. "Take her straight to Emma," he directed Sebastian. "She'll know what to do. I'll ride for a doctor. We need this girl alive."

Ah, yes, so you can torture my ink formula out of me.

I said nothing as Sebastian carried me back to Stranje House. I decided to play dumb, pretend delirium. It wouldn't be hard. The searing cold and throbbing pain made it difficult to think, let alone speak. But as he mounted the steep path up the cliffs, the climb jostled my head, and I moaned involuntarily.

He lengthened his stride once we got to level ground and I settled into his arms. If only he would've kept silent. "Wake up, Miss Ruffles."

Ruffles. Ohhh, the evil wretch.

He shifted me against his chest. "Come on, you little termagant, I know you're in there. Say something clever. Or ridiculous. Anything. Perhaps you might tell me why a young lady would dabble with invisible-ink formulas?"

Dabble? I almost erred and said it aloud. *Dabble*, indeed! My experiments constituted a great deal more than mere dabbling. How dare he? Furious, I clenched my jaw. The effort cost me. A whimper escaped.

"Miss Fitzwilliam?" He stopped walking. Sunlight filtered across my eyelids. I felt him staring at me. The rascal bent close and blew a lock of hair away from my face. "Georgiana?"

The audacity of the man—addressing me by my Christian name. I kept mum. I even managed not to shiver when he brushed the side of his finger all tickle-y and gentle against my cheek.

"Damn it," he whispered. "Wake up." He took off at an even faster pace than before. "You're no good to me dead."

No good to him dead.

How very moving. The milk of human kindness must've

soured completely before he'd had his sip. Never mind that the man smelled of fresh linen and sunshine, he truly was a despicable wretch. The bruising pace he set nearly made me shriek with pain, but I bit my lip, refusing to give him the satisfaction of knowing I'd awakened. I'd rather pretend to be in a coma for the rest of my life.

Sebastian pushed past the grim butler of Stranje House. "Where's your mistress?" He whisked me into the foyer. My feet brushed against a flower arrangement on the entry table. "Speak up, man, where's Miss Stranje?"

"The ballroom, my lord. But you can't—my lord, wait!"

We were nearly up the stairs by then. The old fellow hurried after us, sputtering like an overheated teakettle. Sebastian kicked open the ballroom doors and strode in.

I peeked cautiously through my eyelashes, and nearly shrieked in horror. Tess, Jane, Sera, and Maya, all of them were bound with ropes to straight-backed chairs, cloth gags tied across their mouths. At the center of this ghastly semicircle stood Madame Cho, steadily thumping her stick, and consulting a timepiece. She must be punishing them because I'd escaped. I moaned.

Miss Stranje took one look at us and snapped her pocket watch shut. "Good Heavens."

Sebastian headed straight for her, carrying me like a dripping rag across the ballroom. "I believe *this* belongs to you," he said flatly.

This? He'd relegated me to a *this*?

Her heels clicked briskly against the wood floor as she hurried to us. "I've got men out searching the roads and inns for her. We'd assumed she'd run home. Why is she wet? What happened?"

"We found our boat run aground, nothing but splinters, and

her sprawled out in the rocks with a head wound. Captain Grey has gone for the sawbones."

But Miss *Sadistic* Stranje was already plowing none-too-gently through my matted blood-soaked hair, found my injury, and was ascertaining the exact dimensions and tenderness. It felt the size of a small thumping rabbit to me, but she declared it, "A sizeable goose egg. Has she explained herself?"

"No." Lord Wyatt shifted me higher in his arms. "Aside from a moan here and there, she's been unconscious."

"Hmm." The Queen of Cruelty peeled back one of my eyelids and arched her brow. "Oh, you're awake. How very good of you to join us, Miss Fitzwilliam."

No use trying to dupe her. I gave up my pretense and glanced past her, at my fellow students, bound and gagged. "What are you doing to them? It's not their fault. They had nothing to do with my running away." I sounded like a bleating baby goat, and so forced some strength into my voice. "You cannot mistreat them this way. I shall see you hang for it." I attempted to shout that last bit, only to shrink back, wincing with pain. In a less boisterous manner, I warned, "I saw that girl's bones." At her blank stare, I added, "The dead girl in the pink gown."

"Bones? Pink gown? What dead girl?" Miss Stranje laid her hand against my forehead. "What are you going on about?"

I thought I saw Tess and Jane exchange a flickering worried glance. But my head hurt so badly, any minute I expected everything to go black. Next it would be my bones rotting in the cave, wearing nothing but this muddy night rail. I closed my eyes.

Miss Stranje heaved a sigh. "She must be delirious."

"I'm not." I forced my eyes open to squint at her. My arm flopped out and I pointed at the girls squirming in their ropes to get free. "How can you be so cruel?"

A muffled sound came from Jane.

"Girls!" Miss Stranje clapped her hands. "You're running out of time."

"No. *Please*. Don't hurt them." I gestured weakly, my energy flagging. "You can't."

She clucked her tongue at me, and spoke to Sebastian in somber undertones. "She must have a fever. Would you be so good as to carry her up to the dormitorium?" With those clicking heels of hers echoing in my head, Miss Stranje tromped ahead of us to the door. "Madame Cho, I leave you to handle the situation here."

Situation? She meant the girls. But they didn't deserve Madame Cho's stick. "Don't beat them." My plea fell on deaf ears.

"Greaves, warm some blankets, and send up broth."

We climbed the stairs, me silent, Sebastian grim-faced. At least, he had the decency not to say any more rude things to me. By now, I expected his arms must be sorely aching, having carried me all the way from the beach. I gave him credit for not complaining. With each step, pinpricks of light flashed at the edge of my vision. I bit hard on my bottom lip to keep from whimpering. Before we reached the dormitorium, the flashes dissolved into a blind stupor. I don't recall Sebastian leaving. I do vaguely remember someone tugging at my hair with a cloth and a comb, and a stern-faced man listening to my chest with a cone. One of the girls, Jane, I think, spooned broth into my mouth. After that, there was only sleep, dark and seemingly endless sleep.

Not restful.

A fitful, meandering miasma—over and over I relived the previous night, running in dark passages, drowning in waves, crashing on rocks, and wolves standing over me. Finally I dreamed of a huge black stallion with flames snorting from his nostrils. A mysterious stranger rode the ferocious beast. Lest the horse trample me, I ran as fast as I could, but never seemed to escape. When I turned to see him, the rider bore down even harder, laughing at my terror. Flames illuminated his face and I saw that it was that wicked devil Sebastian.

Thrashing at the covers and gasping for dear life, I opened my eyes. "Agh." Morning poured in as someone threw back the curtains.

"About time you woke up, slugabed."

I blinked. Tess stood silhouetted in the too-bright window. A small kitten licked my cheek, the tiny tongue tickled as she washed away the sweat of my night terrors. I squinted, grateful for the affection, relieved to have escaped wolves and a fire-breathing stallion. A wee pink nose sniffed at me, white whiskers waved merrily, and tiny red eyes—

I screamed.

It's true. I admit it. I squawked like a Sunday chicken and shook madly at the covers, sending the vile creature skidding across the floor.

"Stop!" Tess scooped up the rat and cuddled him in the crook of her arm. "He meant you no harm."

Had I not been half out of my mind at the time, I would've sworn that rat squeaked something in response to Tess's ridiculous speech.

"Did that . . . that *thing*," I said, and pointed, still clutching the covers. "That vermin spend the night on my bed?" I wiped my cheek. "I thought it was a kitten."

"I daresay, Punch is as good as any kitten and twice as smart. He sensed you might be lonely. Fine way to repay his kindness."

The other girls were up and dressed, staring at me. I remembered the gentle touch of Punch's tongue on my cheek and felt a little ashamed. There had been some comfort in it, even if it was from a rat.

"Are you well enough to get up?" Jane sat down on the edge of the bed.

My head hurt, but it didn't throb like it had yesterday. "Yes, I think so. How long have I been sleeping?"

"Since yesterday." Sera tickled the rodent as it tumbled and twisted in Tess's arms. "The doctor said to let you rest, that you'd be right as rain in the morning. Although, what is right about rain, I'll never know."

"And you? What did they do to you?" I asked, looking closely for new bruises. "Did Madame Cho beat you?"

Exchanging furtive glances with one another, they didn't answer.

"You can tell me. I've found a way out. We can escape. There's a cave—"

Jane patted my hand. "We know all about the cave, Georgie. It's all right if I call you that, isn't it?"

It was odd that she would ask permission now, after having freely used my given name in the attic. I nodded.

She straightened the edge of the quilt, not looking at me squarely. "Well then, Georgie, we all think it was awfully good of you to stand up for us the way you did."

Sera murmured agreement, and Maya said, "Most kind."

Tess shrugged. "Yes, fine. It was all plummy and sweet of you. But now it's almost time for breakfast. Do you plan to come with us or shall we send up more broth?"

My stomach grumbled at the notion.

"I believe we have our answer." Maya's cheery voice rippled through us like a wind chime, lifting the mood. She opened my trunk and pulled out a sprigged muslin morning gown trimmed with mourning lavender and black. Although I looked ghastly in it, it would have to do. "Perhaps you would like to wear this?" She sounded uncertain.

Sera grimaced at the ugly gown, but grabbed my hand. "First, I believe you might benefit from a quick rinse in the Feetham machine."

To my astonishment, Miss Stranje's establishment boasted of an indoor privy. Not only that, the room contained a Cumming's sliding valve water closet. I had begged my parents to install one of these brilliant new mechanisms at our estate. My venerable parents warned me to stop filling my head with nonsensical ideas. "Chamber pots," they said, "have served the aristocracy of England for centuries. It gives the servants something to do during the day."

Another contraption stood in the privy. The Feetham machine was nothing short of a miracle.

"Climb in." Sera ordered.

Mouth still agape, I obediently stepped over the edge of a copper tub into the center of a four-legged contraption of pipes supporting a cistern overhead.

"Clothes." Sera pointed to a stool on which I might place my night rail. Meanwhile she took hold of a hand pump and began working it vigorously. "Pull the chain, but I must warn you—"

Too late.

Eager to see it at work I yanked on the handle. "Awk! Cold. Cold." Cold water drenched my head. I practically leaped out.

She laughed and handed me a sponge and soap. "May as well finish washing up."

I did so with all haste. A very reviving experience. The warm towel afterward had never felt so good. Unfortunately, my curls frizzled tighter than ever. Corkscrews, my mother called my wild curls. No use trying to smooth them out. Only with excruciating effort and a hot iron could they be tamed. Thank goodness the machine had washed out the blood and sand. I sighed, grabbed a ribbon from my portmanteau, and tied back my tangled mop.

Maya helped me pull the dress over my head, and tie the side tapes. I took the opportunity to ask, "Why were all of you tied in chairs? What did Madame Cho do to you?"

"If you plan on coming with us, stop talking and hurry up." Tess sniffed impatiently. "You've taken too long already. We aren't allowed to be late." She deposited Punch with Judy behind the secret panel and latched it. "I, for one, do not intend to miss breakfast."

I jammed on my kid slippers and followed Tess and the others downstairs, wondering what was in store for me. Considering my quite literal fall from grace, what would Miss Stranje do to me? I had no desire to spend the day locked inside a metal sarcophagus lined with sharp nails.

Six

MY STUDIES

Outside the breakfast room, I stopped, smoothed back my hair, straightened my spine, leveled my chin, and glided into the sunny yellow room with as much dignity as Anne Boleyn on her way to the chopping block.

"Good morning, Miss Fitzwilliam." Miss Stranje's lips twisted in a mocking smile. "Nice of you to join us via the customary route. I'd rather expected you to pop in through one of the secret passages. Heaven knows, there's bound to be at least one that leads to this room. What say you, Tess? By my reckoning, you've explored most of our hidden tunnels."

Tess stopped scooping eggs onto her plate and glanced guiltily toward a bank of cupboards on the south wall, giving away the answer.

"Ah, yes, through the cupboard. I'd forgotten." Miss Stranje nodded and pointed to the trays of food on the sideboard. "Do help yourself to kippers and eggs, Georgiana. We've much to discuss this morning."

My stomach growled enthusiastically at her suggestion, thus thwarting my desire to remain dignified. I hurriedly filled a plate with several slices of hothouse oranges, three sausages, a serving of curried eggs, and a whortleberry scone dripping with butter and honey.

The tantalizing smells nearly drove me to madness. It had been a full day since my last real meal. Forgetting my manners altogether, I dove into breakfast with the enthusiasm of a stable lad. Only after several mouthfuls did I regain sanity. They were all looking at me. I rested my fork properly and dabbed at the berry juice and butter on my lips. "Lovely scones. Quite good."

"I shall convey your praise to Cook," Miss Stranje said coolly, and turned her attention to the other girls. "You may all attend your various pursuits this morning. Except you, Jane. The steward would like a word with you, something about which fields ought to remain fallow." She waved her hand airily, dismissing the details.

Jane simply nodded, as if fallow fields were a perfectly normal topic of conversation for young ladies.

Miss Stranje spread jam on a slice of toast and leveled a scolding gaze at Tess. "Miss Aubreyson, It has come to my attention that you have not been as circumspect during your morning exercise as one might hope. Have you forgotten the terms of our agreement? You are not to be observed."

Tess dropped her spoon. It clattered to her plate. "How did you find out? *He* told you?"

"Lord Ravencross? Heavens no."

"Then how?" Tess collected her spoon and stared at her food as if the answer must be hidden in her curried eggs.

We all leaned forward like eavesdropping Nellies awaiting Miss Stranje's reply. She took a bite of toast before answering. "You nearly got yourself trampled to death. Did you actually think that fact would escape my notice?" She gazed pointedly at each of us. "As mistress of Stranje House, it is my duty to be aware of all that passes here. *All*."

It struck me that Miss Stranje moved about this house with more skill than even Tess. Given the knowing slant of her eyes, I doubted even the secret room above our bedchamber was a secret from her.

The shrewd hawk-like expression evaporated from her features. "I trust you will be more discreet in the future?"

With a terse nod, Tess stabbed a sausage.

Our headmistress read from a note in her hand. "Maya, your music instructor begs leave to arrive a half hour late."

She set the note on a silver tray bearing several other missives. She sorted through the pile and abruptly snatched one from the bottom of the stack. She broke the seal, quickly unfolded the letter, and read intently. The contents seemed to unsettle her. She said nothing but refolded the paper into a tight square and tucked it in her pocket.

Selecting another card from the pile, she tapped her finger against the gilt edge. "Enjoy your day today, ladies. For tomorrow, it looks as though we must entertain guests. Our neighbor, the delightful Lady Pinswary, intends to pay us a visit."

Sera dragged a piece of potato around her plate. Maya sighed mournfully. I judged by the tight press of our headmistress's lips and everyone else's sagging countenances that Lady Pinswary was not actually delightful.

"Here's another treat for you, a visit from friends your own age. She will be accompanied by her daughter, Miss Pinswary, and her niece, Lady Daneska."

Sera winced.

Maya heaved an even deeper sigh.

Jane pushed back her chair, and brushed against Tess as she

rose. I would've sworn she whispered into Tess's ear on her way to the sideboard where she scooped another kipper onto her plate.

"I saw that, Jane." Miss Stranje frowned and tossed the card onto the tray. "Really, my dear." She sniffed. "A little subtlety would not go amiss."

Jane's shoulders straightened and she spun around. "My apologies. It was clumsily done. I shall endeavor to improve."

Tess set down her cup with a jarring clunk. "Jane has a point. She wonders why you're allowing them in the house? Frankly, so do I. Especially that conniving little traitor. Why don't you tell Lady Pinswary and her devious niece that we are not at home? Countess or not, you know Daneska is trouble."

The force of Tess's outburst shocked me. I expected Miss Stranje to fly into a stern rebuke, or Madame Cho to thrash Tess with her stick. Instead, everyone in the room just sat there looking glum. Everyone except our headmistress.

"I can think of three very good reasons why that tactic would be a mistake." Miss Stranje cracked the shell of her boiled egg with a swift whack of the spoon. "Seraphina, would you care to speculate as to my reasons?"

I popped an orange slice into my mouth, thinking that it wasn't difficult to guess. She couldn't very well tell a *countess* to go away. It simply wasn't done. Even I knew that much.

Sera quietly set her fork on her plate. "One," she stated matter-of-factly, "if you do not allow Lady Daneska to visit she will assume it is because you have something to hide. She will double her efforts to find out what is afoot."

"Precisely. And?"

"Two. By allowing her to visit you have an opportunity to misdirect her."

Ah-hah! Misdirection. So that's how our headmistress kept

her treatment of young ladies a secret from the authorities for so long. I might find an ally in our visitors. This Lady Daneska must've gotten wind of Miss Stranje's methods.

"Go on." Miss Stranje scooped out her egg and salted it.

"Thirdly. During the conversation, it may be possible to trip her up, perhaps lure her into a slip of the tongue. She might unwittingly disclose some tidbit that would be . . ." As if embarrassed to continue, Sera glanced sidelong at me. "Um . . . useful."

Useful for what? Did Miss Stranje collect gossip with which to blackmail her neighbors—more infamy to hide her despicable behavior?

Sera did not stop at only three reasons. "It would also prove illuminating to ascertain the purpose of her visit."

Miss Stranje tilted her head with something akin to respect in her expression. "Yes, and what purpose do you suppose she might have?"

"I suspect Lady Daneska has several objectives." Again, Sera looked sideways at me, this time she did not appear embarrassed or guilty. "Not the least of which is curiosity about your new student."

"Well done." Miss Stranje whisked out the folded note again and read it silently.

"Your last assumption is impossible," I argued. "I only arrived night before last. No one even knows I am here."

"Oh, she knows." Jane spoke this to a spoonful of peaches laced with cinnamon. "She probably knew you were here before your coach turned down the drive."

Tess nodded.

"Without a doubt." Miss Stranje smiled with a wickedly arched brow. "You all know what this means, don't you?"

The others nodded.

"Disarm them." Jane forced a smile. "Make them excessively comfortable."

"Play the innocents," Sera whispered to me.

"Yes," our headmistress confirmed. "To that end, before Lady Daneska's arrival tomorrow, please assist Georgiana in selecting more appropriate attire." She flicked her hand in my direction. "See if you can do something with her hair."

I shrugged, all too accustomed to my appearance being a source of consternation.

Miss Stranje tapped the note against the table and studied me. "We shall be serving tea to our guests. I trust your mother instructed you on the proper behavior for such occasions?"

Oh, yes, my mother had instructed me on proper behavior while taking tea, proper behavior at dinner, at soirees, assembly rooms, and even at card parties. Mother had instructed me over and over, but on every occasion found me clumsy, ugly, and socially inept. I answered Miss Stranje with a fraudulent smile, "Yes, certainly."

"Excellent." She stood abruptly. "Now, if you've finished your breakfast, Georgiana, come with me. It is time we attended to your studies."

Tess and Maya looked askance at each other. Were they worried?

My studies?

I followed our headmistress into the hall feeling certain her use of the word *studies* was a euphemism for torture. She meant to punish me for last night's behavior. Clearly, Miss Stranje's educational theory relied heavily on pain. No doubt she was planning to whip the stuffing out of me until I dared never disobey her again. She would do all this under the guise of turning me into a more pleasing daughter for my mother.

Go ahead. Torture me. I will never become a simpering, pudding-headed, marriageable Miss. *Never.*

I clamped my lips together in absolute defiance, but my clammy palms spoiled the effect. So, I wiped them against my skirts and marched onward to my doom.

We had descended the main staircase before I realized the discipline chamber wasn't in this direction. Unless Miss Stranje possessed two torture chambers, I might not be getting stretched on the rack this morning. Confused, I tried to guess my fate.

Attend to my studies . . .

If she meant to stick me in a room with that dragon, Madame Cho, and force me to learn Chinese history, I would leap out of the nearest window, cut off my hair, don boy's clothing, run to the nearest port, jump aboard a frigate, and join the crew. Not a perfect plan, I'll admit. But surely it would succeed better than last night's escape.

My studies?

Miss Stranje's task was to reform me into a biddable young debutante. What studies did that require? *Oh, please God, do not let it be a dancing master.* I could not bear the humiliation of crippling another skinny Frenchman. Monsieur Fouché had howled louder than a cat with his tail caught under a chair when I tromped on his ankle. Mother had to pay him double his fee just to get him to stop squealing.

I slowed my pace, from a resigned march to slow plod. *Not dancing. Please, not dancing.*

"It isn't dancing, is it? Because I simply won't—"

"Heavens no." Miss Stranje led us through the foyer into the west wing corridor. I breathed a sigh of relief and picked up my stride to match hers. With a slight sniff and a no-nonsense tone she said, "Dancing class is on every other Thursday. Next week we will be mastering German folk dances."

I groaned and slowed my steps again. We passed a gallery of family portraits, unmistakably Miss Stranje's relatives. Their sharp-beaked features did little to cheer up the dark-paneled hallway. I shivered, unable to escape their uncanny lifelike stares. They glared down at me as I walked beneath them, judging, though they were long cold in their graves.

"Do stop dawdling, Georgiana." She waited beside a door at the far end of the hall. I caught up as she pressed a key into the lock and turned the handle. She stood back and pushed the door open.

The ancient floorboards creaked as I stepped inside. Mullioned windows allowed in ample light and yet there was a row of lamps dangling from the ceiling so the room might be used after dark. A stillroom lay before us—unlike any stillroom I'd ever seen. Filled with wonder, I stood with my mouth hanging open like a stunned codfish. I couldn't stop myself from rushing across the room to a long worktable set with the most amazing equipment I'd ever seen.

I had only dreamed of such contraptions. I'd read about equipment like this in Antoine Lavoisier's chemistry books. But to see them, not in a drawing, but in real life—I could scarcely breathe.

I touched my finger to a set of brass measuring scales. They bounced in reaction. I jerked my hand back and inspected a distillation tube connected to a copper beaker atop a heating platform. The damper on the small oil burner could be opened or closed to perfectly control the heat. *Remarkable.*

Miss Stranje stood at my elbow. "The copper tubing can be removed," she said, and pointed to the clasps on the rim of the beaker.

"Where did you get it?" I marveled.

"A gypsy caravan came through last month. Their tinker did respectable work so I commissioned him to make that and some of these other devices."

"But why?"

She pointed to several small glass beakers. "These I procured from a glass blower in London." She pointed to a bank of small drawers on the side wall. "You'll find the bins filled with various minerals. I wasn't certain which you needed so I ordered an assortment."

I rushed to the small drawers, pulled several open, and couldn't believe my eyes. Sulphur. Magnesium. Saltpeter. Copperas. Precious cobalt.

"This was my grandmother's stillroom." Miss Stranje inhaled deeply. "The smells never fail to remind me of her. I still remember her teaching me to distill rose oil and make almond extract." She picked up a worn marble mortar and pestle. "This was hers."

I pulled open a bin marked "mollusk shells," fine iridescent shells that could be ground into purple powder. How did she know they were a component in so many dyes? Then, I spotted my books stacked on a small desk beside the cabinet. My books! *The History of Persian Alchemy*, a treasure my brother had procured for me, and *Lavoisier's Manual*. Even my notes were laid out, unwrapped, unpacked from my trunks—without my permission.

"Why!" I spun around. "Why have you done this? My parents hired you to purge this sort of thing out of me, to rid me of my, my . . ." I was going to say *defects*.

She watched me, waiting without mercy to see how I would describe that which my mother hated in me.

My stomach twisted into a sickening knot just as it had last night. Except, this morning, it tightened around sausages and curried eggs. I refused to get sick. I would not humiliate myself in front of her. So, despite the squeezing knot in my belly, I clamped my lips together and swallowed hard. If only I could run from the room and curl up in a corner somewhere. Maybe then, I wouldn't feel like retching. But my stern headmistress stood between me and the door, searching my face for weakness, waiting for me to say those torturous words. *My defects.*

I would've preferred the rack. Thrusting my chin into the air, I said, "My eccentricities."

"*Eccentricities?*" The corner of her mouth angled up slightly. "Is that what you call it? I should rather have thought of it as the workings of a brilliant mind."

I blinked. No one, except my brother, had ever said such a thing about me before. Wary, I edged away. "I saw your torture chamber. I know what you do in this school."

"Do you?" She feigned innocence.

"Yes. Everyone knows your reputation. I daresay there are hangmen considered more merciful."

Her shoulder lifted in a minuscule shrug.

"I saw with my own eyes. Bruises and cuts on the other girls. Manacles. Whips. Jane locked in a spiked mummy case."

She squared her shoulders. "The chamber has its uses."

"Oh, yes, I imagine so." My chest heaved with indignation. "Useful for reforming brilliant minds into unexceptional ones. For ridding your students of their eccentricities."

"Do you really think such punishments could accomplish all that?"

Her question caught me off guard. I drew back. *It wouldn't work on me. I would rather die.* "No," I admitted.

She waved her hand at the laboratory equipment. "And this? Do you think this is a devious plan to rid you of your *eccentrici-*

ties? A clever ploy—if you are free to experiment, science will lose its appeal?" She waited for me to respond. When I didn't, her mouth twitched into a smirk. "Of course, if you'd prefer to have a go on the rack, I'll simply have to oblige you."

I blinked, unable to find my bearings with her.

"Come now, Georgiana. Do you want to work on your formula, or not? It occurred to me that with the proper equipment you might not burn down any more stables."

True. With proper equipment, that fire would never have happened. Was this another tactic? Apparently she was quite fond of misdirection. "I know what you want," I said. "You want me to finish the ink formula for Lord Wyatt and Captain Grey."

"Yes." A tiny hint of admiration softened her features. "That is precisely what I want."

"Why? What makes you think my ink is anything of value?"

"Your mother's letters were quite explicit about your experiments."

A *lie.* "Impossible." I squinted and crossed my arms. "Until the fire she never cared one wit about anything I did. She wouldn't know anything beyond the fact that I was working on an invisible ink. Her letters would've been full of complaints. Nothing substantial enough to merit all this." I waved at the equipment.

The intrepid Miss Stranje pressed her lips tight, buying time to construct another untruth. I gave her no quarter. "What does Miss Grissmore have to do with any of this? If you have harmed her in any way—"

"Hardly!" She glanced up sharp at that, like a hawk discovering the mouse in her claws had rather pointy teeth. "Miss Grissmore and I are former schoolmates. She came to me after your parents turned her out without a reference."

"Oh." I cooled considerably and turned away, toying with one of the brass weights for the scale. "Thank you for that. She didn't deserve such poor treatment. Grissy was an excellent teacher."

Miss Stranje took a deep breath and proceeded with a softer tone. "She speaks rather highly of you as well. She convinced me that you are capable of developing an ink. On the strength of her recommendation I procured this equipment."

"I see." Except, I didn't see. I couldn't see any more than a blind man in an apothecary shop. Miss Stranje and Miss Grissmore were friends. *Impossible.* Everything suddenly felt topsy-turvy. My assumptions were all called into question. I kneaded my temple. "Very well, you've explained *how,* but you've still not told me *why.* What do you intend to do with my ink?"

"A prudent question." This response did not come from Miss Stranje. I spun toward the deep voice. Sebastian and Captain Grey stood in the doorway. The captain approached us. "Well done, Miss Fitzwilliam. It is right that you should ask." He bowed. "I'm relieved to see you have recovered from your mishap."

"Captain, how good of you to come." Miss Stranje met him with rosy warmth. The two grasped each other's hands as if they were lifelong friends, and just as quickly stepped apart, blushing and awkward.

Miss Stranje tried to hide her reaction by introducing them to me. "Captain Grey, Lord Wyatt, you've already met my new student, but under . . . how shall I say . . . under less-than-appropriate circumstances. Please, allow me to properly present to you, Miss Georgiana Fitzwilliam."

I dropped into a curtsey elegant enough to please even my mother, wishing the whole time that my wretched hair did not resemble a stork's nest smushed into one paltry white ribbon. But it did. There was no help for it, and because there is no sense trying to pretend one is a silk purse, when one is, in fact, a sow's ear, I quickly dispensed with the niceties.

"Pleased to meet you, Captain Grey." I intentionally took no notice of Sebastian. "Now, if you will kindly explain what it is you want with my ink, and why I should trust—"

"Georgiana!" Miss Stranje cut me short. "You will not take that rude tone. Captain Grey is a man to whom we owe much. It is only his generosity and goodwill that allows us to live here. This house, the grounds, the cottages and adjoining property, all belong to him."

The gentleman shook his head. "No, no, my dear Miss Stranje, you must not credit me with such virtues. It is not generosity on my part. You are a most excellent overseer. The estate flourishes under your guidance and your students' contributions." He caught his breath and stepped back from her. "By rights the house ought to be yours. Your father would have left it to you, if it were not for that abominable entailment, or if you'd had a brother. . . ."

He stopped. Warmth colored his cheeks. His mellow voice caught and his easy manner turned awkward and unexpectedly boyish. "It is the least I can do."

Clearly, generosity had little to do with the matter. *Remarkable*. Poor earnest Captain Grey appeared to be in love with my scheming headmistress.

"There you have it," Miss Stranje resumed lecturing me. "Captain Grey deserves our utmost respect. You may not demand answers of him as if you were the local magistrate."

Oh, if only I were the magistrate. This school and her malevolent discipline chamber would be banished from England. I silenced myself, clamped my lips together, and turned my thoughts to how I might finagle the truth out of them as to what they wanted with my ink.

Captain Grey clasped his hands behind his back and paced a step or two before stopping in front of me. "It is right and proper that you should ask these questions, Miss Fitzwilliam. It is crucial that your formula be guarded. In the wrong hands, it would be a dangerous tool." He took a deep breath. "I will explain our interest."

"Proceed cautiously, Ethan," Sebastian warned. He leaned against the doorpost, his arms crossed over his chest as if he was bored. "She is, after all, a girl. And girls must talk. *Incessantly*." He uncrossed his arms and strolled toward us. "They tend to do so without regard for the importance of secrecy."

Oh, that topped it. I couldn't keep a secret? Bird's-nest hair or not, I confronted his high and mighty lordship. "I sincerely doubt the topic of invisible ink will come up while chatting with my friends about how many ruffles to put on my next ball gown."

Sebastian brazenly perused my sprigged muslin morning dress with so critical an eye that obviously he doubted I'd ever worn a ball gown.

No matter that I hadn't. I certainly could have, if I'd ever had the slightest interest in such frivolous things. Which I did not. In light of his scorn, I decided to have a ball gown made for me just to spite him. Although, how it would spite him, I wasn't quite certain.

Oh, confound it all! The man was muddling my thinking.

Captain Grey clapped Sebastian on the shoulder. "In that case, I shall leave the explanations to you." He bowed to me, a veritable saint compared to his brutish companion. "Miss Fitzwilliam, I leave you in the capable hands of Lord Wyatt. Not only is my nephew an able attaché, he is, like yourself, a student of science. It may please you to know that he is acquainted with the author of one of your books. When Sebastian was a very young lad, he and his father helped Monsieur Lavoisier's wife smug—" He stopped and cleared his throat.

"Pardon me. What I meant to say is he and his father helped her *transport* out of France some of Monsieur Lavoisier's writings and equipment."

Sebastian crossed to the other side of the table and lifted a small glass beaker, turning it round and round in his fingers. "Captain Grey exaggerates my part. I only helped my father carry away a few sacks and provide a diversion. But I remember her. A brave intelligent woman, Madame Lavoisier. Without her, we would know nothing of these instruments." He set down the flask with a reverence that surprised me. "Nor would you have his notes. After her husband's capture, the revolutionaries confiscated almost everything. *The Republic does not need scientists or chemists*, that's what they said, right before they beheaded him." He flicked his finger against the flask. "They guillotined both her husband and her father on the very same day."

We stood in morbid silence. I could not keep from pressing my hand against my throat.

Captain Grey nodded farewell and Miss Stranje took his arm. They headed for the door. Surely she didn't intend to leave me here alone with Sebastian. It wouldn't be proper. "You're leaving?"

"Captain Grey and I have business matters to discuss. You won't be alone, Miss Fitzwilliam." She tilted her head toward the corner. "Madame Cho will act as my emissary."

It was then that I realized Madame Cho had slithered into the room without my noticing. The old dragon sat in the corner watching me with her cold lizard eyes. Sebastian took off his coat, flipped open my Persian alchemy book, loosened his cravat, and rolled up his cuffs.

"What are you doing?" I asked.

"What does it look like I'm doing?" He continued to roll up

his sleeves. "If you're not planning to use this equipment, I most certainly will."

"You can't simply assume command here. This is my laboratory."

"Is it?"

Not mine. Not exactly. I spared a covetous glance at the equipment table. "You promised to explain why you want my formula."

"I did not," he said, and turned his attention to the Persian book.

"I heard you. You told Captain Grey—"

He scoffed at me. "I know exactly what I said. I told him to proceed cautiously, because girls talk too much."

I reached over, shut my Persian manual, and clutched the fragile old book to my bosom. "And *boys* talk too little."

Obviously, he wasn't a boy. I had only emphasized the word to annoy him, and it did. He flinched ever so slightly, but enough that it pleased me. He deserved a set-down.

"I suggest you explain," I said.

If he thought his measly glower would frighten me, he was wrong. My father, with his grizzled skin, lionlike side whiskers, and bulbous nose, possessed a far more terrifying frown. Sebastian had a fine straight nose, a defined jaw, with smooth inviting skin. His eyebrows, although they sat at a wicked brooding slant, weren't nearly as fierce as my father's bushy ones. I met his gaze with steady ease. I even managed a triumphant smile.

He exhaled noisily. "How do you expect me to explain it to you? You couldn't possibly understand." He waved my bravado away. "Impossible. You're completely ignorant of world affairs. An *innocent*."

He spat the word at me, twisted it, as if being innocent meant I was vulgar and indecent. Suddenly, his hard stare made me uncomfortable in a way my father's never could. I backed away, brushing against the scales, sending the sensitive trays bobbling noisily. The sound of the clinking brass tumbled through my belly. I couldn't meet his gaze.

I swallowed and sucked in my discomfort. "Why do you think I've been working so tirelessly to find an invisible ink?" I wasn't about to tell him about my brother's death. That was too personal for the likes of him. I jutted my chin. "I'm well aware of world affairs."

"Well aware?" He scoffed. "Do you have any idea what's happening on the continent at the moment?" He sounded exasperated with me.

I stiffened my spine, as I had seen my mother do a thousand times. "Certainly. Napoleon has surrendered, he abdicated his throne, and they've banished him to Elba."

"Oh, very good. Even a chimney sweep knows that much." Madame Cho chuckled softly.

"At least, we finally have peace," I defended.

He shook his head and muttered, "Peace."

For no reason at all, I felt like crying. I was not stupid. And this . . . this boy was not going to make me feel like a simpleton.

"Very well then, if I am so ignorant"—I shoved past him and snatched my manuals and notes away—"so disgustingly innocent, I suggest you enlighten me."

My cheeks burned. That had come out all wrong. I only hoped he would ignore the more torrid implications.

Madame Cho coughed discreetly.

His lips parted. He stared at me, as if I stood before him as naked as his forearms. I rubbed mine, feeling unaccountably chilled. Silence bristled between us.

With a smirk, he relaxed. "Peace, Miss Fitzwilliam." He held up his hands in mock surrender. "As Captain Grey explained, I am a diplomatic attaché. The captain and I are charged with protecting certain European dignitaries. We require your ink in order to exchange sensitive messages when the need arises. The old codes and our current ink formulas are too easily detected. There. That should be explanation enough."

I clutched the books to my bosom. It was exactly what I'd suspected. "So, you are a spy."

"No. A diplomatic attaché."

"Which is a fancy way of saying a spy."

He shook his head. "That bump on your head must've injured your brain."

"Your concern is touching," I said, pointing out that he hadn't yet asked after my health. "But you needn't worry, my brain is quite well. Well enough to deduce the obvious."

"Apparently not, since you are sorely mistaken. I am a member of the Office of Foreign Affairs, a diplomat, as was my father, and his father before him."

He explained all this using the same tone and forbearance Miss Grissmore had used when explaining higher mathematics to me when I was only ten. I found his overblown patience both entertaining and annoying.

"As such," he continued, "I am sworn to protect Britain's interests and that of her allies. If, on occasion, that means I must go about my task quietly and without drawing attention to my identity, I only do so in order to fulfill my duties as a sworn protector of King and country."

"*Quietly*. Yes, I see," I said, tapping one finger against my lips. "Because, clearly, you *are* a spy."

The muscles in his jaw knotted and he drew in a long irritated breath. "And *clearly*, you lack even the most basic skills in diplomacy or tact."

My cheeks flamed up again. He'd struck too near the mark. I thrust my chin up proudly, unwilling to tolerate insults from him. "If by that you mean I lack skills in deception and trickery, then you are right. If I possessed those arts I wouldn't be locked away in this hellish place, would I? And you wouldn't know anything about my ink."

"Hellish? Stranje House?" He frowned at me, his mischievousness evaporated. "You don't know what hell is, little girl. I see no guards at the doors or bars on the windows."

"No, but you did see daughters of the realm gagged and tied to chairs."

"That was . . ." He clamped his lips together. "Ask your friends about that."

"I did. They wouldn't say anything."

"Well, ask again."

"Are you aware of the fact that Miss Stranje keeps a discipline chamber filled with torture devices?"

"Oh, that . . ." He caught himself, buckled his jaw, and crossed his arms. "In your case, I suspect a good spanking now and then might prove useful."

"You're just like her. Uncaring. Heartless. Arrogant—"

"Enough! If you think this is such a terrible place, why do you not leave?"

"I tried."

"Yes, and you wreaked havoc on a perfectly good boat. Next time try taking a dryer route. There's the door. The road is a half mile due north."

I stepped back, unwilling to confess I had nowhere to go—no one who loved me well enough to shelter me if I did leave. I bit down on my lower lip to keep from betraying myself with angry tears. He was no gentleman to be so cruel.

He swore under his breath. "I'm sorry. That was badly done. Look here, Miss Fitzwilliam, we have gotten off to a bad start. Might we not just begin work on the ink?"

I shook my head, unwilling to look at him until I had my emotions under control. "Not unless you explain. Fully."

"It is all so complicated."

I said nothing to that.

"I can't tell you everything. These are matters of state. What I am at leisure to explain, you could not be expected to understand."

Wishing to heap burning coals on his foul head, I found the courage to face him squarely. "Then I suggest you put to use all that diplomacy and tact you claim you have, and help me understand."

He drew back, as if I'd surprised him. That wicked eyebrow of his arched up as he stood there assessing me. After a prolonged and uncomfortable silence, Sebastian's shoulders relaxed and I saw his resolve weakening.

"I learn quickly," I offered as a salve. Although, why I should soothe his rude temperament, I didn't know. I suppose some treacherous part of me wanted to prove my worth to him. He continued to brood in silence. The man stood nearly three feet away from me, yet I could smell the freshly pressed linen of his shirt and, I swear, I could almost taste the damp morning mist that had settled in his hair.

"Very well." He exhaled abruptly, and his manner softened. "A far cry from peace—Europe is in chaos. So many nobles were executed during the Terror or killed in the war, that much of the ruling class of Europe is either dead or in hiding. Spain, Portugal, Italy, the entire continent is plunged into a dangerous upheaval. Borders are in dispute. Economies destroyed by the war. Europe is unstable—a beast without a head, wounded, thrashing in pain."

He turned and leaned against the cabinet, staring out the window at the brilliant midmorning sky. A sparrow leaped from the branches of a flowering pear tree and fluttered past, completely unconcerned about the volatility of Europe.

Sebastian glanced over his shoulder at me, sadness darkening his features, and I saw how he thought of me. I was like that sparrow, flittering to and fro, blissfully ignorant of the monstrous happenings in the rest of the world.

"Were you there when they beheaded Monsieur Lavoisier?" I bit my lip. It was a dreadful question. It had nothing to do with the matters at hand, but it sprang from my mouth before I could retract it. Seeing such horrors might explain the hardness in him.

He paced. I didn't think he would answer, but he stopped beside me and said quietly, "Not Monsieur Lavoisier. I was a child, only five. Captain Grey exaggerates my part in all that. I only helped carry a few sacks and provided a diversion. But a few weeks later, they caught my father and, although he was a diplomat to the French government, dragged him away and executed him for crimes against the Republic. I shouldn't remember, but how can I forget? The shriek of the blade falling and . . ." Sebastian stopped and squeezed his eyes shut.

I swallowed, waiting, afraid to breathe, regretting having brought him needless pain.

When he opened his eyes the hardness had returned. "You've distracted me with pointless memories. I thought you wanted me to explain why we need your formula."

I could scarcely move, much less nod.

Squaring his shoulders, he towered over me. "What I am about to tell you must be kept in strictest confidence. You will never tell anyone." He grabbed my shoulders. "*Anyone.* Do you understand me? Lives depend on you keeping silent. My life."

I ought to have felt angry that he handled me as if I were a wayward child. I didn't. I felt afraid. Afraid, because his touch sent my pulse flapping faster than a frightened sparrow. But, instead of running away, I wanted to draw closer. I wanted to slide my hand over the place that hid his heart and soothe the trouble there. Heat flooded up my neck. I stared blindly at his shoulders, not daring to look up, and yet I couldn't stop thinking of his face, his searing blue eyes, his mouth so close to mine.

A hundred questions I wanted to ask him. He'd seen his own father beheaded. Why had he been allowed to witness such a terrible thing? Had his mother held his hand as they watched? I inhaled sharply. Or had he lost her, too? How had they escaped France? And after all that, why did he follow in his father's footsteps? For his sake, I stuffed a fist into the mouth of my curiosity.

"Swear." He stood over me, waiting, demanding my promise of silence.

"I give you my word."

He glanced at Madame Cho. "And you." She looked up from her embroidery and nodded as if such vows of silence were commonplace for her.

Sebastian released me and shifted uneasily. "Rulers and ambassadors from all over Europe are planning to gather for a council, a congress of sorts, in Vienna."

I'd read something in the London *Times* about a historic meeting to take place on the continent. I nodded, encouraging him to continue.

"Their goal is to hammer out a course of action to restore order and economic stability to Europe. There is strong disagreement about how this should be achieved. Many leaders are determined to restore the ruling aristocracy and the royal families.

You can imagine how this infuriates the populists and revolutionaries, especially those in France."

He massaged the muscles of his forearms as if it might relieve some of his tension. In a low voice he added, "We've heard rumors of a plan to assassinate these heads of state while they are all gathered so conveniently in one place."

I backed away. "This can't be true. No one would do such a dishonorable thing."

"I assure you, Miss Fitzwilliam, it is true. There are those to whom honor does not matter." His face darkened and his eyes narrowed with anger. "They have banded together, dedicated to one purpose: restoring Napoleon to his throne and uniting all of Europe under one crown."

My mouth formed an O. Now I understood. "The Order of the Iron Crown."

He squinted sideways at me. "How do you know that name?"

I pinched my lips together not wanting to admit to eavesdropping. I glanced up to the ceiling and that was clue enough.

"Of course." He groaned. "The tapestry. You overhead us."

"Yes, but what's more important is how did you hear of this plot? Have you told the proper authorities?"

"Slow down." He warded off my rapid questions. "You already know more than you ought. It's my job and Captain Grey's to uncover such plots. All you need to know is that if you give us your formula for invisible ink many lives will be saved. The inks we have at present are too easily exposed by applying heat. Lately, we've had to rely on codes—a grave risk. The Order has deciphered several of them. Consequently, men have died. Good men." Sebastian paused and raked through his black curls, clenching his jaw muscles. "In one case, our man and his entire family were murdered for helping us."

"I'm so sorry." I flinched at passing off someone's life with so light a sentiment. I attempted to change the subject. "I imagine it is extremely difficult to distribute new codes without them being intercepted by your enemies."

"Exactly." Some of his ire cooled. "It's vital to the safety of hundreds of dignitaries, their families, and their entourages, that we have a means of exchanging messages covertly."

His life hung in the balance as well.

My throat tightened and I had trouble swallowing. We had a *very* big problem. "You do realize my formula isn't perfected yet?" My shoulders sagged under the confession of my failure.

"So I heard." He surprised me with a wry half grin. "An explosion, was it?"

I shrugged, preferring not to think about that day. I wanted to please him and he needed me to succeed. The leaders of Europe were in danger. *He* was in danger. Dwelling on my past mistakes wouldn't help any of us.

When he started to chuckle at my embarrassment, I thrust the Persian text at him. Laughing at me wouldn't help, either. "We ought to get started," I said brusquely.

Seven

ASHES

I opened my notes and brushed away ashes and charred flecks of paper left from the day of the fire. That whiff of burnt paper, although only a hint, billowed into a remembered blaze of singed horsehair and smoldering straw. I nearly choked, but instead gulped air. Despite my dry throat, I slowly breathed out the memory. That's all it was, just a memory. Nothing more. I had work to do, and no time for nonsensical phantom smells.

"Turn to my marker," I told Sebastian, embarrassed that my vocal cords crackled like an adolescent boy's.

"Which marker?" Snippets of paper protruded every which way out of the Persian book

I flipped it open and pointed to a passage on transmutable dyes. "There. We will begin where I left off." I showed him the recipe on the singed pages of my notebook. We compared the ingredients to the chemicals described in the Persian text.

"See here, where it says *red salt*. I'm not certain what that means. At first I thought it referred to copperas, copper crystals.

But then I got the idea to mix cobalt with saltpeter, potassium nitrate. That's what I was doing when—"

"Why? Cobalt is blue." He frowned and rubbed the stubble on his chin while he pondered the recipe.

"Yes, of course. But when you mix it with a nitric acid, such as saltpeter, cobalt turns red." I was eager to explain more, especially because he paid attention. Sincere attention. His skeptical smirk had vanished. He leaned across the worktable; listening, considering my hypothesis.

Listening. *To me.*

No one had ever done that. Not really, not with that kind of respectful consideration. Oh, our old cook used to let me sit at the table and theorize to her while she kneaded bread—but she was half deaf. Mother never even feigned interest. She usually yawned and glanced at the ceiling before shooing me away, exasperated with my *harebrained* ideas.

Sebastian, with steady blue eyes, waited to hear more.

I swallowed hard, trying to keep my heart from flinging itself up into my throat. Childish of me to react so excitedly, simply because someone was polite enough to listen. "The acid causes the cobalt to crystallize—into red crystals. That might be our red salt."

"Possibly." He stroked his thumb across his jaw, considering the idea. "Unfortunately, saltpeter, being the chief ingredient in gunpowder, poses a bit of a risk when heat is applied." He brushed a fleck of ash from my book. "Although, I suspect you already know that." His impish eyebrow arced up, mocking me just a little. "Plus, I question whether the ancient Persians would have known how to convert cobalt into red salt."

I prickled up. "They knew." I concentrated on the ancient text struggling not to openly confront him. "Why must people always assume we moderns knew more than any of the previous cultures? It simply isn't true, evidence proves otherwise."

I bit my lip, suppressing the impulse to argue the point further. I wanted to maintain the delicate connection I felt with him, so I turned the page. Shoulder to shoulder we leaned over the books. Heads together, we hypothesized as to what other ingredients the ancients might have described as red salt.

And all the while, my skin tingled under the gentle breeze of our companionability. I doubt any lover's poem would have teased my ears more sweetly than our discussion of iron oxides and magnesium.

At length, I exclaimed, "That's it! We'll use ammonium to emulsify ferrous sulfate. That must be the answer." I rushed to locate the ingredients.

"Mmm. Perhaps." He still studied the text. "Although I'm concerned about what will happen when we apply heat."

"Ever the skeptic, aren't you. It's worth a try."

He straightened. "Not skeptical. Cautious."

"Light the burner," I ordered, hunting through the element drawers. "Ah, here it is."

I measured out the ingredients and set the mixture atop the stand. The burner worked beautifully, exactly like a chafing dish but with a more intense flame. While Sebastian stirred, I went through the remainder of Miss Stranje's chemist's chest, pulling out each little drawer, searching the contents of every box for any element that might be construed as red salt.

A few moments later, I fanned my hand in front of my nose to drive away the stench from our mixture. It smelled worse than rotten eggs. Sebastian coughed. I felt sorry for him standing over the pot stirring.

"Ghastly smell." I held my nose and squeezed past him to open the window, but stopped when he coughed again. This time his shoulders hunched and he barked so spasmodically I feared he might lose the contents of his stomach. I patted him between the shoulder blades, and commenced coughing quite violently myself.

White acrid smoke puffed up from the bubbling mixture, stinging my nostrils. A glance at the fizzling brew and I realized my mistake. "They're reacting!"

Sebastian reached through the suffocating smoke and shut off the flame. I covered my mouth with the collar of my dress and slammed a lid over the pot, and yet smoke continued to pour out around the edges. I rushed to the window, but the rusted latch wouldn't budge. Sebastian tried the next window, only to be overtaken by another coughing fit. Pounding and thumping, I yanked on the handle, and finally got the stubborn latch to give way. But it stuck and I only managed to pry it open a few inches.

By that time, Sebastian had turned an alarming shade of gray. Desperation twisted his features. Any second he would collapse. I caught his arm over my shoulder and we stumbled toward the door. Just as we rounded the worktable all of his weight fell on me. I tipped, and we slid to the floor. Sebastian would die if I didn't get him to fresh air immediately.

"Madame Cho," I screamed. "Help!" But she was already out the door, gasping, and fanning away the fumes with the silk she'd been embroidering.

I wriggled out from underneath him, grabbed him under the arms, and tugged with every ounce of strength I had. I pulled his limp body toward the door. Madame Cho shuffled back, holding the silk over her mouth, and took hold of his arm. Together we dragged him into the hall.

"Shut the door," I shouted, not wanting the fumes to asphyxiate the entire population of the school. I checked Sebastian for signs of life. Faint breath sounds came from his mouth, and his chest expanded slightly. He was alive.

Barely.

Think, I ordered myself. The fumes had been acidic. How could we counteract it in his system? I remembered a note in Lavoisier's book.

"Milk," I said, grasping Madame Cho's arm. "Quickly! We need a pitcher of milk and two eggs. No. Three egg whites." Her face screwed up, as if she thought I'd lost my mind. "To neutralize the acid. Mix the whites in milk and we'll make him drink it. Hurry!"

Instead of arguing, she vanished down the hall with surprising speed. I dragged Sebastian farther from the stillroom, farther from the fumes seeping under the door, farther from the poison that was killing him. If I could haul him all the way out into the garden, the fresh air might help. I tugged and pulled, coughing with every step. At last, I yanked open the side door. Steps. Too many steps for me to drag him safely down without giving him a concussion. A wracking cough overwhelmed me. Wheezing, I sank against the doorpost and propped his head on my lap.

Without thinking I slid my fingers into his black hair, smoothing it back from his forehead. My freckled hands looked so shabby against his raven black hair and smooth white skin. Too white. I jerked my hand away.

No longer gray, Sebastian looked like a stone angel in the graveyard, washed bone white in the sun. Pale and unearthly. All wrong. Where was his devilish sneer? His teasing grin? The cold *gone-ness* of his features made me shiver.

"Come back," I whispered, and fell to coughing momentarily. I'm not the sort of girl who falls apart in a crisis. Nor do I blubber pointlessly. Not me. The moisture in my eyes was merely a reaction to the acrid fumes. That's all.

"Breathe," I ordered, and fanned fresh healing air toward him. "Breathe." I gave his shoulders a shake. "You mustn't die. You can't. I will not permit it."

As if he heard me, Sebastian lurched up. Immediately, he commenced a brutal coughing spasm. I braced his shoulders. At the end of it, he slumped into my lap breathing in loud gasps. "Stay calm," I said, sounding very authoritarian even to my own ears. "Try to breathe evenly."

I thought he said, "Ha." Or it could've been "Huh?" No, in retrospect, I'm fairly certain he uttered a derisive "Ha."

"Conserve your strength," I urged. "Don't talk. Just breathe."

His impudent smirk returned. He ignored me. "You . . . are . . ."

"Hush," I cautioned. "No need to thank me."

His eyes widened.

"After all," I said. "You caught me when I fell from the spy hole, and yesterday you carried me up from the rocks." I coughed briefly. "Turnabout is only fair."

Sebastian's pupils rolled upward. I thought he might lose consciousness again, so I patted his cheeks. "Take a deep breath. Stay awake."

He shook his head and inhaled deeply, exactly as I'd instructed. Only it brought on more coughing. "You are"—cough—"the most"—cough—"vexing"—he wheezed—"dangerous"—cough—"girl"—cough—"I've ever—" cough, cough, gasp.

He had the audacity to flop back against my lap as if I was his personal feather pillow. *Fine.* I certainly didn't want to hear the rest of his rude comments anyway. The mocking glint in his eyes gave me a nearly uncontrollable urge to shove him down the steps.

Fortunately for him, at that very moment Captain Grey and Miss Stranje came running down the hall toward us, followed by Madame Cho and a footman carrying a sloshing pitcher of milk. I felt relieved that they did not arrive pelting me with angry shouts of "Murderer!"

Captain Grey knelt beside me and braced Sebastian into a more upright position. He asked simply, "What happened?"

"She—"

"Fumes," I interrupted, before Sebastian could publicly condemn me. "The chemicals we mixed reacted and formed a poisonous gas."

Captain Grey nodded as the footman arrived with the pitcher and a glass.

"Egg whites?" I asked as the fellow poured.

"Yes, miss. Already in the milk."

"Good." I indicated the glass should go to Sebastian. "Drink this. It will help neutralize the effects of the acidic fumes."

Sebastian reached for it, but his hands shook. Captain Grey guided the milk to his protégé's lips. After gulping most of the contents, Sebastian exhaled loudly and once more began to accuse me. "She—" He coughed.

I slumped and gave up trying to silence him. No sense prolonging the inevitable. My days of experimenting were at an end. Sooner or later the captain and Miss Stranje were bound to hear about my colossal blunder.

Stupid, *stoopid*, impulsiveness. I wanted to bang my head against the wall. If only I had thought it through more carefully before flinging ingredients into the pot. Sebastian had warned me. It was like the fire all over again. I'd leaped before thinking. I could hear my father scolding me. *Reckless little fool.*

Miss Stranje fixed her attention on Sebastian. Concern bleached out her sharp features. I'd nearly killed her benefactor's nephew. I expected her to horsewhip me soundly or lock me in the mummy case. At the very least, she would send me home with a note scrawled across my forehead—hopeless. What did it matter? I couldn't feel any more disgraced than I already did.

I edged up against the doorpost, so I might stand and face my accusers. It occurred to me I could run away. It didn't matter that I had nowhere to go. Running would free me from this wretched moment, from the aftermath of this whole bloody mess.

I managed to push all the way to my feet. Had I been steadier, I might have taken off like a fox fleeing hounds. Except, I was dizzy.

The garden wobbled and tipped at an unnatural angle. Light hurt my eyes, so I focused down the length of the cool dark hall. Still the earth did not hold as steady as it ought.

"She—" Sebastian cleared his throat. "Saved my life."

I wondered for a minute if my hearing had become as unreliable as my sight.

"Pulled me out," he wheezed.

Captain Grey turned to me and smiled solemnly. "Thank you," he said. "I owe you a debt of gratitude."

I didn't deserve his gratitude. I shook my head, refusing his thanks. Another mistake, shaking my head made the entire world spin.

"You're not well." Miss Stranje grabbed hold of my shoulder and eased me down beside Sebastian. She signaled the footman to refill the glass. "Drink some of this milk."

"I'm fine." I pressed my hand against my eyes to stop the spinning. "I didn't breathe in as much of the fumes as he did."

Sebastian pushed the glass at me. "Drink."

Had he really told them I *saved his life*? It wasn't true. He had it right the first time, I'd nearly killed him. I was dangerous. First, the fire in my father's stables. Now, this.

I lifted the glass to drink, but a liberating blackness swallowed me up.

Eight

APPARITIONS

I have no memory of how I got from the hallway to my bed. It seemed as if I floated up the stairs in a whirling darkness. I saw faces along the way. Hideous faces. Stern faces. Wild, mocking, laughing faces. Now that I am rational again, I believe they were merely the portraits hanging in the hallway, the faces of Miss Stranje's disturbing ancestors.

Like the three hags in *Macbeth*, these apparitions cackled and chanted at me. "Boil, boil, toil, and trouble . . ." They stirred a cauldron of bubbling red liquid. The pot hissed and spit burning prickly droplets onto my skin. A cloud of vapor encircled us. "Your fault. Not smart. Red hair. Red salt," they chanted. "Worthless brain and freckled heart, silly little oak wart."

The witches twirled around me in dizzying circles, cackling. Again and again they sang that maddening ditty about my worthless brain and oak warts. One of them resembled Madame Cho, except her eye sockets were plugged with milky unseeing stones and she wore the black hood of an executioner. I turned to run and collided with the chopping block of a guillotine. The blade hovered above my head.

"No! No!" I screamed, hiding my face from the steel edge plummeting toward me.

"Wake up, child. Wake up." Miss Stranje drew the covers away from my neck.

No guillotine. No witches. No hags. Although Madame Cho stood next to the bed, arms crossed, silent, dark-eyed, wearing a judgmental frown. I could tell she blamed me for the poisonous fumes. And why shouldn't she?

As usual, I'd rushed into an inaccurate conclusion and my experimenting landed me in trouble. The hags were right—my brain was worthless. If only I'd been born a simpleton with brown hair, a good girl without freckles and absolutely no interest in ancient chemists. If only I could rip out my overactive curiosity and trade it in for an interest in embroidery, maybe then my mother's friends would smile at me. Maybe then my mother would love me.

"You've been asleep a very long time. You need fluids." Miss Stranje pressed a glass of milk to my lips. "Drink."

I sipped obediently. "I didn't intend—"

"Hush." She set the glass down with an irritated plunk.

"Sebastian?" I rasped.

She stiffened at my use of his familiar name. "Lord Wyatt," she corrected. "He rested comfortably through the night, and is recovering."

"I didn't mean to harm—"

"Stop." She inhaled deeply. "I know you didn't intend to hurt him. Next time, think carefully before you act."

Madame Cho emitted a low grumble of agreement.

"I *did* think." My voice croaked like a rusty frog. "I was trying to make the ink."

"And did you?"

"No." I sank against the pillow. "I failed."

"You failed yesterday. Try again tomorrow."

"Tomorrow?" I'd been so certain she would punish me or send me home.

"Yes," she answered curtly. "Unless you're suggesting there is no solution to the problem?"

I was suggesting no such thing. I studied her, not sure how to answer, frustrated by the way she turned my words against me. "There *is* a solution. The Persians had a formula. So, did the Greeks. Pliny, the elder, refers to an invisible ink. I just don't know if I can—"

"You just don't know?" She didn't yell at me, but it felt as if she had. "Georgiana, this is not a child's game."

No, it wasn't a child's game. It had *never* been a game. Oh, yes, it's true, in the past I took childish risks, but my intent had always been deadly serious. I couldn't fight Napoleon with a musket or a knife, but I had hoped to do this one thing—I hoped to make certain no one else lost their brother because a dispatch got intercepted by the enemy. I didn't want anyone else's world to grow as lightless and lonely as mine.

I leaned up on my elbows and chewed my bottom lip. But everything had changed. Before, the ink had been only a plan, an idea, a hope. Now lives hung in the balance. *Sebastian's.* The other diplomats. The leaders of Europe. I shuddered. My shoulders hunched. What if I failed again?

She stared at me, scouring my soul. "Either you are up to this challenge, or you are not." Her words came at me like eagle claws. "Which is it?" she asked in a menacingly soft voice.

Which was it, indeed?

I wanted to run away again, not from her, from myself, from the confusion pummeling my head. Some cowardly part of me wished I could forget about Pliny's invisible ink forever. At the same time new ideas tumbled through my mind.

Oak warts.

Why had the old hags chanted about oak warts? Oak galls. What did they mean by it? I knew, of course, the hags were only a figment of my imagination. *They* didn't mean anything. It had come from some far corner of my own mind. Oak galls, the round misshapen growths on oak branches, when ground to a fine powder, were used in making many types of ink.

Was there a way I could turn ink invisible, and then use a gall-based developer to bring out the color? Seed pods of ideas took root and germinated in my mind. A new theory bloomed and treacherously whispered, *what if . . .*

Eager to test the idea, I sat up straighter. My head felt heavy as an anvil. Two words hammered against it. *What if.*

What if always came at a price.

Those two words were the reason I had to continue my experiments. Those insidious words meant there would never be approving smiles aimed at me. *What ifs* insured there would be no good-daughter pats on my head from my father. My mother would continue to dislike me. *What ifs* promised no ball gowns in my future. No suitors bestowing adoring looks on me, least of all Sebastian.

It didn't matter. I could not escape the *what ifs* any more than I could stop breathing or rip off my arm.

"Yes." I lifted my head and looked directly at her, straight through the foolish water blurring my vision. "I will find an answer."

"Good," she said, only she didn't sound pleased. She thrust a handkerchief at me. "Dry your eyes, Georgiana." She shook her head and her mouth twisted in sympathy. "You are a rather stubborn case, aren't you?"

I didn't understand her meaning. Madame Cho, on the other hand, was easy to understand. She chuckled—a dry unfriendly grunt. I guessed what that guttural sound meant. It meant she thought I needed a bamboo cane applied to my backside.

"Stubborn how?" The room joggled a bit as I leaned up, but at least it didn't spin as it had before.

"I'm too busy to explain at the moment." Miss Stranje consulted a small clock she pulled out of her pocket. "You have slept through an entire day. Lady Pinswary is about to descend upon us this afternoon." She slipped the timepiece back into her pocket, smoothed down her skirt, and turned just as Sera and Jane rushed into the room.

"She's awake." Sera hurried to the bed and stared at me.

"I overheard the maids say she would never recover." Jane focused on our headmistress for answers.

"Servants tend to exaggerate. See for yourselves. She's doing quite well. "

Miss Stranje adopted a more businesslike manner. "At any rate, she'll have to do. We've no time to waste. Lady Daneska and her aunt will arrive all too soon, and since one of the primary purposes of her visit is to scrutinize our new student, we must set our minds to the task of making her appear presentable."

Presentable.

"Ha," I scoffed, and wished them best of luck in that endeavor. If presentable meant anything beyond making me clean and tidy they were going to be sorely disappointed. "My mother has tried for nearly sixteen years and met defeat at every turn."

The three of them gathered around, studying me as if I were a fireplace mantel they wished to decorate for Christmas. Miss Stranje tilted her head to one side, contemplating the daunting job before them. "Seraphina, you're the artist. What color would suit her best?"

"Let me see . . ." Sera tugged the bedroom drapes open wider, came back and inspected me under the full glare of the sun. Tapping her finger against her chin, she squinted at me. "Hmm, I should think blues would complement her eyes. As well as certain shades of green. We ought to steer clear of pinks. And avoid stark whites."

Jane sorted through my armoire. Apparently a servant had unpacked the contents of my trunks. "There's not a stitch of blue in here. Or green."

Of course not. I could've saved her the trouble of checking. Everything I had was either white with purple sprigs or lavender. A color in which I looked abysmal. I'd begged my mother to allow me to stay in black. I hadn't felt ready for half-mourning anyway. But she insisted that white or sprigged muslin were the only suitable fabrics for a young lady. I'd always felt rather like a snow-covered strawberry toddling into the room wearing one of her frosty confections. My poor mother winced every time she saw me.

Jane shut the doors on my wardrobe with finality. "Nothing in there will suit."

My mother would have burst a blood vessel if she'd heard Jane's assessment of my wardrobe. "What?" she would cry. "All that money spent on seamstresses, for naught?" After a lengthy tirade, my mother would fall silent and fix me with an expression of painful disappointment. Her plan to marry me off to a duke doomed to failure. It was, after all, my fault.

Jane did not lament. "You and I are much the same size. I have a blue-and-white striped sarcenet gown that would do very well for the occasion." She collected it from her armoire, draped it across the bed and pulled it up under my chin. "See."

"Yes, just the thing," Miss Stranje declared.

"Humph." Madame Cho gave us a curt nod and shuffled out of the room.

Sera spoke directly to me, acknowledging me as a person, rather than a scarecrow they were attempting to dress. "It's a lovely color on you. Brings out your eyes."

No matter how handsome the blue stripes might look on me, I knew I would never be anywhere near as beautiful as Sera.

Maya dashed into the room, amber and scarlet robes billowing behind her, like wings on a brightly feathered bird. She rushed to Sera, breathing hard from her haste. She looked me over and confusion lit up her face. "She is not dying? A maid just told me—"

"Heaven's no." Miss Stranje tsked. "She's a bit dizzy, that's all. Now, I really must attend to other matters. I leave you girls to figure out what to do with her hair." She took one last look at me, frowned, and added, "I'll send a maid to help."

I groaned.

Jane pointed at the flute clasped in Maya's hand and suggested, "We might try snake charming."

They chuckled behind their hands, but I wasn't much amused at being likened to Medusa with a head full of snakes.

Sera untied my ribbon, raked through the tangles with her fingers, carefully avoiding the bump that was still tender on the left side, and twisted my hair back. She scooped it up and turned every which way to see the effect. "Perhaps if we minimize any decorations near the neckline, her hair will form an attractive pattern to please the eye."

"Doubtful," I grumbled. "My hair might poke someone's eye out, but please it? Never."

They ignored me. Jane shook her head. "We could scrape it all back and leave a few curls around her face."

Sera let go and my hair tumbled out like Moses's burning bush.

"I have a pomade we might try," Maya suggested.

"It's no use," I said. "My mother has tried every possible pomade or fixative. Sugar water only makes it worse. Potato starch is a disaster. Lard. Beeswax. Duck grease and egg whites. Rose oil . . ." I stopped ticking off failed attempts to tame my hair and threw up my hands. "Unless you are a magician, all we can do is tie it back and hope for the best."

"Hope is the best kind of magic." Maya trilled a few notes on her flute. "I will get the pomade. You will see." From her armoire, she retrieved a filigreed chest painted bright turquoise, yellow-orange, and vivid red. Reverently opening it, she lifted out an earthenware jar of cream. It smelled heavenly.

"What is it?" I asked.

"Flowers from our garden in India. Ginger, almonds, and honeysuckle." She breathed in deep over the jar. "The smell of home. Many women in my country wear this. It is an old recipe. My grandmother made it." Maya's gaze drifted to the far wall. I could tell she was seeing not our sedate oak-paneled dormitorium but the colorful blossoms of a faraway garden, and a grandmother who no longer lived.

"I can't take this." I handed it back. "It's too important to you."

She pushed the jar into my hands. "Use it. I will enjoy having the fragrance of home near me. Perhaps later you can help me make more."

I nodded, silently thanking her for such a kindness. Even if my hair could not be tamed, it would smell wonderful. Maya tucked up into the window seat and, bathed in afternoon sun, she played her flute while Jane and Sera wrestled with my obstinate locks.

As they worked, I heeded Sebastian's advice and asked, "Why did Miss Stranje have you all bound and gagged in the ballroom?"

Maya stopped playing the flute. All work on my hair paused. It fell so quiet I could hear birds outside our window. Jane took a deep breath and smoothed pomade through my hair carefully avoiding the bump. "We were practicing."

"Practicing?" It made no sense.

Sera laughed uncomfortably. "Escaping out of the ropes, of course."

"Exactly." Jane brushed out a curl, and Maya's flute rippled cheerfully as if they were done explaining.

"Why?"

Jane pinned down a curl and stood back with her hands on her hips. "Why must you ask so many questions?"

Having heard that criticism all my life, I bit back my irritation and pushed onward. "It is a perfectly reasonable question. Furthermore, I don't understand why you continue to protect Miss Stranje with your silence."

"Very well," Sera said matter-of-factly. "We were practicing because one never knows when one might need to escape from being bound to a chair."

I'd never heard anything so absurd, but Jane nodded as if it was a completely rational explanation.

"Tess is the only one who succeeded within the time limit," Sera offered up this glowing praise. "Clever girl slipped out of the gag without even untying it."

"I would've done," said Jane, "but my knots were so tight I broke a fingernail." She held it up for us to commiserate.

"See here," I said, fed up with their lack of forthrightness. "You can stop pretending. I saw the skeleton in the cave. I demand an explanation."

"Demand?" Jane tugged on a lock of hair.

"All right. It's not a demand. I would very much like to know what's going on here."

Jane smoothed down the hair she'd tugged. "Mollie, you saw Mollie. That's the name we gave the bones."

Sera combed out a snarl. "That cave was used for smuggling long before any of us were born. In all likelihood that skeleton belonged to a smuggler from a hundred years ago, and judging by the size, it was a man."

"But . . ." I pulled away for a moment. "It had on a dress, a pink gown?"

Jane smiled mischievously. "One of my castoffs. A few months ago Tess and I snuck down on a lark and dressed it. What did you think of the sign?" She whispered in a spooky voice, "Beware the hangman's waltz."

"A joke!" Angry, I stood up, scattering pins everywhere. "How could you? I was terrified."

Jane had the decency to look guilty. "Not a joke. *Not exactly*. It was meant to ward off intruders." Under the force of my glare, she added, "Tess's idea."

"I should've guessed." My hands balled into fists.

"A bit of fun, that's all." Jane picked up the scattered pins.

With a gentle hand Sera pressed me back into the chair, and pointed to the doorway. "Hush, Abigail is coming."

I sat and brooded silently. Nothing was as it seemed in this place. Everything was upside down and wrong side out. I felt completely at sea. After my disastrous experience in the rowboat, that phrase held considerably more meaning.

Abigail came and went, carrying water and towels, bringing ribbons and combs, picking up hairpins, offering advice, and finally leaving us to our own devices.

I'd had years of practice sitting perfectly still while my hair was being tugged, pulled, unsnarled, brushed, ironed, pinned, and plastered into place. Today, by far, proved the least painful and most successful. After they slipped the blue dress on me, Sera held up a mirror to show me their handiwork. My anger evaporated.

I gasped. Surely another girl stared back.

Unless Maya had charmed my stubborn curls with her flute playing, the pomade had worked a miracle. My rebellious frizzles were transformed into soft shiny waves. Jane had scooped up my curls and pinned them back loosely, allowing a fullness that flattered my face. Instead of making me look like a garish sore thumb, the cornflower blue dress complimented my hair, and gave me the look of an exotic colorful bird. More like Maya, or Sera, or even Jane.

"You *are* magicians," I whispered, still scarcely able to believe it.

"Very pretty." Maya set her flute aside. "Well done, ladies."

Sera and Jane bowed like troubadours in a traveling circus. The clock on the mantel chimed and Jane immediately straightened. "It's getting late. Has anyone seen Tess?"

No one answered.

"We can't delay any longer. It would be just like Lady Daneska and her aunt to arrive early to catch us off guard."

"Go," Maya said. "I will stay here and help Tess get ready." She retreated to the window seat and draped her robes over her head, hiding under an elegant hood, and made the song of a faraway songbird float from her flute.

"Come." Sera grabbed my hand. "We'll wait and watch from the Hamlet hole."

Nine

BATTLES IN THE
DRAWING ROOM

Hamlet hole? Wait." I slipped out of Sera's grasp. "What am I supposed to do, exactly? And why does Lady Pinswary wish to meet me?"

"I suspect her niece is behind this visit. Lady Daneska is curious," Sera said.

"Why should she be curious about me? And why did Tess call her a traitor?"

Jane looped her arm through mine and tugged me to the door. "You ask a great many questions. We'll explain everything later. For now, we really must go. I'm certain I heard someone in the main hall."

Thus far, in my experience here at Stranje House, people rarely explained later. They had more of *wait-and-see-for-yourself* policy. We hurried downstairs and turned sharply into an understair closet.

"Come along." Jane darted into the closet. Which could only mean it was another . . .

"Oh, no." I balked and clutched my skirts. *Spanking bad luck these secret passages.* "I don't want to ruin your lovely gown mucking about in another narrow dusty—"

"It's all right." Sera urged me forward. "Everyone knows about this one, even the servants. See. They've swept it."

The passage was narrow but tidy. We stopped in a nook barely wide enough for the three of us. "We call this Hamlet's hole," explained Sera. "You remember, in *Hamlet* how they hid behind a curtain or a screen to spy on one another?" She slid open a wooden panel to reveal a silk painting mounted across the opening. "This lets us see in, without being seen, and eavesdrop on the evil about to befall us in the drawing room."

"You do remember the scene in *Hamlet* where Polonius gets stabbed hiding behind a curtain?" Jane hid her amusement behind her half smile.

"That's not funny." Whatever evil was about to take place here had to do with me, not her.

"Oh, piffle. One can choose to be sour and afraid, or we can poke fun at our trouble." She demonstrated her philosophy with a finger to my ribs.

"I doubt those are our only available choices."

In answer, she pressed her troublemaking finger to her lips warning me to be quiet.

We studied Miss Stranje's drawing room through the backside of an Oriental silk painting of two dancing cranes, a line of Chinese writing, and a few spindly trees. The brushstrokes hardly obscured our view at all. Darkness concealed us, but we had a perfect view of the sunny parlor. The gilded furnishings, the sea blue Turkish carpet, the vase of flowers on the mantel, the entire tableau lay before us in impressive detail.

Miss Stranje sat in a chair next to the fireplace with mending on her lap and a sewing box beside the chair. She looked the very picture of domestic tranquility—a clever ruse. The butler ushered in a guest who could not possibly be Lady Daneska.

Our headmistress set aside her mending and stood to greet a young gentleman. He limped into the room and bowed curtly.

"Oh, my," Jane murmured. "Is that . . . ? It is. It's *him*, isn't it?"

"Lord Ravencross," Sera mouthed in awe. "I knew it. He's—"

"So much younger than I thought he'd be," Jane whispered. "And taller. So much more—"

"Yes." Sera took a quick breath. "Exactly as I'd imagined." She exhaled slowly.

Lord Ravencross wore a simple linen shirt with no vest, the way a young farmer would, rather than a lord. A plain brown coat strained over his muscular shoulders. His limp, rather than making him seem weak, made Lord Ravencross appear stronger, a man to be reckoned with, powerful. Dangerous. A man who could not be stopped, not even by a severe injury.

No short stylish Beau Brummel haircut for him. His mane of dark hair had been raked back, soldier style, into a simple leather thong. He looked completely out of place in a drawing room. But he had those eyes, deep brown and wounded. The kind of eyes that made a girl wish he would turn and look at her. Only her. He could melt steel with those eyes. But right now they were rimmed with gray, and I guessed Lord Ravencross had been harassed all night by a guilty conscience.

He stood at attention, like a young officer lecturing his troops. "Let us come straight to the point, Miss Stranje. I may have injured one of your . . ." His rigid posture broke and he hesitated as if searching for the right word. "Er, that is to say, one of your . . ."

"One of my guests?" suggested Miss Stranje.

"Guests?" He alerted on her terminology. "I thought they

were your students. Thought you ran some sort of school for problematic chits?"

She shrugged. "However do these rumors get tossed about? Do I look like a schoolmistress?" In that coy manner of hers, Miss Stranje settled back into her chair and gestured for him to be seated on the sofa.

I swear I have never seen a man who looked as much like a trapped wolf as Lord Ravencross. He clamped his jaw tight and glanced wildly about the room as if the brocade couch had intentionally boxed him in. To make him feel more at home, the flowers would have to be thrown out, the damask curtains ripped down, and the whole place changed into a dark cave. "Confound it! Is the girl injured or not?"

"Won't you have a seat, my lord?" Miss Stranje waited very primly.

He raked back a lock of hair that had escaped its moorings, and limped over to the couch, but did not sit.

"Would you care for some tea?" Miss Stranje's left brow cocked in an irritatingly smug manner and humor tainted her voice. "I daresay you'll be more comfortable if you actually lower yourself onto the cushion."

He sat but refused tea. "Miss Stranje, I beg you will answer the question. Is the girl hurt or not?"

She plunked down the teapot. "Yes, I believe she may be. Perhaps you ought to see her and judge for yourself." She rang a hand bell and Madame Cho, who I suspected had been lurking in some hidden corner of the room, appeared almost instantly. "Please fetch Miss Aubreyson to the drawing room."

"No." He shot up from the couch as if she'd dumped hot coals in his lap. His lame leg rammed into the tea table and set the china to clattering. He clenched his teeth and hobbled sideways to where there was more room to pace. "I don't need to see her. If she's injured, just tell me and I'll pay for the damages."

But it was too late. Madame Cho had hurried away.

"Ah, I see. You view the young lady as one would a chipped saucer." Miss Stranje held up a cup and saucer, making a pretense of inspecting it. "You have the idea a few sovereigns will patch up the damage and ease your guilt." She clucked her tongue the way one does at a naughty boy.

"Guilt has nothing to do with it. The fault was not mine." He waved away the cup she offered. "She ran into my horse. Not the other way 'round. Running like a ruddy savage, she was, and on my land, too."

"I see." She set the cup on the table and laced her fingers neatly in her lap. "That explains your distress. A young lady *running*. Oh, my!" She sniffed and shook her head. "And on your land, too."

"That has nothing to do with it. You don't understand at all, damn it. She fell, and I"—he stopped pacing and rubbed the back of his neck—"I may have been a trifle abrupt with her."

"You, my lord? Abrupt?" Miss Stranje asked, all innocence and sugar. "I cannot fathom such a thing."

"Must she tease him so?" Sera whispered in Jane's ear.

"It's for his own good," Jane answered in hushed tones. "Watch what she's doing. It's masterful."

Masterful? High praise to give a woman who was making her guest squirm. What earthly good would such treatment do him?

Jane observed my confusion and leaned next to my ear to explain, "She's helping him face what he did wrong."

"Yes, fine. I was *abrupt*," Lord Ravencross snapped, pacing ferociously. "And it is possible I may have said a few curt words, as well."

"Curse words, you say?"

"Curt words," he corrected. "Hasty. I spoke without thinking."

Just then Tess appeared in the doorway of the drawing room. Lord Ravencross froze to his spot on the Turkish carpet and stared.

"Oh." Sera inhaled sharply, and clutched my elbow. "She looks . . . she's—"

"Astonishing," I breathed.

Tess filled out the vanilla lace gown in ways I never could. She had breasts. The neckline on her gown left no doubt of that fact. She didn't look sixteen, or even seventeen. She looked eighteen, shapely and elegant, a diamond of the first water. She certainly didn't look like a girl who rose before dawn every day and sprinted across muddy sheep pastures, or a girl who climbed through grimy secret passages and kept a pair of rats for pets.

"Come in, my dear." Miss Stranje stood and motioned to Tess. "Lord Ravencross, may I present Miss Tess Aubreyson."

Lord Ravencross appeared to be just as stunned at Tess's change in appearance as we were. He swallowed hard, drew back his injured leg, and bowed quickly. "You are well, I see."

Tess didn't answer. She simply curtseyed, very prim, very formal, and very unlike Tess.

Miss Stranje needled him further. "You do realize, my lord, that not all wounds are outwardly visible." It was another of her twisty-turn-y comments. Did she mean Tess's hurt feelings after being left to fend for herself in the mud? Or the emotional scars Lord Ravencross must surely be hiding?

"I admit it was badly done." A lock of dark hair fell across his eyes. "I should've made certain she hadn't twisted her ankle, or—" He didn't have a chance to finish.

"Pardon me, miss." The butler edged into the double doorway and in a formal monotone addressed our headmistress.

"Your guests have arrived. Lady Pinswary, accompanied by Lady Daneska and Miss Alicia Pinswary."

"Thank you, Greaves." Miss Stranje stood and smoothed out her skirts. "Show them in."

Lord Ravencross's guilt evaporated instantly. He broadened his stance and stared at the doorway like a wolf bracing against attack.

Lady Pinswary didn't wait to be shown in. She shoved past Greaves. A buxom woman clad in a gown of mahogany brown bombazine, she sailed into the room like a warship entering a placid blue harbor. A broad-brimmed hat, decorated with fruit and fowl, sat at a jaunty angle on her head. Any minute I expected the pile of cherries, flowers, and stuffed bluebirds to tumble off the side.

She disregarded everyone else in the room and headed straight for Miss Stranje. "Thank goodness we've arrived in time," she bellowed in a nasal tone. "We've come to warn you—"

"Auntie Prue, être à l'aise, ma chère tante. We need not shout the alarms. See our friends, they are unharmed," said one of the young ladies drifting in behind Lady Pinswary. Despite the French, her accent crystallized from the snowy mountains of Prussia. "Miss Stranje will think we buy our manners at the Piccadilly market, yes?" She said all this in such charming tones that Lady Pinswary stammered incoherently for a moment, but then her shoulders relaxed into silence.

"Daneska," Jane hissed, and stared hard at the young lady.

"She's exquisite," I whispered, and suddenly felt inadequate, a country bumpkin in comparison, or as my mother would say, *a peasant.* I chipped at one of my ragged fingernails.

Sera nodded and quietly added, "Too beautiful for her own good."

I jumped back as Lady Daneska turned sharp and glanced up at our screen as if she'd overheard us. Just as suddenly she gave us a saucy wink and whirled away. The silk on her lustrous dress swished like winter snow whipping against a cold wind—all glittery sparkliness.

"She knows we're here," I whispered.

"Yes." Sera's voice drooped with sadness. "She was once one of us."

"What—"

Jane pressed a finger against her lips again, hushing me.

The other young lady, Miss Alicia Pinswary, was lovely in her own way, with flawless skin and perfectly coiffed dark hair. She entered the room with her chin up and quite dignified even though she toted a fluffy little black and white spaniel puppy in her reticule.

Both girls wore the latest fashions, shiny exotic silks made up in daring French styles. But poor Miss Pinswary was like a serviceable teacup standing next to a dazzling crystal goblet. Lady Daneska captivated the attention of everyone in the room.

Except the puppy, who barked eagerly at Tess.

Amid the dog's antics Lady Daneska spotted Lord Ravencross. She caught her hand to her throat and stifled a small gasp. It was barely noticeable, but I would've sworn her fair skin blanched even whiter for a moment. She recovered and quickly turned to greet Tess.

"Tess, my darling girl," she cried, and followed this affectionate greeting with an exuberant hug and kiss.

Tess remained rigid as stone.

"It has been much too long." Lady Daneska caught our friend's cheek in her gloved hand. "Look at you, you are become most lovely." After giving Tess a pointed inspection, she grinned. "Almost you look civilized. No, that is not quite right. How does one say . . ." She frowned, struggling with the language. "*Tamed*. Yes, that is the word. Tamed."

"I assure you, Daneska, I still bite on occasion."

She grinned. "Always with the wit." When Tess refused to grant her even the hint of a smile Lady Daneska's mouth formed a perfect O. Like a wounded kitten, all helpless and sad, she pouted. "Never say you are still vexed at me? Not after all these many long months."

Tess didn't answer or move a muscle.

Miss Pinswary's puppy, however, barked at a more excited pitch and tried to wriggle out of the reticule.

With an annoyed little huff Lady Daneska said, "I see you still have the effect of *magnétisme* on animals. That much, at least, has not changed." In a whiplike movement, she delivered a hard flick to the puppy's nose.

His bark instantly changed into a yip, and then a muted whimper. "Daneska!" Miss Pinswary clutched her whimpering pup protectively.

As if she'd done nothing at all, Lady Daneska ignored her cousin's outcry and continued, "Come now, Tessie, it is not like you to hold the grudge."

"Don't call me that."

"Unless you had one of your terrible dreams about me. You haven't, have you? Not about me?"

Tess ignored the question and left Daneska standing alone in the middle of the room. She went to comfort the whimpering dog who waggled happily and licked her fingers.

"Never mind." Lady Daneska dismissed Tess with a wave of her hand. "What does it matter? Is only silly dream, yes?" Her accent got heavier. "These things mean nothing, nothing at all." But she looked worried, a golden-haired cherub with a frown marring her porcelain brow. Then, in one quick breath, her face cleared and she laughed—a delicate laugh, an angelic trill—so light the sound floated on the air like the tinkling of a crystal chandelier being raised. Altogether too perfect.

"Why is she worried about Tess's dream?" I asked.

Jane and Sera exchanged furtive glances, but gave me no reply. The three of us watched in silence as Lady Daneska approached Lord Ravencross. "It is the pleasant surprise, *ma bonne chance*, to see you here, my lord."

She stood very close to him and dropped into a deep curtsey. I'd never seen a curtsey like hers. It was so charming and engagingly done that before I realized it, I was mimicking her movements.

Jane nudged me and whispered, "Practicing seduction, are we?"

I straightened immediately. She was right. Lady Daneska had arranged herself at such an opportune angle that Lord Ravencross could not help but see directly into her cleavage. And that clever dress of hers—all shimmering silk and fluttering organza—was cut so low I blushed to think how much of her bosom he had in view. The gown was a sensuous shade of lavender, not old-lady lavender, it was a frothy purple that shifted colors depending upon the light, and it was trimmed seductively in black. Which meant— "Oh, my goodness, she's in half-mourning."

"Her father died last year at Leipzig." Jane held my arm and leaned so close her breath tickled my ear when she spoke. "Not that she was excessively fond of him. Except for the fact that, during the march through Prussia, Napoleon made her father a duke, which in turn elevated Daneska to a countess, she had very little good to say about him."

I mouthed my question, "Did her father send her to Stranje House?"

"No." Jane caught her lip for a moment. "He sent her to live with Lady Pinswary, her mother's sister. It was Daneska who insisted she must come to Stranje House."

"Why?"

"To study English manners. Or so she said." I could tell Jane knew more, but she merely shrugged.

Lady Daneska remained deep in her curtsey with her hand extended up to Lord Ravencross, as if she was Anne Boleyn awaiting King Henry to raise her from submission.

"Minx." Sera scowled. "She has him completely flustered."

Lord Ravencross stared at Daneska's proffered hand as if it were a three-eyed fish and he had no idea what to do with it. His gaze shot to Tess—Tess, whose lips were pressed together in obvious vexation.

I nudged Sera. "Has Lady Daneska formed a tendresse for Lord Ravencross?"

"Hardly," Sera said. "She despises him."

Given her coquetry, how could that be? "But that curtsey?"

I bent my head to hear her soft reply. "Study her face when she doesn't think he's looking. Watch closely. There. Did you see it?"

A flash of pure venom distorted Lady Daneska's features, but only for the briefest instant, then it vanished, replaced by her bewitching smile and glimmering teeth.

I was speechless.

"Sera sees everything." Jane glanced sideways at me. "Daneska resents him taking his brother's place. She was quite, er, *fond* of the late Lord Ravencross."

A hundred questions raced through my mind, all of them beginning with *why*. But I knew they would have to wait.

Lady Pinswary aimed her massive prow at Lord Ravencross. "We never expected to see you here, my lord. We heard you were wounded in the war, but I see it was all a hum. You look perfectly fit to me." She paused to sniff. "Pity about your brother. We shall miss him. *He*, at least, had the good sense to wear a cravat when making calls." Over the end of her stubby nose, she peered at him. "I see you're out of mourning already. Rather soon, isn't it?"

Miss Stranje cleared her throat. "My lady, one cannot properly evaluate the depth of another's grief by the color of their clothing." With an upraised eyebrow, she glanced at Lady Daneska. "It is a woefully unreliable custom. Clearly Lord Ravencross is deeply distressed by the loss of his brother. As are we all."

Lord Ravencross's jaw tensed. He could not seem to find any point in the room on which to focus comfortably. "I assure you, this was not a social call," he blurted. "And now, if you will excuse me, I shall see myself out." With that he limped rapidly toward the exit, but hesitated in front of Tess. "I am relieved you were not injured."

"Not completely uninjured, my lord." She looked up at him without even a wisp of girlish timidity, or any concern that everyone was eavesdropping on her remarks. "You said some rather harsh—"

"I—I . . ." He clamped off the stammer. "Have you forgotten? It was you who startled my horse and nearly got yourself killed."

"An accident. And your horse shied only a little. You spooked the poor creature more when you bellowed at me. That's why he reared again. It was your foul temper that nearly got me killed."

He clenched his jaw, glanced over his shoulder at their spellbound audience, and snapped a curt bow to Tess. "My apologies. However, as my temperament is unlikely to improve, I suggest you stay well away from my property. Or next time you may not be so lucky."

Before Tess could respond Lord Ravencross thundered out into the hall, loudly demanding the servants bring him his blasted hat.

Lady Daneska flounced to the sofa and settled herself squarely in the middle. "Such a pleasant fellow, that one."

Lady Pinswary huffed at Tess. "You needn't have driven off the only eligible male for miles around." She whirled to her hostess. "Clearly, Miss Stranje, you are failing to teach this one any manners."

"I shall make a note."

"Take my advice, girl." Lady Pinswary navigated to the large chair beside the tea table. "If you want a husband you model your behavior after my Alicia, or my niece."

Tess snorted at that and dropped into a straight-backed chair near the door.

Miss Stranje directed Miss Pinswary to a seat and asked her guests, "Would you care for some tea?"

Lady Daneska surveyed the biscuits and sweetmeats laid out on the table. "But this is lovely. You are the perfect hostess, Miss Stranje. Always thinking ahead." This last bit of praise she delivered with a sly peek at our headmistress. "And you remembered strawberries! My favorite." The impertinent girl seized one from the plate with all the familiarity of a family member, plucked the stem and popped it in her mouth.

Lady Pinswary waved away the offer. "No, no. We haven't time for tea. We're here on an important errand, a matter of life and death."

Alicia Pinswary held her dog tightly in her lap as she squeezed onto the far end of the sofa beside Lady Daneska.

"Oh, Auntie, there is always time for tea, is there not?" Lady Daneska mewed. "Look at all these delicious sweets. Our dear Miss Stranje has made *le grand effort* to please us. It would be rude for us not to partake, yes?" She placed a small ginger cake in the center of a plate and held it out to entice her aunt.

Her aunt eyed the platters of crumpets and chocolates on the table and the cake her niece held out. "Well, they say ginger is soothing for the stomach, and molasses is exceedingly good for the bowels. Oh, very well, if you insist." She snatched the plate.

"Good." Lady Daneska beamed. "Now, we can all sit together and have the pleasant chat." I would've sworn she waved her fingertips at us in our hiding place before her gaze whipped toward Tess. There it was again, that split second of anger before her expression shifted. "We are friends, are we not? Breaking bread? That is what friends do."

Tess sat mute in the chair.

Miss Stranje handed Lady Daneska a cup of tea laced heavily with cream. "Have you had word from your family? In light of the current political situation, how do they fare?"

Lady Daneska's shoulder lifted in a half shrug. "They have a saying on the continent, what Napoleon *giveth* the Vienna Congress *taketh* away. I expect they will dissolve my father's duchy. When next we meet, I fear you may be reduced to addressing me as a simple miss." She laughed again, that perfect trill, like the strumming of frozen harp strings.

"I assure you, there are far worse things." Miss Stranje offered her a platter of shortbread biscuits. "However, I was inquiring after your father's family. They are in danger, are they not?"

"Oh, that." Daneska accepted one of the cookies and added a few strawberries to her plate. "That is why they sent me here, to England, where I am safe."

"And yet you went back?"

"Not to Pomerania." She shot back and arched, like a startled cat.

"No? I had thought . . ." Miss Stranje studied her former student. "But of course, now I remember. You accompanied the former Lord Ravencross to Saxony, before his most unfortunate death." Brash of Miss Stranje to mention such an indiscretion.

Lady Daneska snapped the shortbread in half. Crumbs scattered across her lap. She made a great show of brushing them away, as if a morsel of dry cookie would ruin her gown forever.

Miss Stranje shook her head mournfully. "He died at Mockern, did he not?"

The puppy wriggled from Miss Pinswary's grasp, intent on lapping up a crumb or two from Daneska's dress. He yipped when she rewarded him with a quick swat.

"Dani!" Miss Pinswary scooped him up and cuddled him to her breast. "Toby meant no harm." She cooed to the dog and Lady Daneska ignored her completely.

"It is all this talk of war. It is too much sadness." Lady Daneska brushed the remaining crumbs to the floor. "We must speak of less distressing matters. Auntie Prue, you brought a letter you wish to discuss, did you not? Something about a fire."

Lady Pinswary had just bitten into her second ginger cake. "Hmm, oh, yes." She set the plate down and held up one finger before digging through her reticule. With a great flourish she produced the missive and paused to dab crumbs from her lips, before saying, "My cousin wrote to me. You are housing a criminal, one Georgiana Fitzwilliam." She glanced up making certain all eyes were on her. "An arsonist."

Arsonist.

It felt as if Lady Pinswary had rammed the prow of her ship straight into my stomach.

Wondrous quick my status dropped from *wayward daughter, lacking in social skills and having too many disturbing interests,* to dangerous criminal.

Sera leaned close. "Don't worry. Most of us had thorny reputations that chased us here."

"Look at Daneska," Jane hissed. "Sitting there taking it all in, trying not to smile. Wicked little cat."

Sera absently twisted a ribbon from her dress around one finger. "I'm not sure Dani can help herself."

Jane issued a hushed order to Sera. "Stop giving her the benefit of the doubt. And you"—she fixed her gaze on me—"don't underestimate her. Daneska learned to scheme before she left her nurse's teat. And she probably bit that off on her way out."

"Why are you so upset with her? What did she do?" I asked.

"She betrayed us," Jane snapped, almost too loud. "And England." Softer, she added, "She overheard things she shouldn't have and ran straight to him, to Lord Ravencross's older brother. The two of them rushed off to warn Napoleon. Lord knows how many men died because of her."

"You mustn't be so hard on her," mumbled Sera. "Her father's life was at stake."

"She never cared one wit for her father. It was his title she cared about. That and her attachment to Lord Ravencross's brother." Jane crossed her arms.

"We don't have any proof," Sera insisted.

"You're too soft." Jane's hands balled into fists. "It didn't take much for him to get Dani to play the traitor, did it? For all we know she was involved with him before she even came to Stranje House."

"There's no evidence of that."

"My instincts are evidence enough." Jane turned to me. "If Captain Grey hadn't warned the allies to change strategy, Leipzig would have fallen to Bonaparte. As it was, eighty-four thousand men died."

Eighty-four thousand.

"In three days. The field is still red with their blood."

I gulped in horror. My mother never allowed talk of battles. All those men, wounded and dying. Young men like my brother. *Boys.* Some of them no older than me.

"I hate war," Sera said softly.

I shuddered and could only nod.

Below us, Miss Alicia Pinsway stroked Toby and looked worried. "Is it true? Is this fire-starting girl, this *arsonist* really one of your"—she reached for a square of cheese and nervously fed it to her dog—"your young ladies?"

"I don't think arsonist is the appropriate word." Miss Stranje defended me, for which I felt exceedingly grateful.

Lady Pinsway reached for another cake. "It is someone who starts fires—"

"I'm aware of what the word means," Miss Stranje said.

"Then I cannot fathom why you would allow such a dangerous creature to reside under your roof. Your forbearance is foolhardy in the extreme. It says here, the girl set fire to her father's barn and burned the place to the ground. My cousin's orchard as well. Destroyed the entire crop."

Squire Thurgood's apples. I moaned.

"Good heavens, Emma, the child might put a torch to our entire neighborhood. We could all be killed in our sleep."

"In our sleep. Oh, dear. That would, indeed, be a tragedy." Miss Stranje set her teacup on its saucer. "We really ought to be awake for such a momentous occasion."

Lady Daneska snickered and her cousin smiled behind gloved fingers.

"Don't be impertinent." Lady Pinsway shot a quelling look at both girls. "I don't know what you are playing at, filling your home with these troublesome girls. But I know for a fact your grandmother wouldn't want you consorting with criminals."

"You will kindly leave my grandmother out of this."

"It's for her sake I've come today. It's my duty to warn you. Have done with this Miss Fitzwilliam! Send her packing. We can't have her sort here in Fairstone Meade, it won't do, won't do at all." She exhaled loudly, stuffed a large piece of ginger cake in her mouth and sagged back against the chair.

Lady Daneska twirled a strawberry by the stem. "We must not leap to the hasty judgments, Auntie Prue. Her papa's stables may have caught fire by accident, no? Even so, I must confess, I'm most curious about the young lady." Her shoulders scrunched up in glee. "I would very much like to have a look at her. Wouldn't you, Alicia?"

"Oh, yes." Her cousin nodded, combing her fingers through Toby's fur. "I'm all agog to meet her."

"Don't see why," grumbled Lady Pinswary. "The Fitzwilliam girl is a menace. It says so right here." She waved the crumpled letter.

Miss Stranje patted Lady Pinswary's hand. "I'm certain once you meet her it will put your mind at ease. You'll see her and know immediately the young lady has no wish to murder any-one in their sleep."

Miss Stranje gestured to Tess. "Miss Aubreyson, will you please fetch Miss Fitzwilliam."

Lady Daneska rushed to add, "You will come back, won't you? I want to hear about . . ." But Tess had already hurried out of the room. ". . . your dream." Lady Daneska's words withered like leaves on a winter breeze. She smiled as if nothing were amiss and put another strawberry in her mouth.

"It's time." Sera nudged me and we turned to leave Hamlet's hole.

"Wait. We have more visitors." Jane grabbed my arm and yanked me back. She pointed. "That's Captain Grey and the fellow with him is Lord Wyatt. You might remember him, he found you and carried you back to the house yesterday."

I'd imagined Sebastian still in bed suffering the ill effects of the fumes. He looked a trifle pale, but walked tall and steady. Clearly his strength had returned. Relief nearly drowned me.

Sera whipped back to peer at the newcomers. "With a face like that, how could you not? He's positively byzantine."

"Byzantine?" I asked.

Jane's eyebrows arched. "Like a Greek god."

A wicked twinge of jealousy knotted my shoulder muscles. Except, I shouldn't be jealous. Jealousy was an impractical notion. Completely illogical. Utterly pointless. Especially in this instance, Jane's and Sera's looks far outshone mine. Plus there was the blindingly beautiful Lady Daneska, who at that very moment was performing another of her vulgar curtseys for Sebastian's benefit. The vixen lifted her hand up to him like Cleopatra.

Cleopatra's asp.

I'm not so foolish to imagine I could compete with any of them for his attention. My neck kinked into even tighter knots. Why should it matter to me if he fell in love with one of them? It didn't.

"Yes, I know him well," I said, with an unwarranted tone of proprietorship. "Lord Wyatt is my laboratory assistant."

Ten

SEEING RED

"Your assistant? And you kept this a secret? Selfish girl."
Jane's wide smile belied her hushed scold.

"Leave her be. I would've kept him to myself, too." Sera sighed.
"What's it like working alongside him?" Sera was kind and good-
natured; she deserved better of me than petty jealousy.

"Come with me and see for yourself," I said. "Lord Wyatt
behaves toward me in a decidedly arrogant manner."

"That's peculiar. He's usually so amiable." Sera leaned closer
and looked at him again. "Even so, you must agree, he is excessively handsome."

"Is he? I hadn't noticed."

Sera smelled the fib before it even escaped my lips. Her eyebrows shot up, but at least she had enough grace not to call me
on it. Jane rapped my arm in a wordless rebuke. We studied the
two men a moment longer. Captain Grey became a silent senti-
nel behind Miss Stranje's chair. Despite Lady Pinswary insist-
ing she could make room for him on the sofa beside her niece

and daughter, Sebastian stood near the far window, gazing across the room at the Chinese screen as if he knew we were watching.

"Very well, you're right," I whispered. "Lord Wyatt is tolerable looking in a dark, roguish, Byronlike manner."

With a sideways grin Jane pushed me out of the spy hole. "Go on. Miss Stranje is expecting you any minute. I'll stay here and watch."

Sera and I left the shadowed safety of the hidden passage. In the foyer, just outside the drawing room she stopped me. "Wait. Let me check you." She turned me around and brushed dust off the back of my gown. "Remember to smile sweetly no matter what is said about you." She smoothed down a stray curl at my temple and pinched my cheeks. "There. You look quite presentable."

I cringed. Earlier, I would've been pleased to hear anyone pronounce me *presentable*. I'd doubted such an outcome was even possible. Now I longed for more.

Was I that homely? Could she not have said *pretty*? Or at least *charming*?

Next to her, I felt like a great, lumbering, blue-striped gargoyle. I wished she had refused my invitation to come with me to the drawing room. Sebastian would be so enthralled by her loveliness he would never even look at me. "Are you coming in with me?" I asked.

"Of course." Sera smiled brightly. "I'll be right by your side."

Exactly what I feared.

We entered together, fairy princess and gargoyle. I found it difficult to fix my eyes anywhere but on the carpet.

I knew Lady Pinsway would take one look at me and decide I was indeed a vile arsonist. That would distress Miss Stranje. The dog would leap from Miss Pinswary's lap and try to bite my ankles. Sebastian would be captivated by Seraphina and wish she were the chemist instead of me. Lady Daneska would laugh and throw strawberries at my face. It was all going to go very badly, very badly indeed.

Two boots appeared on the floor in front of me. I glanced up. *Sebastian.* "Miss Fitzwilliam." He bowed. "A pleasure to see you looking so well, quite charming in fact."

Charming?

Had he read my mind? Sebastian had never bowed to me before, not properly, not like a gentleman to a lady, and certainly not without insulting me. I was so stunned by his behavior I would've forgotten to curtsey if Sera hadn't nudged me in the ribs. As I did, he said under his breath, "What, only one ruffle?"

The wretch. His gallantry burst like a soap bubble, proving the compliment he'd given me was counterfeit.

"She has red hair." Lady Pinswary squawked like a hen laying an egg. *"Red!"* As if the color of my hair was an evil omen— the harbinger of *kill-you-in-your-sleep* fires.

Lady Daneska smiled broadly. The dog yapped at me. Miss Alicia Pinswary appeared to be somewhat bored. She said, "I don't know why you were in such a rush to meet her, Dani. She doesn't look dangerous at all."

Miss Pinswary's remark was rewarded with a quick pinch from her cousin. She squeaked like one of Tess's rats and rubbed her thigh.

"Miss Fitzwilliam." Our headmistress signaled for me to come forward. "These ladies have received a troubling letter about you. Please put their fears to rest by explaining how your father's stables caught fire?"

Surely Miss Stranje didn't expect me to tell the whole of it. These ladies wouldn't approve of my explanation any more than my parents had. And what about the ink? I'd promised to keep it a secret. Lady Daneska thrummed her fingers against the sofa cushion. A sly smile played at the corner of her mouth and her arctic gaze held a barely contained eagerness. She would pounce the minute I tried to lie.

I stood, knees trembling like a common criminal on trial. My tongue turned to sand. I swallowed, raised my chin and tried devilishly hard to appear at ease. Unfortunately, no words found their way to my mouth. Not a one.

"As I understand it," Miss Stranje prompted, "you were trying out a new recipe, were you not?"

She astonished me. It was true. And yet not. I breathed in the reprieve. "Yes. Exactly. A new recipe."

"You were cooking?" said Miss Pinswary with considerable astonishment. "In the stables?"

"How very odd." Lady Daneska's lips pursed. "Is your family so poor you have no kitchens?"

Miss Stranje cocked one eyebrow expectantly.

I had a ready answer to that question. Ready, because it was the pure truth. "We have a very fine kitchen, my lady. But our cook, you see, wouldn't allow me in. Earlier that day I had attempted a similar recipe, and she complained that my concoction stunk up the place. I felt certain if she would just allow me to adjust the ingredients, the recipe would come out right. But, she said no, and banned me from the kitchen."

Lady Pinswary nodded sympathetically. "Cook doesn't let me in my kitchen, either."

"Hmm, this is most confusing." Lady Daneska continued tapping the sofa, with one finger, soft and slow, like rain dripping off the roof. "You don't look like the sort of young lady who would enjoy the . . . how do you say, activities *domestiques*."

Her finger stilled and she sighed. "Do you also like the sewing, and the sweeping, and the scrubbing of the floors?" She said all this in a disinterested singsong tone, and glanced over her shoulder, batting her ridiculously long eyelashes at Sebastian.

"No," I said a trifle too loud. "Just recipes. I like trying out new recipes."

Her eyes sparked and her attention whipped back to me, claws out. "Do you mean to say, you were so . . . what is the word? Determined? Yes, that is it. You were so *determined* to boil up this new concoction, as you called it, that you built the cooking fire in with the horses and the oxen?"

"Yes." I shifted nervously. I saw where she was going. I couldn't tell her it had been because a *what if* had whipped me mercilessly and driven me to experiment. I had to try. I had to know—at any cost.

"But how foolish." She shook her head and twittered, a frozen trill plucking at my raw nerves. "You seem to me a most bookish sort of girl. I would not have thought you stupid."

Foolish at times. But not stupid. I wanted to slap the sneer off her perfect face. Instead, I simply glared at her. She stared back, winter-sky eyes, barely blue. Blue would've held too much warmth. "And I would not have thought you rude," I said sweetly. "You appear to be a more polished sort of girl."

Miss Stranje made a little noise, I might have guessed it a stifled laugh, but her features wore no expression at all.

Sebastian cleared his throat and charged into the uncomfortable silence. "I thought all young ladies tried their hand at cooking now and again. Isn't it required study for females?"

"Oh, yes," Sera agreed a little too eagerly. "Miss Stranje insists we all learn how."

Lady Daneska's face went through a number of intriguing

twists. It was like staring into a crystal the way her face fractured and reshaped itself, first angry, then charming, next shrewd and flirtatious. All in the space of a mere second.

"Lord Wyatt," she cooed. "You know much more about females than this, I think." She patted the seat beside her. "Come. Sit. We will speak of the feminine cooking skills. Yes?"

Heat flooded my cheeks. She'd managed to make cooking sound seductive.

Sebastian laughed appreciatively and remained standing by the fireplace. "I'm afraid I have little interest in such things—wouldn't know a compote from a cantaloupe."

Everyone in the room chuckled. My cheeks cooled and I took a deep breath.

Lady Daneska shrugged and spread the silk of her skirt over the place she had offered to him. "I am most curious, Miss Fitzwilliam. There is an excessive amount of straw in a stable. You, I think, would not be ignorant of this. Why did you not build the cooking fire out of doors?"

"Yes," Lady Pinswary demanded. "Why didn't you?"

Alicia Pinswary's dog barked as if expecting an answer, too.

"It was raining." *Lightly misting really, but I couldn't allow water to corrupt the ink formula.*

Lady Pinswary sniffed. "Surely, your mother keeps a stillroom where you might try new recipes?"

"No, my mother has no interest in such things." *Nor in my need to experiment.* "I had thought if I kept the flames low there would be no danger." My shoulders sagged and I shook my head in shame. "But, as you said, there was too much straw. Dried bits of it floating everywhere. A spark ignited, and . . ." I stopped the tale there. No sense explaining that my formula burst into flames. That would ruin the illusion that I'd been cooking up a pudding of some kind.

I cringed, remembering how flaming muck had splattered everywhere. Until that very moment, I'd blotted out the memory of the fire snaking across my worktable and spilling onto the floor. Nor had I remembered the orange flames licking all around me, the crackling tongues of fire gobbling up straw. I'd forgotten screaming for our grooms as I tried to beat out flames with a horse blanket. Forgotten how the smoke seared my nostrils and stung my lungs. Forgotten slapping at the embers alighting on my skirts. How in heaven's name had I blotted out the high-pitched whinnying of the terrified horses as we flung blankets over their heads and urged them out to safety?

Mine wasn't simply a failed experiment. The grooms could have been killed. The horses. All of us. Burned alive.

"Are you unwell?" Sera asked.

I couldn't answer. The parlor moved in dizzying wobbles. Sebastian rushed to my side and guided me to a chair. I sat down, breathing in stops and starts, stunned, shocked, but most of all, repentant. No wonder my parents wanted to be rid of me.

I am a menace.

Lady Daneska stared at me, no doubt judging me for the fool I was. "You must tell us, Miss Fitzwilliam, what was this most important recipe for which you were willing to risk everything."

There it was. The one question I couldn't answer honestly without telling her about the ink. "It . . . I—"

Miss Stranje cleared her throat loudly.

"Enough questions," Sebastian ordered. "The trauma of recalling those tragic events has overset Miss Fitzwilliam. We ought not to tax her anymore with these painful memories."

Lady Daneska's attention snapped to him. "How very solicitous of you, Lord Wyatt. I did not know you were so well acquainted with Miss Stranje's new guest."

"We've only just met. But surely anyone can see—"

"Yes," she said, and smiled, looking quite satisfied. "Anyone can see."

She knows.

Except, she couldn't. It was impossible. She could only guess all this had something to do with him. *Does she know Lord Wyatt is a spy?* Supposing she did, she couldn't possibly know what I'd been brewing that day. Not unless my mother unwittingly . . .

I turned to Lady Pinswary. "Pray, did your cousin say anything more about the accident?" The minute the words escaped my mouth I wanted to grab them and stuff them back down my throat. I sounded far too desperate.

Lady Daneska gave her aunt no opportunity to answer me. "No, no, Miss Fitzwilliam, poor dear, you are too overwrought. We must have no more questions about that dreadful day, *n'est-ce pas?* Only look at Lord Wyatt, your knight most chivalrous. I think he would bite off our heads if we dared ask more, no?" She stood up and smoothed out her skirt. "I fear our fifteen minutes have flown by."

Lady Pinswary set down her plate and followed her niece's lead, flicking crumbs off her gloves as she stood. She steered her daughter in Lord Wyatt's direction. Miss Pinswary curtseyed prettily.

"You must pay us a visit, my lord." Lady Pinswary nudged her daughter closer, but the puppy started to bark. Sebastian backed away and Miss Pinswary darted to the door. Her mama gave up and turned to me. "I trust you won't do any more cooking while you are here in Fairstone Meade?"

I blinked. Only yesterday, I'd been boiling up a new emulsion. How could I answer truthfully?

Miss Stranje smiled. "Not to worry, my lady. I keep a well-appointed stillroom should Miss Fitzwilliam decide to try out another new recipe."

Lady Daneska gave Sera a farewell kiss and said quietly, "*Adieu.* You will tell Tess and Jane that I forgive them, yes?"

Sera tilted her head, puzzled. "If you mean you want me to ask them to forgive you, that is something you must do for yourself."

"No matter." Lady Daneska waved away Sera's dispute and laughed carelessly, sounding like small icicles shattering against stones. She turned to our headmistress. "My dear Miss Stranje, what interesting company you keep."

"High praise coming from you, my lady."

"Yes. Most interesting. You like playing with the hornet's nest, I think." She strolled toward the door but stopped beside me. "And to what end, I wonder." Lady Daneska studied me with all the warmth of a feral cat. "Miss Fitzwilliam, you are a curiosity. We shall visit again when you are less indisposed or—is the word discomposed?" She shrugged and with a cheery grin said, "My English, it is so bad. Ah, well, *c'est la vie.*"

On the contrary, I'd begun to think her English was perfect, except when she chose to play at French.

Lady Pinswary sniffed and looked down her bulbous nose at me. "Heed my advice, young lady, and take up knitting. Less peril for the rest of us."

I meekly nodded.

"I don't know." Sebastian rubbed his chin skeptically and in a deadly serious tone said, "Those needles look awfully sharp."

Lady Daneska gave him a playful tap on the arm and her pert little lips turned up in a beguiling smile. "With you, always the clever remark. *Le danse du sabre.* We must meet again, my lord, soon."

He smiled back.

I wanted more than anything to throw a chair cushion at her. And at him, too. I caught Miss Alicia Pinswary watching me too intently. She quickly looked away and made a fuss over stuffing her pup into the reticule. But there was no mistaking that vicious little grin she tried to hide. She'd observed my jealousy. No doubt, she and Daneska would have a jolly good laugh about that on the way home.

I wanted to crawl under the sofa and never come out.

Miss Stranje curtseyed in farewell to Lady Pinswary and Lady Daneska. "Do come again. Your visits are always so very"—she paused—"diverting."

Daneska laughed, but for the first time it sounded genuine. No delicate heavenly peal, this was a scratchy crow of triumph.

Eleven

SHE KNOWS

Lady Daneska left me drowning in uncertainty. As soon as Miss Pinswary and her yapping dog made their exit, I dropped onto the sofa. "I failed. She knows."

Miss Stranje pressed a finger to her lips, waiting until the sound of the front door shutting echoed through the drawing room. She seemed distracted. Where was her scold? I expected her to berate me for not being discreet enough, for tipping my hand. Instead, she rubbed her palms against her skirt as if wiping away grime.

Captain Grey caught her elbow. "You're worried."

"No, I'm pleased." She smiled up into his concerned face. "All in all, I think it went quite well, don't you?"

He stared at her thoughtfully for a moment. "That isn't precisely how I would've summed it up. Miss Fitzwilliam is right. Lady Daneska knows something."

"She does." Lord Wyatt gripped the frame of the settee. "What's more, Miss Fitzwilliam stumbled upon a pertinent question. What else might have been in that letter to Lady Pinswary?"

Stumbled. I did not stumble upon it. It was a perfectly logical question. I crossed my arms and frowned, not that the scoundrel would notice.

Miss Stranje shook her head. "In all likelihood it was only her busybody cousin, spreading a piece of spiteful gossip. *Surely.*"

I hoped she was right. "Mother detests my experiments. My scientific pursuits are an embarrassment to her. Weighing that into the equation, I doubt she would have mentioned that one of my experiments caused the blaze."

"That would also explain why your neighbors suspect a more malicious motive." Miss Stranje brightened. "There you are—a perfectly logical conclusion."

Logical. See there, Sebastian, not everyone dismisses my mental capability as mere stumbling.

"Come now, we've nothing to worry about." Miss Stranje absentmindedly caught Captain Grey's hands in hers. "Lady Daneska is only conjecturing at this point." She glanced down at her fingers wrapped around his, flushed pink, and let go of him immediately. Captain Grey's hands remained extended to her a moment longer, as if he thought she might grasp them again.

Instead, she whirled to face me. "Miss Fitzwilliam, you did quite well today, especially for someone with no training."

"I did?"

"Yes. I must say, your quick thinking impressed me. *The cook wouldn't let you in.*" She smiled, looking almost girlish. "A brilliant tactic."

"It was the simple truth," I confessed. "Not a stratagem."

"Ah, I see." She nodded. "The truth can be highly effective."

Effective? For what? Deception? I struggled to grasp her meaning.

"We were fortunate today. Lady Daneska, for all her cleverness, inadvertently revealed more than she realized. Although, it is rather evident that she is . . ." Miss Stranje's confident words trailed off, her brow creased again.

"Up to something," Sebastian finished for her. Deep in thought, he paced and muttered as if no one was really listening, "Obviously she'd like to put an end to your school, but there was more."

Sera held a throw pillow on her lap and toyed with the fringe. "Something to do with Lord Ravencross."

"Undoubtedly." Sebastian tapped the back of our sofa as if marking several facts and then resumed his pacing.

The captain shot him a quelling look and led Miss Stranje to her chair. "Let us put the matter aside for a moment." He leaned over the tray of food and rubbed his palms together. "What do you say, ladies? Shall we enjoy some tea and biscuits?"

Sebastian ignored Captain Grey's attempt to distract Miss Stranje. "Did you notice? At one point she looked as if she'd like to run Ravencross through with a pike."

Sera nodded. "Yes, when she wasn't shamelessly flirting with him."

Head down, still treading a path on the Turkish carpet, Lord Wyatt grunted in agreement. "Of course, she would hate him, wouldn't she, if she was privy to the circumstances of Lucien's death."

Lucien? "Lord Ravencross's older brother?" I wondered. "How did he die?"

Sebastian glanced at Captain Grey, who nodded permission.

"It's not a secret," Sebastian began. "We tracked Lucien, who was, of course, Lord Ravencross at the time, to a farmhouse in Mockern north of Leipzig. Gabriel, his younger brother, was encamped nearby with a unit of the Royal Horse Artillery. We snuck him behind the lines, hoping he could meet with Lucien and make him see reason. Regrettably, Lucien did not appreciate his younger brother's intrusion. After a heated exchange, he got angry and drew his sword. Slashed Gabriel's leg to the bone." Sebastian grabbed his own sword hilt. "Gabe had no choice. He had to fight back. By the time we broke in the house Lucien was dead and Gabriel lay barely alive. We pulled him out before Lucien's men had a chance to finish him off."

"His own brother," I murmured.

"It was awful." Sera nodded. "Tess saw the fight in one of her nightmares."

Why had the former Lord Ravencross turned against England, I wondered. "What made him so furious he was even willing to murder his brother?"

Captain Grey cleared his throat. "Enough of this."

There were a dozen more questions I wanted to ask. Had Lady Daneska been in love with the former Lord Ravencross? In what capacity had he served Napoleon? However, this was not the time to ask, and I doubted any of them would indulge my curiosity.

I suddenly realized this line of conversation meant Sebastian and Captain Grey had observed Lady Daneska talking with the present Lord Ravencross, even though that conversation occurred before they entered the room. Which meant they, too, had been watching, but from where?

Twisting and craning my neck, I searched the walls for another tapestry or silk hanging they might've been hiding behind. I caught Sebastian observing me. He pointed. "Screen beside the mantel."

I squinted at the ornate ductwork. I'd thought it merely a heat vent, but the metal grid would provide a perfect vantage point. "Of course." I tried to appear sophisticated and not at all surprised.

"Tea," Captain Grey reminded all of us. Sebastian bristled as he settled on the sofa beside me. Miss Stranje silently poured. After we were all served, Captain Grey said very softly, "Something else is troubling you."

Miss Stranje nodded. "A note arrived . . ." Captain Grey pulled his chair closer to hers and they conducted a hushed conversation.

That left the three of us, Sebastian, me, and Sera, sitting there drinking tea in awkward silence. The shortbread cookies looked ridiculously small in Sebastian's large hands, and the dainty teacup looked like a toy.

I sought for a topic we might discuss. "I'm pleased you're not still suffering ill effects from the fumes."

He gave me a cavalier shrug.

"I worried you might be confined to your bed for several days."

"What? Sit in bed and miss seeing you in your finery? Never." A twitch in his cheek betrayed him.

He was making sport of me. What a widgeon I was, to think he actually found me *charming*. There was no sense pretending I was and always would be the proverbial sow's ear.

"This isn't *my* finery," I explained matter-of-factly. "This dress, the taming of my hair, everything, must be credited to others." I gestured to Sera. "Here is the artist primarily responsible for my transformation." I sat back and allowed her to accept proper recognition.

"A marvel, Miss Wyndham." He raised his cup to Sera. "I'm astonished. All that wildness so admirably tamed. A remarkable exhibition of your skills." He delivered this remark with a roguish grin as if it was all just polite conversation.

Sera laughed.

His words were half compliment and half insult. Or more accurately: one-third compliment and two-thirds insult. I refused to let it rile me. Mostly because I knew it would please him too much if I did.

I inhaled deeply and changed the subject. "I've been thinking—"

"About ruffles?"

"No. About oak galls."

"I see. And do you plan to paint them pink and dangle one from each ear?"

"How amusing you are." I pretended to yawn. "For your information, my lord, oak galls are a common component—"

"Of ink. Yes, I know." He lowered his voice, lost his mocking edge, and glanced over to see if Sera was listening to our conversation.

"I believe I'll take a turn about the room," she said with a wink at me. "The paintings in here are quite fascinating. They merit closer study."

In a near whisper I continued, "Normally, powdered gall is suspended in a solution of iron salts. The iron reacts and causes the dark purple color to appear. But *what if* . . ."

There was that phrase again, *what if,* the one that doomed me to a life alone. I shifted uneasily, wishing he would gaze at me with such skin-tingling intensity for a reason other than my theories on invisible ink.

"What if we"—I licked my lips and tried again—"what if *I* made a base out of colorless iron salts? A gall emulsion could be sponged over it later to develop the message."

"How the devil would you make a colorless iron emulsion?" he asked.

"By applying heat to copperas. The minerals should separate and leave a clear iron. If not, I can try adding sulfur or perhaps potash."

He mulled over the idea, pinching his dark brows together. My fingers itched to reach out and smooth away his frown. At last he nodded and his face relaxed. "It might work. The trick will be getting the liquid iron salts to dry invisible and remain nonresponsive to heat. It's certainly worth a try."

I set my teacup on the saucer. "I'll collect some galls in the morning. With all the oak trees on Stranje House grounds, I'm bound to find enough for the experiment."

"Very well." Sebastian finished his shortbread. "I'll walk over from the dower cottage first thing in the morning to help."

"No!" I blurted, thinking of how helping me had nearly cost him his life. "I can do the experiment alone. You mustn't expose yourself to more fumes. It's an unnecessary risk." Immediately, I wished I hadn't said it.

"You consider *that* a risk? You think I need you to protect me?" He looked incensed. "Me?"

"Yes. No. What I mean is . . ."

He shook his head, his eyes darkened, and his jaw bunched up at the corners. I wished I could swallow the last thirty words back down my throat.

I was as annoyed at myself as he was, but for different reasons. While it was true I didn't *need* his assistance, I did *want* his company. Oh, why had I told him not to help me? Because I am absurdly practical, that's why.

If only I'd kept my dratted mouth shut for once. Infuriating though Lord Wyatt was, I rather enjoyed the sensation of my heart fluttering through my belly every time he turned his wicked blue eyes in my direction. I certainly didn't like him frowning at me. I'd much rather he harassed me.

"Of course not," I said. "Obviously you are accustomed to taking much greater risks."

Under the force of his stern inspection, I clamped my lips shut and waited, fidgeting with the fabric of my skirt, hoping he would counter my refusal of help and insist on hunting galls with me in the morning.

He didn't. He kept studying me with that inscrutable expression of his.

So, naturally, I blurted out more inanities. "You said it yourself, yesterday. I can be rather vexing at times. And dangerous. Even though Miss Pinswary doesn't think so, the fact of the matter is; you're right. Yesterday's fiasco proved it." I pressed my lips together, *finally* locking them down after completely ruining any chance of seeing him tomorrow.

"I see." He seemed to relax. "I did say that, didn't I?" He grabbed a handful of almonds. "It's true. You *are* quite vexing." He worked his jaw muscles, shifting between a dimpled grin, a frown, and an annoying smirk. "Yes, and dangerous. Nevertheless, I must face the danger."

He lifted his gaze to the imaginary distance, and posed in an attitude of martyrdom. It was truly ridiculous. I rolled my eyes. "For pity's sake."

He clapped one hand over his heart in the manner of a pledge. "It is my sworn duty to suffer all manner of vexation for King and country. Even the red-haired, hot-tempered variety."

"Oh, aren't you noble." I crossed my arms and slumped back against the sofa.

The wretch inclined his head, acknowledging the compliment, even though he knew perfectly well I hadn't meant any such thing. Then he tossed an almond into his mouth, chomping it with boyish gusto.

I found it odd that he didn't attempt to look past me and watch Sera as she drifted around the room studying the flowers and paintings. He had, of course, bowed graciously to her when we entered, but as far as I could tell he had never insulted her as he did me. In short, he treated her respectfully. I envied her.

Captain Grey's voice rose above the noise of my brooding thoughts. "Why must you refuse help, when it is offered?"

We all turned at the sound.

"You know I'm grateful." Miss Stranje placed her hand over his. He stared at her gloved fingers resting on his tanned roughened hand. She leaned toward him in an earnest, almost pleading manner, a manner that seemed completely foreign to her nature. "Exceedingly grateful. But, it's a day's journey, too much of an imposition for you. Especially with the diplomatic ball so near. No, she's my sister. It falls to me to set things right. I'll travel to Shoreham as soon as the arrangements can be made and deal with the matter myself."

"I don't like it, Emma. Creditors don't behave like gentlemen. Thieves and brigands, the lot of them."

"Thieves and brigands I can manage. It's my sister who troubles me." She sighed and sat back. "You mustn't worry. If I leave at first light, I can complete the business and return by evening. You already do so much for me. To do more would be unseemly. You know what people will think."

He set down his cup and saucer with a plunk. "I have no interest in their opinion. More to the point, there is and always has been an offer on the table."

Sebastian cleared his throat reminding them that Sera and I were listening to their private conversation. Both turned sharply in our direction. Miss Stranje lowered her gaze, and Captain

Grey stood abruptly. "It is past time Lord Wyatt and I took our leave."

Sebastian rose and bowed to us. "Thank you for the pleasure of your company, ladies." With that short dismissal, they strode out of the room, leaving the place as bleak and hollow as an empty theater.

Miss Stranje stood. Her neck was red and blotchy, and agitation rumpled her normally inscrutable features. Our intrepid headmistress appeared to be suffering. I wouldn't have believed such a thing possible. Except there it was, her lips pressed thin, her brow doing all manner of contortions.

"You will excuse me." She hurried past us with a stilted gait. "I have the megrims."

I did not doubt her head ached. Sera watched with an anxious expression as Miss Stranje hurried away. Taking the seat beside me, she whispered, "The captain has distressed her even more than Lady Daneska did."

"Yes," I agreed, and peered up at the Chinese screen wondering if Jane still watched us. I'd been so preoccupied I'd nearly forgotten we were being spied upon.

Sera chewed her bottom lip pensively and took a sip of her now cold tea. "There's nothing we can do for them," she said. "But you, you are a different matter altogether. You like him, don't you?"

"Who? The captain?" I played the innocent. "He seems a very honorable man."

She pursed her lips. "Don't fib. I can always tell."

I relented. "Oh, very well. You mean Lord Wyatt. Yes, of course, I like him. Why wouldn't I?" The minute I said it, I thought of several very sensible reasons why I shouldn't care for him at all. For instance, the way he insults me at every turn.

"No, I mean you *really* like him."

"Yes, he's quite useful in the laboratory." I picked up a small square shortbread biscuit and stared at it, noting the uneven angles, wishing it were a perfect square, but it was, after all, merely a baked good, and baked goods did not ordinarily form perfect squares.

"Georgie"—she shook her head at me —"there's no use denying it. I can see how you feel. It's evident in so many things. Your fingers trembled when you reached for an almond at the same time he did. You watched him sideways over the rim of your teacup. Even now, as we speak of him, a pink flush is climbing your neck."

"Fine." I slouched against the back of the sofa. "You've caught me out. I cannot help myself. I *do* like him." I thumped the place where he'd been sitting with my fist. "I do. Although why I should, with that acerbic tongue of his, is beyond me."

Sera held up a finger. "I can give you one very good reason." She had my full attention.

With an elfish grin she said, "If he turned one of those smoldering looks on me, the way he did you, my knees would give way entirely."

Smoldering look? Did she mean his teasing smirk?

Jane practically danced into the room. "A vastly entertaining afternoon." She whirled around the couch and snatched the imperfect shortbread right out of my hand. "Why, Miss Fitzwilliam, what have you done to poor Lord Wyatt to captivate him so completely?" She chuckled and flung herself into Miss Stranje's chair.

"Don't be absurd." I reached for a chocolate. "Nothing could be further from the truth. You've mistaken a bully's delight in teasing for captivation. Did you not notice the way he ridicules me at every turn?"

Jane snorted. "Oh, he's interested, my girl."

"I don't see how you can draw that conclusion."

"Have you no brothers?"

"Two." *Still alive.* "But they are grown and have no time for me."

"Ah, well then you must take it from me. He wouldn't trouble himself to tease you if he wasn't intrigued." Jane popped the biscuit into her mouth.

She was right. Where my older brothers paid me no heed, Robert had teased me. *Often.* I'd always known he meant it good-naturedly. Still, I wasn't certain Sebastian's teasing was the same. It felt different somehow.

Sera clarified, "That's the way men are."

Jane must have noted my skepticism. "On the subject of men, you're going to have to take my word for—"

Madame Cho barged into the room, rapping her bamboo cane at all of us. "Sit like ladies!"

Twelve

ϾASE OϜ ΤΗΕ AϾϾΙDΕΝΤΑℒ SPY

We corrected our posture immediately, apparently not enough to satisfy Madame Dragon. She jabbed her stick in the direction of the clock. "Enough lazy. Change clothes. Help Cook. Now!" She chased us out of the drawing room, scuttling along behind, chasing us up the stairs with her stick like a giant crab nipping at our heels.

In the privacy of our dormitorium we changed into work dresses. Jane said, as she helped untie my tapes, "Sera was telling the truth. Miss Stranje expects us to learn to cook. She believes every young lady ought to understand the work of the house. We learn by doing."

"Rather convenient, don't you think?" I muttered. "This way she saves money on servants."

"That's not why." Sera brushed out her flaxen hair and quickly plaited it. "Miss Stranje says we must always be prepared to adapt ourselves to any situation in life. Besides, we may not always be able to depend upon servants." She tied a ribbon around her braid. "One never knows what the future might bring. Tess has foreseen awful things in her dreams. London in flames, cannonballs falling from the sky, buildings crumbled, and—"

"Well, I don't mind domestic chores." Jane cut off Sera with a cautionary frown and a quick shake of her head.

"What an odd school this is." *If it was a school at all.* I had serious doubts on that score. I knew three things for certain.

One—Stranje House was no ordinary finishing school.

Two—nor was it the cruel reformatory gossip purported.

Three—Miss Stranje was up to something and we girls were to be part of it. Although, I had yet to lay hold of exactly what that something was.

I hung Jane's beautiful dress in her wardrobe, giving the lush striped fabric one last smoothing, and decided to try procuring information via a different tactic. With a forlorn sigh I said, "I suppose household chores are not so bad. At least we aren't being horsewhipped or locked inside a mummy case."

Jane rolled off her stockings and pulled on a pair of serviceable woolen socks. "You do realize that was all a ruse?"

"But I saw blood. *Your* blood."

"Yes. I suppose you did." She slid her feet into a pair of brown work boots. "Those tines are rather sharp and, on occasion, I might be a bit clumsy." Jane smiled with a little too much sympathy.

I froze. Watching her, feeling like a complete ninny, because I had a fairly good idea of what she would say next. "It wasn't, was it?"

"No. I'm afraid that was a wax packet of beet juice and paint."

"Burst for my benefit." What a gullible little fool I'd been.

"No," Sera said. "For your parents' benefit."

"My parents? But why? They would've been perfectly satisfied knowing Miss Stranje planned to slap my wrists with a ruler if I got out of line. Or cane me with a willow branch."

"Not good enough." Jane slipped a blue work pinafore over her shoulders. "Miss Stranje had to be certain they wouldn't interfere. *At all.* For any reason. No poking their noses in to see how you're coming along. She had to make sure they wanted to be thoroughly rid of you."

"Jane!" Sera scolded.

"Well, it's true."

"A little kindness in the telling wouldn't hurt."

Jane blew air through her lips. "You should talk, Miss-gloom-and-doom-cannonballs-falling-from-the-sky. I'm sorry but cod liver oil tastes fishy even if it's taken with a spoonful of sugar—fishy and confusing. May as well take the facts as they fall. I prefer the truth, plain and straightforward. I'm sure you feel the same way, don't you, Georgie?"

Did I?

Yes. Wasn't I the one always wanting answers? If so, why did those answers suddenly feel so difficult to accept? I sank onto the bed and tried to look at the facts without feeling dizzy.

"I never get a simple answer from any of you." I stared at Jane, waiting until I had her full attention. "If you like straight-forward truth, I believe you've come to the wrong school."

"*Touché.*" A smile played at the corner of Jane's mouth as she finished lacing her boots.

I didn't feel triumphant, just weary. It had been a tiring few days. I wanted to crawl under the bedcovers and stay there for a good long while. Instead, I silently slipped into a work dress.

"Come along," Sera tugged on my hand. "You'll like Cook." Her eyebrows lifted as if she was letting me in on another private joke.

Everything was humorous to them. Duping me. Skeletons in

dresses. A torture chamber that wasn't a torture chamber. Our school that wasn't a school. Or maybe it *was* a school, only not for reforming us into marriageable misses. No, Miss Stranje was transforming us all right, but the question was, *into what?*

"Look at us, headed to the scullery. You, Jane, she has you meeting with a steward. Does she intend for you to become a scullery maid or a farmer? What is Miss Stranje planning to make of us? Scientists? Thieves? Spies?"

Sera let go of my hand. She and Jane stopped and turned to me.

For once, Jane's normally flippant manner was gone. "Yes."

"Which?" I scoured their faces praying for the truth.

Sera nodded at Jane. "Tell her."

"All of those things." Jane stood taller, every inch of her solemn. "And more."

"More? What more?" It was incomprehensible. What kind of life was I embarking upon? "No more roundaboutation. Tell me!"

Jane huffed. "She's teaching us how to navigate in society."

"Because we're different," Sera explained with considerably less agitation than Jane. "Miss Stranje teaches us how to manage polite society—"

"So we don't stick out like odd ducks flapping about atop the beau monde's plum pudding."

Sera shot Jane a quelling look. "Miss Stranje believes we can adapt to society's strictures, blend in, while secretly improving our talents and unique abilities. The fact that many of our skills might prove useful for poking around in foreign affairs—"

"Phfft." Jane scoffed and rolled her gaze to the ceiling.

"Is merely an added bonus. Most of us think the challenge is—"

"A great deal more intriguing than needlepoint." Jane grabbed my arm. "There. Is that plain enough for you? Now we have to get down to the kitchen or Cook will fillet us in place of the fish."

"We'll explain more later, but for now we must hurry." Sera genially took my other arm and we hurried down the hall. "It will be all right."

Would it? It felt as if I were tumbling in the ocean again.

One thing I knew for certain. My life would never be the same. Maybe that wasn't such a bad thing. I glimpsed something, something shimmering with possibilities. Maybe, just maybe, Stranje House would be a way out of the tight-lidded box into which I'd been born.

"I find cooking quite relaxing." Sera patted my shoulder. "You'll enjoy it."

Cooking. Yes. That, at least, was something predictable, normal, something with which I felt reasonably familiar.

At home, the kitchen had been my favorite place in the house. A warm cozy room, it always smelled of fresh-baked bread and simmering soups. Florrie, our cook, was a congenial little Cornish woman who insisted on pristine white walls and plenty of windows for light. She had always been ready with warm buttery shortbread or a steaming bowl of savory stew and dumplings when I snuck into her kitchen.

Similarities between the two kitchens ended at good smells and ample sunlight. Stranje House's cook was the most terrifying woman I'd ever seen. Well over six feet in height, she probably weighed twenty stone. A burly, double-chinned woman, with snow-white hair and heavy black eyebrows set in a permanent scowl. She wore a bloodied apron cinched tight around her waist, which only emphasized the fact that she was built like a hay wagon.

With a mighty thwack, Cook brought her cleaver down and

severed the bone of a lamb shank. She pointed the bloody cleaver at us and shouted, "Yer late! If 'erself hears about this they'll be hell to pay."

She waved her weapon at Jane. "You—fetch leeks and slice 'em for soup."

Next, she aimed it at Sera. "Potatoes, peeled and quartered."

Oh, yes, this was quite relaxing.

They hurried off and Cook stared down her steel blade at me. Lamb's blood oozed off the broad blade and dribbled onto the cutting board. "An' who 'ave we here?"

Despite her coarse dialect, she commanded my full attention. I bobbed a quick curtsey. "Miss Georgiana Fitzwilliam, ma'am." I cringed, thinking I'd sounded like a cowering parlor maid.

"Georgie, is it? Well, I don't like the look of you. Too green about the gills. Yer as gray as month-old bread. Take yerself off." She waggled the cleaver at Madame Cho. "Away with 'er. I'll 'ave no sick 'uns in my kitchen." She followed this edict with a series of bone-splitting staccato whacks as she chopped up the rest of the lamb shank for stewing.

I blinked, astonished to see Tess in the far corner of the room. She, who not an hour earlier had appeared in the drawing room with all the dignity of a duke's daughter, stood at the scullery performing the lowest of tasks, scrubbing out a large pot.

Sera rounded the corner, her arms laden with potatoes. "Go on, Georgie, rest. We'll bring you a bowl of soup later."

"Out," ordered Cook.

Madame Cho didn't whack the floor with her stick the way she would have done elsewhere. She waved her arms, shooing me out of the kitchen as one would shoo a crow out of the garden.

I followed orders and trudged back to the dormitorium, my head spinning, only I had no time for sleep. Whatever else was going on in this madhouse I had a responsibility to Sebastian. I focused on the one constant in my life at the moment—the ink.

As soon as Madame Cho left the bedroom I pushed back the covers and dug out a sheet of parchment and a graphite stick from my armoire. I needed to calculate the ratio of iron salts to water, and figure out what temperature to heat the green vitriol before it would turn clear. I had to figure this out as quickly as possible, lives depended on it. I pictured Europe's leaders gathered in a room discussing economics. Suddenly cannonballs explode the walls. Assassins burst in and slaughter everyone. The room becomes a bloody horror of severed limbs and heads.

What if Sebastian got captured or killed because I failed to solve this problem? I shook the sickening images out of my head.

Ink. I concentrated on making ink. I scratched through hypotheses proven wrong, calculated ratios, and jotted notes on a new formula. If only I had my textbooks from the laboratory so I could double-check my figures.

My eyes drooped and my head ached. Perhaps if I rested for only a few minutes I might feel well enough to sneak out later, retrieve my books, and complete the calculations. A short nap, that's all I needed. Fifteen minutes, maybe twenty, then when the others went in to dinner, I would wake and steal out to the laboratory.

I laid my head on the pillow and surrendered to oblivion.

I awoke to a faint gray light filtering through the gaps in the drapery. I blinked, trying to get my bearings. A bowl of leek soup rested on the night table. Surely I hadn't slept straight through to morning, and yet there was no other explanation.

Tess tiptoed beside the bed and scooped up the white rat tickling my cheek. I didn't scream this time, but I did awaken fully, sit up, and push back the covers. She deposited Punch behind the secret panel and headed to the door to leave.

"Wait," I called, rubbing sleep from my eyes. "I want to go with you."

She seemed surprised at that. "Why?" she whispered.

"I need to hunt for oak galls."

"Galls?" She frowned at me as if I had gone completely mad.

"You know, those round ugly growths on an oak branch." I curved my fingers showing her the approximate size. "They're caused by wasps and—"

Jane moaned and pressed a pillow over her ears.

Tess shushed me with a finger to her lips and whispered, "I don't have time to wait for you to dress." Lifting the edge of the draperies, she peered out. Rays of dove gray and kitten-tongue pink wafted into our room. Heralds of dawn. "It will be sunup soon. This is the only time I'm allowed to run." She seemed agitated and tense. "I'm going. Don't wake Sera and Jane."

"But—"

Sera stirred in the bed next to me. I glanced across the room and noticed Maya's bed was empty. When I turned back, Tess had already vanished from the room.

I dressed, gulped down the cold leek and potato soup, slipped on my shoes, and hurried outside. Wisps of morning fog twirled and eddied through the garden like dancing ghosts, brushing each blossom with cold droplets of moisture. Morning larks trilled their hodgepodge symphony, punctuated by croaking frogs and sleepy crickets.

I rounded the corner and there was Maya, sitting cross-legged in the center of the veranda. Her eyes were closed, her face tilted east, where the sun nipped at the gray fading edges of night.

She appeared to be deep in prayer or meditative thought. The wolves lay stretched out beside her. They raised their heads and watched me approach. As I tiptoed past, Phobos got to his feet and trotted to my side.

"Good dog," I said softly, grateful he hadn't raced toward me with teeth bared. I hoped he really was a dog and not a wolf. I also hoped someone had fed him recently, preferring that he not make a meal out of my leg. Thoughts yammered through my head because that's what always happens when I'm nervous. "Um, thank you for keeping me warm after I hit my head." *And not eating me.* "Awfully good of you. Probably saved my life."

The ruddy animal grunted as if he understood and walked alongside me. We traveled across the grounds in companionable silence. I headed for the nearest copse of trees. In the dim light, I noticed the outline of an oak deep in the thicket. I plunged into the heavy undergrowth with Phobos right behind me. As I pushed deeper, thorns scratched my arms. The brambles grew so thick I couldn't wriggle between them to reach the oak tree.

We backed out and went farther north to a more promising stand of oak. This time Phobos didn't follow me. He lay down and waited while I pushed aside elm saplings, dodged nettle, and plowed through scrub alder, only to meet a roadblock of prickly holly so dense not even a weasel could squeeze through. I tore the hem of my dress getting out.

I smacked my hand against pink blossoms on a hawthorn bush, sending up a spray of dew and petals. "A few measly galls— that's all I need."

Phobos grunted in agreement. We hunted farther north where I spotted a large old oak in the distance. It grew near the hedgerows marking the property line. We walked nearly a quarter mile to the far corner of the property, slogging through tall grass, following a muddy sheep path. In retrospect, I realize it must've been on the line of Lord Ravencross's property. It stood beside a tall, neatly groomed hedge, and, unlike the Stranje House grounds, which were largely unkempt and left in a natural state, someone had taken a scythe to the tall grasses and weeds at the base of this tree.

There weren't any galls on the lower branches, but I noticed several promising specimens on a limb about fifteen feet above my head. My mother would have applied a switch to my backside if she knew I was about to scramble up a tree. "I simply cannot tolerate such unladylike behavior," I could hear her say. "Why must you be so impulsive, Georgiana? These outlandish experiments of yours must stop. No more jumping out of windows. You shame me. You shame your entire family." Then Mother would nod and direct the housemaid to go at my legs again with the switch while she continued to scold me.

Ah, well, what did it matter? I'd endured the switch for less important reasons. What choice did I have? To make the ink I had to have those galls. To get the galls I needed to climb the tree. Ladylike behavior would simply have to wait. The lives of European leaders were at stake. Sebastian depended on me.

I glanced around. The early hour and the dim light would keep me safe from prying eyes. Stranje House stood in the distance, so obscured by bushes and trees that I couldn't even see the garden porch. Nor could I be seen clearly from any other house round about.

Curiosity peaked Phobos's ears as he watched me slip off my shoes. I wiggled my bare toes against the tickly grass, and grabbed hold of the lowest branch. Using my feet to push against all the grooves and crevices of the knobby bark, I pulled myself up and scrambled onto the first branch. Pleased with my progress, I maneuvered to a standing position and tucked my skirts up into my stays so that they hung just above my knees, and scaled another branch.

Phobos put his forepaws on the trunk and issued a quick yip. Ordering me down I supposed. "Hush." I ordered. "Sit." He dropped back.

I succeeded in hoisting myself up onto the next bough, but it looked a very long way to the ground. I stayed on my belly. All I needed was to go out five or six feet to that promising clump of leaves, where I counted at least four large galls. With my legs hugging each side of the gnarled branch, I inched along on my belly out to the smaller branches and that cluster of leaves.

That's when I saw Tess on the other side of the hedge. Running. And Lord Ravencross galloping his horse across his neatly mown grounds on a dead run collision course. Just as I was about to shout a warning, he pulled up short, swung off his brown stallion, and marched up to her like a great growling bear. "I warned you not to run on my land!"

Tess stopped and leaned forward to catch her breath. "You knew full well I would be here. I always run here. The grounds at Stranje House are too wooded."

He pointed his riding crop at the fields stretching beyond the hedges. "Then run on the sheep pasture at the back."

"Can't. Lambs start chasing me and that upsets the ewes." She straightened and planted her fists on her hips. "Aside from that, you practically dared me."

"I did no such thing. I told you to steer clear of my property." He slapped his riding crop against his palm threateningly.

"I distinctly remember you saying, *or else*."

"*Or else* next time you might not be so lucky," he recited. "It was a warning—not a dare."

"Was it?" Tess didn't even flinch. Nor did she back down. "Suppose I draw a line right here." She dragged the toe of her shoe across the grass between them. "If I say, don't step over that line or else I might do terrible things to you, what would you do?"

"I wouldn't put up with such nonsense." He promptly stepped over the line.

She glanced down at his feet. "Exactly my point." Ravencross's horse pranced over and nuzzled Tess's neck. She stroked the big brown's nose and gently pushed him aside. "You would want to know exactly what I planned to do about it, wouldn't you?"

The stallion pushed between them again. This time he whickered and thrust his muzzle into her hair.

"Zeus! Stand down." Ravencross shortened his hold on the reins and stepped his horse back. "What in blazes have you done to him? Either you've got apples hidden in your hair or you've bewitched the animal."

Tess shrugged. "You're far too jaded to believe in magic, my lord."

"At least you've got that much right," he grumbled, but then in a louder, angrier voice he demanded, "Are you going to get off my grounds or not?"

"If I were you, my lord, I would not shout or make any sudden movements." She nodded toward Zeus who had arched his neck and was blowing through flared nostrils. "Your stallion is taking a defensive attitude on my behalf."

"What the devil?" He turned to Zeus. "Maybe I ought to rethink that witch idea."

"Maybe you ought." She shook her head and stared off into the distance, away from him and his horse. "I've been accused of it before, on several occasions. And, I might add, by men older than you. Men who ought to have been long past silly bedtime stories."

Frowning, he led his agitated horse to the nearest tree and

looped the reins into a clove hitch. The stallion tossed his head and pawed the ground. Warily, Ravencross returned to Tess and the line she'd drawn. He stood far too close to her. "Well then, what am I to do with you for trespassing?"

She glanced down to his feet, standing just barely on his side of the line. "How should I know, my lord? It was you who dared me."

"I've a good mind to take my riding crop to your backside."

She tilted her head speculatively. "Now, there's an amusing idea." She glanced around his shoulders at Zeus pawing the ground. "If I promise not to cry out, there is a slim chance your horse won't dash you to pieces."

"Stand down, Zeus," he called at his stamping horse. "You agitate him."

"It is you I agitate, my lord. Your horse is simply confused by your anger, because he senses something else."

A wary stillness fell upon both Zeus and Lord Ravencross.

"He senses what I can see plainly writ on your face, my lord. That scowl does not hide your feelings so well as you might think. I know what you want from me."

I covered my mouth to silence a sharp intake of breath and nearly slipped from the branch. How did she have the nerve to say such a bold thing to him? Perhaps she didn't realize what she'd said. Or how flirtatious it sounded. Either way, if my mother had heard it, she would've condemned Tess as a brazen hussy and given her the cut direct for the rest of eternity. As for me, I felt a growing admiration for her and could not look away. Tess had pluck. I couldn't wait to see what she would do next.

Ravencross studied her for the longest time. "Now it is you who is daring me."

"No." She stepped back. "I am merely doing what I do every morning. Running."

"No, you're not. You, my girl, are playing with fire. And I suggest you stay well back." He dragged the heel of his bad foot across the grass, emphasizing the line between them.

She shook her head. "You ought not tell lies, my lord. In your heart you are *begging* me to cross that line."

I could not believe it. Tess did precisely that—she stepped across it. They stood only a hairsbreadth apart. Exactly as a wolf strikes, with a growling flash, Ravencross grabbed her shoulders and pressed his mouth over hers.

Tess eagerly kissed him back.

I gasped, and clutched the bark of my tree so tight some of it broke off into my fingers.

Lord Ravencross pulled away abruptly, still gripping her shoulders, and straightened to his full height. "You see," he snarled in a rough voice, "I never beg for anything."

"Not out loud," she answered calmly.

"Never." He let go of her. "Not even silently."

"Then you believe your own lies, for I have never seen a man so hungry for love."

He paced sideways and glared at her. "You know nothing of such things. What can you know of anything? You're just a child."

"We're nearly the same age. I'm seventeen, and if ever I was a child, my lord, that childhood ended long, *long* ago." She said it quietly and with such profound sadness that even Zeus whickered sympathetically.

Lord Ravencross softened his tone. "Nevertheless—"

She interrupted him. "And I learned all those many years ago to stop listening to what people said, and listen instead to what they mean. Some people speak with honey and intend to serve us poison. You, my lord, speak with thorns but yearn for cake."

"You don't know anything about me." He backed away from her, his chest heaving as if she'd punched him. "You"—he pointed his riding crop unsteadily—"are a witch."

"More lies," she said, and took off running.

As Lord Ravencross watched her go, he brought the crop down, slapped it hard against his thigh, and slowly limped to his horse.

Thirteen

ᴄAUGHT

"If you intend to fall on me again, I would appreciate a warning." Sebastian stood on the ground below. He and Phobos stared up at me expectantly.

I closed my eyes and pressed my forehead against the rough bark, and hugged the branch even tighter. *Why?* I asked the fates. Why could I never get away with even the smallest of indiscretions? And it would be Sebastian who came upon me while I was straddling the upper branches of a tree with my dress hiked up to my thighs. Embarrassed beyond words, I tried to scoot my skirts down to cover more of my legs, but nearly lost hold of the branch.

A wicked grin dimpled his cheeks. "What, may I ask, are you doing up there?"

"Hunting oak galls," I said, trying not to sound mortified while tugging at my dress, and hoping my naked legs would escape his notice.

"Hmm . . ." He tossed several plump galls in one hand.

"Looked to me more like you were daydreaming. Communing with the birds, are you, Miss Fitzwilliam?" He made a whistling bird noise.

Could my humiliation get any worse? I prayed he didn't know I'd been spying on Tess and Lord Ravencross. I know I ought to have scrambled down the tree the instant I overheard them talking. Or at the very least, I should have looked away and gone on about my business. Except it had all happened so quickly, and I was worried for Tess and . . .

Oh, very well, I admit it. There's no excuse for my behavior. Drat my curious mind. I'm a scientist. I observe. Study things. Draw conclusions. I had to know what would happen between them. The sad truth is, I couldn't have looked away any more than I could've flown off that branch.

"How do you propose to get down?"

Naturally, I planned to climb down. But how to do it in a ladylike manner, while a gentleman observed, posed a prickly dilemma.

"Do stop fiddling with your dress. Otherwise, you're going to come down the hard way."

He was right again. I grabbed the branch just in time. "It's only that I . . ." *Oh, bother! I'm half exposed right now and that makes me more uncomfortable than the thought of falling.*

"I hadn't anticipated an audience." I went back to adjusting my skirts.

"That much is obvious. Don't stand on ceremony on my account." His *not-so-subtle-ha-ha-to-himself* chuckle was exactly what one would expect from one of Satan's dark angels. "I assure you, Miss Fitzwilliam, I have seen female legs and feet before. Although, I must admit, yours are shaped quite splendidly."

I jerked my bare calves up into my skirts, hiding them as much as I could.

"But I digress. We must return to the problem of your descent. Shall I climb up and help you down?"

"No. If you will turn your head I believe I can manage quite well on my own, thank you."

"Yes," he said coolly. "I've witnessed several times how well you manage on your own."

"That is unfair."

"Allow me to offer you a compromise. What if I close my eyes and hold out my arms thus." He stuck out his arms directly beneath my branch. "That way, should you slip I'll be halfway prepared. I must confess. The night you fell from the spy hole it was more of a lucky catch than skill on my part. A split-second grab for the best." He snapped his fingers to illustrate. "Had I missed . . ."

He shook his head mournfully, but ruined the sympathetic effect with a wry twitchy grin. "If I'd missed, the world would be minus one gall-hunter." He smirked, as if picturing me splattered on the Elizabethan chest was frightfully amusing.

"I've had enough of your mockery. Act the gentleman for once and close your eyes."

He complied with his arms extended. Phobos barked as if he expected me to fall, too.

I seriously doubt Lord Wyatt actually closed his eyes because he moved beneath me as if anticipating a fall. *The rascal.* Nevertheless, I crept along the branch, and kept a firm grasp while lowering myself onto the next limb. All the time I wondered exactly how much of my person he could see from his vantage point. I quickly edged over to the trunk, clutched it, and slid into the V of the tree. At that juncture I held my skirts together with one hand and jumped to the ground. Luckily, he caught my shoulders and kept me from stumbling and landing smack on my face.

"Thank you," I gasped. What was it about his hands that seemed to warm me through and through, and simultaneously left me breathless? I looked up into his face and remembered Tess kissing Ravencross. I couldn't help myself, I wanted Sebastian to do the same to me.

"Are you quite all right?" He studied me with the concern of a brother for a sister.

I sighed and glanced at the grass beneath our feet. Phobos washed my leg with his tongue. It tickled and I shivered. *No, I was not okay.* I wanted Lord Wyatt to kiss me. And that was highly improper.

"You're blushing," he said, steadying me while I slipped on my shoes. "You needn't fear," he confided in earnest. "I won't tell a soul that I found the beautiful Georgiana Fitzwilliam climbing a tree barefoot. Your secret is safe with me."

Beautiful?

"You promise?" I asked.

He laughed and hugged me for a brief wonderful second, then let go. He tilted his face down to mine and, as we gazed directly into each other's eyes, he said with almost believable seriousness, "I solemnly swear."

I knew he was agreeing not to tell anyone about me climbing the tree, but for one wondrous moment I pretended he was promising that he thought I was beautiful.

The merriment left his face and he blinked. His mouth softened.

And *I knew.* I knew, in that instant, he thought about kissing me.

Sebastian stepped back and cleared his throat. He plucked the galls out of his pocket. "Here." He thrust them at me. "I found these on the way over."

"Thank you," I caught my breath and scooped the galls from

his palm. "These will do splendidly." I smiled. I wanted to dance, wanted to whirl, wanted to fling my arms around his neck. For one glorious instant he'd thought about kissing me.

Me!

The sound of thudding footfalls interrupted my delirium. I turned to see Tess running up the park toward us. Inwardly, I cringed for at least a dozen reasons. For one thing, I'd been spying on her. For another thing, she looked remarkable in her running dress, like an ancient warrior goddess, wild and free and carnal, like a . . . a . . . she-wolf.

That was it! Suddenly, I understood why she and Ravencross were attracted to each other. They were perfectly matched. Be that as it may, my immediate concern was keeping Sebastian from falling prey to her animal magnetism, because I certainly *did not* look like a warrior goddess. Or a goddess of any kind. Especially not with oak leaves stuck in my hair, scratches on my arms, splotches of mud on my torn skirt, and twigs poking out everywhere.

I handed the galls back to Sebastian, knocked a beetle off my bodice, plucked twigs and bits of bark out of my white muslin skirt, which is, by the way, a very impractical fabric for climbing trees.

Tess caught up to us before I had removed even half the debris. I blew an errant curl out of my eyes and said, "Good morning." Smiling, as if nothing were amiss.

"Breakfast is in half an hour," she said tersely. "And you"—she glowered at me and Sebastian—"don't leap to any hasty conclusions today." With that, she ran past us.

"Hasty?" Sebastian called after her.

"Conclusions?" I asked.

Without answering either of us, or even looking back, she sprinted away, pounding the ground with hard thrashing strides.

"What's she going on about, do you suppose?"

"I haven't the vaguest idea." I wished he would not stare after her so intently. I glanced up, surprised the sun had climbed so high. I wasn't sure if I had the right to invite guests to Miss Stranje's table, but it was nearly the breakfast hour and it seemed rude not to offer. "Would you care to come in for breakfast?"

"No, thank you. I ate at the cottage with Captain Grey. However, I would like to go to the stillroom and begin working on our experiment."

Our experiment. I smiled.

"We haven't much time. Two days from now, I need to have a working formula. Lady Castlereagh is hosting a ball in London and many of the diplomats with whom we exchange information will be in attendance. It is the perfect opportunity for me to distribute the new ink, if we have one, before they return to the continent."

Two days' time. It wasn't long enough. Not with my success rate being what it was. I stopped walking and stared at him. "Only two days?" I repeated, hoping I'd heard him incorrectly.

He nodded and gently removed the galls from my hands. "I'll get started, shall I? I could grind these. I noticed a mortar and pestle on the work table."

"They must be crushed very fine and sifted." *Two days.* Could it be done? What if my latest idea didn't work? Still bewildered, I mumbled, "Two days to accomplish so much?" And then . . . then he would leave. Only two days left with him.

"It will be all right." He dropped the galls into his pocket.

It wouldn't. It wouldn't be all right. Even if I succeeded in making the formula, I would never see him again. *Ever.* He would be off in Vienna, and I would be stuck here.

"You're cold." He chafed my arms, but my chill wasn't from the brisk air.

"So short a time. I'm not sure if I can—"

"You can. You will. We're very close to an answer." He cut me off and whipped out a clean kerchief, dabbing at a small abrasion above my elbow. "Look here. You've scraped your arm."

"It's nothing."

"I'll decide that," he said, as if he were so much older and wiser than I. As if I couldn't tell a gash from a minor cut. Nevertheless, I stood and quietly allowed him to attend to it.

"These things must be cleaned out to avoid infection. This is what comes of you climbing trees," he scolded. "There was no need. I made it perfectly clear I would be here to help."

"I didn't think you'd come." I liked him leaning close to me. I liked the comforting smell of freshly ironed linen on his neck cloth and the inviting scent of honeyed scones on his breath. Only two days, I mourned silently.

"Widgeon," he chided, and tied his kerchief around my arm. "I told you I would be here."

"You say a great many things, my lord. And I never know which are said in jest and which are serious." He looked up from bandaging my arm and gave me a singularly confusing grumble.

Properly bandaged, I headed toward the house. "You will find cheesecloth in a drawer along the back wall," I said, "for sifting the powder."

"Yes," he responded, matching me stride for stride. "But, Georgiana, tell me something."

His pensive tone made me stop. His coat sleeve brushed against my arm. "Back there, under the oak tree, you wanted me to kiss you, didn't you?"

"Me?" How dare he ask such a thing? Never mind that it was true. One simply did not ask rude questions like that. "No. Heavens, no. Of course not." I took off at a bruising pace, barely able to keep from running. Phobos loped happily along beside me, tongue hanging out, oblivious of my embarrassment.

"My mistake," he called after me.

"Yes."

Mistake. Mine, apparently, not his.

My heart slid down into the vicinity of my toes. It felt as if I kicked the poor abused organ with every step I took. Yet, I hurried even faster to get away from him. If I could've dashed away without seeming like a shame-faced schoolgirl, I would have. As it was, I scurried ahead of him into the garden, darted up the steps, and called over my shoulder, "I really must hurry. Don't want to miss breakfast."

As if I hadn't lost my appetite entirely.

The moment I got through the door, I did run. I took the stairs two by two, up to our dormitorium and collapsed face-down on my bed. If only I could hide there for the rest of the day. Except I wasn't alone. Tess stood across the room. I groaned, pressed my face into the goose feather coverlet, and yanked a pillow over my head. Even buried under all those feathers, I heard her footsteps as she walked up beside my bed.

"I saw you in the tree." She poked my shoulder. "Spying on me."

I groaned again, wishing this morning and its wealth of humiliations would go straight to blazes. "I'm sorry," I said, but my apology was muffled. Shoving the pillow aside I lifted my head. "I am sorry. Truly I am. It was a dastardly thing to do. I didn't mean to spy on you. Not really. I was in the tree, and . . . oh, rubbish!" I smacked the pillow. "It just happened."

"Never mind." She exhaled loudly. "Everyone spies on everyone else in this house. No reason why you should be any different than the rest of us. In your case, I suppose it's only fair. After all, I don't need to climb a tree to spy on you. I've spied on your life more than you have mine." Tess winced, as if spying on my life saddened and exhausted her.

"What do you mean?" I sat up. "You've seen me in dreams?" She nodded.

A hundred questions popped into my mind. "When? Last night? Before I arrived, or after? What did you see?"

"Before." She folded her arms across her chest, shielding herself from my interrogation.

"I don't understand. If you'd already seen things about me in dreams, why did you ask Sera what she saw about me?"

"It's complicated. I haven't time. Suffice it to say, Sera sees what *is*. I see what *will be*." Tess turned to walk away. "Or what *might be*."

"Wait." I sprang off the bed and grabbed her arm. "What did you dream about me? Tell me."

She shook my hand off with a warning glare that made me back away. "It isn't like that. I only see glimpses. A jumble. Flashes. All I can tell you is don't act in haste today."

"Haste?"

"Yes. Don't leap out of windows before you've thought things through."

"You dreamed about *that*?"

"About you smashing into a tree. Breaking an arm. The bone splintering." She grabbed my arm where the old fracture was still tender. "Yes. I lived through that moment with you."

No wonder she was ill-tempered. "Not my finest moment," I said by way of apologizing.

"But isn't that what you do, Georgie? Jump before you've figured out the tree is too close. Underestimate how fast straw catches fire." She let go of my arm and pointed her finger at me.

"It's simple. Don't act in haste. And don't let Lord Wyatt leave until tomorrow afternoon."

I rubbed my arm and watched her head for the door without looking back.

How could I make Sebastian do anything? I wasn't his keeper. What was I supposed to do? Tie him in a chair and sic Madame Cho on him? I certainly couldn't keep him here by any other means. According to him, even the thought of kissing me was a mistake.

Fortunately, he wouldn't leave until the ink was done. That wouldn't be until tomorrow afternoon at the earliest. At the rate we were going, it might be never.

Tomorrow would be here all too soon.

Fourteen

EXPERIMENTING

I picked at my breakfast, forced myself to swallow a few morsels, and pushed the rest around the plate. After Miss Stranje excused us I slipped quietly into the laboratory. Sebastian was working intently at the table and Madame Cho sat in the corner chair embroidering a long piece of green silk.

He glanced up from sifting brown powder. "There you are. I thought you'd never get here. The galls are pulverized and almost ready. What solution do you plan to suspend them in?"

His all-business attitude suited me just fine. I'd made a lifelong habit of focusing on my experiments rather than expecting warmth from the people around me. If that was the way he wanted it, I could do that now without any problem.

I answered Sebastian in a perfectly calm voice, without a hint of the wild emotions thrashing about in my chest. "Before we know what to put in the gall suspension, I'll need to finish my calculations and formulate the clear iron ink base."

I went straight to work scribbling ratios and mixing a test

solution. I didn't want to take a chance of asphyxiating him again. So this time I stood at the burner, heating the iron salts in a pot of water. I stirred until the minerals began to dissolve. He leaned over my shoulder, watching. I ignored the way his nearness made my skin prickle and tingle just as it does before a lightning storm. I also ignored his low rumbling murmurs of approval when the mixture began to boil. I paid no attention when his arm brushed against mine as he reached around me to adjust the burner. Although, he really ought to have asked me first. Never mind that the heat needed a reduction, I was in charge here. This was my domain. He ought not to think he could anticipate my needs.

When he tucked a piece of my hair behind my ear, it was outside of enough. He had no right to touch my person in such an intimate way. He was my assistant, not my brother, and certainly not my lover. He'd made that abundantly clear this morning. "Don't," I snapped.

"It was in your way," he said matter-of-factly.

"I've grown accustomed to looking through my hair. Must you stand so close?"

"Would you have me miss the most interesting part of the experiment?"

I exhaled my irritation. "No. I suppose not. But I would prefer if you stood beside me, instead of breathing down my neck. It feels as if you are a great hulking giant about to thump me should I do anything amiss."

"What an odd thing to say." He sounded genuinely surprised, almost offended. Still he didn't budge from leaning over my shoulder. In fact, his breath tickled even more, warming the sensitive skin just below my earlobe. "Young ladies have never complained about it before."

"Young ladies enjoy you breathing down their necks, do

they?" The stupid question popped out before I'd thought it through. I cringed the minute it escaped my lips.

"Prodigiously," he said into my neck.

I couldn't stop the shiver it caused. "You know what I meant."

He stood so close, that I felt his soundless chuckle through the slight vibration of his chest against my shoulders.

Madame Cho, our vigilant chaperone, cleared her throat pointedly.

He backed away slightly. "I assure you, it's true. I've done the research. You appear to be the only female in all of Christendom able to resist my charms." He'd said it in jest, and yet I realized the depressing truth—there were bound to be scores of women in love with him, beautiful women, seductive women, like Lady Daneska.

I stared at the bubbling mixture, scowling. "I suppose you left London littered with broken hearts." I'd tried to sound glib, sophisticated, witty, maybe even a little bit flirtatious. *Stupid, stupid girl.* No sooner had I said it than I wanted to smack my mouth, because I most certainly did not want to hear about his conquests.

"No." He moved to my side and shook his head solemnly. "No broken hearts in London on my account." He rubbed his jaw, stroking freshly shaved whiskers, arousing the scent of his shaving soap into the air between us. "Mind you," he added, "the continent is an entirely different matter."

I had the oddest reaction. I wanted to sock him in the belly, or slap that cocky smirk off his face. Either way, it is lucky for him that I had to keep stirring.

"Look." He pointed at the mixture. "It's getting more transparent."

I'd been staring at the iron salt solution but not seeing it at all. It did look somewhat clearer, but still retained a greenish yellow tint. He leaned close and, I am embarrassed to report, I studied the color of his skin and the way his dark hair curled around his earlobe, rather than the murky liquid in the pot.

"Uh-oh," he said, and jerked back. "It's turning brown. What's happening?"

"Drat!" I grabbed a cloth, pulled the vessel from the heat and stared at the now reddish brown contents. "I let it go too long. We'll have to start again."

He tossed the contents out the window and I started the measuring process again. This time I watched the mixture more carefully as we heated it. Once more it failed to stay transparent.

"Sulfur," I suggested. "We should try a dash of sulfur."

We did, and it seemed to work. Until, at the last minute, it turned a disheartening ochre color. Next, we tried potash and hypothesized that if we kept the temperature exactly right we might succeed. No. Again and again, we tried. And so it went, until the day stretched long, and we were both rubbing at our temples in frustration.

When the light outside our window waned from widow's gray to funeral black, Sebastian lit a candelabra. A footman brought us a platter of meats, cheese, bread, and fruit. I grabbed my notes and tucked up on a bench along the wall. There had to be an answer somewhere. Sebastian flipped the Persian textbook open on the tabletop and leaned over it, dragging his fingers through his hair as he searched for an answer. "We're so close." He thumped the table. "It only needs a small push and we'll have it."

He was right, but I knew from experience that finding a solution as complex as this had been known to elude scientists for years, even decades. That troubling thought made me thumb through my notes even more frantically. I stopped on a set of papers with numerous scribbled-out passages. A few months ago I'd experienced a great deal of frustration because the Persians were so inconsistent in identifying their ingredients. For instance, they might call iron salts green vitriol, copperas, or even alum. They used these names interchangeably, despite the fact that there are notable differences between those substances.

I shoved a mass of unruly red curls back from my face and stared at the flickering candles. "We can't be certain exactly what the Persians meant by copperas."

He tossed me an apple. "It has to be iron salts, because we know they react with gallotannin to make ink."

I shrugged and bit into the apple, the sweet juices invigorated me. I squinted at a note I'd previously scratched out. Hope flared. Except we'd had so many missteps that day, I dreaded another wrong turn. I barely offered the suggestion aloud. "Ammonium."

He glanced up, like a hound alerting on a scent. "Did you say something?"

"What if we add ammonium? To minimize oxidation." I struggled to read the scratched-out note. "Two months ago I wrote a note that says ammonium applied to copperas produces blue crystals and leaves behind a white fluid. White might dry close enough to clear."

"Worth a try." He clapped his hands together, invigorated by the possibility. "I'll mix," he offered. "You keep reading. You might run across something else we should try."

"Very low heat, I should think." I didn't know if he heard me or not.

He nodded, absently opening storage drawers, hunting for ammonium, measuring water and iron salts. I leaned my head against the wall and watched him work while I finished off the last of my apple.

Sebastian was as much a riddle to me as invisible ink. An insufferable devil one minute and a brooding angel the next. The man jested mercilessly, and yet I knew he hid a dark wound in his heart. I couldn't imagine how a child could bear seeing his own father killed so brutally. But he cloaked his grief so effectively that, except on rare occasions, it seemed almost as if the tragedy had never occurred. He didn't behave like an injured animal. He wasn't brooding and angry like Lord Ravencross. What was it in Sebastian's makeup that allowed him to survive and even thrive, despite a scarring childhood? I concluded that Captain Grey must have been an extraordinary guardian.

I sighed, watching him work. One thing I knew for certain, the man was too striking in appearance for his own good.

He hummed softly as he poured ingredients. "Read." He pointed the measuring spoon at the papers in my lap. "You can gaze adoringly at me another time."

I jerked upright. "I was doing no such thing."

Madame Cho grunted, an eerie sound that almost resembled a chuckle. Sebastian simply raised one eyebrow at a jaunty angle.

"I wasn't gazing at you, *adoringly* or otherwise." I sniffed and bent over my notes. "Be sure to keep the heat low."

"Aye, aye, General."

"You may as well leave the window open. The ammonium is going to stink." Barking orders made me feel in control again. "And for pity's sake, if it does start to smoke remove it from the burner right away. I'm too tired tonight to drag your enormous carcass out of here again."

"*Enormous*, I am not enormous," he muttered, tapping the copperas out of the measuring spoon onto the scale. He stopped and squinted at me, a picture of concern. "But now that you mention it, you are looking a bit peaked. Perhaps it's time you toddled off to bed with the rest of the youngsters."

"I'll not *toddle* anywhere. This is my laboratory and I won't be dismissed." I flipped to a new page and pretended to be deeply engrossed in my old notes. "Aside from that, I am not a child." The minute I said it I realized it sounded exactly that, childish.

"The lady doth protest too much, methinks."

"Shakespeare. How droll." I sighed and tsked, trying to sound as if I was above all his nonsense. "If you must know, my lord, I am sixteen. An adult." Old enough to have a season in London. Old enough to be shipped off to Stranje House and abandoned to the care of strangers. For that matter, old enough to marry. Several girls in my village had married at fifteen. Not that it was of any importance. I swallowed and caught the corner of my lip between my teeth. Because, of course, I would never marry.

"Sixteen?" He set down the measuring spoon and studied me speculatively. "That old?" He smirked as if it was all a big joke. I hated him for that.

"Yes, *that* old." I turned away from the burning look in his eyes, which was probably nothing more than candlelight reflecting off his pupils. "Perhaps it is you, my lord, who ought to toddle off to bed. I know how much you elderly folk value your rest."

Without so much as a smile at my jibe, he asked flatly, "How much ammonium?"

I checked my notes. "One dram, I should think. If that doesn't work, we can add more later."

He concentrated on measuring. I skimmed through more pages cataloging past experiments, analyzing my failed recipes, searching for something I might have missed, some glimmer of hope. Why wouldn't the solution turn clear?

I was so absorbed in scouring my notes, I didn't notice Miss

Stranje enter the room. "I take it you have not found the answer yet?"

Immediately, I swung my feet off the bench and corrected my posture. Even though Madame Cho had been sitting in the corner all day, she so seldom looked up from her stitching that I'd relaxed and lowered my guard. I glanced at the old dragon's straight-backed chair and was shocked to see she had left her post. I must have been more absorbed in reading than I'd thought. "No. No answer yet."

"A pity." Miss Stranje sniffed stoically. "Unfortunately, you must put aside your work until tomorrow. Past time you went to bed, Georgiana."

I expected Sebastian to smirk at that, but he didn't. He stirred the ammonium and iron and frowned. He must've been thinking the same thing I was.

"We have so little time," I explained. "Less than two days."

"Only one day now," he added.

"We're so close to an answer, perhaps if we had another hour or two?" I asked.

She glanced at the pitch-black windowpanes. Raindrops pattered against them, clinging to the glass. Candlelight caught on the droplets making them shimmer like golden pearls. She flipped open her pocket watch and shook her head. "You've been up since dawn, and it is already long past a reasonable hour to retire."

My attention whipped to her. How did she know I'd risen at dawn? How much of my morning adventures had she observed? If she'd seen me climbing the oak tree with my skirts tucked up above my knees, nothing showed on her face. There was no narrow frown promising punishment, no menacing arched brow, no shame-on-you pursed lips. Nothing. Instead she calmly said, "A rested mind is a fruitful mind."

"I'll finish up here," Sebastian offered. "You've had a trying day."

I imagined him saying, *toddle off to bed, little girl,* and wanted to throw my notes at him.

He continued stirring. "If this doesn't work, I'll add more ammonium."

"The ratio ought not exceed two parts copperas to one part ammonium," I warned.

He nodded. "Failing that, we'll continue the experiment in the morning."

Outnumbered, I heaved a resentful sigh. "Keep precise notes."

I slapped the stack of papers on the worktable and Miss Stranje marched me away like a prisoner being hauled off to prison. She led the way through the dark hall holding aloft a single taper in a small brass holder. Wind moaned through the mullioned windows and the walls creaked. A draft swept through the hall and the flame guttered, casting an unsteady orange glow against the dark paneling.

A tidal wave of isolation washed over me. The house, the night, and the storm threatened to swallow me up. I wanted to run back to the laboratory, back to the light, back to Sebastian. Instead, I quickened my steps to keep up with her and remain in the small flickering orb of our lone candle. In the distance, a clock chimed the hour. "If we were in London, I would be allowed to stay out much later than this." I argued with more than a little irritation in my voice. "I've heard some balls are not even over until it's nearly dawn."

"We are not in London."

"All the same, is not this experiment more important than staying up late to dance and flirt at some foolish ball?"

"An interesting argument," she said impassively. "But if, as you say, staying up excessively late is foolish when practiced in London, it would be no less foolish to do so here."

I hurried up the stairs behind her. "I thought you wanted me to produce the formula at all costs."

"Not at the risk of your life. The fumes compromised your health yesterday. Testing your stamina tonight hardly seems a wise course of action." She clucked her tongue. "The death of a student is always so ticklish to explain to the authorities."

If she intended to be humorous, she missed the mark. I returned to the issue. "Working late wouldn't kill me."

"A mistake in mixing chemicals might."

"But other lives *are* at stake here—more important lives than mine." *Sebastian's for one.*

Miss Stranje stopped and held the candle up nearer to my face. She looked quite perturbed about my last argument. "Are you God? Who else is equipped to make such a judgment?" she asked. The candle exaggerated her harsh features. She became almost gargoyle-like frowning at me so intensely. "Listen to me carefully, Georgiana Fitzwilliam. It is impossible to know the importance of one's life. You have no way of knowing what effect you will have on mankind."

She lowered the candle and proceeded up the stairs. "Sleep, Miss Fitzwilliam. Sleep is of paramount importance now. Morning will be here soon enough. We are both tired and I have a long journey to Shoreham ahead of me tomorrow."

She stopped in her tracks and huffed as if she hadn't intended to say that last bit. I remembered her argument with Captain Grey. Clearly, she wasn't looking forward to this trip to see her sister. I itched to know more about it, but she straightened her shoulders and returned to her customary businesslike manner.

"You may resume your quest first thing in the morning, after your mind is rested. We simply cannot afford for you to make another potentially fatal error. When you are tired, you are far more likely to rush to a faulty conclusion."

No one had ever debated so rationally against me before. It was refreshing and annoying at the same time. With a defeated mumble, I asked, "Are you always this sensible?"

"Sensible?" Her candle flickered. For an instant, I thought I saw her smile. "No. Not always. I'm afraid I have been accused of acting rather impulsively at times. Not unlike yourself."

"Hard to imagine *you* jumping out of an attic window strapped to a kite."

"I might surprise you. I understand more than you think. Which brings me to a point of some concern."

She stopped on the landing and turned, waiting for me, lowering the candle so that I could see my way up the stairs. I froze, startled. The candle illuminated a roaring lion's head carved on the balustrade. The beast seemed to burst out of the dark, his mouth open, teeth bared, and his thick tongue protruding. She walked on leaving me in the dark with the lion. I hurried to catch up. "A point of concern about what?"

"I must ask you to proceed cautiously in your dealings with Lord Wyatt."

I raised my hand in a pledge. "I promise not to asphyxiate him ever again."

"How very good of you," she said in a dry humorless tone. "But you know perfectly well that isn't what I mean."

My stomach somersaulted. Had she guessed the way I felt about him? How much had she observed that morning? She couldn't possibly know that I'd wanted to kiss him. She waited for my response, saying nothing to alleviate my frantic unasked questions.

"Cautious how?" I blurted.

We reached the dormitory floor and she slowed her steps. "Lord Wyatt is a young man of intellect and action. A soldier. A strategist. For these reasons, he studiously avoids matters of the heart. He does not bestow his affections easily. You must not wound him. He has experienced enough hurt for several lifetimes."

"Me?" *Wound him?* Could she not see how utterly impossible that was? The hour was late, but not so late that she should suddenly begin talking utter nonsense. "It is unlikely that I should ever hurt *anyone* in that regard."

"You think not?"

"I'm certain of it. I harbor no false hopes in that direction. Indeed, contrary to what my mother may be plotting or planning, I shall never marry."

Her shoulders sagged and the candle guttered for a moment before she steadied it. "Not an easy resolution to keep." She spoke as if from experience. I wondered if a similar resolution was the obstacle between her and Captain Grey. "It is understandable if you believe you need to remain unmarried so you can pursue a higher calling, but you are young yet. It would be best not to decide such a weighty matter at your age."

"It isn't a higher calling. I'm simply facing facts. I'm practical, if nothing else. All things considered, given my peculiar interests, and . . ." I gave her a cavalier shrug, and tugged on one of my wild curls. It flashed like fire in the candlelight. "It is highly unlikely that anyone would ever fall in love with me."

As we approached the dormitorium, I stopped, knowing that by this time the other girls would have slipped out of their beds and gone upstairs to the attic. I didn't want their secret discovered because of me. I lunged for the knob and wedged myself between her and the door. "I'll go in alone. I can see well enough in the dark. I wouldn't want the candle to awaken the others."

Her lips pursed and one eyebrow tilted up. Fortunately, she stepped back. "As you wish. But you are mistaken."

"Mistaken? How?" Did she know the girls weren't in their beds?

Wind howled through the landing window, and her candle flickered almost out. I only caught a glimpse of her worried expression. "You underestimate your appeal, Georgiana. It would be easy for someone to fall in love with you. Especially someone who uses his head for something other than holding up his hat. I ask only that you do your best to avoid engaging Lord Wyatt's affections." She turned, as if that put an end to the matter.

"Wait. Why?"

She paused and bowed her head. Her back still toward me. "For both your sakes. His line of work is not conducive to relationships." She glanced back at me, pain etched across her features. "He's a young man, Georgiana, far more likely to make dangerous mistakes if his heart is foolishly tangled up elsewhere."

As she walked brusquely away, she said over her shoulder, "As it is, I'm afraid he's already halfway in love with you."

I tightened my grip on the doorknob, and despite the cold draft, sweat made my palm stick against the brass.

Miss Stranje strode away, leaving me enveloped in darkness. Yet my thoughts blazed as bright as a stable fire, leaping wildly and licking at my consciousness with hot orange tongues. Was she right? Could it be true? A hundred counterarguments raged through my mind, and yet one question rose above them all, one outrageous demand that could not be silenced.

Only halfway?

Fifteen

KISS FAREWELL

O nly halfway." I sighed into the darkness.

In answer, a deafening crack of thunder shook the walls of Stranje House. I dashed into the room and discovered I'd been mistaken about more than just Sebastian's feelings toward me. The girls were already in bed, asleep. As I undressed, I heard Sera breathing evenly. Despite the storm battering the windows, she didn't even stir. None of them did. Lightning shot blasts of white through slits in the curtains. One of the flashes illuminated Punch's albino fur as he cowered atop the blankets, next to Sera. When I pulled back the covers and slid into bed, he crept hesitantly up beside me. His silly whiskers tickled my shoulder as he risked coming closer.

"You're frightened, aren't you?" I whispered, feeling sorry for the poor quivering mite. I had no idea how Sera and the others could sleep through the storm rattling the whole house. He nosed up to my cheek and gave me a grateful lick. I tentatively petted the rat's back. It wasn't as unpleasant as I'd expected. His short hair and plump tummy reminded me of my father's fox-hound puppies.

He stopped quaking and curled up on my chest, calming down as I stroked his back. "Miss Stranje says Sebastian is halfway in love with me," I confided, and experienced a rush of jubilation, followed by stomach-grinding despair. I sighed. "How does one go from halfway to whole in only one day?"

Despite Miss Stranje's warning not to wound Sebastian, I was as much at risk of getting hurt as he was. More. And to what end? After tomorrow I would never see him again. Falling in love was pointless self-torture. "I refuse to waste another thought on him. Ever."

Punch responded with a rat-size kiss on my chin. Probably the only kiss I would ever have. I closed my eyes and tried to blot out the image of Sebastian's dark hair, his cobalt-blue eyes, and the intriguing beard shadow on his jaw.

Thunder blasted right above our roof and startled Punch. Sera moaned and tucked deeper into the covers. Between the bone-shaking noise of the storm, a rat quivering on my shoulder, and my own restless thoughts, sleep eluded me. I stubbornly forced myself to stop thinking about silly things, like the curve of a certain person's earlobes.

Instead, I concentrated on invisible ink, calculating ratios in my head and toying with other ways to achieve a clear iron salt base.

Three things happened at the exact same time:

The clock chimed three.

Lightning flashed outside our window.

Inspiration struck with as much force as the thunder that followed.

I scooted Punch into the hollow of Sera's back and whisked out of bed. I had to get back to my laboratory. I didn't worry about changing out of my nightgown. Sebastian would be long gone by now. I draped a shawl around my shoulders, put on my shoes, and tiptoed out of the room. A crash of thunder had me dashing down the hall. I whipped around the corner, nearly slid into that awful lion's head at the top of the railing, and scurried down the stairs. I didn't stop running until I entered the long dark hall. Bursts of lightning sent wafts of ghostly gray down the corridor, illuminating Miss Stranje's ancestors' faces. As I hurriedly walked past them, they all seemed to peer down at me with her same hawk-like intensity, frowning, questioning, evaluating. I wished they would all sit back in their frames and leave me alone. I could almost hear their feathery voices calling my name. "Georgiana."

Something moved in the darkness.

I heard my name again, only louder this time. "Georgiana?" The ghostly voice came from the shadows in the hallway.

With all the grace of a startled rabbit, I squeaked and nearly jumped out of my skin. Before I knew it, he had hold of my shoulders. "Sebastian," I said, sighing with relief and clapping a hand over my heart.

"Who did you think it was? And what in heaven's name are you doing up?"

"I couldn't sleep. An idea came to me." Flustered, I rattled on like a crazy woman. "I thought for certain you'd be gone. Gone from the laboratory, I mean. I need to try one thing. I have a theory that might solve the problem." I stopped for a breath. "The ammonium didn't work, did it?"

Lightning flashed, and I saw him staring at me as if I'd gone raving mad. "No."

I pulled out of his grasp and opened the door to the still-room. He followed me in. "Surely you don't intend to work at this hour?"

I nodded. "Yes. Just one quick test, to see if my new theory works. I won't be able to sleep unless I try it. One more experiment and then, I promise, I'll go back to bed."

The windows allowed the glory of the storm to radiate into the room. More glorious than a fireworks display over the Thames. For just a second it captivated our attention.

He muttered, "I shouldn't allow this."

"You don't have a choice. If you make me leave, I'll only pretend to go, wait until you've gone, and sneak back in."

"Obstinate child."

"I told you before, I'm not a child." I struck a match and lit the candelabra.

"I can see that." He tilted his head and peered at my nightgown as if he could see through it in the candlelight.

"Don't be ridiculous. I daresay this night rail covers far more of my person than any of those ball gowns you keep talking about." Nevertheless, I pulled the shawl around me protectively.

He stopped openly studying me and sighed. "A pity. I suppose the memory of your lovely legs dangling from an oak branch will have to suffice."

His words startled me. *Lovely?* Was I? The wicked curve of his lips made me feel unaccountably weak. I found it difficult to take a breath. That feeling returned, that unbearable yearning, and the fluttery sensation in my belly. I wanted him to kiss me more than I'd ever wanted anything.

Ever.

So much so, the very idea seemed to make my lips swell for want of his.

"Georgie," he warned, and backed away. "I'm not made of stone. This is a highly improper situation, and if you continue to look at me that way, I can't . . ." He shook his head slightly, and stood back as if I were a leper.

Heat rushed into my cheeks and shame blazed through me. I fumbled with the measuring spoons. "I haven't the foggiest idea what you're talking about."

He folded his arms across his chest, stern as a Methodist preacher, and I was afraid he planned to deliver a sermon on my wanton behavior. Instead, he said, "Tell me about this idea of yours. How did you know the ammonium didn't work?"

I measured water into the mixing vessel. "It almost worked though, didn't it?"

"Yes." He exhaled gloomily. "It changed to a pale yellow. But no amount of ammonium would make it clear. I tried twice more." He handed me the packet of iron salts.

Eager to share my new idea with him I burst out, "Alum."

"Alum?" he repeated, giving the idea to germinate. "Used in tanning, isn't it?"

"Precisely. Dyers mix it with iron salts to mordant wool before adding the color."

"Oh, I see." He nodded. "Because it renders iron salts colorless in preparation for dyeing."

I nodded.

A slow smile spread across his face. We grinned at each other like two children on Christmas morning. He struck the flint to light the burner.

A half hour later, as I stirred the liquid over low heat, crystals formed and drifted to the bottom of the pan. He stood next to me leaning over the pot. "It's working."

"I think so, I can't tell in this light." I took it off the heat and placed it under the candelabra. We stared at it. "It's clear." I whispered, worried it would suddenly turn dark.

We watched scarcely breathing.

"It worked," he murmured, and then practically shouted, "It worked! You're brilliant."

"Yes, I know."

He laughed.

So did I. Unaccustomed to frivolity, I moved on to issuing orders. Exhaustion rendered me incapable of restraining my bossy nature. "Write out three or four test messages while I mix up the gall emulsion." I pointed at my ink pot. "Then write over the invisible message with India ink so we can see what the gall emulsion does to standard ink. You'll find clean sheets of foolscap in my folio."

Apart from a salute, he went straight to work with no further mockery. I smiled to myself. The excitement of our success had caused him to forget about sending me off to bed—a lucky turn of events, because I'd never be able to sleep now. He tore sheets of stationery in half while I dissolved the gall in water.

As he scrawled a test message on one of the papers, glancing sideways at me while writing. His furtive expression made me suspicious of what he might be saying, but he quickly moderated his features and stacked the messages.

"No, no," I ordered. "Spread them out. They need to dry thoroughly for the test to be accurate."

"Tsk, tsk, you must address me properly, as my lord, remember?" He mimicked Miss Stranje's scolding voice as he spread out the papers. "Thus you would say, *my lord, would you please be so good, and kind, and tolerant, and forbearing, as to spread out the test papers so that they might dry thoroughly?* At this point, if you were a well-schooled young lady, you would flutter your long lashes and demurely add, *if you will do me this one kindness, my lord, I will be forever in your debt.*"

My mouth opened in search of an appropriate response, but nothing came. So I closed it and did something I never do. I giggled. I blame it on the lateness of the hour. Exhausted, elated, whatever the cause, I succumbed to giddiness. In fact, I shook so hard with nearly soundless laughter that I sloshed a bit of gall solution over the edge of the pan.

"Oh, no, Miss Fitzwilliam. This is not a proper response at all. You shall have to do better." He aped Miss Stranje's mannerisms perfectly. *"Else how shall we punish you for this effrontery to womankind?"*

"A turn on the rack?" I suggested. "Horsewhipping?"

The mirth on Sebastian's face changed to stone.

I didn't understand what I'd said to offend him. "She has one, you know," I said defensively. "A rack, I mean. And a horsewhip."

"Torture is not a jesting matter."

Yet it had felt good to speak of the torture chamber concealed in the underbelly of Stranje House, to mock the evil it represented. Then I remembered the horrors he must have seen as a child. What other grisly sights had he witnessed even more recently? My cheeks burned as they did so often around him.

"I'm sorry."

He nodded, still withdrawn and stone-faced.

Was his hardened countenance because he'd been tortured? "Have you ever . . ."

A grimace of pain crumpled his features, silencing me. I dared not ask. Some secrets are too dark to share.

We worked under a woolen blanket of awkwardness, until he held one of the sheets of paper over a candle flame, and said, "I'm checking to see if heat makes the message appear."

I stopped work and came close to watch. Wind rattled the windows. The candle guttered and flickered noisily. We stared at the seemingly blank paper. Waiting. Hoping. At last, he nodded with satisfaction and held it up to the light for me to see. The invisible writing was so faint that, with diversionary writing laid atop it, no one would ever be able to see it.

"So far, it's a goer." He shifted up onto his toes and drummed his fingers on the worktable. His excitement cast off those earlier shadows. No more prickly wool between us. Eagerness radiated from him like heat from the candle. Almost breathless he said, "Let's see about the developer."

My hands trembled as I lifted the pot from the heat, hoping the results wouldn't disappoint him. "It's ready." I dipped a small sea sponge in the brown liquid. "Which note would you like to test first?"

He passed one of the papers to me, crossed his arms and held his breath, watching me with his lips pressed tight. I dabbed reddish brown fluid over the invisible message, and waited a moment before blotting the page with a dry cloth to soak up the excess moisture.

We stepped back and watched as the iron slowly reacted with the gall. Faint words appeared on the page. He breathed out a huge sigh of relief. "We're close. Try it again," he urged. "Only this time apply more gall."

I did, and the results were gratifying. Brown words materialized on the paper, clear and easy to read.

"You've done it," he whispered, staring at the message. Then he nearly shouted, "By all the saints and angels, you've done it!" He picked me up in a bear hug and whirled me around. We knocked the scales and corner of the cupboard as he spun toward the window. "I can't believe it. Do you know how incredible this is? Do you have any idea how long I've waited for an ink like this?"

"It's well after midnight," I said. "Six days?"

He laughed and loosened his grip, allowing me to slide down his chest until my feet barely touched the floor on tiptoes. With one hand he gently smoothed a flock of wild curls back from my face. "So many deaths could've been prevented if you'd been born a few years sooner." He stroked the sides of my head. "There's so much going on in here."

Through my nightgown, I felt the muscles of his chest constrict. My forehead brushed against the rough stubble on his jaw. He held me so close that I could almost taste the warmth of his lips as he smiled at me. Hours ago, he'd loosened his neck cloth and shed his coat. My arms rested around his shoulders clutching the rumpled linen of his cambric shirt. He kept holding me, studying my face as if he saw something remarkable there.

Joy washed over me. It was as if all the hidden messages inside me had suddenly been revealed, as if everything about me that had always seemed peculiar and awkward finally made sense. I felt truly happy for the first time ever. I never wanted to leave his arms.

But Sebastian *would* leave me. Soon.

Sadness crushed me like a pestle grinding a gall against the stone mortar. There would be no tomorrow for us. He would leave for London as soon as we mixed enough ink. I lowered my gaze from his lips and tried in vain to straighten his disheveled neck cloth, but the folds had long since lost their ability to stand. So had I. If he hadn't been holding me, I would've crumpled and fallen to the floor.

Sebastian lifted my chin, and without a word, with no reprimand for looking at him with mooncalf eyes, no mockery, no teasing, he brushed his lips against mine. It was no more than the fluttering of a hummingbird's wing. Then he pressed them against my forehead, kissing me on the head as if I was a child he was kissing good night.

"I will come back," he whispered.

I said nothing. Simply held him, knowing his words were a lie spoken out of kindness. At least, he felt that much. *Kindness.*

An instant later, his mouth found mine. This time it was no child's kiss. It felt as if he poured years of hunger and longing, thousands of heartbreaking secrets into me, into this one urgent moment. I didn't know whether to weep or explode with happiness. I never wanted to let him go. I kissed him harder, wanting to keep him with me forever.

Sebastian pulled back and took a deep ragged breath. "Georgie," he called my name in a husky gasping whisper. I opened my eyes and he wore such a pained expression I tried to get closer to him, to comfort him. But he held me away and shook his head. "We can't. I can't do this. In the name of all that's merciful, Georgie, go away."

Go away?

My father's customary dismissal. "Go away, child." My older brothers' greeting when they visited. "Go away, runt." My mother's weary refrain. "Go. Away."

Go away.

Stunned, I stumbled back. What had I done?

He turned away from me and leaned onto the windowsill like a man praying, his head in his hands. "I don't form attachments. I can't. No entanglements." He hid his face from me and said all this with cold certainty. "It's less painful for everyone." When he said those words, I detected a slight tremor, and couldn't help but think of the little boy who watched his father murdered on the guillotine. Less painful for him.

Still bowed, still articulating each word in an unfeeling monotone, he said, "You deserve more."

To that absurd claim, I laid my soul bare. "And yet, you have already given me more than I have ever had." The truth shamed me, but I stood and faced him squarely. I would rather accept the humiliation than allow him to banish me on such feeble grounds.

He rubbed at his cheek and mouth as if he wanted to scrub my scent off his skin. "I can't." He whirled around, glaring at me like an enraged angel. No, like the devil I'd first met. "Don't you see?" he growled. "I'm not in a position to—" He stopped trying to explain. "For God's sake, go to bed. I don't want to argue the matter. I'll mix more test batches myself. Check drying times. Different papers. I can't concentrate with you here. Go! Now."

Like everyone else in my life, he wanted to be rid of me.

"It's you who should go. You have your ink. You have what you came for. We already know it works. Make as much as you need and leave. That way you'll never have to see me again."

I backed toward the door, my shoulders heaving as I gasped for air in violent gulps. Was it shame suffocating me? Anger? Or was it grief? I didn't know. It all mixed together and bubbled up into an inscrutable toxic froth that made me tremble.

I could hardly speak. "My notes." I pointed with a shaking finger. "Try to follow them properly." Bumping into the door, I groped pathetically for the handle, and left.

In the dark hall, I sagged against the door, pressing it shut. I heard the muffled sound of his footsteps on the other side. There was a slight movement of the handle as he took hold of it. Except he didn't turn the knob. Instead, there was a soft thud. I felt the vibration through the wood, and knew he had leaned his forehead opposite mine. I heard him say my name, but it didn't make the pain go away. No, in fact, I had to wrap my arms tight against my stomach, pressing against the turmoil, as I stumbled away from the laboratory.

The storm had abated. There were no more eerie blue-gray flashes to light the way. Cold, shivering, I pulled my shawl tighter around my shoulders. As I trudged past Miss Stranje's relatives, my eyes adjusted to the dark and I saw every one of their shadowed faces. Instead of chiding me, they seemed to mourn with me as I walked away from the one truly warm moment of my life.

Even the lion at the top of the stairs no longer frightened me. *Go ahead.* I thought. *Devour me. Rid the world of my noxious presence.* There are things in life worse than dying. For instance, this chilling apathy that spread like a canker into my limbs.

With slow heavy steps I made my way into bed. I did not give way to tears, not even when Punch nuzzled my chin, not even when the house moaned in sympathy. I stared at the ceiling, numb. Tomorrow, I would beg Madame Cho to clamp me onto the rack and turn the wheel. Maybe a good stretching would snap the feeling back into my soul.

Somewhere before dawn I must have slipped into a coma-like sleep because I awoke to Tess shouting at me.

"Wake up!" She shook me as if the house had caught fire. "It's happened. It's all gone wrong."

Sixteen

FAILURE AND SUCCESS, THOSE TWO IMPOSTERS

Iow could you let this happen?" Tess stood beside my bed in her nightclothes, her hair uncombed and matted. Wild-eyed, she glared at me like some sort of madwoman from Bed-lam. "What happened? What have you done?"

"What are you going on about?" I muttered groggily.

"I told you not to do anything in haste."

I shook my head trying to comprehend her meaning. Did she know I'd let Sebastian kiss me? Even if she did, it was none of her business. Tess, of all people, had no right to say anything. "Leave me be." I pulled up the blankets and wriggled deeper into the pillow.

"You were supposed to stop him. Now he's gone. The night-mare is back." She shoved me. "Get up!" she yelled, rousing the others.

Sera turned over. "What's the matter?"

"It's happening again. It's like it was before she came," Tess said in a ragged voice.

Sera sat up and grabbed Punch, holding the squirming rat the way a frightened child clutches a rag doll. "Are you sure?"

"Yes." Tess tugged my arm, dragging me out from under the covers. "Quickly. You have to do something or it's all going to go horribly, horribly wrong. Hurry!"

"Stop." I jerked out of her grasp and sat on the edge of the bed, lowering my throbbing head into my hands. It felt as if a cannonball had collided with my skull. "At least, let me dress."

"There's no time." She thumped my shoulder. "Come now, or he'll die."

My stupor vanished. I looked up into her distraught face, afraid to ask, "Lord Wyatt?"

"Yes."

Fear jolted through me. I dashed out of the room with Tess hard on my heels. We tore down the stairs and sprinted through the hall. I flung open the laboratory door, expecting the worst, expecting to find his asphyxiated body lying on the floor, but the room was empty. My work table looked tidy. The tools gleamed as if he'd scrubbed all night. Early morning sun drifted in through the windows. Everything at peace. Except Tess.

"He's gone," she murmured, "to London."

"I know." *Gone.* The paralyzing sadness of the night before crept back into me.

Her shoulders sagged. "You were supposed to keep him here longer." She glared up at me. *Furious.* "Why didn't you keep him here one more day? Just one more."

"I couldn't." My hands squeezed into tight fists, fingernails digging into my palms, helping me hold steady, and not yell at her. "Lord Wyatt wanted to be rid of me. No doubt, he wanted to get as far away from me as possible."

"I don't understand." She blinked rapidly, shaking her head.

"No. I saw him with you yesterday. Clearly, he had feelings toward you. I was certain he wouldn't be so quick to leave."

"Why does everyone keep mistaking Lord Wyatt's feelings toward me?" I glanced around the room empty-handed. Nothing with which to prove my point. "He feels no—" I lowered my voice. "He *felt* no particular affection for me. Aside from that, he has urgent business in London. He would've left today regardless of anything I did, or didn't do."

I flicked my finger against the scales, and sent them clinking and bouncing. "Anyway, what difference does one day make?"

"Everything." Tess frowned at me, her eyes rimmed with sadness and dark circles. "The difference between kingdoms rising and falling. Life and death. *His* life and death."

"Not Sebastian," I begged in barely a whisper. *No!* I silently screamed. He might want to be rid of me, but the thought of his death pressed down on me, gravity times a thousand, crushing my chest, forcing my knees to buckle. I gripped the worktable. "It can't be. How? Why?"

She sat on the long bench, tucked up, hugging her knees. She pointed to the window sill. A half-sheet of paper rested beneath a small pot of reddish brown liquid. "See for yourself."

"This is how it begins." She rocked slightly. "Tyranny. Decades of war. Thousands dead."

I stared at her and chewed the corner of my lip. I'd admired Tess from the start, reluctantly, but there you have it—she inspired awe. I envied the way she always seemed so aloof, so remarkably confident. Even if her confidence was, at times, tinged with hostility. This morning, her whitened pallor and distraught wide eyes frightened me more than if she held a dagger to my throat.

She'd withdrawn into herself, turned inward by visions of

destruction and death. The way she stared at the letter, I suspected she already knew the contents.

My feet felt brittle as icicles. With hesitant steps, I approached the windowsill. My fingers trembled as I slipped the paper out from under the bottle of gall. There, written in India ink, Sebastian had scrawled a note in bold hard strokes. This portion of the letter anyone could readily see, this was the *diversionary writing* as he called it—the ruse.

> *Dear Miss Fitzwilliam,*
> *I pray you will be so kind as to excuse my early departure. Captain Grey and I have numerous duties in London that require our immediate attention. As you can see, I completed our experiment and prepared flasks for the purpose we discussed.*
> *I wish you well in your future endeavors. May I say, it has been an honor to make the acquaintance of a young lady who has more than flounces and fripperies occupying her thoughts.*
> *My best regards,*
> *Lord Wyatt*

Another set of words resided between those lines, a secret message meant only for me. Written in fainter ink, it read:

> *Dearest Georgiana,*
> *You must forgive my harsh words last night. The situation caught me off guard. I couldn't think clearly with you so near. My baser instincts wanted to rule.*
> *First, I cannot thank you enough for this ink. It will do more good than you could imagine. As you might've guessed, after London I go to Vienna. How long my sojourn there will be, I cannot know. Second, I must warn you, Georgie. Do*

not expect other gentlemen to behave with the restraint you
witnessed in me. Exercise caution around other men while I
am away. No kissing.
    I shall be extremely unhappy if I hear of you breaking any
other hearts.
    Yrs, Sebastian

He was teasing, of course, about breaking hearts. I hadn't
broken his. If I had, he might still be here. I wanted to smile at
his words, but the warmth they generated vanished under a
deadly chill.

Sebastian's secret message wasn't hidden at all.

Neither of us had applied the gall solution, and yet the faint
writing was clearly legible, every word exposed. My invisible
ink had darkened on its own. Sunlight streaming through the
window may have developed it, or may have reacted with a
chemical in the paper. It didn't matter. Sebastian was headed to
London, and tonight he would distribute an invisible ink that
would betray everyone who used it.

I whipped around to Tess. "We have to stop him."

She rocked, pale, unmoved.

I ran and shook her shoulders. "Tess, listen to me. Lord
Ravencross's horse—you must get him to lend it to you. I have
to ride for London straightway. I can't explain why. It's a secret,
but I need you to get me a horse."

She stared blankly at me.

I shook her again. "Tess, I need a horse. Any horse. Now."

That seemed to wake her up. "You can't."

"I can. I must. I have to warn Lord Wyatt or terrible things
will happen."

"No. You can't leave yet. Think it through. We only have one
hope." She frowned. "You have to make an ink that works."

After my colossal failures in the past few days?

"There isn't time." I gave her shoulders another shake. "We have to stop him. Now! Before he gives it to his men. He'll get caught. They'll *all* get caught."

"No!" She jerked out of my grasp and buried her face in her hands. "Listen to me. I've seen that path. If you don't make an ink that works, too many people die." She looked up, eyes pleading. "Too many. Him, others, ambassadors, kings . . ." She tried to suppress a moan and started rocking again. "If they die, you can't begin to imagine what happens here in England, *and* on the continent."

She rubbed her forehead, hard, as if that might scrub away the images she saw. "I warned you! Why didn't you listen? Everything was going so well. The dreams had stopped. If only I'd seen this. If I'd known Sebastian would leave I would've tied him down." She gritted her teeth. "If only he would've waited. You would've figured it out today. *Today.*" She slapped her hand against the wooden bench. "That's how it was supposed to be. It was supposed to be *today.*"

"You can't know that." Frustrated and angry, I shouted at her. "Formulating a new ink could take months."

"You only have today."

I clutched Sebastian's note in my fist, and glanced wildly about the workroom. "Even if I do find a solution today, how would I get it to him?" A few moments ago my course of action had seemed so clear, a simple matter of running him down on the road and warning him that I'd failed, that the ink didn't work. Now, everything seemed infinitely more difficult.

Impossible.

Tess stood and stared down at her feet showing beneath the hem of her night rail. "I only know what happens if you don't. You have to do it, and then we must take it to him."

"How? He's in London. There's a ball tonight, with diplomats, dignitaries and . . ." I shook my head and backed away. "No. It's impossible. We must get word to Miss Stranje. She'll know what to do. Madame Cho—"

"No!" She grabbed my shoulder and wrenched me close. "You can't. Miss Stranje won't get back in time, and I've seen what happens when Cho sends word to London. It makes things worse. Much worse."

She drew me close to her face, so close I smelled her terror. Acidic. Suffocatingly sweet. Almost metallic.

"If Madame Cho stops him from delivering the ink, Sebastian dies in Vienna." She stared at me, looked straight through me into another time, a place of horror. Her eyes opened wide. Whites showed all around. "Hundreds slaughtered in a single day."

"What? How? Tell me what happens. Maybe we can—"

"It isn't like that." She made a low keening noise. "It comes in snatches. Flies at me like a flock of mad birds, flapping in every direction, beating against my skull. If this happens, then that happens, and this. Never in a neat organized line. It crashes over my head in rolling waves. Bomb bursts of pain. Fragments."

Her fingers dug into my shoulders, holding on, as if she might fall. "You don't understand. I live what happens. A blast shatters Sebastian's ribs. Rips through his side. I've gasped with him as he silently screams for air, holding his bloody entrails in his own hands." Her voice dropped. She squeezed her eyes shut and lowered her face. "Dying isn't easy. All those wretched regrets as life oozes away."

How did she keep from going mad? I tried to pull out of her grasp.

She blinked, color washed back into her cheeks, she drew a quick breath and let go. "Not just him, Georgie. Hundreds. The sound of their wailing tears at my soul. How can I make you see? Bloody battles. The destruction. Shall I tell you about the starvation? Orphaned children—"

My heart rabbited around my chest, thumping, lost. I didn't know which way to turn. Where to run. "What can I do? How do I stop it?" I pleaded, knowing if I failed again, I would never banish my guilt.

"Bring him an ink that works. It's the only path open to us. I've seen the others." She voiced this fragile hope with quiet determination. "We'll leave as soon as you're done."

"But how—"

"I'll get a horse. You"—she pointed at the table—"make the ink."

Sera stood quietly inside the doorway, watching us, holding a familiar pair of shoes and my muslin morning dress in her hands. "I brought your clothes." She held them out to me. When I didn't take them, she set the pile on the table. "We'll explain to Madame Cho that you have more experiments to do. Maya and I have knife-throwing lessons this afternoon. We'll keep her so busy she won't suspect anything. Jane will bring you something to eat and assist you."

Maya followed Sera into the room and the three of them stood around me in a solemn circle, like mourners at a funeral.

"You all know about the ink?"

Sera worked the toe of her shoe against the floorboards. "Our training wouldn't be worth much if we hadn't figured it out."

"You must never breathe a word of it to anyone else," I warned. "Swear on your lives—not a word."

"You have our promise," Sera said, taking the blood oath for them all. "We'll help you as much as we can."

I glanced at the worktable and ran my fingers through my

hair. After a lifetime of failures, of jumping too soon, of foolish blunders, and wrong assumptions, too much depended on me getting it right for once. "What if I fail again?"

Maya reached for my hand. "You *will* find the answer, Georgiana." Her voice vibrated through her fingertips up my arms, and flowed around me like a hypnotic flute, smoothing out my agitation. "You are a woman of much courage. I know this. You will go to London, and you will do what must be done."

Sera nodded as if she believed it, too.

I bowed my head trying to escape Maya's trance. Could I really formulate an ink that worked in so short a time?

She kept hold of my hand, gazing steadily into my eyes "I believe you will do this." Her words were airy notes of hope that sailed straight into my heart.

"You will." Sera stood beside Maya. Her face not as serene as Maya's. "You must."

Tess slipped out of the room. The others followed, leaving me alone in the middle of a desperate nightmare. Yet, there was a chance, a mathematically improbable chance, but a chance nonetheless, that I could set my mistake right.

I bent over my notes with an urgency and determination I had never felt before. I studied the formula. An hour later, I realized exactly where my error lay. As usual, I'd overcomplicated things. The solution was so simple. Iron was bound to darken when exposed to any number of elements, sunlight. It was uncontrollable. Alum, alone, was the answer. I knew it with as much certainty as I knew I was still standing on the floor in my bare feet.

How had I missed it last night? I swallowed, remembering exactly why. *Sebastian.* The ache in my chest expanded. I remembered his arms holding me and his lips covering mine. But Tess had made me see his death, too, and that was unthinkable. I would concentrate as I'd never concentrated before.

I quickly pulled on my clothes. It only took a couple of hours more to create the new formula. By the time Jane brought food, I'd already mixed and heated a batch of clear soluble alum. "What did you tell Madame Cho?"

She set down the tray. "I explained that you insisted on working without interruption, and that I would bring you food and provide assistance if you needed it."

Ah, yes, the truth can be highly effective. "Did that satisfy her?" I snatched a muffin, took a bite, and tossed it back on the plate. It may as well have been wood shavings. My appetite was gone. I measured gall for the developer solution.

Jane rubbed her arm absently. "She got that quizzical look on her face. You know, the one that means she didn't believe me."

"It was nothing less than the truth. I certainly don't want any interruptions and I do need your assistance."

"How can I help?"

I pulled out several sheets of foolscap from my folio, tore them in half, and half again, so that we had a dozen test papers. "Write something on each one using India ink."

Jane checked the nib of the pen. "She's bound to notice when you're gone this evening."

"Not if we're careful."

"We'll need more than caution on our side. Luck, I'd say. What do you want me to write?"

"Anything. A quick line or two on each of the papers."

She thought for a moment and set to work. By the time she finished, the new invisible ink formula was ready to be tested.

Jane had jotted several farming instructions on each. "Leave the west field fallow. Plant beans in place of wheat in the east field," and so on. I quickly perused the papers and glanced up. "Are these ways to improve crop yields?"

She nodded.

"Brilliant." I had a new appreciation of our Jane. "We must discuss this when I return from London." *Assuming I did return.*

She smiled. "I thought you might find it interesting."

Between the lines of her list, I used the clear alum ink to pen a short invisible apology to Sebastian for putting him in danger. On successive pages, I apologized to the Prince Regent of England for making an error on my previous formula.

I waved one of the papers bearing my hidden confession over the burner, heating it. I laid another in the sunny window. All afternoon we repeated the process, using different types of paper. I sprinkled water on some notes, dirt on others, spilled wine on them, salt, vinegar, and candle wax. This time, I wasn't taking any chances. I intended to expose the ink to light, time, heat, and anything else that might cause it to inadvertently develop. With a grimace, Jane reluctantly spit on one of the notes—thus providing me with a saliva test.

All the while, I kept repeating over and over in my head. *Don't let anyone die because of my mistakes.*

I imagined the diplomats and their families who might suffer because of my failed ink, because I'd jumped to conclusions. Miss Stranje was right. *Impulsive.* Tess was right. *Hasty.*

One face, above all those nameless others, haunted me, one whose features I knew by heart. The thought of Sebastian locked away in a dungeon, or dying in the ghastly way Tess described, set me to pleading even harder for a reprieve. *Please, God, if you're there, spare them.*

"What are you thinking about?" Jane wiped out the pot so I could start a fresh batch of invisible ink.

"My mistakes." I stirred the gall emulsion.

"Don't you wish there was a way to turn back time? There are so many things I wish I could go back and do differently."

"You?" I turned down the heat on the burner. "But you always seem to know the exact right thing to do."

She shook her head. "Not always, or I wouldn't be here, would I?"

"What could you possibly have ever done wrong?" I poured the solution into a cooling vessel.

"Everyone makes mistakes," she said pensively.

I handed her the spoon. "But if you *could* go back in time, what would you wish to do differently?"

She shrugged. "Bragging cost me everything. If I could turn the clocks back, I would keep my successes to myself."

I checked on the papers in the windowsill, holding each of the notes up to the light, inspecting them for any telltale signs of the invisible writing. I didn't understand Jane wanting to hide her successes. It was my failures I desperately wished to escape. "Whyever would you want to hide your accomplishments?"

She stirred the emulsion, cooling it down. "My parents were killed in a coaching accident," she explained. "They left us with a nearly worthless estate. My older brothers, gamblers, the pair of them, had no use for our ancestral home apart from the meager allowance it provided. They abandoned me, left me with a handful of servants to get along as best I could." She shrugged. "So, that's exactly what I did."

Her chin jutted up and excitement elevated her voice. "Thomas Coke's farm is situated near my family estate. His ideas on animal husbandry were the talk of the neighborhood. I listened closely to what he said, asked questions, and convinced our steward to implement his new methods. It worked. Our farm flourished. By the second year, the estate income doubled."

Pieces of the puzzle began to fit. "Is that why you consult with Miss Stranje's steward? You're advising him?" I hunted through the cupboards and found a dozen small vials to hold the new ink.

"He's Captain Grey's steward, but, yes. We've made significant improvements here in less than a year."

Truly amazed, I plunked the bottles on the table. "That's remarkable. Surely you don't regret any of that?"

"What I regret, is having *told* anyone. You see, I invested the extra capital from the estate and tripled our gain. It turns out I have a passable ability to manage finances."

"Tripled it? More than passable, I should think." I checked the dampened note. It had finally dried and still showed no signs of the invisible writing *Success.*

"If only I'd kept that news to myself, things would have gone along famously." Jane glanced at the evening sky darkening outside our window. "We have to hurry." She fanned the developing solution to make it cool faster.

I thought of my two older brothers. Sadly, they were nothing like Robbie. They cared only for trifling with ballet dancers, parading about town like peacocks, and gambling at White's. Easy to guess what would happen without my father's reins on their pocketbooks.

"You told your brothers?" Poor Jane. I glanced up from preparing the bottles, holding my breath, dreading her answer.

"Yes. I thrust my success under their noses. Scolded them for their excesses. Tightened the purse strings. I badgered them about wasting their lives and squandering money on cards and light-skirts." Jane handed me a funnel. "How stupid I was to think they would listen to me, their little sister." Her lips clamped into a hard-buttoned line.

"They sent you away, here, so they could plunder the estate, didn't they?" My hand trembled as I poured invisible ink into the dozen small vials.

"It'll be all right, Georgie." Jane steadied the funnel for me. "I should've anticipated it. I knew what they were. If only I'd kept my foolish mouth shut."

"No." I shook my head. "No one could've predicted such deceitful and irrational behavior." I pressed corks into each of the bottles.

"That's just it, I could've. Pride blinded me. I was so certain they'd be impressed. So certain of their gratitude. So certain they would listen to me." She smiled mirthlessly. "Undoubtedly, by now my dear brothers have run through their funds and bankrupted the estate. Any day, I expect Miss Stranje to tell me there is no more money arriving to pay for my education."

I packed the vials into a small box, and cushioned them with cotton wadding. "At least when that happens, you will get to go home."

"That is the *last* thing I wish to do." She stepped back and stared at me as if I'd run mad to even suggest such a thing.

I blinked and clutched the table with both hands, hanging on for balance. With a shock, I understood. I no longer had a desire to return home, either.

Seventeen

THE CASSANDRA
COMPLEXITY

Jane!" Sera burst into the stillroom. "Tess says to run straight-way and find a ball gown that'll fit Georgie." Pausing to catch her breath, Sera turned to me and thrust a flour sack into my hands. "Here, I wheedled this out of Cook. It's food for your journey. Cheese, apples, and sliced chicken. "

"Thank you." I set the bag on the table. "However did you get anything more than a crumpet out of that terrifying woman?"

"Cook isn't so bad."

I knew better.

"Sit." Sera pointed to a chair. "I'm supposed to fix your hair."

"There isn't time for that nonsense," I said.

"It's a ball. They won't let you in the door looking like this."

She was right. "Very well, but hurry." I dropped onto the chair.

Maya scurried in, her arms laden with brushes and combs, ribbons, a mirror, and her miraculous pomade. They set to work, weaving, plastering, and binding my troublesome locks into a splendid Grecian coiffure. They were sticking the final pins into place when Jane returned carrying a satchel.

"My best gown." She opened the top so I could see a tuft of green silk embroidered with beautiful white scrollwork.

I stood up ready to go. Grateful for their help, I spoke without thinking, "Thank you. You've made me feel like Cinderella." Except she hadn't put thousands of lives in danger.

"This is no fairy tale." Jane closed the bag and frowned. "It's more like you're Cassandra running to warn the Trojans about the big wooden horse full of soldiers who plan to burn the city." She pressed the bag into my hand. "Let us hope you have better luck than she did."

I needed more than luck. I caught the corner of my lip. Too much hung in the balance.

Sebastian's life.

Our homeland.

Tess's prophesy led me to suspect Napoleon might yet find a way to proceed with his plans to attack England. Although, banished to Elba, we ought not underestimate the Emperor Napoleon's reach. As Father put it, the man didn't know when to give up. I couldn't help but picture my family estate taking cannon fire, and Stranje House under siege. My knees suddenly felt like boiled leeks.

"This way." Sera hastened me out the side door. She pointed to a coach waiting at the far end of the drive. I'd expected a horse. In fact, I'd expected to see Tess astride Zeus. The idea of hanging on behind her while we galloped that huge stallion all the way to London had been daunting.

I ran down the drive and the coach door swung open. Lord Ravencross, a very angry-looking Lord Ravencross, sat across from Tess inside the coach. Despite his scowl he looked remarkably handsome in his dress uniform. "Get in," he barked, offering me a hand without lowering the steps.

I clambered up, attempted to dodge his knees, bumped first the door and then his bad leg, as I lugged in Jane's satchel, my reticule carrying the ink vials, and the bag of food. Finally, I settled next to Tess. Neither of them greeted me. Tess leaned against the far corner with her face turned away from both of us. Lord Ravencross yanked the door shut and rapped on the roof. The coachman sprang the horses.

"I thought we were going on horseback?" I asked.

They said nothing in response. They did, however, exchange venomous glances at each other before turning to stare out of opposite windows like two brooding children.

"Thank you for the use of your coach, my lord." I gripped Jane's satchel beside me as we went over a rut in the road. "Did you tell your coachman to hurry? Did you explain that lives depend upon it?"

He nodded and cast a sidelong look at Tess.

I needn't have worried about speed. We traveled at a breakneck pace. The carriage practically flew down the rutted road, bounding over bumps and potholes and veering sharply around curves. I held the ink cradled in my lap and with my other hand clutched the ceiling strap to keep from bouncing off the seat.

For nearly an hour, no one said a single solitary word. The atmosphere inside grew more and more tense with every mile. The seats were of fine leather, soft, luxuriously padded, and the carriage well-sprung, but given the hostility crackling between Tess and Ravencross, riding on horseback may have been more comfortable, after all.

By the time we hit the outskirts of London, the night turned black and deep with fog. Our coachman slowed the horses to accommodate for limited visibility and increased traffic as hundreds of carriages converged onto the too-narrow streets. Our speed reduced to a crawl. Too slow. I tapped my foot. If only it didn't take forever to get across London. Bouncing my leg impatiently, I considered getting out and running ahead to clear the path. But of course that would only succeed in getting me trampled or lost in the fog.

Desperate for a distraction, lest I go mad with anxiety, I grabbed the food sack and slung it onto my lap. "Sera packed food for our journey. Meat, bread, and cheese."

I held it open to Tess. No reply.

"She finessed it out of Cook. No mean feat, as I'm sure you must realize." I had no stomach for any of it, but perhaps she did. I continued to hold out the bag to Tess. "We do have a long night ahead of us."

She shrugged and said nothing.

"Are you hungry, my lord?" I fished out an apple and offered it to him.

He shook his head in curt refusal.

"Very well." Tess smacked her hand against the leather seat and snatched the apple out of my hand. "I'll have one of those."

The way she held the apple made me think she planned to heave it at Lord Ravencross. But she didn't. She held on to the apple and threw words at him instead. "For your information, *My Lord High-and-Mighty*, I was only going to borrow Zeus. You know perfectly well I would have brought him back in the morning."

Lord Ravencross turned, and despite the dim light, his eyes seemed to blaze as he narrowed them solely on her. "You are aware, are you not, that it is customary to hang horse thieves?"

"Then hang me." With a haughty toss of her head, Tess chomped into the apple.

It was my duty to intercede. "My lord, this entire situation is my fault. Tess would never have tried to borrow your horse if I hadn't begged her to do it. Which I would not have done if this weren't a matter of grave importance. Extremely urgent—"

He turned an almost desperate expression on me. "Do you think I would be carting the two of you off to London for any other reason?"

I shook my head and regretted breaking the silence.

He glanced sideways at Tess. To my surprise, a splash of yearning and boyish tenderness weakened his features, betraying him. "She wouldn't tell me anything, other than Lord Wyatt's life depended upon me and it was my duty to King and country." Clearly, his reasons for escorting us had more to do with Tess than King or country. An instant later, his face hardened into his customary mask of anger. "I owe Lord Wyatt a debt of some consequence"—he glowered at his lame leg—"so I could hardly refuse."

Tess munched on the apple and didn't say another word until we rumbled across the cobblestones on Queen Street. As if Ravencross had never said a cross word to her, Tess chirped as gaily as a lark in summer, "Thank you for your escort, my lord. You may set us down at the corner of St. James's Square."

He bristled at her request. "I think not. What do you intend to do, beg admittance at Lady Castlereagh's door? The servants will toss you out on your ear."

"I have no intention of *begging*," Tess said, lingering on the last word.

He shifted uncomfortably, frowning at the haughty tilt of her chin.

"Well, I don't mind begging," I said, collecting the satchel into my lap. "We need to hurry. I will plead for the both of us."

"No need." Tess hefted a small carrying case at her feet and announced with pride. "I brought a rope."

"A rope?" Lord Ravencross and I exclaimed simultaneously.

My stomach cinched into a tight knot. This did not bode well. "What do you intend to do with a rope?"

Tess jabbed me with her elbow. "I'll thank you to show a little confidence. I've gotten you this far, haven't I?"

Actually Lord Ravencross had gotten us this far, but I had no desire to argue. "How—"

"It's simple." She smiled, looking quite pleased with herself. "All we need to do is slip around back and find a dark section of the building. Then I'll scale the wall to the third-floor balcony."

Ravencross snorted. "Brilliant."

"I'll have you know, *My Lord Grouchy-Bear*, I happen to be particularly adept at scaling walls. I have done it before."

"Oh, of that I have no doubt, *Miss Horse-Thief*."

She shrugged. "I'll climb the wall and then hoist you up, Georgie. We'll change into our ball gowns in the dark of the balcony and enter through the deserted bedroom."

Unable to hold back any longer, I said, "Climbing the wall does not seem a practical plan. What if you fall? And hoisting me up with a rope . . ." I shook my head. "What makes you think the bedroom will be deserted?"

"Bound to be," she said with utter confidence. "Because everyone will be attending the festivities in the ballroom. And there you have it." She snapped her fingers. "Easy as peas on a knife. We'll slip in and blend with the other guests, locate Lord Wyatt, and proceed with the business at hand."

Ravencross closed his eyes tight for a moment, and to his credit he composed himself before speaking. "Outstanding plan." He clapped—two dull pats of his gloved hands. "And if you get caught? You do realize that breaking into the minister of foreign affairs' home would be considered treason."

The leather seat squeaked as Tess squirmed beside me.

He leaned forward and stared directly at her. "In which case, when I caught you in the stable with Zeus, I may as well have strung you up myself and saved *King and country* the expense of a hangman." He stared at her neck, as if distracted by the ghostly specter of an imaginary rope.

Tess's hand fluttered to her throat, but she quickly withdrew it and crossed her arms defiantly. "I suppose you have a better idea?"

I earnestly hoped he did, because hers was a disaster, and the best I could come up with was slipping in through the servants' entrance.

"Yes." He sat back and crossed his arms, too. "Next year I'll be twenty-one, old enough to take my seat in the House of Lords. Lord Castlereagh needs all the supporters he can get. I think my title should be enough to gain us admittance."

"Marvelous," I practically shouted. "No dangling at the end of a rope."

"I can't guarantee that much," he said. "Leave it to her to have your necks in a noose before the night is out."

"At least we don't have to scale the foreign minister's wall," I murmured.

Tess shrugged. "I'd been rather looking forward to that part."

Lord Ravencross opened the driver's trap. "Take us to my town house."

"Why?" Tess demanded.

"So you can change into your gowns in privacy. What else?"

"No!" I blurted. "There isn't time." At this very moment, Sebastian might be handing out the wrong ink.

"I see," he said. "And yet, you thought there was time for you to sneak around the house and scramble up a rain gutter?"

"Don't be absurd. I wouldn't have used a rain gutter," Tess huffed. "Much too noisy. I would have climbed the brick—"

"No more arguments." It was my turn to smack the seat. "To save time we can change in the carriage."

He shook his head. "There isn't enough room in here. Aside from that, what do you expect me to do, close my eyes?"

Tess held her hand over her breast and feigned surprise. "Heavens no, my lord. We would never expect you to be so gentlemanly."

"What then?" he growled.

"My dear *Lord Ogre,* if you would be so kind as to step outside and stand guard I'm certain there's ample room for Miss Fitzwilliam and I to manage a change of wardrobe."

He snorted in disbelief. "Reduce me to keeper of the door, will you? Very well, *Your Royal Bossiness,* I shall comply." He pulled on his forelock, as if he was the lowliest of servants.

Tess inclined her head in a queenly fashion.

Lord Ravencross flicked open the coachman's transom and ordered, "Pull onto a side street, a quiet one, and stop." He slammed it shut and scowled.

The coach turned and rolled to a stop. Ravencross climbed out and cast a warning over his shoulder. "Be quick about it. I can't skulk out here all night like a ruddy brigand."

We dressed hurriedly, helping each other ease the gowns over our heads and tying tapes that were difficult to negotiate in the cramped space. I pulled on a luxurious pair of white elbow-length gloves. Tess fastened around my neck a string of pearls that Jane had generously packed in the satchel. She'd also lent me a small beaded reticule into which I carefully stowed the vials of invisible ink. We were ready.

"Oh, my," I said when I took stock of my companion. "You look beautiful."

Tess smoothed out her gown, a clever combination of diaphanous white silk flowing over her shoulders and sides, with a cornflower blue panel running down the center. It was, however, cut fashionably low, and revealed a great deal of her bosom. I shrugged. Such was the Parisian style. She looked stunning in it and would provide a useful diversion for my night's errand. With Tess in the room, I could go about my business without attracting any notice at all.

I opened the door and summoned Lord Ravencross. With a nod he instructed the coachman to take us to St. James's Square and climbed in. He took one look at Tess and his cheeks flamed. He tugged at his collar.

"Would you like me to straighten your cravat for you?" Tess asked.

"No," he snapped.

Aloof and as elegant as a swan, she elevated her chin. "As you wish."

He eyed her cleavage and took a deep breath. "I've half a mind to rip the ruddy cloth off my neck and use it to cover up your . . ." He waved at her breasts. "Haven't you something to hide those . . . What I mean is . . . Bloody hell, you're practically naked. I'll be forced to call out at least a dozen men before the evening is half over."

"It was not my intention to distress you, my lord."

I rather thought it might have been her exact intention. She plumped up the lace at the sides of her breasts. "There. Is that better?"

Whether it was better or worse, I couldn't tell. Poor Lord Ravencross could not look away.

Tess seemed rather pleased at his response. "I fail to see why you should call anyone out on my behalf. You aren't my brother, nor any relation at all. I don't see that it is any of your business if another gentleman lays his eyes on my . . ." She paused, waiting for him to tear his gaze away from the exact spot in question. "Person."

He growled and shoved back against the seat.

"Speaking of relationships." I called their attention to the business at hand. "How do you plan to explain our connection? What excuse will you give as to why you are escorting us this evening?"

"Don't need an excuse," he muttered.

"You could introduce us as your cousins," I suggested. "Among the peerage everyone is related somehow or other. In fact, it is quite likely you and I *actually* are cousins through my father's line. My uncle is Lord Brucklesby."

"*Brucklesby.*" He made my uncle's name sound like a sour word and muttered something else, which sounded suspiciously like "That old goat?"

I wasn't certain, because our carriage finally rolled to a stop in front of Lord Castlereagh's imposing town house and my thoughts turned elsewhere. "Sebastian," I whispered aloud, and touched my finger to the carriage glass.

Eighteen

HARE AND HOUNDS

Lord Ravencross's plan worked. A few moments later, we stood on a lavish staircase along with dozens of other guests waiting to be announced into the ballroom. I tapped my foot against the marble stair and peered up and down the procession hoping to catch a glimpse of Sebastian. He must be here. He had to be here, but where? I stretched up on my tiptoes but couldn't see over the gentlemen's shoulders, or ladies' voluminous turbans and billowy hair arrangements. In this awful crush how would I find him in time?

Tess edged close and warned us in a low voice, "Daneska will be here."

Lord Ravencross rumbled with disapproval. She laid her hand on his arm. He stared at her white glove resting on his dark sleeve.

"This is important, my lord. You must stay away from her. Whatever you do, avoid her at all costs."

He frowned and looked confused. "I have no interest in Lady Daneska."

"I am well aware of that," she said. "It's your dislike of her that worries me. It would be best if you did not cross paths tonight."

"I will not run from her," he snarled.

"You mustn't take that attitude." Tess let go of his arm and tilted her face up to him, pleading. "She already wants vengeance. We cannot risk making her angrier."

"You can't possibly think I fear her."

"I wish that you did." Tess shook her head. "You don't know what she's capable of. I do. Daneska is no fool. She won't attack *you*. Not directly." Tess pressed her lips together. "She'll go after someone you . . ." She looked away and red rushed into her cheeks. "Someone else."

His eyes widened. "She wouldn't," he whispered softly.

"I'll stay away from you. Perhaps she won't guess. . . ."

He frowned. Hard lines brought the wolf in him to the surface. "Even she would not be so bold."

"I beg to differ, my lord. You do not know her as well as I do."

He grumbled and turned away.

Tess leaned close and whispered in my ear. "You must stay away from her tonight, too. Otherwise, she will destroy everything." By the intensity in her eyes I knew she had seen Lady Daneska play a part in this nightmare. "Run if you have to. Heed my words. Run."

I nodded quickly.

"Oh, this is hopeless." Tess turned pale. "Impossible." Her shoulders sagged and I feared she would fall to the floor and under the heavy agony of knowing too much.

"It will be all right." I grabbed her hand and clasped it tight, speaking quietly but in a voice firm enough that she would draw strength from my words. "We fixed the ink. That was *impossible*. Yet, because of you, we did it. This will be easy in comparison. We will deliver it to Sebastian and leave. We can do this. Look, we are almost to the receiving line."

She shuddered. "May God help us all."

Our turn arrived to be announced. I swallowed air and felt a bit nauseous. The page shouted us in a booming voice, "The Earl of Ravencross, his cousin, Miss Georgiana Fitzwilliam, and her companion, Miss Teresa Aubreyson."

Fortunately, most of the guests in the room took little notice of us. We made our way down the receiving line where Lord Ravencross bowed elegantly and introduced us to Lord and Lady Castlereagh. Tess and I curtseyed deep. I quaked in my shoes, meeting the leader of the British House of Commons under false pretenses. Lord Ravencross rapidly distracted Lord Castlereagh with a friendliness I hadn't thought him capable of, while we pressed forward away from Lady Castlereagh's curious glances.

Lord Ravencross asked our host, "I wonder if you might help me. I'm looking for a particular friend of mine, Lord Wyatt. We served together on the continent."

Lord Castlereagh studied Lord Ravencross with greater interest. "I know the man. Fine fellow, Lord Wyatt."

"Bit of a muddle," Ravencross confided. "I agreed to meet him here earlier, but I arrived late, you see. Wouldn't know where I might find him, would you?"

I pretended to be disinterested, averting my gaze to the dazzling company swirling across the dance floor. All the while, my ears were keenly tuned to every word they said. That's when I spotted Daneska on the other side of the ballroom surrounded by admirers. She glanced pointedly in our direction.

"I've a fair notion," the foreign secretary spoke cautiously, "I saw Wyatt and several of his friends headed out the side door. If I know the gentlemen, they wanted a quiet place to smoke cigars, and perhaps drink a glass or two of brandy." He nodded toward the west wall of the ballroom. "Probably went downstairs to my study. No doubt they found the good stuff stashed in my desk."

I gazed up at the ornate ceiling. Clearly, Sebastian had rounded up his contacts for a secret meeting under the foreign secretary's roof. Ravencross thanked our host, bowed, and we took our leave of the reception line.

"I have to get to that study," I said to Tess from the side of my mouth. She nodded and drifted away to join a circle of young ladies and gentlemen, greeting them as if they were old friends. One fellow bowed over her hand and looked on the verge of asking her to dance.

Ravencross growled under his breath and marched straight for Tess and her group of acquaintances. He parted the circle and glowered at them like a towering Hessian mercenary about to whip out his saber and cut down each and every one of them.

He provided the perfect diversion I needed to find my way to the side door. Turning, I nearly collided with Miss Pinswary. Had she overheard what I said to Tess? Her eyes narrowed on me. "Miss Fitzwilliam, what a surprise to find you here."

"Miss Pinswary." I dipped in a quick curtsey. "I did not see you standing there."

Her face hardened. "Well, I noticed you. How could I not, green is a rather daring color for a young lady, don't you think?"

I glanced down at Jane's dress. The silk was beautiful, but she had a point, green is not customarily a debutante color. "I borrowed it," I murmured.

"No matter." She waved away my explanation. "Truthfully I envy you. Anything is better than this pasty white thing my mother and Daneska inflicted upon me. It's all right for Dani, isn't it, white sets off her golden skin. It turns mine to ash."

"Oh, no, you look quite lovely." I attempted to sidle away.

She squinted at me. "Where are you going? Mama will have an apoplexy when she discovers you are here." Miss Pinswary did not look troubled at the idea of her mother having a brain hemorrhage. "Her cousin has convinced her you ought to be brought up on charges of arson." She glanced around unconcerned about my criminal nature. "Where is your Miss Stranje? I didn't hear her announced."

Thankfully, at that moment Tess joined me.

Miss Pinswary forgot all her questions. She raised her chin several degrees, flipped back a lock of hair, and sniffed. "What a clever gown, Tess. Quite *French*. And here I thought Miss Stranje was supposed to be reforming all of you into respectable young ladies. See how poor Lord Ravencross pants after you like a lame wolf. Perhaps I am mistaken in the sort of lessons Miss Stranje gives."

Tess curtseyed before answering. "Comments of that sort are beneath you, Alicia. You mustn't allow your cousin to poison your better nature."

Miss Pinswary pinched up like a dried lemon.

Just as if they hadn't exchanged a single harsh word, I heard Tess ask in a solicitous tone, "Where's your little dog? Did you bring him?"

Alicia's sour countenance dissolved. "I wanted to." She sighed. "But Dani and my mother wouldn't allow it. He's no trouble in my reticule. Truly, he's not. Poor baby, he's bound to be miserable without me."

I edged back and Tess stepped in front of Alicia to prevent her from following me.

"He is an adorable little mite." Tess clucked her tongue in

genuine sympathy. "But surely you will be dancing too often to watch over him as well as you would like. If he escaped and scampered under the dancers' feet . . ."

I slipped quietly away and hurried toward the west wall of the ballroom. I was almost there when off to my right I noticed Lady Pinswary sailing through the crowd straight for me. I skittered behind a large group of matrons, but she towered over everyone and aimed her sights directly at me. I headed for the thickest clump of guests I could see. Despite three ridiculously large ostrich feathers bobbing from her coiffure, the woman bore down on me with the determination of a crazed hunter, practically shoving peers aside in her quest to run me aground. No doubt she planned to grab my ears and give me a vicious shake the minute she was within arm's length.

I dashed off, keeping as low as possible without looking absurd, and finally evaded her. I looked toward my goal, the side door, and saw Lady Daneska headed in my direction. Like a queen taking a stroll through a garden, she wove gracefully in and out of the crowd. Clever fox, she smiled and fluttered her fan at the gentlemen, when all the while she was sniffing after a hare.

Well, this rabbit planned to give her the slip. I dashed behind a cluster of people and tried to blend in. I spotted a servants' entrance in the paneling behind a bank of potted plants. Even if Lady Pinswary or Lady Daneska saw me, neither of them would dream of following me through a servants' door.

At the same moment I cracked opened the door, a trumpet blared, and the page announced, "His Majesty, Prince George, Regent of England."

As the entire company turned to observe his entrance and bow low, I whiskered through the side door and shut it tight behind me. For good measure I flipped the latch before taking off down the secondary hallway.

Breathing easier, I ignored the quizzical expression on a footman's face and, as if I knew exactly where I intended to go, hurried toward the more lighted end in search of a staircase leading downstairs.

In my rush from the hall into the west foyer, I tripped over an outstretched foot. It sent me stumbling into a side table, where I nearly toppled a Chinese vase. My reticule clanged against it and I prayed none of the ink vials had broken.

"Hey ho, cuz," said the owner of the offending foot. I recognized the bully's drawl immediately. It was one of my uncle Brucklesby's obnoxious sons.

"Good evening, Roderick," I said through clamped teeth as I righted the vase. Turning to greet my smirking cousin, I discovered, to my great displeasure, not one, but two cousins leering at me. "Freddie." I nodded, acknowledging my uncle's youngest son.

Freddie, three years my senior, liked to think he was too good to breathe the same air I did. He lifted one of the coiled ringlets hanging over my shoulder with two fingers, as if it was a loathsome caterpillar he meant to squish. He let it fall and circled me like a tomcat does before pouncing. "Can this be our own little Georgie?"

"Nah," said Roderick. "This girl is almost passable. Our Georgie is a wild-haired little urchin, too busy reading books to be caught dead in a ball gown."

I brushed the stupid ringlets back and folded my arms, trying to imitate my mother at her irate best. "Lovely to see you two, but I'm afraid I must be going. Isn't there a housefly somewhere whose wings you haven't plucked off?"

"Zounds! But the chit has grown a sharp tongue. I'm

wounded." Freddie pressed a hand over his breast in mock anguish.

"No one says *zounds* anymore, Freddie. Last century. Completely passé." I shook my head pretending a great deal more sophistication than I felt. "Now if you will kindly step aside I have business to attend to."

"What business?" Like a pair of stray dogs, they circled tighter. "Come to think of it, where's your da?" said Freddie. "Don't recall seeing him or your brothers on the guest list. But then he isn't an earl, is he?"

I shrugged. "I doubt you are privy to Lord and Lady Castlereagh's guest list."

Roderick imitated his brother's inquisition-like tone. "Uncle Henry doesn't know you're here, does he? And why are you roaming the halls? Up to something, aren't you?"

"Dangerous for a young girl to be caught alone, even in a place like this." Freddie pinched my arm.

I jerked away. "I'm not alone. I have an escort and a companion with me. I was simply making my way to the ladies retiring room. I don't need an escort for that."

"Oh, I don't know." Freddie sneered, leaning in to sniff my hair. "Never know who might be lurking—"

"Hold on." Roderick straightened, as if his head might explode. "I've had an idea."

"Huzzah," I said. "I shall notify the *Times*. Now if you will please step aside." I tried to shove past him.

"Hold up, cuz. You could be of use to me." Roderick flicked my ringlets back over my shoulder so they hung across my breasts. He grabbed both of my shoulders and studied me as if I was a bug on a pin. "She's not altogether disgusting, is she? What do you say, Freddie? I might use her to make a certain young lady jealous, eh?"

Freddie shrugged. "Might do."

"Come on, then." Roderick grabbed my arm and tugged me in the opposite direction I wished to go. "You shall stand up with me on the next set."

"No! I can't." I wrenched my arm out of his grasp, but he seized it again.

"Leave me be, Roderick. I'm not going to dance with you."

"You will." He held my arm so tight that I had no choice but to drag alongside him. "Duty to family, and all that. If you won't, I'll—"

I didn't have time for his threats. "I told you, I *can't*." I twisted out of his hold.

"She's right." Freddie shoved me against his brother. "Remember, Rod? She broke her dancing master's foot. Or was it his leg? Can't remember. But I do remember Uncle Henry had to pay off the bloke so he wouldn't put the story all about town."

I couldn't help it. My hands curled into tight fists. I wanted to pummel them both within an inch of their lives. If they weren't so much bigger than me, I would have. Nearly spitting with anger, I said, "There you have it, I'm an abominable dancer. So, let me go."

"I'm not afraid of a bruised foot." Roderick grabbed my arm again. "Come along. I need you to make Amanda Crimwall jealous."

A man behind us cleared his throat. "I'm sorry to disappoint you, gentlemen, but Miss Fitzwilliam has promised the next set to me." Without turning I knew who spoke.

Roderick let go of my arm and spun around. "Lord Wyatt." He backed away as if confronted by a great towering dragon.

Sebastian held out his arm to me and I quickly accepted his escort. The moment we were out of earshot, he hissed down at me angrily. "What the devil are you doing here? More importantly, what are you doing with those two miscreants?"

"I have the great misfortune of being related to those two miscreants, as you call them. They're my cousins. And I am here because the ink you took with you is a disaster. It develops on its own if exposed to light."

He stopped short, as if we'd run headlong into an invisible brick wall. "Are you certain?"

"Upon my life, yes! The note you wrote me, *the secret one*, I read it without applying the gall solution."

"Can't be." He shoved a shock of black hair away from his brow and started to pull away. "I've got to retrieve the ink. I just finished giving it—"

"Wait." I held on to him and pressed my reticule into his hand. "I brought you a replacement. This one works. I tested it thoroughly. Give this one to your men."

He stared at the emerald green purse in his hand. "You've already corrected the formula?" He opened the drawstrings and checked inside. "And you made more."

I shrugged off his amazement. "It was a minor adjustment."

"You're certain this one works?" He looked worried.

"Yes. I'm absolutely certain." I wanted to put his mind at ease. "I wouldn't have made the mistake last night except I was tired, and because . . ." I caught the corner of my lip, before admitting the truth. "I was distracted."

He swallowed and nodded without looking at me. "About that—"

"Don't." I shook my head. "Please, don't say anything."

"Very well." His features tightened. He set his jaw. "I've got to hurry and deliver this to my associates." He glanced down at me, stiff, apologetic. Standing close, he held the reticule in one hand and toyed with my gloved fingers with his other. Knowing

I might never be this close to him again, I savored the smell of his shaving soap and the hint of brandy on his lips. The edge of his cheek by his ears flushed scarlet. He murmured, "It grieves me to leave you so soon."

And yet, he was already backing away. *Farewell* caught in my throat. I couldn't say it. My fingers dropped away from his.

"Stay away from your cousins." He issued the stern order from the stairway, once again all business. "They're not to be trusted."

He needn't tell me. I'd suffered enough at their hands on holidays and family visits to know that my dear cousins had graduated from torturing toads to making life miserable for anyone within their purview, especially me. I nodded.

Sebastian cast me a final wistful look over his shoulder and hurried away. *Gone.* Perhaps forever. The light in the hall seemed to dim. All I felt was cold.

And alone.

And dreadfully unbearably sad.

I turned to go back to the ballroom and Lady Daneska stepped out of the shadows.

Nineteen

CUTS LIKE A KNIFE

W hat a delightful surprise to find you here, Miss Fitzwilliam." She came closer. I stood frozen to the spot. My stomach spiraled down into a bottomless pit. I remembered Tess telling me to run. But I couldn't leave, not without knowing how much Daneska had overheard of my conversation with Sebastian.

She looped her arm through mine as if we were the best of friends. "It is very odd, I think, that you should give Lord Wyatt your reticule. Is this a new custom? If so, I have not heard of it." She winked at me.

The champagne on her breath, her French perfume, the sugary starch holding her hair in place, all of it wafted hot and sweet and suffocating over my face. She watched closely as the worry devastated me. She'd overheard at least part of the exchange.

"What was in your reticule, I wonder? Love notes?"

Perhaps she had not heard everything. I took a quick gasp of air. It was then I realized I'd been holding my breath. "I beg your pardon, my lady, but I must return to the ballroom. I've been away too long. Tess will be worried."

She laughed softly, one of her airy, treacle-y, horribly perfect little trills. I tried to ease out of her grasp, but she held on and genially guided me down the hall. "I expect you are right." She nodded. "Tess is indeed excessively worried. I will take you to her straightway."

"But the ballroom"—I tried to extricate myself—"is back the other way." She entwined her arm around mine so that I could not pull free without being inexcusably rude.

"No, no." She shook her head. "The ballroom smells of smoking candles and old men's farts. We must not go back there. Besides, my aunt, she is searching for you. She thinks you snuck away from Stranje House bent on mischief. According to her . . ." Daneska lowered her voice and mimicked her blustery aunt perfectly. "Miss Fitzwilliam is a rotten apple. A deranged creature who ought to be locked away in an attic. *Forever.*"

My mouth opened, but I had nothing to say.

"Oh, yes, it was quite comical. You should have seen her, Georgiana. You don't mind if I call you that, do you? She nearly turned purple when she saw you in the ballroom. I don't blame you for slipping out. The roly-poly Prince can be so tiresome, don't you think? You did say you wanted to find Tess, did you not? She slipped out right after you." Daneska chuckled deep in her throat. "I am afraid she is upstairs on a silly goose chase. She worries I locked you in a closet. Ridiculous, no?"

This was a trick, a lie. I knew it by the too-smooth way she said it. We stood before the backstairs, and I refused to go any farther.

"Come. We will find her together. The three of us will have an amusing tête-à-tête. Much more entertaining than that stuffy ballroom, I think." Daneska, with her blond curls and large eyes, had the ability to look genuinely sincere and almost girl-ishly innocent.

I questioned whether Tess might actually be upstairs. Other-wise, she would've come and found me by now. Still, I balked.

Daneska urged me onto the first step. "What did you say was in your reticule? Oh, yes, now I remember. *Ink.*"

My stomach shrank into dark prickly despair. She had over-heard.

"Now why would a young lady carry ink in her reticule? It is most confusing." She shook her head. "I certainly do not carry ink in mine."

My rapid breathing must surely have betrayed me, but I hur-ried up beside her, my gaze flitted nervously to hers. "One never knows when one might need to write a letter," I said, falsifying a friendly nonchalant tone.

"Ah. I see." The corner of her mouth twitched. "Oh, don't look so worried, Georgiana. I already knew about your pre-cious ink."

I turned sharp at that.

She smiled, catlike, and ever so pleased with herself. "After our little conversation the other day, I was terribly curious." She tapped her chin. "What had you been brewing in your papa's stable? What could be so important that you would take so great a risk? Naturally, I sent a friend to your family estate to find out."

I practically chased her up the next few stairs, praying every-one at home had kept their mouths shut. Especially my mother. I had to know. As much as I wanted to bite the question back, I couldn't. "Surely, you didn't send someone to speak with my mother—"

"Of course not. I would never dream of asking her. Oh, but your cook, now that is a different matter. An amiable woman,

your family cook. Quite susceptible to the charms of a handsome vegetable seller."

I nearly sank to my knees. I clung to the balustrade for support.

Cook.

I'd told her all about my experiments. She'd indulged my
prattle so patiently while kneading bread or dicing carrots. She
had been my only confidante.

Daneska curled her arm around my waist and helped me
up the next few steps. "Has the intrepid Miss Stranje failed to
teach you so simple a trick? Tsk, tsk." She sounded genuinely
concerned. "My dear girl. If you want to know something, ask
the servants. They know all."

Now I understood why Miss Stranje kept so few of them.

The top of the stairs led to a hall of servants' bedrooms. I
pushed out of her grasp. Pickpocket-quick, she snagged my arm,
wrenched it behind my back, and forced me ahead.

"Let me go, Daneska." I wriggled like a mongoose trying to
get free. "If you already know about the ink, what do you want
with me?"

"You wound me, Georgiana. I merely desire the pleasure of
your charming company."

"I'm not charming." *The formula.* She didn't have the exact
ingredients. She couldn't have gotten that from Cook, at least
not all of it.

I marveled at how Daneska could make her voice sound so
pleasant. "I thought you might like to exchange recipes. That is
what friends do. You share yours with me, and I will share with
you the ingredients of a lovely Romanian apple cake."

Always mocking.

I shook my head, and tried to copy her glib tone. "I'm afraid
my recipes are a bit too complex to explain to the likes of you."

She forced me to turn, nearly twisting my shoulder out of the socket. Face-to-face, her pale eyes darkened, and she hissed, "Don't pretend to be superior to *me*, Georgiana Fitzwilliam. You are *nothing*. Long before you came, I was one of them, you know, one of Miss Stranje's clever castoffs." She yanked my arm. Hard.

"No. You *chose* to come to Stranje House." I gritted my teeth, refusing to let her see how she hurt me. I don't know why I said that, nor why her choosing to come to Stranje House was an important distinction. But it was. She was not one of us. Daneska had never been cast off. She didn't know what it was like. And then I realized . . . "Miss Stranje didn't choose you."

Her expression tightened. Rage whipped across her features and blew away as if by a cold wind. In that instant, I knew Daneska was capable of murder. She pinned me to her side and marched us forward.

"Why?" I ventured. "Why did you want to be at Stranje House?"

"I was bored."

"That's all. You were bored?"

"*Naturellement.* Have you met my aunt? I needed *something* to pass the time. I thought it would be entertaining to study Miss Stranje's clever tricks."

"You knew what the school was before you came?"

She jerked my arm. "You ask too many questions."

"So I've been told." I stomped on her foot.

She winced and doubled over but instead of letting go, she tightened her hold. "Come along, Georgiana, don't be difficult. Poor Tess is up here all alone. If you want to help her you must come with me."

"She wouldn't have come alone. Lord Ravencross would not—"

"He's not Ravencross," she snarled. "Don't call him that."

She shook with sudden rage. Even through gloves, her claws dug into my skin.

"What should I call him?"

"*Nothing*. Less than nothing. A dog." She took a calming breath and reverted to the icy smooth voice she preferred. "Do you really think he would go alone with a young lady into the servants' bedrooms?" She grunted at my naiveté. "He may be a cur, but even he would not compromise Tess like that."

"Perhaps not. But he will come looking for her if she doesn't return soon. Just as Lord Wyatt will look for me."

"Oh, my dear girl, I'm counting on it. Although, for the moment, Lord Wyatt is too busy. He's off playing his annoying little games with everyone's lives."

She twisted my arm until I feared it would break, and stuck something sharp into my side. "This is what *I* keep in *my* reticule." She whispered next to my ear. "A dagger is much more useful than ink, no?"

Yes. Infinitely more useful. I gulped back terror, anger, and wished to heaven I had a knife of my own at that very moment—a big sharp one.

"Such an elegant little blade." She twisted it, taking a moment to admire the wretched thing. "It would be a pity to soil it with your blood. Now, be a love, and open the door."

I yelped, as the point bit through the skin on my ribs.

"Quiet." She pressed the blade deeper.

"I thought you didn't want to soil your knife," I said, and gritted my teeth together to keep from crying out as I turned the knob. The door swung open. A small oil lamp flickered atop a bureau. I knew instantly Tess *had* been there. But she was gone. An empty chair sat in the middle of the small room, cords coiled loosely around the base. A still-knotted gag lay on the seat.

"Tess?" Daneska barely uttered aloud. Her panicked gaze flitted to the corners of the room.

Her hold on me weakened. I jabbed my elbow into her ribs and sprang sideways, lunging for a pitcher on the washstand. Something. *Anything*, I could use to bash her over the head.

She grabbed my hair. My head snapped back. Next thing I knew her knife was at my neck.

"I should slit your throat for that. A pity I need you alive." Her fingers pressed hard against the soft place right below my ear. Her paralyzing grip made me dizzy, unable to speak or move.

If she wanted me alive, she needed to stop squeezing my neck. The room turned into a mass of bright swirling spots with an ever-expanding dark center.

"Sweet dreams, Miss Fitzwilliam."

Blackness.

I have no idea how much time passed before she slapped my cheek, rousing me. Daneska's face swam before my eyes. "Wake up, sleepyhead. This is no time for napping. We are about to have visitors."

I struggled to find my way out of the murky depths of unconsciousness, but I couldn't move. She'd tied me into Tess's chair, and bound my hands securely behind me. In its stupor, my mind wandered backward to one of Jane's cryptic remarks, "One never knows when one might need to escape from being bound to a chair." Oh, how I wished I'd had a few of Miss Stranje's peculiar lessons.

The ropes chafed my wrists as I tried to wriggle free. Through my grogginess, I heard someone in the hall demand, "Where is she?"

There was a scuffle. A few moments later two men came in,

wrestling a third man between them. Daneska shut the door and held up a lantern.

I inhaled sharply. "Sebastian!"

"Tut, tut, Georgiana, that's Lord Wyatt to you." She flaunted her knife the way another woman might waggle her fan at a beau.

Sebastian stopped struggling. His gaze flew to her and landed on me. Although he now had a wad of cloth tied in his mouth, gagging him, nothing could silence the panic that suddenly screamed through his eyes.

"Over there," Daneska ordered. "I don't want him near the door."

Two large footmen dragged him past my chair and held him against the wall by the window. Surely they couldn't be Lord Castlereagh's servants. Too burly. They looked more like sailors or dockworkers disguised as servants so they might slip into the ball unnoticed. They were hired thugs, not gentlemen. They couldn't possibly be knights of the Order of the Iron Crown. Napoleon would have granted that title only to gentlemen of means and members of the aristocracy.

When Sebastian tried to say something to me, one of the brutes punched him in the gut. I shrieked, but Daneska clapped her hand over my mouth and pressed the point of her knife against my throat. I felt the sting as the point pierced skin beneath my chin.

"Be a good girl, and do as you're told. A proper young lady does not scream." She said this with a lilt in her voice as if it pleased her enormously to be teaching me manners. She withdrew her knife. "There. That's better. Now we can all be friends."

Not in a hundred years. I glared at her.

"I'll wager you can guess what I want? You see, by the time

we found him, Lord Wyatt had already doled out your lovely ink." She shook her head. "Well, except for two last vials. He smashed those. Most uncooperative, don't you think? But then our Sebastian is a very naughty boy. Aren't you, my darling?" She drew her finger along the bottom of his jaw. "I daresay your valet will be most annoyed, that ink is bound to leave a nasty stain on your coat pocket."

His neck cloth had been lost in the scuffle. Daneska pouted and trailed her fingers intimately down his neck. "Poor Sebastian. It is too bad you are so . . . how do you say, *krótkowzroczna?* Shortsighted. Our Emperor Napoleon will soon be free and all of Europe will unite under the Iron Crown. What a pity you have chosen to fight against us." She slid her fingers into his shirt where it hung open and torn. "Perhaps I can change your mind."

It clawed at my skin the way she flirted with him in the middle of abusing us. I must've huffed at her impertinence. She snapped her attention to me like a dog on a scent.

"You're jealous." She grinned.

I tried to wriggle free. When that wouldn't work I inched the chair forward hoping the leg would pinch her toes.

"Oh, *poor thing.* Did he talk sweet to you? Of course, he did. But you are too clever for that old trick. You knew he only wanted the ink. You didn't actually believe his sentimental rubbish, did you? Oh . . ." She tittered.

God forgive me, I hated her. I may have growled. Some noise came from my throat.

She laughed again. "But I can see you did. How deliciously gullible you are."

Even though she still stood next to Sebastian, it felt as if she was strangling me. Her hand wandered brazenly inside his shirt. I wanted more than anything to slam my fist into her revoltingly beautiful face.

"I know Lord Wyatt quite well," she purred. "He has a rather, er, how do you say . . . *vigorous* reputation with the young ladies. Surely, you didn't think a little red-headed peahen like yourself would snare such a prize?"

My heart slammed into my stomach. I thought I would be sick. It wasn't true. It *couldn't* be true. I looked at Sebastian. Pleading with my very soul for the truth. It shouldn't matter. Not now, when we were both probably going to die. And yet, it did. I desperately needed to know if he'd only been using me.

I cannot explain how, but where words might have failed to reassure me, Sebastian conveyed the truth in a single expression of his eyes. He told me more in that one wordless moment than he could have using a thousand words.

With cold clear certainty, I said, "You're a liar."

"*C'est la vie.*" She acted as if it didn't matter, but her eyes darkened and her lips pressed tight. She closed her fist around his shirt and ripped it open. Buttons clattered across the floor. Fast as a snake strikes, she slashed her blade across his chest.

I shrieked as an arc of dark red blood bloomed on his chest and ran in rivulets down his belly.

Daneska clamped her hand over my mouth. "The wound, it is not so very deep. Not yet." She sizzled poison in my ear. "You caused this small problem, yes? The Order, also, has a small problem. Coincidently, your fault, too. So unless you want small problems to become big problems . . ." She wiped the bloody knife across my bodice, taking care to make certain some of his blood smeared onto my breasts. "You will tell me your formula."

There was a low rumble from Sebastian. He shook his head warning me not to say anything. Daneska nodded, and her servant slammed Sebastian's head against the wall.

"You must not listen to him, Georgiana. He is a man. Men are always so impractical. It is the women of the world who must live with the mess men make of it, no? This is between you and me." She used the knife to indicate the two of us.

Ruthless witch. Your blade still drips with Sebastian's blood.

"We are pragmatists you and I. You are a scientist. Very practical. Me, I am practical, too. I want what is good for Europe. Peace and stability. The Order of the Iron Crown will unite the continent and stop all this pointless bloodshed. Your English King, he cannot promise peace or stability. Poor mad King George, he cannot even keep his own mind right side up."

I had no answer for that. It was the sad truth.

"Ah. See. You know I am right." She grinned and tapped my shoulder with her knife. "His foolish son, Humpty Dumpty Prince George, is no better. Your parliament, they made this fat buffoon Prince Regent of England. The fool. Your ruler gambles and chases skirts while his government makes war all over the world—America, India, Africa. You must ask yourself, what do these men want?"

I did my best to look confused. As long as she talked she wasn't hurting Sebastian.

"I will tell you what they want—the greedy swine. More and more for England." She spit air through her lips.

I seethed, struggling to keep a mask of feigned interest. My brother had died fighting to free the continent from the very tyrant she worshipped. I knew the truth. She cared nothing about the welfare of anyone except herself. Daneska wanted *more and more* for Daneska.

She narrowed her gaze, scrutinizing me. "Your eyes—little mouse—they tell all. You are the skeptic." She aimed the dagger over her shoulder. "It's him, isn't it? The charming diplomat has convinced you. Foreign service. Ha! A joke. *La grande farce.* Sebastian is England's pawn. Always sneaking around sticking his nose in where it does not belong. Always making trouble."

She screwed the blade through the air, twisting the point toward me. "The Order needs to know what mischief he and his pesky friends are playing at so we can keep it in check. You understand, yes?"

I nodded, frantic to keep her talking. I could practically taste how bitterly she hated him. Any second she might turn her venomous blade on him again.

She frowned and stood back. "This was a simple matter until now. Their codes were easy enough to decipher. But now, my dear"—she lifted one of my curls over my shoulder and arranged it against my décolletage—"now you have invented an undetectable ink."

My fault. I upset the apple cart. Jane was right. I was dangerous. I ought to have stayed in the corner doing needlepoint.

As if she could read my mind Daneska said, "How very remarkable you are." She smoothed her fingers along the skin of my neck and shoulder.

Sebastian groaned. I saw by his expression how desperately he hoped I would not give away the secret. Or was he afraid for me? Perhaps both.

Daneska whirled back to him and dug the point of her knife under his chin. "So, you see, the Iron Crown wants your little ink and I'll have it one way or another." Blood ran down her blade.

"Stop!" I blurted. "He can't tell you anything. He doesn't know the formula. I had to change it before I came. That's why I'm here. The one he helped me with is useless."

Sebastian's shoulders sagged and he closed his eyes. I'd said the wrong thing. But I couldn't let them hurt him anymore.

"I knew that much by your conversation in the hallway. Now, if you would be so good, I need the recipe." She shoved the dagger deeper and blood spurted onto her gown. She grimaced.

"That is going to stain," she murmured, but then focused on me. "Now, you were saying . . ."

"I'll tell you."

Sebastian struggled with his captors and shook his head. Daneska forcefully rammed her elbow back into his abdomen. She didn't even turn around or blink. He bent forward with a groan, but she continued to smile pleasantly at me. "Do get on with it. Then we can all go home from this wretched smelly little room and be happy."

He warned me off with his eyes.

She gestured to the big one. He struck Sebastian in the face and blood spurted out of his nose. "No more," I begged. "I said I would help you. Why are you hitting him?"

"Because, my friend, you are not talking fast enough." She whirled behind me and grabbed my hair, twisting it around her palm, coiling it so tight I thought it might rip from my scalp.

Her ruffian slugged Sebastian again and split open his cheek. We were so close I could almost feel his skin tear. I whimpered.

"Hurts, doesn't it? Watching someone you care about suffer. You can make it all stop."

"I don't have the exact measurements. I'd need my notes."

The other man slugged Sebastian in the ribs. He crumpled against the wall. She yanked my hair, cranking my neck back so far, that I looked at her upside down. "Georgiana, you are trying my patience. Your cook assured my man that you were the smartest little thing she'd ever laid eyes on, and that you had a memory longer than the King's Road. That is a direct quote. Quite in awe of you, your cook was. So, you see, you must do better than to say you can't remember." She let go.

Sebastian slumped to the floor with the next blow. Why did he not moan? Why? Was it so I wouldn't tell them? Did he think I couldn't see how much it hurt? He should not have been so brave. His courage made me love him more, made me feel each blow all the more keenly.

"Pulverized gall," I said, loud enough to make them stop.

Sebastian shook his head and struggled to sit up. He tried to shout at me through his gag. But I couldn't let them hurt him anymore. "And alum."

She crossed her arms. "You must not lie to me, Georgiana."

"Don't you need a pen and paper to write this down?" I asked.

She inspected the tip of her dagger. "My little dumpling, you are not the only one with a good memory."

"I see." With a sigh, I continued. "Two parts copperas."

"Copperas? What is that?"

I groaned because it was such a good question. Why couldn't she be stupid? It might've taken the Order of the Iron Crown years to figure out the meaning of that one component.

Just then, the latch broke and the door burst open. Lord Ravencross flew into the room. Tess rushed in right behind him.

Daneska signaled the biggest footman. He yanked Sebastian to his feet and dragged him to the window. I shouted for Tess, but it was too late. Daneska's henchman heaved Sebastian over the sill and shoved him out of the third-story window.

I screamed.

Tess kicked the footman between his legs and the oaf doubled over and swung wildly for her. She brought both fists down on top of his neck and he collapsed. She grabbed him by the hair and slammed his face into the floorboards.

Daneska hung on to the curtain and leaned out the window. No doubt she derived some grizzly pleasure from making certain she'd killed Sebastian. I roared with anger, but stopped mid roar. Daneska jumped.

Impossible. I struggled to scoot my chair closer.

"Hold still," Tess ordered. "I'm trying to untie you."

As soon as my ropes were off, I rushed to the window. A hay cart rolled through the narrow alley below bearing the prone body of Sebastian. Daneska sat beside him on the hay. That sneaky cheat! She'd *known* the cart was there. She'd planned this mode of escape the whole time.

I yelled to her. "Let him go!"

"Come and get him," she jeered as the dray turned out of the alley. I could've sworn she gave me a flippant farewell wave, but the moonlight was weak, and I could not escape the last image I'd had of Sebastian's face, battered, bleeding, and desperate.

"We have to go after them."

I whirled around just in time to see Lord Ravencross plow a conclusive fist into the remaining blackguard. Tess had her knee pressed into the back of the blighter on the floor, and was using my ropes to bind his feet and wrists.

"Hurry! Daneska's taking him away." I dashed past the broken door into the hallway. "We must go now!"

I couldn't wait for them to secure Daneska's men. Sebastian was wounded and probably dying. I raced down the back stairs. There had to be a servants' door to the alley. I startled a maid on the first floor. She averted her eyes, as do maids in all great houses. I grabbed her shoulders and made her face me. "Which way to the alley on this side of the house?"

She trembled with fear, and who could blame her. The blood smeared across my bodice made me look like a murderous mad-woman.

"Speak up, girl!" I gave her a shake.

She pointed to a side corridor. I darted down it and nearly ran face-first into a footman. I backed away, knowing that Daneska might have more spies in the household.

"May I help you, miss?" He looked down his nose, assessing

the disarray of my hair, my bloodied gown, and God knows what else that was horribly out of place.

I decided to take a chance. "Yes! Take a message to Lord Castlereagh. It is of the utmost importance that you give it to him and no one else." He looked at me with far too much haughtiness to be an imposter. "Tell him Lord Wyatt has been wounded and captured by Lady Daneska. You must beg him to notify Captain Grey immediately. She is escaping in a hay cart. I am in pursuit. Can you remember all of that?"

He frowned even more than before.

"Answer me! This is a matter of life and death. Do you understand?"

"Yes, miss." He let go of the indignant air he'd been holding. "This is quite out of the ordinary, but I will carry your message to his lordship." He said something more, I believe it was something about not going out into the night without a chaperone, but I had already run down the passage and burst out of the side door.

I dashed to the corner, turned right and ran across the cobblestones in the direction I'd seen Daneska go. I thought I spotted the cart in the distance. But it was dark and the ruddy London mist made everything look like ghostly drays bearing traitors and wounded spies. The paving stones were hard and sharp beneath my kid slippers and I had no idea where I was going, but I kept running, knowing only that I must find that wagon.

Twenty

YOU WILL NEED ME

I was stumbling and panting for air when Tess caught up with me. Her expression looked grim. That meant I'd failed. The nightmare was still in place. I wanted to scream in anguish. It was grotesquely unfair. *Cruel.* How could so much rest on one failure? One mistake? And dear God in heaven, why must it be *my* mistake?

My stride faltered. I wanted to collapse right there on the street, wanted to crumble into tears of regret, wanted to scream at the perverseness of the universe. But I couldn't. My lungs burned like the fires of hell and my heart felt heavier than a fieldstone, but I knew if I gave up now Sebastian would die. That lone thought drove me forward. The whole continent might sink into ruin because of me, but the truth is I thumped each bruised foot, one after the other, because of Sebastian. Call me selfish, I could not bear the thought of living in this muddled world without him in it. He would surrender his own life to save all those thousands of strangers. I could do no less, to save him.

While a single grain of hope remained, I would not give up. The fact that Tess ran alongside me meant there was still a chance. She scooped my arm and tried to tug me faster, but my short legs were no match for hers.

I pointed ahead, into the darkness. "They turned up there," I gasped. "You're faster. Go!"

She took off and I pressed forward. The sound of hooves clanking against the cobblestones alarmed me. I glanced over my shoulder and a horseman bore down on me. I ran even harder to escape.

"Miss Fitzwilliam!" I knew that voice and slowed my steps. Captain Grey galloped up beside me. His mount shied at the sudden stop but he held out his hand to pull me up behind him. "Which way?" he shouted.

Ravencross and two other men reined in beside us.

"There," I wheezed, and pointed. Ravencross took off after Tess.

But I'd been so far behind, and the night so dark, I couldn't be certain where they'd turned off. "That one. I think." The hesitancy in my voice was unmistakable. Captain Grey barked orders for his men to scour each of the side roads.

The captain and I rode straight to the street I'd indicated. We no sooner turned than my hopes crashed against the bricks beneath us. There were a dozen side streets and alleys. "They could've gone anywhere," I groaned. "We've lost them."

The moon skated out from behind the clouds for a moment, and I thought I glimpsed the back edge of the cart turning down a side street at the far end. "Down there!" He followed my shaking finger and we raced down the street and took the turn, but they were nowhere in sight.

"Of course!" the captain exclaimed. "Hold steady, Miss Fitzwilliam. I know where they're headed."

I gripped the sides of his coat and we took off at a gallop. The smell of the Thames was unmistakable. It reeked of sewage and rotting garbage, and we raced straight into the salty stench.

The banks of the Thames were chaotic; every inch crammed with ships and boats. We had to slow our pace to pick our way around fishing traps, piles of refuse, and broken oars. Even at that late hour, men were in our way, loading crates, hauling racks of fish ashore, and repairing hulls. Torches mounted on docks and a fire heating a drum of smoking pitch obscured our view. I strained to see past the smoke and flickering flames, into the darkness beyond.

"We'll never find her."

He urged his horse onto a quay. "Watch for movement on the water. My men reported a suspicious-looking sloop moored near here. She won't be in full sail."

"There!" I pointed at a ship moving quietly across the water.

"Right." He headed straight down the nearest dock, but the clutter slowed his horse. He swung me down and I ran to the edge of the pier.

"Daneska!" I shouted.

Like Queen of an armada, she stood tall in the port stern, surveying the shore. I wanted to jump in and swim after them, but that would accomplish nothing except my capture or more likely my drowning. Even if I managed to climb aboard, I'd be no match against her four burly oarsmen. "Come ashore!" I yelled. "I'll trade the formula for Sebastian."

"Meet me in Calais." And just like that, she waved farewell.

"No! Wait!" I shouted so loud all of London surely heard. "Come back!"

Her wicked laugh rippled across the black water.

Captain Grey tied off his horse and ran up beside me. I clutched his sleeve. "Do something!" In a mad flash, I remembered the day my father's favorite dog had turned rabid. He shot the bitch rather than let her destroy the rest of his pack. It had to be done. "Shoot her!" I couldn't stop myself from yanking on his coat. "You must shoot her!"

Grim-faced he clasped my shoulders. "Would you have me sign his death warrant?"

I blinked, not understanding.

"How long do you think that hired crew would keep him aboard if she were dead? As soon as they hit open water they'd toss him overboard for fish bait."

He was right. The men at the oars looked like pirates at best. Daneska's ship sailed silently into the black mists of the Thames. My voice cracked with anguish. "But we must do something."

"I'm going after them." He let go of my shoulders. "To Calais."

I shook my head. "But it's a trap."

"Undoubtedly." His torment mirrored my own as he watched her ship fade from sight. I knew then how like a son Sebastian was to him.

"I'm going with you."

"Impossible."

I didn't explain that it was all my fault, that I needed to right my wrongs, or even that I loved his almost son. It would have fallen on deaf ears. Instead, I stated the facts. "You need a counter trap. I have something she wants. I will be your bait."

He said nothing for a moment. Lines of misery deepened on his face. "She wants the ink, yes, but surely you realize she intends to extract much more from him."

I hadn't thought of that. The truth of it set my insides to bubbling; a caustic mix of terror and anger like the vat of stinking tar boiling on shore. "All the more reason to bring me with you."

He squared his shoulders and with a hard sigh said, "Miss Stranje will have my head."

"She is practical. She'll understand I'm the only coin you have to barter with."

He said nothing, but I knew he'd relented. He walked back to his horse just as his two men rode up and hailed him. Captain Grey issued quick hushed orders. I overheard him say something about Miss Stranje. One of them took off with all three horses and the other strode with us down the banks of the Thames. We hurried along the shore, around broken lobster traps, stepped over mooring lines, passed beached fishing gigs, until we came to a good-size dock where we boarded a sleek cutter.

He roused the crew from where they slept under tarpaulins. "Cast off," he ordered.

To his companion he said, "Our best hope is to catch them before they leave the river."

They untied the ship from the pilings and two sailors set to the oars, while another worked on unrolling the sail. We'd maneuvered to the end of the pier and had just caught the flow of the river when I heard Tess shout my name.

She rode on horseback behind Lord Ravencross. At our dock she slid down and ran. She hitched up her skirt and ran even faster. Alarmingly fast. I was afraid she would surely fly straight off the dock and land in the swirling water of the Thames. Lord Ravencross pursued her on horseback, but his mount balked at the change from the sandy bank to the shifting boards of the dock.

Tess leaped off the end of the pier.

I screamed, certain she'd splash into the fast-moving river and drown. Instead, her hands slapped over the side of the ship. I lunged and grabbed hold of her forearms. My mouth gaped open as I tried to pull her up.

"You're going to need me," she rasped, just as if she wasn't dangling over the side of a ship moving at a rapid clip down the Thames.

"Good God!" Captain Grey reached over the gunwale and hoisted her higher.

"Permission to board, sir," she said, only slightly out of breath.

"Do I have a choice?" He heaved her onto the deck and shook his head.

I glanced back to where she'd jumped from. We were now seven or eight meters from the end of the dock. Lord Ravencross sat astride his horse looking as stunned as I felt.

"By all the stars, Miss Aubreyson!" Captain Grey stared at Tess, aghast, and shook his head some more. Finally, he jerked off his hat and raked a hand through his hair. "I've never witnessed a leap that daring. Or foolhardy. Certainly not from a girl. All you need is a cutlass between your teeth, young lady, and you'll have a splendid career as a pirate." He slapped his hat on and went back to hoisting of the sails.

Tess watched him go, and then fussed with her ball gown, smoothing down the soiled fabric of her skirt. "Drat. My best gown." She scrubbed at a smudge of dirt. "I might be able to get that out with a little lemon juice."

I don't know what it was, relief that she hadn't drowned, or amazement, but I felt a sudden overpowering urge to hug her. So I did. To my surprise, she hugged me back. When I finally gathered my wits and let go, she shrugged as if her extraordinary boarding method was nothing at all.

Feeling awkward, I said, "We're going to Calais."

Calais. France. A foreign country. And I'd never been away from home on my own before Stranje House. I knew, without a doubt, Tess was right. I *would* need her.

She nodded.

"Have you foreseen this? In a dream, I mean?"

She shook her head.

"Then why did you jump?" Just thinking of that feat made

both of us glance back at the dock. We could no longer see Lord Ravencross. He and the pier were lost in the darkness and jumble of boats and ships along the bank.

"He'll be angry with me."

I suspected Lord Ravencross was more astonished than angry. From what I'd seen he'd looked shocked and bewildered, and then I thought I'd seen a glimmer of admiration. I couldn't be sure, it had all happened so fast and the river had carried us away so quickly.

"But you said you knew I would need your help."

Her mouth crooked to the side. "Doesn't take a dream to know that much."

Captain Grey brought us two woolen blankets. "It's five hours to Calais. You'd best get some sleep."

"But if we should catch up to them—"

"You'll know," he said curtly, and turned to leave. Then he hesitated and added in a gentler tone, "It's unlikely. Unless we spot them soon, we've no way of knowing what route they'll take."

"Why Calais?" I asked, knowing he was in no mood to answer questions, but if I was to plan, I needed to know.

"Since the war ended, it has become the busiest port in the world. Troops from many nations are there awaiting transport home. It is easy to slip in and out unseen. The city is rife with allegiances to both Royalists and Napoleon. The Iron Crown has a stronghold. A house. Heavily guarded." His shoulders slumped. "That is where she will take him."

He looked so disheartened I withheld the rest of my questions.

Tess and I found a perch atop some boxes away from the slosh and spray and settled in. But for me, sleep was out of the question. I had five hours in which to plan. Five short hours to work out a strategy to right my wrongs. Five hours to regret that I hadn't learned more at Stranje House. If we ever returned, I would rectify that. Top of my list of things to learn was how to swim properly. Oh, and how to escape from being tied to a chair. So many things I could've learned. I shook off those regrets. They wouldn't help me now. For the nonce, I needed to devise a plan.

"Do you know anything about their stronghold?" I whispered.

Tess shook her head.

We fell silent for a long time. The gentle wafting of the river changed hands for the harder slaps of ocean waves against the hull.

"I wish Jane were along," she murmured. "No one can pick a lock as well as Jane."

"That would be handy."

"And Sera," she added. "Sera would be able to take one look at the building and know exactly where they were holding him and what our best approach would be."

"We might try using her techniques."

"I'm no good at it." Tess fidgeted, trying to get comfortable. "I'm always too busy thinking of what might be. I miss nine-tenths of what she sees."

"I might give it a go."

"Phfft. I doubt it." She pulled the blanket up and tried to tuck in. "You're always too busy drumming up your next question."

She rested her head against my knobby shoulder using me for a makeshift pillow. "If Maya were here we could sleep. She would sing to us, or say something comforting."

I didn't say anything. I simply rubbed her hand. Warming it in mine, knowing even Maya's mystical murmurs wouldn't have put me to sleep that night.

I had planning to do.

Twenty-one

STRANGERS IN A STRANGE LAND

I fell asleep! How could I have slept when there was so much to do? So much to figure out? Only the sad fact of the matter was I had absolutely no idea what we were up against, and my strategizing had proved futile and turned into dozing. I woke in a cold damp panic, to the sound of gulls circling above us, screeching my guilt into the gray light of predawn.

We stretched our stiff muscles and hurried to the bow to watch as Calais unfolded before us, a vast maze of canals and waterways with piers, docks too numerous to count, and ships creating a forest of masts. Two forts were visible in the distance, and a giant citadel loomed in the forefront, gray-walled and mysterious. The city itself looked smaller than I'd imagined, a mere village compared to London.

Small, yes, but Calais was crowded and bustling even at that dusky hour of the morning especially near the port. Soldiers in all sorts of uniforms, vendors hawking their wares, and sleepy-eyed vagabonds huddled in corners. We trudged into the city, a pitiful spectacle. Tess and I were probably taken for doxies, if anyone took the time to wonder about the two bedraggled females straggling along behind Captain Grey and his companion. Thank goodness, he hired the first hackney coach he came upon.

The inner part of the city looked surprisingly British. Small wonder considering it had been occupied by Britain for several centuries. We soon ventured into another section of town that looked Spanish in nature, tiled roofs and crisp stucco walls. Captain Grey signaled the coachman to stop. His man climbed out and took an inordinately long time purchasing a newspaper from a lad on the corner. He even perused a few pages.

I guessed we must be near the Iron Crown's stronghold. It had to be the imposing Spanish villa across the way. High walls, and the only way in or out looked to be through the front gate. I glimpsed a courtyard in the center, so I leaned out of the window to have a better view.

Captain Grey immediately tugged me back into my seat. "For pity's sake, Miss Fitzwilliam. Do not tip our hand this early." He heaved a sigh. "We've precious little on our side of the slate as it is."

Another blunder. My stomach was empty but I suddenly felt more nauseous than I had even on the voyage.

When his man, Mr. Digby, as I was later to learn, climbed back in the carriage Captain Grey gave him a questioning look. Digby shook his head. "They've doubled the watch."

Captain sighed. "That means she's already inside. They've increased the guard in anticipation of our arrival."

I leaned forward. "Couldn't we gather some of these British troops and storm in?"

Mr. Digby answered for Captain Grey. "No. We are on French soil, and that house belongs to a Romanian dignitary. The consul is in residence. Any military aggression would be considered an act of war. At the very least, it would create an international incident."

I was perfectly willing to create an international incident. But clearly, they were not.

Captain Grey took one last look at the stronghold. "We may as well find lodgings."

Digby grunted. "The British consulate will be full."

"The Blue Lion is closer, and far more private." Captain Grey opened the trap and gave our coachman directions in flawless French.

As we left, I carefully studied the street. A lighthouse stood at the north end, but to the south we passed an impressive church tower. I guessed it must be a monastery or a convent, although it looked more like a lookout turret with a cross on top. Both were tall enough to overlook the courtyard and if we had a spyglass . . .

"Do you think we might climb to the top of the lighthouse?" I asked.

They all looked at me as if I was daft.

"To have a better look at the stronghold. Unless you think the nuns would let us into the church on this other end."

As if it summed up my choices Captain Grey said, "You're not Catholic."

"I might be," I said. "If they'll let me into their turret."

"We will find quarters first. Then we will decide, Miss Fitzwilliam, whether you are having a crisis of faith or breaking into a lighthouse manned by the French army." He did not smile.

The proprietor of the Blue Lion knew Captain Grey and quietly ushered us to a private parlor reserved for distinguished guests.

They spoke to us in hushed English and I had the sense that this was a place frequented by British "diplomats," as Sebastian liked to call himself. As soon as a serving girl brought us some sausage, cheese, and bread, Captain Grey closed the door and unfolded a map of the city.

Digby pointed to the Iron Crown stronghold. "There might be a side door here, between the buildings. Or in the back."

"If so, they'll be watching it. I'm beginning to see the merit of Miss Fitzwilliam's idea."

Just then, we heard a tap on the door. We all looked at one another in surprise. It couldn't be Daneska; she wouldn't be so bold. Captain Grey pulled it open and Miss Stranje walked in. Directly behind her trailed Jane, Sera, and Maya.

"Emma!" he murmured in astonishment.

"Good afternoon, Captain Grey." She curtseyed just as if they were meeting in a parlor over tea. "Our crossing was a bit choppy, but we made it in fine time."

He made a quick bow and scooted out a chair for her.

"Thank you. Now, if you will please catch me up. What do we know?" Miss Stranje took off her traveling bonnet and leaned over the map.

Captain Grey hesitated, cleared his throat, and jabbed his finger at the map. "We are here. He is being held there."

Tess and I stood very still. I may even have backed away slightly.

"Oh, for pity's sake." Miss Stranje slapped one hand down on the table. "Don't all of you look so surprised to see me." And with one sweeping glare, she took in all of us. "What did you think I would do when I arrived home and found the two of you missing?" Her scolding gaze flew around the room and landed on the captain. "By the time your man brought me word, I had already repacked the carriage and was about to depart for London."

"But how . . . ?" I asked before thinking. Then I noticed Tess frowning at Sera.

"No," Miss Stranje warned her. "Don't blame Sera. She didn't spill a word. Very stoic. You have Lady Jane's practical nature to thank for my arrival."

Jane shrugged off Tess's glower. "Given the situation it seemed the sensible thing to do."

Maya looked altogether different garbed in English clothes instead of her sari, but her voice was as soothing as ever. "Lady Jane is right. We could not allow our Miss Stranje to worry."

Our headmistress planted both fists on her hips. "Did you really think I wouldn't race to your sides the minute I heard?"

Tess sniffed, still miffed at being caught acting on her own.

Jane stood her ground. "You can be cross if you want. Considering what's happened, it's fortunate I told her straightaway."

"Yes." Miss Stranje rubbed her arm, her brow furrowed. "Things have gone from bad to worse."

She frowned at me. Not with her normal *all-seeing* hawk eyes, no, with the eyes of a *shred-you-to-pieces* eagle. "I warned you to proceed cautiously, to think things through. This is what comes of acting in haste."

I cringed. Miss Stranje had no need for a rack. Her words tortured me more than enough.

Seeing my distress, she clamped her jaw shut for a moment. Except she wasn't done with me yet. She gave it one more turn of the crank. "I told you—nay, I pleaded with you, not to engage his affections. This is what comes of it. He ran to your aid without thinking. You made him vulnerable." She fired this accusation straight at me. In front of everyone.

I wanted to crawl under the floorboards, but all I could do was back farther away.

"Em," Captain Grey said under his breath. "He acted of his own accord."

"I suppose." She took a cooling breath and waved away my sins. "Whatever the case, what's done is done. Lord Wyatt must be extracted at all costs. How long has Lady Daneska had him?"

Captain Grey had no need to consult his watch. "Seven hours." He walked to the window, his shoulders drooping. "They've doubled their guard and posted men across the street watching the gate."

She nodded and bowed her head in thought for a moment. "There is still hope." She rose and rested her hand on his shoulder and murmured, "He's strong, Ethan. Well-trained. It will be days before he breaks. We will find a way to get him out."

Days before he breaks. What must he be going through? My stomach lurched. It felt as if we were back on the ship and it had just dropped over the crest of a wave. I had to sit in the nearest chair or fall down. Captain Grey said nothing.

Miss Stranje paced back to the table and drew her finger along the path from the royal docks to the Iron Cross stronghold. "You do realize Louis the Eighteenth will be here tomorrow to reclaim his throne?"

"Tomorrow!" Captain Grey spun around and stiffened, wary and suddenly very alert. "So soon."

She tapped her finger over the docks. "Not for him. It's been twenty-three years since the Bourbons fled France in fear of their lives."

"I know what you're thinking." Captain Grey paced. "There were threats against the Vienna Congress because they recognized his right, but we've heard nothing about a plot directly against him."

"Still." She pressed down the edges of the map, straightening the wrinkles, smoothing the corners. "I cannot think it is a coincidence."

Digby rubbed the stubble on his chin. "She has a point, sir. The Iron Crown must be chafing to see anyone but Napoleon on the throne. Not only that, Louis placated the army by agreeing to a constitutional monarchy, but ask any Frenchman on the street. Most believe the charter is worthless, that the king will go back on his word."

"Jeopardy from both quarters." Miss Stranje met the captain's worried gaze. "If Louis the Eighteenth takes his rightful place on the throne, Napoleon will have little hope of ever returning. You know what that means."

"He doesn't have any hope now! He can't." Jane marched to the map and plunked her hands atop it, as if she could find an answer in the lines and shading. "He's in exile. Banished. He lost. It's over."

"Jane," Miss Stranje said with a soft scold. "The man crowned himself Emperor. I'm afraid his lust for power is boundless, as is that of the Iron Crown."

"God help us. You're right." Captain Grey paled and turned to Digby. "How many men do we have left here in Calais?"

"Precious few, sir. Most are in Vienna. Or watching the ports in London."

"You have us." Miss Stranje stood her tallest and regarded both men evenly despite the alarm troubling their faces.

"But you . . . and they . . ." Digby stammered. "They're just girls."

"Untested." Captain Grey drew in a sharp breath. "Surely, you wouldn't—"

"Nonsense! These particular girls have been tested their entire lives."

We looked at one another, we five. We outcasts. We oddities, who had not exchanged our true selves for a humdrum life in an English sitting room. A fierce current rushed between us, a commonality tying us together with a knot stronger than blood. She was right. We *had* all been tested. Over and over.

I swallowed hard. In my case, I had failed those tests. Repeatedly.

Miss Stranje yanked our attention back to her. "First things first. Lady Jane, dear, hand Tess and Georgiana the parcels we brought for them. Blood on one's gown is intolerable no matter the circumstances." She rubbed the tips of her gloves together noting the grease from the table.

"Highly irregular," Digby mumbled, and shook his head. "No good can come of it."

Miss Stranje ignored him. "You and Mr. Digby must see to protecting the king. That, of course, must take precedence. You have so little time. You will have your hands full trying to discover the vulnerable points and setting up proper protection. That means it falls to the girls and I to extricate Lord Wyatt. The information to which he is privy must not fall into the hands of the Iron Cross. The consequence . . ." She trailed off, pinching her lips together as she observed Captain Grey's distress.

He rubbed his temples and leaned over the table looking pained and weary. "I don't see how you can do it, Em. It's too dangerous. The house is impenetrable."

"Nothing is impenetrable, Captain." She said it kindly, but jutted up her chin. "It merely presents a greater challenge. We shall have a better idea of how to proceed after we have a closer look. If anything happens to Louis it will plunge us into another war. You know I am right."

He stared sadly at her small hand resting on his arm. The ache in his expression made me look away in shared sadness. "I can't lose you, too." He said it so softly that I hardly heard.

"He is not lost. You'll see." She was firm in this, bristle-backed as a wild boar. "Trust us. We will present our plans to you this evening." She turned to us, shooing at us if we were geese in the garden. "Tess, Georgiana, what are you waiting for? You cannot be seen on the street like that. Go to my rooms and change. Quickly. We've no time to waste."

Captain Grey cleared his throat. "Miss Fitzwilliam has had an idea."

I wheeled back to eavesdrop as Captain Grey explained about having a look from the lighthouse or the church tower.

"Or . . ." I interrupted, hoping they wouldn't be angry if I offered a suggestion. "What if one of us were to disguise ourselves as a servant—"

"Can't. She knows us," Jane said. "And believe me, Daneska would notice."

Sera piped up. "Except she doesn't know Maya. Maya came after."

"True." Miss Stranje tilted her head and studied Maya. "It just might work. Are you game?"

Maya's face lit up with pride. "I am."

Miss Stranje fished a coin out of her reticle. "Quickly then, go and buy the scullery maid's clothing. Trade her yours, and give her this for her trouble."

When we reassembled in the private dining room, the captain and Mr. Digby had left to gather their compatriots and set up reconnaissance and protection for the king of France. Maya had turned into a scullery maid. I was astonished at her transformation. The rags she wore even smelled of the kitchen. I thought her disguise was perfect.

However, Miss Stranje and the other girls did not.

They circled her making little adjustments here and there. I knew instantly they'd all played this game before.

Seraphina frowned "Her face is too clean."

"Easily remedied." Tess dragged a finger through the hearth and made strategic smears of soot to sully Maya's striking caramel complexion.

"Her shoes betray her." Jane took them from our subject and scuffed them against the rough charred bricks of the fireplace.

"Hands," ordered Miss Stranje. Maya thrust out her palms. "Your nails are flawless, Miss Barrington. I'm sorry for this, but a man's life hangs in the balance and perhaps yours as well. Tess, your knife, if you please."

Tess unsheathed a dagger from her thigh and handed it over. Miss Stranje shaved the ends of Maya's nails making them jagged and uneven. Then she rubbed them through the grease on the table. "That should do the job. Not so filthy as to alarm a potential employer, but not clean enough to draw suspicion."

"Hair," Sera said with an apologetic sigh. "Far too shiny and clean."

When Miss Strange stepped forward with the knife again, Jane lunged forward to stop her. "Wait. There's no need for that. We can muss it up. Use some ash to dull the shine, and add a few tangles. Let me try." She dug a brush out of her reticule and went to work. "Like this. Then if we pull it back in a braid and cover her head, no one will know."

"We don't want her to get caught," Tess warned. "It must do uncovered as well."

"Give me half a chance, will you."

Jane fashioned, or rather unfashioned, Maya's dark hair and we assessed her handiwork. The cloth scarf and mussy ends straggling out around her dirtied cheeks added an unexpectedly authentic edge to her appearance. "Brilliant. She's a work of art."

"Hmm. A few uneven ends might've been more convincing." Miss Stranje handed the dagger back to Tess. "But it will do."

Maya exhaled with relief.

The rest of us donned deep-brimmed bonnets and dull gray and brown cloaks. Nothing to draw attention. "When do I get a dagger to wear under my skirt?" I asked.

They all stopped dressing for a moment, but Tess was the first to answer. "Not until you learn how to throw one and land it directly in a man's heart without cutting yourself up in the—"

"Not yet." Miss Stranje cut short the discussion.

They hid my red hair by stuffing it under a hideous mobcap and securing that under an enormous coal scuttle–shaped bonnet. She instructed us not to walk together. Maya was to walk alone the moment we left the inn. The rest of us were to remain in clumps of two or three.

Belowstairs, from the Blue Lion kitchen, Miss Stranje purchased a shallow basket of shabby vegetables intended for the refuse pile. She equipped Maya with the basket and sent her on her way with orders to peddle the pathetic wares along the street south of the stronghold.

Maya was one of the most gracious and naturally elegant human beings I'd ever encounter. I marveled at her ability to change into a believable penniless orphan selling limp leeks and moldy onions. And, although no one bought any of her wilted vegetables, one kind gentleman dropped a ha'penny onto her tray.

We watched from various positions. Tess and I stood nearby pretending to listening to a pamphleteer on the corner. There was a large crowd listening to him extol the evils of allowing a Bourbon back on the throne. Although he was pontificating in French, it was not hard to grasp his complaints. We stood at the back edge of the crowd, near Maya, feigning interest in his rant against the excesses of the royal family, pretending to read his pamphlet, and being extremely cautious not to draw attention.

Jane gave the signal. A woman had emerged from the gate of the Iron Cross stronghold. One glimpse at the woman and we knew immediately she must be the cook. A headscarf tied securely under her double chin, her cloak was frumpy but high-quality wool, and she carried an empty basket headed for market. It made perfect sense. Having finished up the breakfast service she would be off to buy for the next few meals.

Maya ran up to her, "*Madame! Oignons? Poireaux?*"

The woman shook her head.

Maya held up a pathetic-looking leek and switched to Spanish. "*Las cebollas. Los puerros?*"

"*Non.* No! Go away." She waved a beefy arm shooing Maya away. Her speech had fallen into English tinged with what sounded like a Flemish or Dutch accent. I couldn't tell.

"Please, madame." Maya followed her and begged, "Four leeks and this fine turnip for one sous? A farthing? *Un centime?*" They neared us. The mellow warming quality of Maya's voice flowed even to where we stood. "Please. You are kind. I can see that."

The woman stopped, hands on hips and inspected Maya's paltry offering. "Child, dat turnip is . . . *uitdrogen.*" She dropped it back on the tray. "Dried up. And what do I want with more onions? Every orphan in de city is selling dem. I've enough leeks to feed ze army. What I need is a good side of mutton."

She turned to go, but Maya gently touched her arm. "Please, madame. My mother was a camp follower, a cook. She died, and now I must sell leeks or . . ." Maya glanced down in embarrassment and shook her head mournfully.

"I see." The woman nodded, knowing what an orphan girl's alternative would be.

Maya, having caught the woman's full attention, sprang into our plan. "Perhaps you need help in the kitchen? I could wash pots, chop vegetables, clean foul, stir soup stock. I did all these things and much more for my mama. I would do this for you in exchange for food to eat and a place to sleep near the hearth."

"Well . . ." The woman rubbed her chin. "With all za extras in the house to feed, I could do with some help."

"A pallet by the fire. That is all I ask. I will work hard, and you will never hear a word from me."

"Ach, dat is something. I don't like ze chatterboxes. Well, den, you come wit me." She grabbed Maya's tray, set it against the wall, and thrust her large basket into Maya's hands. "I can use ze help carrying things back from market." They walked off together.

One of us was in.

Twenty-two

BEST LAID SCHEMES OF MICE AND MEN

As prearranged, once Maya had succeeded in gaining employment at the house, we headed toward the lighthouse. The watchtower wasn't directly on the water's edge. In fact, the beacon sat well back from the actual port, on slightly higher ground than the surrounding flat terrain. The ideal position to withstand torrential waves and guide incoming ships.

And to spy on the Iron Crown stronghold.

A French soldier slouched against the wall by the tower door. He didn't wear the common French uniform. The insignia on his hat, a shako worn at a jaunty angle, bore the city coat of arms, which made me think he must be a guard for the Lord Mayor of Calais. At our approach, he came alert, not as a disciplined soldier having been caught unaware might do. This fellow straightened and preened the way a man does when he sees a group of ladies.

His musket hung on a loose strap over his shoulder, and he strutted forward with his chest out and asked in a friendly manner what we were doing there. *"Bonjour mesdames, que faites-vous ici?"*

Miss Stranje smiled broadly. I'd never before seen her adopt so friendly an expression. I confess it frightened me more than her hawk face. *"Bonjour, monsieur."* Although I would guess Miss Stranje could speak perfect French if needed, she used stilted syllables to laboriously pronounce *"C'est un beau phare."* What a beautiful lighthouse.

"Ahh," he said, with an air of superiority. "You are the English, yes?"

"Oui. How clever you are. And what a magnificent tower."

"Of course." He glanced over his shoulder at the building as if he'd never before noticed its magnificence. "But you cannot be here, mademoiselle. You must go."

"Oh, no," she whined, sounding so mournful I thought she might burst into tears. She ushered us forward. "My girls and I have come so very far in the hope of seeing this marvelous sight. Your fine city must look spectacular from up there." We all nodded vigorously. She pointed up at the balcony around the lantern.

"Spectaculaire. Yes, of course, but . . ." While he looked up to where she pointed, she reached in her reticule and pulled out a gleaming silver shilling. His attention snapped to the coin as it caught the light.

"What harm can there be if you let us in?" she purred. "Please. *S'il vous plaît, monsieur."*

He stared hungrily at the shilling.

"Is the lightkeeper inside?" she asked.

"Non. No. Not until evening. But the stair, it is very . . . uh . . ." He gestured to indicate a severe angle. "How do you say, *escarpé."*

"Steep."

"Yes. Steep." He snatched the coin. "You must be careful." He opened the door with a key that hung around his neck.

The way was, indeed, steep, eight stories of narrow steps spiraling up to the first observation platform. We decided to forego the even narrower stairs that led to the lamp room itself. The view was incredible, dizzying. Gusts of wind slapped our skirts against our legs and threatened to blow off our bonnets, but we could clearly see the villa from where we stood on the balcony. Miss Stranje made a point of waving to the soldier who was craning his neck to see if we had made it. As soon as he waved back and returned to his post, she pulled out her spyglass and handed it to Sera.

Sera trained it on the stronghold. "Third-story window in the middle. Do you see it? It is the only one with the curtains drawn." Sera lowered the telescope and pulled a strand of hair out of her eyes. "That must be where they're keeping him."

Jane nodded. "Makes sense. There are no dungeons or cellars belowground in this area. The water table is too high."

Sera continued her analysis of the stronghold. "There doesn't seem to be a guard stationed inside the courtyard, only the two men positioned outside along the wall on either side of the gate."

Miss Stranje quizzed her. "When we were observing Maya, you spotted the man watching from the café across the way, didn't you?"

"Green cap, gray coat, beard." Sera continued to studying the Order stronghold through the spyglass.

Jane spoke up, "I noticed him, too."

"A second man stood too long outside the watchmaker's shop across from the north corner of the house. Black felt hat, brown coat with a tear on his right elbow, a knife sheath on his belt. I suspect there may have been a third man, south, nearer to Georgie and Tess. But I couldn't see from our position."

Miss Stranje. "Tess?"

"I'm not good at this," Tess grumbled, and then shrugged. "There might have been two. Was it the fellow preaching against Louis the Eighteenth? Or the gentleman in the top hat standing off to the side studying the pamphlet far too diligently."

"Both, I expect." Miss Stranje motioned for the telescope.

Sera handed it to her. "Take a look at the back street. There's no access to the house but I think it would be our best escape route."

I stared at the window where Sera said they were holding Sebastian. So close, and yet it was impossible to reach him. I gripped the railing wishing I was squeezing Daneska's neck. From where we stood, I could see into the courtyard with its idyllic fountain and rustic gardens. It all looked so unbearably tranquil. "If only I had my Da Vinci wings, I could fly into that courtyard at night and—"

"Do you think you would be able to guide those wings of yours any better than you did on your first try?" Miss Stranje sounded deadly serious. I didn't know whether she was scolding me, or if she actually considered the wings a viable idea.

I took a hard look over the railing, and swallowed even though my mouth had suddenly gone dry. "Yes," I answered warily. "I think so. With some minor modifications."

She waited for more explanation.

"The problem was I hadn't expected the kite to carry me as far as it did. Nor as fast. It flew me into our tree before I could steer out of the way. There's no obstruction between this tower and the house."

"But could you steer it well enough to glide directly into the courtyard?"

I swallowed and looked at Sebastian's window, afraid even to imagine what he must be enduring behind those closed curtains. "Yes," I said, clenching my teeth.

Tess grabbed my shoulder and turned me toward her. "Will it hold two people? Because you can't go alone. If there's a fight, what would you do without me?"

Tess was the tallest of us. It would require more wingspan. I hedged, "It might hold two. Depending upon—"

Miss Stranje stopped me, and gently pulled Tess away. "If it comes down to a fight, the household will be aroused and our battle lost before its begun." She took the spyglass from Tess and returned it to her reticule. "If this plan is to succeed, we must use stealth and distraction. It is Lady Jane who must ac company our kite flyer. I'm certain there will be several locks to pick."

Stealth and distraction. Two traits with which I had no experience. "Distraction?"

"Yes. For instance, if I wish to pick your pocket I might hold up a map, like so." Miss Stranje pretended to raise a map in front of my face and pointed to it. "Thus, I might say, *please, miss, can you tell me where the grand watchtower is. I'm so frightfully lost.*"

I grasped her concept and nodded.

"And while you are looking here. I will have reached into your reticule or pocket . . ." She gave me a tap from inside my cloak pocket. Until that moment, I hadn't felt her hand at all.

"And snatched your timepiece." I proudly held up her watch, having removed it during the lesson.

Surprise whisked across her features, but quickly vanished behind her hawk mask. "Hmm, I suppose there's hope for you yet, Miss Fitzwilliam."

No huzzah. No well done. She snatched her watch from me

and said curtly, "What materials will we need to make these wings of yours? And how long will it take to construct them?"

"Tightly woven silk. Something for lightweight crossbeams. Baleen would be ideal." I paused and estimated the time to sew and put it together. "Even with extra hands to help cut and stitch the silk to the support pieces, several hours."

"We should have no trouble procuring baleen in a seaport, and—"

"You're certain this will work?" Jane interrupted our head-mistress. She stared over the railing. "There's no surviving a drop like that."

Death.

Did I dare risk her life, too? I followed her gaze to the ground so very far beneath us. My throat tightened and I couldn't answer.

Miss Stranje patted Jane's hand. "Look up, my dear. Up to the birds soaring through the air. Dwell upon the adventure of it, Lady Jane. *Flying.* I envy you." She consulted her timepiece before returning it to her pocket with a securing pat. "But now, we must purchase our supplies and head back to the Blue Lion to report to Captain Grey. And then, I'm afraid, it is time for Georgiana to carry a note to Daneska."

I took a deep breath. The hardest part of my task would be not borrowing Tess's knife and trying out my throwing skills when we saw Daneska.

We climbed down the tower. After a substantial amount of gushing gratitude, frivolous waving, fluttered eyelashes, we curt-seyed and bid the guard *adieu.* With a puffed up chest he re-sumed his post looking a great deal more officious than he had upon our arrival.

On the walk home Miss Stranje stopped on Rue de Marché and handed Jane several coins, directing the three girls to go and procure several lengthy strips of baleen from the market-place. The two of us stopped into a silk merchant's shop. My French was good enough to understand that she had instructed the clerk to bring us light blue silk. Hadn't she just lectured me on *stealth?*

"We need black," I whispered. "It will be night."

With a brisk wave of her hand, she sent the clerk off for the silk. "If you were Lady Daneska, what time of day would you anticipate"—she glanced about the shop to make certain no one was listening—"*visitors?*" she said cryptically.

My shoulders drooped, knowing the answer. "Night," I mumbled.

"Accordingly, they will increase their sentries at that time, will they not?"

"Then when?"

"We have only one window of opportunity." She pressed her index finger against the counter indicating a flight arcing from the lighthouse to the stronghold. "If they are indeed plotting to . . . *greet* the king as we expect they are, the fewest amount of people will be inside the villa during his arrival. Don't you agree?"

It made sense. "But during the day . . ." *In plain sight. How would we not be seen?* Just thinking about it made my empty stomach curl up behind my liver.

As if reading my mind, she said, "You mustn't worry. No one ever looks up. Aside from that, the distance between the light-house and the villa is fairly short. You said yourself your first kite flew much faster than you'd expected."

The breath I'd been holding escaped in a noisy whoosh. There was no other way. It would have to work.

"I suggest you trust me with the particulars and bend your mind to figuring out how to maneuver this contraption."

The clerk came back with two bolts of silk. One a lovely light blue-gray, and the other a softer watered blue. Miss Stranje proceeded to bargain with the clerk in impeccable French. They wrangled loudly over price, but in the end he acquiesced and we came away with a bolt of watered silk that nearly matched the sky above.

"Why did you dicker so fiercely over the price?" I asked as we walked back to the inn. "Weren't you concerned about drawing attention to our purchase?"

"Ah. Yes. That is precisely why I did it. In France, it is the custom to negotiate vigorously. If the clerk made a fool of me, he would be more likely to brag about it and discuss our purchase in the local tavern. Whereas now, his chagrin at having been bested will ensure he keeps his mouth shut."

At the Blue Lion, Captain Grey told us that King Louis the XVIII was already in Dover. He would set sail and arrive in Calais early in the afternoon tomorrow. For the last six years England had granted asylum and protected the exiled French king. Now, with Napoleon imprisoned on Elba, King Louis the XVIII's exile was over. He would return to France tomorrow and reclaim his throne.

Captain Grey planned to place what few men he had at strategic positions along the route. Later that day, he and Mr. Digby had an audience with the Lord Mayor. They hoped to convince him to minimize the celebration and place soldiers along the route. Or at least, abandon his plan to memorialize the occasion by having an imprint made of King Louis's first footsteps back on French soil. It would be impossible to protect the monarch in a setting of that sort, with tiered seating for spectators, with bunting and draperies on the platform obscuring a possible assassin.

"It's a nightmare. There will be a procession through the streets with musicians and fanfare." Captain Grey slung his kit over a chair. "Anything could happen. But I doubt he'll give it up."

Over a light meal of soup and bread, we confided our rescue plan. Captain Grey leaned on his elbow and massaged his temple, which I'd come to recognize as a symptom of his distress. "Are you certain these Da Vinci wings will actually carry you?"

"They did in the past."

"And if you make it inside, how do you plan to get out?"

Miss Stranje answered for me. "Distraction."

He did not look relieved.

I spooned down some of the broth and tried to sop it with a few bites of bread, but everything turned to prickly stones in my stomach. I gave up and set down my spoon. It was time to face Daneska. We composed a letter and set out for the Iron Crown stronghold.

Captain Grey and Mr. Digby escorted me. We crossed a small bridge over the canal and walked down Rue de Madrid toward the Order's chateau. So that I would be readily recognized, I wore my hair out waving like a red flag of surrender. I carried a carefully worded note, promising the formula, but demanding that Lady Daneska must first prove to my satisfaction that Sebastian was alive and well.

We approached the gates of the Iron Crown stronghold cautiously. Unlike the soldier manning the lighthouse, these guards took their task seriously. They moved from their positions against the wall and with muskets in hand, they blocked our entry to the gate. They looked straight over my head and addressed the captain, "*Que voulez-vous ici?* What do you want, *monsieur?*"

I marched forward and thrust the sealed letter at the one who'd done the talking. "I have an important note for Lady Daneska, *la comtesse Valdikauf.* Urgent. *Comprenez-vous?*" My hand shook as I held it out to him.

He snorted, and looked down his nose at me as if I was no more than a street urchin begging for sous, but he finally took it. *"Prendre du recul.* Step back!"

His companion pushed us into the street with his musket. The man with my letter hurried through the gate and locked it.

We stood there peering through the bars. Waiting. At the far end of the courtyard, Maya sat on a bench near a service door, plucking chickens. She was careful not to look directly at us.

Sebastian was only a few meters away. Any minute I might see him. I fought to keep my hands still and at my sides, so they wouldn't betray my anxiety. When Daneska came out to us, I wanted to appear competent and earnest, not worried and panicked. I glimpsed movement in an upper window overlooking the courtyard. It had to be her. She would be gauging my demeanor, noting who accompanied me, taking her time, making me wait, showing me she had all the control of this situation.

I took a deep breath and stood as tall and confidently as I could. In the end, Daneska did not trouble herself to come out. The guard returned with my note. I did not wait for privacy. I opened it right then and read the words she had scrawled across the bottom. I clenched my teeth and glared at the window where I knew she was watching and chuckling.

BRING YOUR RECIPE AND COME BACK TONIGHT AT SIX.

Six o'clock. With that faint promise, we returned to the inn.

I didn't know how I could bear the hours until we would see him. Every plodding minute stretched forever in front of me. I stared listlessly at the sketch of the new Da Vinci wings. My mind felt like useless sludge.

"Stop dawdling." Miss Stranje rapped my boggy head with her knuckles. "We can't begin cutting the silk until you finish the design. Do you intend to let fear and worry drown you? Are you going to leave him there to die?"

"No," I gasped.

"Then breathe." She poked me in the back, making me sit up straighter. "And get on with it."

Vowing to salvage each lost second, I went to work with renewed intensity. Drawing each line with increased hope. Inking away my anxiety with each measurement. As I envisioned how to make the steering mechanism work, my confidence grew. We *would* get him out.

Jane and I made miniature versions of different wing styles out of parchment and tested them. I'd never before met anyone as good at mathematics as I am. Together we calculated the angle of descent, and designed a simple sling to carry two people instead of one.

We laid out the silk and cut it according to my measurements. Sera, Jane, and Miss Stranje went to work stitching, while Tess and I measured and cut the baleen. I had just finished marking for another cut when the clock chimed five-thirty.

Captain Grey appeared in the doorway. "Time to go."

Twenty-three

TROUBLING DISTRACTIONS

The streets were nearly deserted at that hour. Shops had closed. The working poor had already finished their meager meal. The rich were indoors, dressing for evening, while their servants were busy preparing sumptuous dinners to be eaten late. The air smelled of onion soup, potatoes, and roasting meat. Talk drifted from the houses. Laughter rumbled from the taverns. But the three of us walked in worried silence until the white walls of the Iron Crown stronghold loomed before us.

Captain Grey pressed a steadying hand on my shoulder. "Don't give in too easily. She'll suspect something if you do."

I clutched the formula in my pocket. The wrong formula. The one that would develop on its own in twelve hours. It would look right at first, and that might buy us time. The men in the Order of the Iron Crown wanted more from him than this formula, at the very least they would want the names of Sebastian's men and where they were posted. We reasoned that Daneska and her cohorts would keep him alive long enough to make certain she got an ink from me that worked. Hopefully, we would have him out tomorrow before they discovered that this one didn't.

The guard, who had been so rude to me earlier that morning, came forward and spoke to us in passable English. "Halt there. Wait."

"*Reculez*," the other man barked at Captain Grey and Mr. Digby. We backed up some but not much. Captain Grey stood directly behind me.

I waited, but my heart thrashed like a hooked fish and threatened to leap into my throat and suffocate me. I saw Maya sitting across the courtyard, shelling peas beside the cook. I wished I could hear her calming voice, but the guard noticed me staring in their direction and shouted for them to go inside. They scurried through the servant's door, but not before Maya subtly indicated the side of the villa where they were holding Sebastian. She glanced up as if looking at the exact room. Which meant Sera was right; they were holding him on the third floor.

Daneska emerged from the house, looking relaxed and elegant. She smiled pleasantly and greeted me as if we were friends. "How very gracious of you to stop by, Miss Fitzwilliam. I trust you brought your recipe!"

I held up the folded paper. "First, I must see that Lord Wyatt is well."

"But, of course." She motioned for me to come closer and peer into the courtyard.

A guard shoved Sebastian out of the side door. He staggered forward, his hands tied behind him like a man bound for the gallows. Captain Grey sucked in a ragged breath. A scream caught in my throat. My stomach reeled.

Sebastian's eyes. His beautiful eyes. Beaten until they were only dark slits in bulging scarlet welts. And his lips . . .

"No, no, no," I choked.

Unbidden, I felt them on mine. But now they were bruised, split, and swollen, seeping blood down his chin. His cheeks. The fine smooth skin was now a mass of red and purple lumps. I couldn't breathe. Had I not caught the captain's arm, my knees would've buckled.

Sebastian wore the same torn shirt he'd had on in London, covered in dried blood, gaping open to the cold. They hadn't tended the raw angry cut on his chest. To the contrary, as he stumbled closer I saw fresh lash marks crisscrossed it.

Bile scorched furiously up my throat. I heaved in a bitter gagging breath. Unable to stop myself, I gasped, "Sebastian!"

He blinked, as if the dying afternoon sun was too bright, and tilted his head, straining to see who had uttered his name. He lurched forward the minute he recognized me. "No! Georgie, don't—"

The guard struck the back of Sebastian's head with the butt of his rifle. I shrieked, as he collapsed facedown on the grass.

He lay there, not moving, his hair a mass of dark curls, matted with his blood. I ached to run to him, to smooth them back, to hold his head on my lap and beg his forgiveness. Dear God in heaven, he would not be here if I hadn't blundered.

I grabbed the bars of the gate. "What have you done to him?"

"I?" Her hand fluttered to her décolletage. "I have done nothing."

The guard roused Sebastian. Yanking him up by the arm, he hauled him back into the house. I didn't even realize I was crying until Daneska clucked her tongue. "Dry your tears, *mon cher.* He knew the risks of this business. The recipe, *s'il vous plaît.*"

I could not stop tears from running down my cheeks. But now, they burned with anger. "You will release him."

"Not until after I test the recipe."

"How long?" I held the formula back. "When will you let him go?"

"Soon." She shrugged. "These things take time. I must find a chemist. We are very busy at the moment. We have *important* guests to attend to, and the Lord Mayor has invited all of the nobility to welcome the Bourbon *King* back to France." She cocked her chin, making much of the fact that she was nobility and I was not.

"Yes, yes, you are a countess, so you must attend the royal affair. I don't care about any of that. When will you let him go?" I demanded, slapping the formula against the bars of the gate and withdrawing it.

"I make no promises." She stepped back, arms crossed. "You have seen he is alive. If you want him to remain so, you will give me the recipe. Choose."

As if I had a choice. It was a lie, Like everything else about her. The immaculate deception. I had no choice. None. Lady Daneska held all the cards. I was merely a beggar in her world. So, I slid the paper to her and begged, "Please, Daneska."

She snatched her prize and walked away without a word.

I began to tremble. Captain Grey took me by the shoulders and urged me away from the gate. We had walked to the end of the street before I could speak without quivering to pieces. "She'll never let him go."

"We knew that," he said, still supporting my shoulders. "Which is why you must get him out tomorrow."

I do not recall walking the half mile back to the Blue Lion. *Numb.* I felt numb.

I could scarcely even feel my own feet. If I allowed myself to feel, if I reflected at all upon the bleakness of our situation, or the agony Sebastian must be suffering, I would crumble.

This cold mechanical determination was the only way I

could attend to the work that needed doing that night. I worked with such steely focus I may as well have been made of iron fittings and steel gears. One goal throbbed in my consciousness. *Get Sebastian out.*

After we finished building the wings, Jane and I practiced assembling and disassembling them. The parts had to be compact enough that we could bring them into the lighthouse hidden under our cloaks, and yet easy enough to take apart quickly and hide after we landed. Miss Stranje timed us. "Faster," she ordered, until we had the disassembly down to under a minute. "Better. Now do it again."

We discussed every detail of the plan. Jane and I would be disguised as housemaids. Miss Stranje made us practice how to behave like a proper servant, and what to say if we were noticed in the hallway. Tess would dress seductively in order to distract the guards, if needed, as we flew into the courtyard. We needed to lure the soldier guarding the watchtower to the other side of the building so that he would not notice when a gigantic bird took off from the observation balcony. Miss Stranje insisted she must be the one to do this job. "I couldn't possibly send one of you girls to do that sort of job. It would be highly inappropriate. You are far too young and innocent for such things."

The captain turned sharp at that, broke off his hushed discussion with Mr. Digby and two other men, and marched across the room to our table. "A word, Miss Stranje. If you please."

They retired to a dark corner and engaged in a heated discussion. "Very well," she huffed at the end of it. "I'll use a sleeping potion. But we are running decidedly low on the stuff. Not only that, but now I must stop in at a bake shop to find something suitable to put it in."

"Eminently preferable to the alternative."

She sniffed. "I do hope you appreciate that at this rate, my girls and I will be putting half of Calais to sleep." She returned to us looking miffed, but the corner of her mouth twitched as if she was secretly pleased.

We continued planning. Every detail considered, reconsidered, laid out, and practiced until I thought I would go mad.

Jane insisted on teaching me how to pick a lock. "In case something should happen to me. One never knows."

I thought I was past feeling until that moment. Remembering that Jane, too, would be in danger because of me made the lump in my chest grow even heavier. My fingers turned stiff and clumsy. One of her tools clattered to the floor.

It turns out that picking a lock is more of an art than a simple mechanical process. When I failed yet again, Jane sighed. "I don't understand it. The inn's locks are fairly simple. At Stranje House we practice with dozens of more complex locks."

If I could have taken the lock apart and seen the mechanism, I might've had more success. But it was late, and I hung by a frayed thread. I handed back her tools. "Perhaps I will learn there. For now, you must simply promise to not let anything happen to you."

Miss Stranje pulled me aside and handed me a small vial of laudanum. "You may need this if he is in too injured to move without his crying out. Give him a few drops."

She also showed us how to wrap a strap under his arms so we could lower him by rope. It would not be comfortable.

On my way to bed I stopped in the hallway and stared at the bottle in my hand. Suddenly I was unable to escape thinking of his pain. I remembered his poor bruised eyes. His beaten cheeks. His lips swollen, and split . . . I sagged against the wall and squeezed my eyes shut, trying to banish the image. I must focus on only one thought. *Get him out.*

I couldn't sleep that night. I kept going over our plan in my head. Something niggled at me.

Distractions.

We had planned how to divert the guard's attention at the lighthouse, and a diversion for when Jane and I landed. Indeed, we had a misdirection prepared for every aspect of our mission to get in the villa. But what if we needed a distraction once we got inside the stronghold? I worried it wouldn't be enough to simply pretend we were innocent housemaids.

In the early hours before dawn, an idea roused me to action. I slipped out of bed, dressed, and went down to our private parlor to work.

Captain Grey stood at the window, staring at the gloom, waiting for the sun to breach the horizon.

"Couldn't sleep?" I asked.

He put a brave face on it. "Wanted an early start," he said, still staring at the eastern sky.

"I wonder if I might borrow an ounce or two of your black powder?"

Without a question, he reached into his kit and handed me his powder horn. I emptied a small measure of it into my handkerchief, knotted it securely, and returned the horn to him.

"I don't want to know what that is for, Miss Fitzwilliam." He swallowed hard. "I raised him, you know. Since he was a lad."

I'd guessed as much, but kept silent. There was nothing I could say that would help.

"War will most certainly break out if they murder the king. If it were not for that, I . . ." He pressed his lips tight and fixed his gaze on the horizon. "I have a sworn duty to uphold today. But all my own hopes ride with you. I must confess, I cannot even think of it without my innards turning to stone."

I will get him out or die trying. But I did not say that. Little comfort in those words. Especially coming from me. My failure brought us here.

I stared at the pink beginning to edge up over the rooftops. "I will bring him home to you, sir."

He closed his eyes for a moment and gulped back whatever was choking him. In barely a whisper, he rasped, "I pray God you are right."

"Sun's rising. I must go." He handed me a slender metal flask. "I know him. He won't take the laudanum. Give him this to help take the edge off the pain."

I took it and tucked it in my pocket beside the gunpowder.

Later that morning the Blue Lion servants were astonished when I entered their kitchen. Although my French leaves much to be desired, I somehow managed to convey to them the size bottle I needed—small enough to fit neatly in my pocket, but large enough to hold a cup of oil.

For a tuppence, which I had obtained from Miss Stranje, I came away with a small wide-necked bottle filled with lamp oil, half of a candle, and the loan of a wax melting pot. The servants winked at one another, pleased at having duped me. Considering these items might save my life, and that of Jane and Sebastian, I would've paid a great deal more.

It took a good part of the morning to cook up my distraction. I stirred wax over the fire and dipped my little cloth bag of gunpowder, coating it over and over, until I was certain it was waterproof. This was no small feat considering I could not have the packet anywhere near the fire lest it explode.

Miss Stranje returned from the pastry shop and proceeded to do some rather creative cooking herself. She made a mixture of cream, honey, and laudanum, and drizzled it over an otherwise innocent-looking slice of black currant spice cake. She wrapped this delectable treat and placed it in a small basket to take to the soldier guarding the lighthouse.

We worked in companionable silence until Sera burst into the room. "It's done."

Tess came in behind her, grinning and excited. "You should've seen us. Sera was brilliant. She snatched a salted herring from Maya's basket and held the fish up by its tail. *Oh, my gracious! Where did you find such a beautiful herring, mademoiselle?*" She imitated Sera in a squeaky high voice that I doubted Sera would have used. "The cook was livid. *Put zat fish down. Go away! Shoo! Off with you.*"

Tess laughed. "I didn't think Sera had it in her. She kept hold of that smelly fish, and ever so innocently said, *Is this your fish? My apologies, madame. I will put it down immediately.* Of course the cook couldn't look anywhere except at that herring swinging by its tail. Meanwhile, I slipped the instructions and sleeping draught into Maya's pocket without the cook even noticing."

I couldn't join in their merriment, my heart still thumped slow and heavy from this morning's encounter with the captain. I had no time for mirth. No room for levity. I'd made a solemn vow. *I will bring him home to you, sir.*

Neither did Jane. She sat in the window seat, gazing out at the world as if it was her last day on earth.

"What's wrong, Jane?" Sera went and sat beside her. "You look worried."

"No. Of course not. I'm fine."

Even I could see the anxiety she was hiding beneath that too cheery smile. "You needn't go, Jane." I tried to sound commanding. "I can pick the locks myself." Given my lack of success last night I wasn't certain, but putting her in danger added to the weight that was already pressing my bones to the very center of the earth.

"Nonsense. This is what we've trained for. I'm the best at locks. And you . . ." Here she paused and bolstered her shoulders. "You know what you are doing with this flying thing, and . . ." She waved at my project on the table.

Sera took a closer look at the components. "What *are* you doing?"

I didn't want to explain, but it is hard for me to deny a direct question. "Have you ever heard of Greek fire?"

She shook her head.

"Surely, you've heard of grenadiers?"

"Yes. Elite French troops. Big strong soldiers who bravely tossed bombs by hand." She left Jane and drifted near, watching me dip the wad of gunpowder.

"Not bombs, exactly." I said, twisting the top of the bag into a narrow fuse and threading it through the cork. "They called them grenades."

Miss Stranje buckled the lid on her basket. "You do realize the grenadiers were horribly unsuccessful? Napoleon reassigned the men who survived elsewhere."

"Yes, but Greek fire is not just a glass jug filled with gunpowder like the grenades the French had. This is fire in a bottle." I held up the elegant little flask filled with thick oil.

Sera took a deep breath. Her eyes widened.

"In case we need another distraction," I explained.

The joy drained from Tess's face. "Fire," she murmured, and stared at the bottle on the table as if in a trance. "Perhaps I should teach you how to throw a knife instead."

"Do you think you'd have any better luck than Jane did trying to teach me to pick a lock?"

She grimaced.

"Exactly. This is something I *can* do. Apparently, I am quite deadly with fire."

They stared at me. Grim. All four of them wincing as if I'd just walked over their graves.

And why shouldn't they? After all, it was fire, and I had a rather blackened reputation with the stuff. "I didn't mean *deadly* for us." I set the bottle on the table and shrugged. "We may not need to use it."

Miss Stranje exhaled. "Let us hope not."

Twenty-four

FLY OR DIE TRYING

At the lighthouse, we stood back and watched as Miss Stranje bribed the guard to let us watch the festivities from the observation platform. He took her shilling and obliged. She presented him with the spice cake as a further token of her gratitude, and suggested the two of them watch the king's ship come in to port together. He eagerly accompanied her to the side of the tower where he could keep an eye on the door and still watch the harbor with her.

I wished Tess was with us, but she had already gone with a small cart and taken up her position in an alleyway across from the stronghold. Sera, Jane, and I climbed to the watchtower gallery deck with our equipment and assembled the wings. From our vantage point, it seemed as if the entire town had gathered at the royal docks south of us. At that great height, the crowd looked like a swarm of dark lumps, hats and bonnets rippling and shifting like a hive of bees. Once we had the kite assembled, every gust of wind threatened to lift it off the balcony.

Jane and I slipped into the sling and backed against the tower wall.

"Georgie," Sera said pensively. "Remember when I cataloged your traits?"

I nodded, wondering what that had to do with our leap from the tower.

"I'm sorry for that." She laid her hand on my shoulder as if pronouncing a benediction. "Now that I know you better, I see that you are not only smart, but you are brave and loyal. Above all, I see how passionately you care." She let go and nodded in approval. "In the end, I believe that kind of nobility is rewarded."

Peace rushed through me. And strength. But before I could respond, Jane spoke up, "A fine sentiment. But let us hope this is not *the end*."

"That's not what I meant." Sera looked wounded.

I interceded. "I know what you meant. Thank you." I inched Jane and the kite toward the parapet. All we needed to do was tip over the railing and we would be off. "Are you ready, Jane?"

"Yes." She sounded brave, but her feet didn't move.

She was usually the one to do the instructing, but today it fell to me. "Remember, don't try to stand. Feet up. Head down. So the kite will tip at the proper angle to carry us into the courtyard."

"Yes, I know." She swallowed, nodding too fast. "I remember the plan."

Sera glanced anxiously around the corner, checking the harbor. "The king's ship is coming into port. It's time."

Jane sucked in her breath.

I shuffled us closer. "Hold on. Close your eyes if you must. We're going."

Jane gripped my shoulders for dear life. I leaned over the bar. A breeze caught the underside of the wings and we tipped over the railing. Our sling wobbled as the wind carried us over the edge.

We sagged into the air. Then we lifted. I cannot describe the unnerving sensation of falling and yet not falling. Jane's feet kicked against mine as she did the natural thing, and scrambled to find ground to stand on, where there was none. The nose of the kite tipped perilously high.

"Feet up!" I yelled, and fought to lift mine. I tugged on the cords to angle the nose of the kite downward. We balanced into a glide. A high-pitched hum rang in my ears. It took me a second to realize it was Jane trying to hold in her screams.

The kite was extremely fast. Our hair whipped back from the speed of it. But for those brief seconds, as we skated through the nothingness of air, time ceased to matter.

Jane stopped humming.

We soared above fear. We flew with the perspective of angels. From our sunlit perch in the heavens, my failures did not seem so heavy.

A sickening tearing sound shredded our peace.

The silk frayed.

The upper right side of our sling tore. As we headed down over the red-tiled roof into the courtyard, it ripped completely lose. Jane slid sideways. I've no idea how she kept from shrieking. Glimpsing her white face, I worried she would faint in terror.

"Hang on," I urged, and yanked hard on the left cord.

I couldn't rebalance the wings. Jane's foot dragged against the tiles. Surely, we must have alerted the entire household. I pulled with all my might on the cords. The baleen bowed until it almost formed an umbrella as we skittered off the roof. With a deflating whoosh, we sank into the courtyard and landed in a tumble. Upside down.

I took a deep breath, righted myself, and scrambled across

the silk to Jane. I heard shouts from the street and feared the guards had seen us. But then, I recognized Tess's voice crying out for the men to help her. "Oh, no! Please, *monsieurs*. Help me! *S'il vous plaît*. My cart. The wheel is stuck. *Voulez-vous me faire une grande faveur?* I must get to the harbor to see the king."

As beautiful as Tess was, and dressed in the low-cut aristocratic gown Miss Stranje had selected for this very purpose, I had no doubt they would spring to her aid. Jane crawled out from under the broken wing. "Were we seen?"

I shook my head. "Are you all right?" I whispered.

"I'll manage." Her lips were still white.

We quickly took apart what was left of the wings. Maya peeked out of the service door and scampered to us. We gathered up the braces, silk, and cords, and followed her. Just before we ducked inside, I overheard Tess gushing over the guards' big strong arms, still carrying on as if they had saved her from a dire catastrophe. When it was she who had saved us.

We stuffed the tattered remains of the kite into a cupboard under the stair. Maya held a finger to her lips as we tiptoed up. "Cook and several maids had to stay back from the festivities. I added the laudanum to the soup the servants ate at our noon meal. Most of them fell asleep while they were still sitting at the table. The others . . ." She shrugged and I hoped we wouldn't run across them.

We snuck silently through the third-floor hall and Maya pointed out the door. She pressed her ear to it and listened. "He's alone."

Jane went straight to work on the lock. As fast as if we'd used a key, the latch clicked and the door swung open. The room was gloomy and dark. It stunk of stale air and the tarnished-penny tang of blood.

"I won't," he moaned.

Maya silently closed the door. Jane handed her the rope from our knapsack. I slid back the drapes. Sebastian was on the floor, kneeling on the hearth, manacled and chained to the stone fireplace.

"Won't tell you anything," he mumbled.

I ran to him and gently lifted his chin. "Shhh. Sebastian. We've come to take you home, my love. But you must be quiet."

He raised his head at that, and squinted at me through his swollen eyes. "You can't be here," he rasped. "Oh, of course . . ." His head drooped and hung limp. "I'm dreaming again."

I pulled the flask out of my pocket. "Here. Captain Grey sent this for you. Drink."

He stared at the silver flask. "You're really here?" Then, his eyes widened with panic. "No, Georgie, you've got to get out. If they catch you—"

"I'm going to leave straightaway. So are you. Drink this, it will help." I tipped it to his lips and he swallowed as if dying of thirst. He drew back suddenly. The whiskey must've burned his throat or perhaps the raw places in his mouth. I glanced around the room hoping to find water, but there was none. "Bear up a little longer. We'll have you out soon." I brushed back his curls, wishing my fingers could heal the bruises and cuts.

"More." He nodded at the flask.

I was careful to avoid the split part of his lip as I poured. "Jane, can you get these wretched shackles off him?"

She left Maya to finish looping our slender rope around the windowsill and securing it with a knot tied around the hinge.

Jane inspected the lock on Sebastian's manacle, but the small window let in precious little light and there were too many shadows. "These are more difficult." She snatched a candle and tinderbox from the mantel and set it on the floor beside me. "Light that. I need you to hold it by the lock, so I can see."

Maya opened the window wider and lowered the rope.

Sebastian glanced in her direction and blinked. "Tossing me out another window, eh?"

Even chained up, even beaten purple and covered in his own blood, he teased. He meant to wrench a smile from me. I tried. But that flicker in his eyes, sparking so courageously into the tormented darkness of his pain, squeezed my heart with a fist of admiration. What I intended as a casual chuckle came out as a strangled sob.

"Hold the light steady," Jane snapped.

His shoulders sagged. I was afraid he might fall unconscious, but his head shook. "You shouldn't be here. Too dangerous."

Jane unlocked the first manacle. It dropped off and clattered against the hearth. We all held our breath and stared at the door. I counted in my head. Ten . . . fifteen . . . twenty. No footsteps. Jane exhaled loudly and went to work on the other shackle.

"I'm going to test it," Maya whispered, and climbed out the window on our rope ladder, a series of fat knots two feet apart.

Sebastian flexed his free hand. I rubbed his wrist where the iron cuffs had bitten into the skin. "Help me up," he said.

"Wait. Hold still, my lord," Jane said. "I'm almost done." We heard the telltale click. She slid the shackle off and carefully lowered it and the chain to the hearth. Before I could set down the candle and help him, Sebastian struggled to his feet. Just then, the door swung open and banged against the wall.

I looked up in terror. But it was a familiar face. I sighed with relief. "Lord Ravencross."

The same instant I said that, Sebastian murmured, "Ghost."

I took a closer look. It wasn't Ravencross. It looked very like him, same dark hair and features, except this man was thinner and had a slighter build.

"I thought I heard a noise up here." He held a long-barreled pistol trained at Sebastian. "What's this, Wyatt? Hiding behind a bunch of girls?"

Jane peeked out from behind Sebastian and gasped.

"You," Ghost said. "I know you. You're one of Emma Stranje's brats." He shifted the flintlock and aimed it at her.

Sebastian stepped between Jane and the gun. "They're innocents, Ravencross. Let them go."

I pulled the diversion out of my pocket and lit the fuse, praying it would work.

Praying it wouldn't blow up in my hand.

Just plain praying.

I tossed it at the floor in front of him. It was supposed to shatter. It didn't. It bobbled and rolled like a boiled goose egg beside his feet. He glanced down at my feeble distraction. I jerked Jane and Sebastian toward the window.

Lord Ravencross, or Ghost, *whoever he was,* said, "What in hell is—"

It exploded.

Ghost flung his arms up. The gun went off. His bullet split the window frame over my head. Fire blazed across the floor. Ghost screamed and slapped at the flames on his legs.

Jane leaped over the sill and slid down the rope.

"Hurry, my lord." I pushed Sebastian at the window.

"Go." Sebastian ordered me.

I wanted to say, *Get on that rope or I'll shove you out. I swear I will.* But I heard shouting in the hallway. More men coming. We had no time to argue.

"There's room for both of us." I scrambled over the sill and saw Ghost had already extinguished the fire on his pant leg. He was using his coat to beat out the bank of flames between us.

Sebastian climbed out right after I did. He held on, and although he winced in the process, slid down one knot at a time.

Hurry. At the bottom, my leg shook nervously. He got down and, with his arm wrapped around my shoulder, we half ran, half staggered between the houses to the back street where Tess waited with the cart. Jane and Maya helped him into the wagon. I leaped on, and Tess shook the reins. Just then a guard rounded the far corner of the house.

It must have startled him to see Tess at the other end of the alley. His mouth gaped. He took stock of her cart bearing three housemaids and the prisoner. Still blinking with surprise, he lifted his rifle to take aim.

I lunged to cover Sebastian.

With a shout, Tess slapped the reins. The horse broke into a run. Gunshot shattered the corner of the wall. Dust and stucco stung my arms.

We barreled down the street, Tess turned down a side street so fast the wagon tipped on two wheels. My heart thundered. A moment later, we skidded around another turn. She was following the circuitous route we'd pre-mapped in case we were pursued. After another turn, she reined the horse in to a more sane fast trot and we rushed to the inn.

We'd done it.

"It's all right," Sebastian said, stroking my shoulder. "He wouldn't have had time to reload." He pulled a piece of plaster out of my hair. "And he'd never be able to follow at this pace."

I sat up, embarrassed to have lain against him for so long. Sebastian scooted upright and slumped against the side of the cart. He looked so weary.

"Were you hit, my lord?" I saw no evidence of fresh blood.

He smirked. "I believe you know the answer to that." Then he frowned. "What in blazes were you playing at, Georgie? Trying to take a bullet for me. Little fool."

I took umbrage. He could've at least been grateful. Besides, how did he know I wasn't clinging to him in fear of my own life? "You may set your pride to rest. I wasn't doing it for you. I was fulfilling an oath to Captain Grey. I promised to bring you home in one piece."

"Where is the captain?"

"King Louis has come to Calais to reclaim his throne. Captain Grey and Miss Stranje thought there might be a plot to assassinate him. That's where he is right now, protecting the king."

Sebastian groaned and leaned his head back. "Now, it all makes sense. I wondered why Ghost was here."

"But he was still at the villa. Doesn't that mean that he didn't try?"

"No. He prefers to pull the strings from the shadows. He will have sent someone." Sebastian sagged against my shoulder. "God help us if he succeeds."

I swallowed. "Lady Daneska will be there as a guest of the Lord Mayor. You don't think . . ."

"It won't be her. She likes to watch." I felt him wince, a swift telling shudder.

Had she been a spectator at his interrogations? How much of his torment had been purely for her entertainment? It was my turn to shiver.

Sebastian closed his eyes, but I doubted he slept. The cart was too bumpy. I caught him grimacing now and then, but he said nothing more.

As we drove up Rue du Canal, we could see Miss Stranje pacing in front of the inn. She would've known from the direction we were coming that we'd been pursued. She rushed to the back of the cart. Glimpsing Sebastian, her hawk-like features melted with concern. "Good Lord."

"How do you do, Miss Stranje?" Still slumped against the side of the cart, he pretended to doff an invisible hat.

"A great deal better than you, you young rascal." She glanced both ways to check who was observing us. "Get him inside. Quickly!"

She dispatched a lad from the inn to return the horse and cart to the mews, and bustled us upstairs to Captain Grey's rooms. She shooed us out of the room while she and the inn-keeper's wife tended to his wounds. I paced on the landing out-side the door. She sent me to fetch servants to carry hot water and clean linen. "How is he?"

"Alive. Do as you're told."

I ran down the stairs and brought a kettle up myself. "A girl is coming with linen. They'll bring more hot water as soon as it's heated."

I peeked around her shoulder as I handed in the big copper kettle. He was lying on the bed with only a sheet covering him from the waist down.

She pushed me back. "I need the brown case from my room, the one with the big brass buckle. Be careful with it. Those vials break easily." She shut the door in my face.

Thus it continued, until at last the innkeeper's wife rushed out with a pile of soiled linen, and Miss Stranje finally emerged rubbing her palms on her skirt. "He's sleeping."

I tried once again to peek around her. This time she left the door ajar. "I've treated his wounds with sulfur. He's strong. He'll recover quickly."

I sighed with relief.

"You did well, Georgiana." She murmured something else about the rescue, but her praise was lost to me as I pushed in to have a closer look.

His dark curls made such a strong contrast against the white pillow. With the dried blood gone, he already looked much improved. Although he was still swollen, and sleeping so quietly that I worried. "Shouldn't we send for a doctor?"

"It is difficult to know who to trust in Calais."

He lay motionless. Too still. Until he thrashed from side to side and murmured in his sleep, "I won't. No. No more." Just as he had when we'd found him.

"He's back there. Chained up again." I rushed to his side and took his hand in mine. "No, love, you're safe," I choked. "You're back with *us* now."

He stilled. I looked up at Miss Stranje, desperate, begging her with my very soul to stop his nightmares. But how? She was not magic.

She shook her head and came to my side. Her hand rested gently on my shoulder. "It is not an easy thing loving a man such as this." She spoke in a soft whisper that vibrated with the grief and worry she must feel every time Captain Grey leaves her. In this we were more than teacher and student, we were sisters. And she, I realized, was more of a mother to me than I'd ever known.

With a sad kiss to my forehead, she left me and pulled a chair beside the bed. "You may sit with him awhile. It will do him good. I'll have a tray sent up for you."

Before I could sit, Captain Grey burst into the room. Startled, I jumped back. His frantic gaze dashed from me and Miss Stranje to Sebastian in the bed.

She hurried to the captain and pressed a calming hand over his heart. "It's all right, Ethan. I've seen to his wounds and given him something to make him sleep. He'll be fine in a day or two."

He said nothing. Like a man in a stupor, he walked to Sebastian's bed and dropped into the chair. He tossed his hat to the floor and bowed his head into his hands. An agonizingly raw moment passed before he drew his face up from his fingers. He looked directly up at me. "I am in your debt," he said, his voice hoarse with emotion.

What was I to say? You don't owe me anything. Think nothing of it. It was my fault in the first place. While I groped for the right response, he turned to Miss Stranje. "The king is dead."

"What!" She knelt in front of him and clasped his hands in hers. "How?"

He shook his head. "Shot in the head, not more than ten minutes after he landed. I warned the Lord Mayor not to hold the ridiculous ceremony. He had his mind set on memorializing the king's first steps on French soil. It was the plaque maker, Em. The plaque maker."

His face looked drawn and creased with regret. She pressed her lips to his fingers. "It wasn't your fault. You couldn't have known he was a member of the Iron Crown."

"The wretched band was playing so loud I didn't realize what had happened until I saw the gun smoke. In the pandemonium, the culprit dove into the water and swam away."

"Oh, dear." She stood and began pacing, as was her habit.

"And Daneska had a front-row seat," I murmured.

"We've been combing the shoreline. Every man I have is out there hunting the assassin. The Lord Mayor's soldiers joined the search. Although I doubt their heart is in it. Most of them are former French troops." Captain Grey sat bolt upright. His hands turned to fists against his thighs. "There's no sign of him. Not one bloody trace. This has Ghost's hand written all over it. Too well-planned."

"He was in the villa," I said. "He took a shot at us."

They both looked at me. Wary. Astonished. Disbelieving.

"Good God," Captain Grey finally said, and shook his head.

"Yes, but it matters little. If we don't find the assassin we cannot lay blame for the king's murder on the Iron Crown." Miss Stranje tapped her chin, deep in thought.

"Not that it would do any good. Everywhere I go in the city, I hear cries of *Vive l'Empereur, vive le Napoléon.* The tide turns quickly in France. I've sent a warning to Paris." Captain Grey bowed his head again, fingers raking through his hair. "We failed, Em. There'll be war again."

"Perhaps not." She meant to comfort him, but even to my ears her words rang hollow. "Come. All this talk will not raise the dead king. You're bone tired, and I'll wager you haven't eaten since last night. Miss Fitzwilliam will sit with Lord Wyatt. Won't you, Georgie?"

He looked reluctant to leave Sebastian. "As soon as he is well enough to travel—"

"I know." She returned to being an overbearing headmistress and took him by the arm. "But for now, Captain, come along. Leave this young lady a few moments alone with him. She's earned it."

Skewering me with a backward warning glance, she said, "In his condition, it's not like they'll get up to anything while we're downstairs."

How wrong she was.

She had no sooner closed the door, but what I was covering Sebastian's poor bruised face with soft kisses. I even ventured some daring kisses on his neck. After a few minutes of this shameful abuse, and raising no more response from him than a murmured "Georgie," I sat down. Content to stare at him for the rest of the evening.

Twenty-five

SAYING GOOD-BYE
TO THE DEVIL

The next afternoon Captain Grey and Mr. Digby returned to the inn. Both of them looked haggard and nearly off their feet as they joined us in the parlor. Captain Grey removed his hat and made a grim announcement. "The Lord Mayor has called off the search for the assassin. He's having trouble with dissenters, so he recalled his soldiers to patrol the city.

"There's more." He sat down at the table. "Lady Daneska and a gentleman fitting Ghost's description left by coach last night. According to the report, Ghost appeared to be wearing a bandage on his right leg." The captain looked at me as if I might shed some light on this last comment.

"In a coach?" Miss Stranje took the seat beside him. "Then they weren't going to the harbor? They're not headed to England."

He shook his head. "Inland."

Thoughts of Ghost made me turn to Tess. She didn't know who he was yet. Neither did the present Lord Ravencross. It didn't seem right. Jane gazed in the same direction, probably wondering the same thing.

Later, Jane and I found a moment alone in the hall with Miss Stranje to ask why our Lord Ravencross had not been told that his older brother was alive.

"Consider Gabriel in this matter," she instructed. "He has been a loyal friend to us. A faithful officer in His Majesty's service. He nearly died trying to persuade his brother to change his course. When Lord Wyatt and the captain carried Gabriel out of that farmhouse where he and his brother dueled, they were convinced Lord Ravencross was dead. He lay mortally wounded in a pool of blood so large, that by all accounts, he must surely have died. Would you resurrect him? To what purpose? Treason is a shameful burden for a family to bear. The name Ravencross would fall into ruin. Their properties returned to the king. Their title stripped. Would you have a loyal man disgraced, his reputation soiled forever because of the treachery of his brother?"

"No," Lady Jane answered for the two of us. "Of course not."

"Then I trust you will both keep silent on the matter."

"What of Tess?" I asked. "Shouldn't she know?"

"Would you burden her with this secret?" Miss Stranje snapped "That seems uncommonly cruel, especially caring for young Ravencross as she does. After Tess, who else will you need to tell? There is never an end to such things." She bristled, feathers out, all eagle-faced at me again. "Mind your tongues, and don't lay the weight of such a secret on anyone else."

I clamped my mouth shut to keep from arguing. It seemed impossible to me that Ghost's identity would remain a secret much longer. Surely someone would recognize him and spread the tale. On the other hand, perhaps he valued his anonymity enough to protect it even more than we did.

Having properly scolded us, Miss Stranje marched upstairs to attend to Sebastian, who had become the most unruly, pig-headed patient in history. His swelling reduced considerably, but in some respects, it looked worse. He now had great purple bruises covering both eyes. At least now we could see his eyes. The more he improved, the more obstinate he became. Refusing to drink any more of her herbal concoctions or sleeping potions. Demanding to be let out of bed. Shouting for his clothes. Cajoling anyone who visited into bringing him something to eat.

"I'm heartily sick of broth and porridge."

"But Miss Stranje said—"

"I am not an infant, Georgie."

"I can see that." His bedclothes left little to the imagination.

"A man cannot survive on mush." He smacked the bedding. His bruised and red scarred shoulder muscles rippled under that thin nightshirt. "Georgie! You're not listening. I need something to eat. A leg of mutton or—"

Miss Stranje stomped into the room. "Out," she said to me, and pointed at the door. By that evening, she threw up her hands and allowed him to come downstairs and dine with us in the parlor.

We were all supping when a messenger arrived from Paris. I was able to observe my ink at work as Captain Grey scooted back the dishes and laid the letter on the table. He daubed developer over the page of writing. A hidden message emerged between the lines. It was gratifying to witness the ink at work, but disheartening to read.

It turns out secrets are often unpleasant things.

It is with deepest regret that I inform you; King Louis the XVIII's brother, Count of Artois, acting Regent of France, has abandoned the throne. He fears for his life. We were able to remove Artois and his family out of the palace through an underground passage. He is in disguise and fleeing Paris this very night.

Count of Artois made the decision to leave the palace after receiving an urgent missive from his son, Charles Ferdinand, the Duke of Berry. I gather from those closest to Artois, his son was unable to maintain the loyalty of his troops. He barely escaped with his life and is believed to be on his way to Ghent.

Mobs have surrounded the palace, demanding Napoleon's return to Paris, hurling stones, and shouting for what's left of the Bourbon family to be put to death. Palace guards only halfheartedly hold the mob at bay. I sincerely doubt they will hold the palace for much longer.

By the time you receive this, Paris will have fallen.

Paris fallen.

We stood in stunned silence. I reread the letter a second time. Captain Grey's men came and went from the parlor throughout the evening, bearing reports of mob activity on the streets of Calais. Dissenters gathered in pockets around the city and were becoming increasingly difficult to disperse.

All of Calais was restless that night. The public house across the street stayed loud long into the early hours of the morning, with rowdy laughter, military songs, shouting, and brawls. From our bedroom window Jane and I stood and looked out over the city. We saw bands of men carrying torches in the streets. Followed by the unsettling sound of troops called out by trumpet.

Jane reached for my hand. "God save us all when Napoleon learns of this."

. . .

Sleep came in fits and starts. In the morning Tess woke up sweating and screaming. I rushed to her side. She was trembling. "What is it? What did you dream?" I feared the answer. What if I had made another terrible mistake?

Still breathing in stops and starts, she leaned her forehead against my shoulder. "No. It's not that. Ever since we rescued Sebastian, it's as if the future is shifting and changing. Like dark shapes moving in a snowstorm. Only glimpses. Napoleon on a throne. Ships. Horsemen." She shivered and buried her face deeper in my shoulder as if she could hide. "This was something else. *Someone* else. I dreamed about Lord Ravencross. Except, it was . . . *impossible*. It couldn't possibly be true."

Jane and I exchanged anxious glances, both of us silently fearing her dreams might reveal what we had sworn to keep secret.

She pulled away. "I'm worried about him—that's all." The confusion troubling her features nearly broke me.

I nodded. Unable to speak without telling her the truth.

A maid scratched at our door bearing a message from Captain Grey summoning us to the private parlor. We dressed and hurried downstairs. Although the sun shone, that morning felt sullen and gray to me. A gloom hung in the air as we entered the room.

"We've no other choice," Sebastian was saying. He and the captain stood side by side staring out the window. At our approach, they turned. The captain looked grave, distant, arms at his side.

Miss Stranje drew in a quick breath and stiffened.

He bowed. "Miss Stranje, young ladies." The captain cleared his throat, and greeted us as if he was addressing us from the quarterdeck of a brig. "We cannot express the depth of our gratitude for what you have done for us."

Mr. Digby applauded. "Hear, hear."

Captain Grey took a deep breath and continued, "However, the city is no longer safe. It will not be long before the Lord Mayor will not be able to contain the riots. British citizens will be at risk. It is time for you to return to England, to Stranje House."

Through this soul-sinking speech, Sebastian watched me intently. I started to protest, that we couldn't leave them yet. "But—"

It was small, the shake of his head. Perhaps no more than a warning tilt, or a lifted eyebrow. Whatever the case, it was enough to stop me.

Captain Grey finished dismissing us by saying, "Lord Wyatt and I must take our leave of Calais as well. A courier brought news early this morning that Napoleon has escaped Elba. He is marching to Paris."

We gasped at that. Tess most of all.

"We will accompany you to your ship, and set sail ourselves as soon as we see you safely away."

Where are you going? I wordlessly begged Sebastian for answers.

Are you well enough to undertake another dangerous mission?

How long will you be away?

Will you ever come back?

He bowed his head. Closing off my silent pleas.

Miss Stranje glanced at me. Pity in her eyes. Understanding. These were the bitter pointless questions we must swallow back and choke down. She gave my hand a quick squeeze. "Thank you, Captain. We will be ready within the hour."

Breakfast was a silent solemn affair. Over in mere minutes. Valises were stuffed and packed into the waiting carriage, and before my heart had even stopped tumbling downhill, we arrived at the dock.

Too soon.

The harbor was busier than an ant hive that morning, scarcely leaving room for our carriage in the throng. We disembarked and made our way down to the pier. Sera, Maya, and Jane boarded the ship straightaway. Tess paused beside me and grasped my arm for a moment before going aboard. "You got him out, Georgie. It's time to go home."

Home.

I sighed. What home?

Not my parents' house. They wanted nothing more to do with me, and even if they did, I didn't belong there anymore. Isn't home the place where you are understood and wanted? Miss Stranje stood off to the side, speaking earnestly with Captain Grey. Just then, her sharp gaze darted to me. Attentive. Concerned. That's when I realized I knew *exactly* where home was. I belonged at Stranje House with the other unusual girls.

I belonged.

I don't know why that thought made tears gather in my eyes. Sebastian came to me with a hard-set expression that I knew meant bad news.

"You're going to be gone a long time, aren't you?"

He didn't answer right away, toyed with his cuff before saying, "That's just it. We have no way of knowing."

"Are you certain you're well enough?" I couldn't keep the worry and sadness from my voice.

He nodded solemnly.

"Safe journey." I caught my lip to keep it from trembling. I didn't want his last remembrance of me to be of my face crumpled and weepy.

"None of that rubbish Daneska said was true. You know how I feel about you, don't you?"

I did know. I couldn't help but see the truth. It was there in his blue eyes, true as God's hand in the sky. "Yes."

There were so many things I wanted to say to Sebastian, but Miss Stranje had already gone aboard, and Captain Grey stood patiently on the dock. Any minute they would leave. *He* would leave. "My lord, I—"

"Don't say it." He guided me to the gangway. When he let go of my arm, I almost reached up to smooth back those dear strands of black hair that had fallen across his brow. His nose, which had always been so straight and perfect, now bore a bruised lump in the middle. I wanted to run my fingers over it and coax it back to its normal beautiful arrogant ridge. Except I couldn't. That would have been far too intimate.

He stared down at me, the corner of his mouth quirked up wickedly. "Memorizing my features, Georgie?"

Embarrassment warmed my cheeks. "You flatter yourself, my lord."

He smirked.

Why must he vex me at a time like this? I might not see him for . . . too *long.* Even if it was only a few weeks, it would be too long.

There could be no good-bye kiss here, not with Miss Stranje and the girls standing at the gunwales waiting for me, watching. Sebastian wanted to kiss me. I could see it in his speculative glance at my lips. He reached for my hand. I thought he meant to hold it, to press it affectionately, the way lovers did in books.

He didn't.

He opened my hand, placed a small round object into my palm, and closed my fingers around it. "This was my father's," he said. "Take care of it for me."

I stared at the pocket watch in my hand. When I looked up,

he was tipping his hat and backing away from me. "Keep it safe until my return."

I didn't know how those few words could be filled with so much promise. But they were. He would come back to me. It meant more than a kiss. More than a furtive lovers' farewell. He trusted me with his most valuable possession, his father's timepiece. It may as well have been his heart.

Miss Stranje called, "Come, Georgiana. It's time to go home."

Still, I couldn't tear my gaze away from Sebastian. He was right. I *was* memorizing his features, the line of his broad shoulders, the way his dark hair curled over his collar, his sure easy stride. I treasured each and every detail, determined to hold on to them as tightly as I held his father's watch in my fist.

"You'll see him again," Tess whispered in my ear as we stood at the railing, waving farewell. "You changed things at least that much, Georgie."

As he and Captain Grey walked away to the carriage, the devil glanced back and winked.

Afterword

Dear Reader,

Although there were attempts on King Louis the XVIII's life, in reality he was not assassinated. He returned to France via Calais on April 24, 1814, to reclaim his throne. As in the book, the Lord Mayor did commission a brass casting made of the king's first footstep on French soil and erected a column to memorialize his return. But Louis the XVIII's triumphal return was short-lived. Napoleon escaped Elba and King Louis had to flee France once again. Napoleonic sympathizers destroyed the monuments in Calais, but they have since been replaced.

The Stranje House series explores possibilities. What would the world be like if King Louis had been assassinated and Napoleon had regained power? Throughout history, we run across pivotal moments like these. Moments where everything hinged upon a single act or a lone decision.

For instance, there was a button salesman peddling his wares near Waterloo. Wellington asked him to carry a message to one of his brigades that had fallen out of position. Without that button seller's help the battle would have shifted in Napoleon's favor. What if the button salesman had decided to sell his buttons elsewhere that day?

What if the French hadn't given George Washington enough money to keep the colonists fighting Britain? France's finances would not have been severely depleted and the French Revolution probably would not have taken place. The colonies would have gone the way of Canada. Slavery would've been abolished just as it was in Britain. The Northern states wouldn't have imposed export taxes on the South, thus preventing a brutal civil war.

Domino effect.

History is rife with singular events that changed everything. *What ifs.* The historical background in the Stranje House series is partially true and partially an alternate history—a *what if.* What if the decisions of one young woman altered the course of history?

What about you?

Have you ever experienced the ripple effect of one small decision in your life? Will your next decision inadvertently change the world?

Kathleen Baldwin enjoys hearing from her readers. You can contact her through her website, and also find other goodies there: book club guides, a Regency glossary, excerpts, and more extras.

KathleenBaldwin.com

Acknowledgments

I must shamelessly steal a cliché: it takes a village to make a good book.

This series would not exist without the perseverance of my extraordinary agent, Laura Langlie. Her devotion to Stranje House is nothing short of legendary. Laura, you persisted, you never stopped believing, and you found the exact right publisher and the perfect editor for our baby. Thank you. If Miss Stranje ran a school today, she would recruit you.

Susan Chang, my fearless editor—I am in awe. Thank you for having a bigger dream for this story than I did. I didn't think that was possible. Thank you for pushing me further than I ever thought I could go. You are the perfect editor for me, which makes me the luckiest writer in the world.

My amazing friends, sisters of my heart, thank you for riding the roller coaster with me and working so diligently to polish Stranje House. You are exceptional people and I love you all. Patience Griffin, oh ye of the starred *PW* review, thank you for providing morale booster shots and indulging me when I needed cheesecake. Special thanks to Carole Fowkes, for getting out your dark crayons and shading my story world. Rae-Dawn Brightman, I'm always grateful for your amazing gift of clarity and your gentle way of questioning. Susan Anderson, kudos for magically untangling sentences. Commander Wayne Hill, thanks for wading through all the historical girly stuff in between tours of duty—salute! Bill Payne, we miss you, and thank you for showing us the way of the purple pen.

Elizabeth Fairchild, brilliant historian and outstanding Regency author, thank you for reading and providing historical tweaks. Nina Romberg, Gretchen Craig, and Sylvia McDaniel, dear friends, fabulous authors, and a super support system, thank you for discussing the writing life over guacamole and chips.

Credit and appreciation go to Jim Griffin for researching the Order of the Iron Crown, and to James Griffin for beta reading and falling in love with Lady Daneska.

Lastly, but not least, words cannot express the gratitude I feel for my family and the support they give me. I'm extremely fortunate to have a technophile genius for a brother. Thank you, Gordon, for computers, amazing software, and topflight security. Thank you to my sons and daughter . . . you vacuumed and cooked while I was too busy writing, you spent hours and hours developing my various websites, yet you still found the time to inspire, encourage, and cheer me on. You all amaze me. I am the luckiest mother ever.

My faithful and loving husband, you are so much like Sebastian, always off fighting tyrants. This book is dedicated to you. You are the greatest supporter a girl could have. When you heard Tor bought this series, you were so happy you jumped up and down. In that moment, my heart overflowed. Joy means so much more when shared with you.

Read on for a sneak peek at Tess's story,
to be told in Exile for Dreamers,
Book 2 of the Stranje House series.

Y ou can't go." I blocked Lord Ravencross's path. "They'll kill you."

"We all have to die sometime." He grasped my shoulders and moved me aside.

"It needn't be today." He let go, so I said it louder. "Not today." *Please.*

He strode down the hall and I followed. "Very well then, if you won't listen to reason at least let me ride with you. They might not attack two men."

"You may think this is a clever disguise." He cut a hard ruthless gaze over my trousers and coat. "Look at you, Tess. Inside of two seconds any fellow worth his salt would be able to tell you're a female."

He tromped away. "I can't catch them and protect you at the same time."

I snapped, "You wouldn't need to. I can protect myself."

"*You* will stay here." He charged out of the room with a pistol in his hand and another tucked into the crook of his arm. "Miss Stranje," he bellowed. "Muzzle your pup!"

My heart pummeled against my chest as he rushed downstairs.

"Let him go, Tess." It was Sera who came to me, not Miss

Stranje. She tugged on my arm. If it had been anyone else I would've jerked away, but Sera understood.

I squeezed my eyes shut against the anguish threatening to make me ill. "I saw them murder him," I whispered. "This morning. In the woods. I saw it."

"I thought as much." She smoothed back my hair. "But now that you've warned him, it won't happen."

"You can't know that for certain."

"It's a fair assumption. Your visions saved Sebastian and all those other men in Vienna."

I kept my voice low so Georgie wouldn't overhear. "We don't know that for certain either. Events changed in Calais, but we don't know what has happened since. There's been no word from Captain Grey or Sebastian for almost a fortnight."

Sera straightened. "This morning you saw what would happen if Lord Ravencross hadn't been warned. Now that you've told him, everything is changed. He's riding out armed. *He* is going after *them*."

I backed away from her. If only I could stop seeing clubs beating against his skull, knives slicing into his chest, and blood, all that blood, *his blood*, and him collapsed in it with no life in his eyes, then maybe I could believe her. *Maybe*.

"Girls!" Miss Stranje called sharply. "If you will all gather around we shall have our first lesson on guns this morning." She announced this in the same manner any other headmistress might gather her students to discuss the proper way to pour tea. But ours pushed open a window that looked out over the park and held out the basket of guns. "Suppose my quarry were to dash across the park in that direction." She pointed across the drive to the far side of the front lawns. "At that distance a small pistol will be of little use. So I will select the pistol with the longer barrel. Why do you suppose that is?"

Georgie piped up. "The elongated barrel will cause the bullet to fire under more pressure. Thus it will go farther and the trajectory will be more reliable."

"Precisely." Miss Stranje knelt on the floor and aimed the gun out of the window. "The longer barrel will also provide a more reliable sight."

Georgie knelt down beside her. "Yes, of course. That makes perfect sense."

Miss Stranje tilted her head to one side, peered down the length of the pistol, and kept talking. "When you aim at moving target, keep the sight slightly in front of . . ."

Palms sweating, only halfheartedly listening, scarcely able to stand in one spot, I kept watch out of the other window. With shaking hands I trained the telescope on the far corner of the north field. Waiting. Watching for Lord Ravencross to come riding along the path.

Maya protested, "Surely, we will never be called upon to use such deadly weapons. We have other methods at our disposal."

"One must not limit one's arsenal," Miss Stranje said. "If your persuasive voice would suffice in every situation, Maya, you would not be at Stranje House, would you?"

"I . . . she . . . that was my inexperience." Maya rarely lost her composure. The off-key notes of pain in her normally melodic voice were unmistakable. She fidgeted with the black pelisse she'd donned for this excursion. "With more training and practice I might have prevailed. Surely, you cannot be suggesting I ought to have shot my stepmother?"

"No." Miss Stranje exhaled loudly, still sighting the gun. She adjusted her position at the window. "Although it is a rather intriguing thought, is it not?"

Maya gasped.

Jane patted Maya's shoulder. "She doesn't mean it. You mustn't take everything so literally."

Georgie studied the angle of Miss Stranje's gun. "I can think of a situation in which a pistol would've come in very handy."

I remembered well the night she had in mind.

Miss Stranje said bluntly, "That, my dear, might have proved a grave error. I fear Lady Daneska would've disarmed you and used the gun against you. She is very well trained."

Georgie sniffed defensively but held her ground. "You trained her. You can train me."

"We shall see." Miss Stranje explained how to sight down the barrel of the gun.

I could not concentrate on her lesson. I stared through the telescope at the far corner of the field where the murderers lay in wait. It was a small thing, that hare bounding out of the adjacent woods, but prickles rained over my scalp and arms. My hands shook. I clenched the scope so tight it's a wonder it didn't break. The next instant a flock of birds winged skyward.

I didn't need a vision to tell me what was going on.

"Ambush!" I shoved the scope at Sera. "It's not just the men in the woods between the estates. More are hiding in the back field." I snatched the double-barreled pistol from Miss Stranje's basket and dashed out of the study.

Miss Stranje called after me, ordered me to stop. I ignored her, took the stairs two at a time, yanked open the front door, and ran. In the freedom of men's trousers I almost flew. I blazed straight and true across the field to the place where they planned to trap him.

I was too late. Lord Ravencross cantered Zeus along the far path headed straight for disaster.

A SCHOOL FOR UNUSUAL GIRLS

A Stranje House Novel

Ages 13–17, Grades 8–12

ABOUT THIS GUIDE

The Common Core State Standards–aligned questions and activities that follow are intended to enhance your reading of *A School for Unusual Girls*. Please feel free to adapt this content to suit the needs and interests of your students or reading group participants.

Prereading Activities

1. *A School for Unusual Girls* is set in an alternate nineteenth-century Europe. "Alternate histories" are works of fiction in which recognizable historical figures have experiences different from those recorded in history books, and notable events end differently and lead to different futures. Ask each reader to imagine his or her own present if the outcome of a recent historical event had been different. For example, what if the current president had lost the last election? Or, what if Steve Jobs had not invented the iPhone? Write a journal-style essay describing today, paying particular attention to details that would be affected by this "alternate" historical outcome.

2. Invite students to discuss the way international events, such as tensions in the Middle East or global warming, affect their lives. Do they read about such worldwide issues in the newspaper or online? Do they worry about these problems? Do they have family or friends who have had to travel to countries experiencing political unrest? Do international events affect their family dinner table conversations, their classroom studies, their daily lives, or even their reading choices? Why or why not?

Supports Common Core State Standards: W.8.3, W.9–10.3, W.11–12.3; and SL.8.1, SL.9–10.1, SL.11–12.1

DEVELOPING READING AND DISCUSSION SKILLS

1. The novel is narrated in the first person by Georgina Fitzwilliam. How do you think this point of view affects what readers learn about Stranje House, the politics of eighteenth-century Europe, and notions of love and trust? Is Georgina a reliable or an unreliable narrator? Explain your answer.

2. Do you think Georgina's parents have a right to send her away, particularly to Stranje House, as the story begins? Why or why not?

3. What is Georgina's ink formula? How does she begin to realize its larger significance after she arrives at Stranje House? How does her own family's experience of loss in war impact her commitment to creating invisible ink?

4. Who are Tess, Jane, Sera, and Maya? What is Georgina's initial reaction to them when they meet in the dormitorium? Why are the girls so cryptic in their early interactions with Georgina?

5. At the end of chapter 4, Georgina notes, "I may be odd and peculiar, I may be freckled and unlovable, but there's one thing I know for certain about myself, I am good at making plans." (p. 52) What do these lines tell readers about Georgina's sense of confidence and about her insecurities? What other key moments in the story counterpoint these two aspects of her personality?

6. At the end of chapter 4, Georgina admits, "I'd a hundred times rather face rats and spiders in the darkness than the monstrous truths Jane had unleashed." (p. 68) What are the "monstrous truths"? How might Georgina's actions be understood in light of this admission?

7. In chapter 6, Georgina discovers what she is meant to study at Stranje House. What did she expect her education to be like and what is the reality? How does Georgina's relationship with Lord

Sebastian Wyatt evolve as they work together to perfect her ink formula? How does the dynamic between them affect their scientific work?

8. How does Georgina's perception of Miss Stranje change in chapter 9? Who is Lady Daneska? Why does she know so much about Stranje House? In what ways is she dangerous to Lord Ravencross, to Lord Wyatt, to Tess, to Miss Stranje, and to England?

9. How does Georgina feel when she realizes that her mother wrote to Lady Pinswary about her behavior? Have you ever had the experience of hearing adults discuss your academic, athletic, or artistic skills, or your future? How did you react to this experience?

10. How does it seem that Lucien, the first Lord Ravencross, died? Could one argue that the author uses the dynamics of the Ravencross family to reflect the complex dynamics of eighteenth-century Europeans, in terms of being for or against Napoleon's return from exile? Explain your answer.

11. In chapter 12, Georgina muses ". . . Miss Stranje was transforming us all right, but the question was, *into what?*" (pp. 172) How would you answer this question?

12. What surprising realizations does Georgina make while on her morning hunt for oak galls? How does Sebastian's rescue of Georgina from the oak tree cause a shift in their relationship? Why isn't Tess angrier about Georgina's spying adventure? What vital secret does she reveal to Georgina?

13. Why does Georgina fail to follow Tess's instructions to prevent Lord Wyatt from leaving for London too soon? Does she also fail to follow Miss Stranje's warning "not to wound" Sebastian, Lord Wyatt, as well? In what ways?

14. Are all of the girls' "unusual" talents intellectual, like Georgie's? How might you describe an ability like Tess's dreams? How are Tess's dreams and Georgie's ink research interwoven?

15. Do you think Georgina endangers herself and others with her unwillingness to share what is happening to her emotionally?

What advice might you give to Georgina about her secret-keeping tendencies? Explain how you might interpret the entire novel as a study about secret-keeping on many levels.

16. How does Lord Ravencross help the girls gain admittance to the party in London? What do Georgina and Tess realize about Daneska as the party proceeds? What happens when Georgina finds Sebastian and how does this information broaden her focus from personal romance to larger diplomatic and military affairs?

17. Who journeys to Calais? How does each traveler participate in the plans to rescue Sebastian and thwart the Order of the Iron Crown? How do Georgina's relationships with the other Stranje House girls change in Calais?

18. Are Georgina and her friends successful in carrying out their rescue plot? Who is Ghost? What do the girls learn about the fate of King Louis XVIII at the end of chapter 25? What risks does Europe face at the novel's conclusion?

19. Describe the relationships between Georgina and Lord Wyatt, between Tess and Lord Ravencross, and between Miss Stranje and Captain Grey. What do you think forms the core connection for each of these couples? How does each couple deal with the tension between their attraction to each other and their sense of responsibility to the larger world? Explain your answers.

20. What does Georgina come to realize about her "home" at the end of the novel? How might the notion of home—on the individual, social, and even international level—be explored as a key motif in A School for Unusual Girls? How might you define the word "home" for Georgina? Could you apply a similar definition of "home" to its use in your own life? Why or why not?

Supports Common Core State Standards: RL.8.1–4, 9–10.1–5, 11–12.1–6; and SL.8.1, 3, 4; SL.9–10.1, 3, 4; SL.11–12.1, 3, 4.

DEVELOPING RESEARCH AND WRITING SKILLS
Character

1. Georgina often feels misunderstood in the course of the story, but she comes to learn that she shares these feelings with other Stranje House denizens. From the perspective of Tess, Jane, Ms. Stranje, or another character, write at least four journal entries, including one reflecting on Georgina's arrival at Stranje House; one recounting some of the reasons you yourself live at Stranje House; one discussing the dangers of dealing with Daneska; and one after the adventures in Calais.

2. In the character of Sebastian, Lord Wyatt, write a letter to Miss Stranje, thanking her for introducing you to Georgina and discussing your concerns for both of your futures, diplomatically, scientifically, and otherwise. Or, in the character of Captain Grey, write a letter to Miss Stranje asking for her hand in marriage and explaining why you think she should finally agree to this proposal.

3. *A School for Unusual Girls* depicts the experiences of Georgina and others who seem to be misfits in terms of their social and intellectual abilities. With friends or classmates, discuss the term "unusual" as it is used in the novel. What type of "unusual" status do you think would be most challenging for someone your age? Is there a difference between feeling different on the inside and being perceived as a misfit by those around you? Are there some benefits to being "unusual"? Role-play a conversation between the Stranje House scholars and their friends in which each character shares her perspective on being different.

4. Review the novel, noting the words used to describe Georgina and her friends' differences, such as "unusual," "exceptional," and "frightening." Add other synonyms as desired. Using a computer-design program, stencils, or letters cut from periodicals and glued onto paper, create a word collage or other graphic art display inspired by your language study.

Setting and Background

5. Create a Reader's Companion booklet for A *School for Unusual Girls*. Include a timeline of key events in early nineteenth-century European history, biographical facts about Napoleon and Sir Isaac Newton, information about mourning traditions of the era, and any other information that might be helpful to future readers. Make sure to annotate historical events that had different outcomes in the novel (such as the death of King Louis XVIII, which did not happen in real history).

6. Go to the library or online to learn more about the history and chemistry of invisible ink. With friends or classmates (and adult supervision), try making your own invisible-ink formula based on your research. Be sure to record your test results through note taking and taking photo images of your process. Create a Power-Point or other multimedia-style presentation about your discoveries to share with friends or classmates.

7. As part of the plan to rescue Sebastian, Georgina builds a new set of "wings" to transport herself and Jane. Go to the library or online to learn about the flying inventions of Leonardo DaVinci. Then, imagine you are a reporter for *The Times* of London in 1814, and word has gotten back to you about Georgina's "flight." Write an article for your paper comparing her invention to the ideas of DaVinci and considering what potential the technology may hold for the future.

Plot

8. Key to the plot of A *School for Unusual Girls* is the fact that Stranje House is not at all as it initially seems. Write two brochures for the school: one that Miss Stranje might hand to angry parents dumping off their daughters, and another that she might offer to scholars and others interested in a place that educates young women to play critical roles in international affairs.

9. The Order of the Iron Crown was established by Napoleon Bonaparte. Go to the library or online to learn about Bonaparte's

organization. Then, write a short essay explaining the historically accurate details about the Iron Crown that can be found in the novel. Or, in the character of a Napoleonic sympathizer, write a speech explaining the importance of the Iron Crown for the future of Europe. If possible, present the speech to friends or classmates.

10. *A School for Unusual Girls* is an alternate history, mixing historical facts and real people with fictional characters and outcomes. Go to the library or online to learn the real history of Napoleon's return from exile, known as the "Hundred Days of Napoleon." Use your research to brainstorm ideas for a sequel to the novel. As author Kathleen Baldwin fictionally kills King Louis, what "alteration" would you make to real history to move your plot forward? What title would you give the next book? Write two to three paragraphs describing your ideas, followed by an outline of the first five to ten chapters of the story.

Themes

11. Author Kathleen Baldwin explores the tension between love and responsibility. Create a poem, set of song lyrics, or a visual-art composition reflecting this tension as it is presented in the novel.

12. Secrets, on both personal and political levels, drive both internal (emotional) and external (action) plots of the novel. Select one critical secret kept by a character in the novel. Write a one to three page essay explaining the origins, motivations, and repercussions of the secret on the character who keeps it and others in the novel.

13. With friends or classmates, create a brainstorm list of reasons for and against secret keeping. Can secrets be divided into different types? Is it all right for government leaders to keep secrets? Individually, or in small groups, write a short summary of the results of your discussion.

Supports Common Core State Standards: RL.8.4, RL.8.9; RL.9–10.4; RL.11–12.4; W.8.2–3, W.8.7–8; W.9–10.2–3, W.9–10.6–8; W.11–12.2–3, W.11–12.6–8; and SL.8.1, SL.8.4–5; SL.9–10.1–5; 11–12.1–5.

About the Author

KATHLEEN BALDWIN loves adventure in books and in real life. She taught rock climbing in the Rockies, survival-camped in the desert, was stalked by a cougar, lost an argument with a rattle-snake, took way too many classes in college, fell in love at least a dozen times, and married her very own hero. She's written several award-winning Regency romances for adults. *A School for Unusual Girls* is her first historical romance for young adults.